DEATHTRAP

A CROSSBREED NOVEL

USA TODAY BESTSELLING AUTHOR

DANNIKA DARK

We are each our own devil, and we make this world our hell.

- Oscar Wilde

Chapter 1

"SO THIS IS THE PLACE you keep raving about?" Christian asked, running his dark gaze over the diner and giving it a judgmental stare.

I smiled and continued examining the menu. "The fate of your meal lies in the hands of whether or not Betty McGuire likes you."

He leaned in tight. "Betty sounds like a real joy. I already told you I'm not ordering."

"Oh, you're ordering. I don't care what you get, but Ruby's Diner saved my life more than once, so show a little respect."

He snapped open his laminated menu. "In that case, is there anything that hasn't been marinated in lard?"

I set my menu aside and gazed out the window. Condensation formed along the outer edges from the humidity and contrasting temperatures. Winter had arrived early, and a light dusting of snow blanketed the city, making even the filthiest streets pure again. It was an accurate representation of my life since joining Keystone.

Working for Viktor Kazan was an evolving lifestyle adjustment. After closing my first official case only a month ago, I'd taken Viktor's advice and used the downtime to get my head together. I needed it, especially after discovering that the detective I'd gone out on a date with was the serial killer we'd been hunting all along. But downtime between job assignments was by no means a vacation. Viktor had given me a stack of cold cases to review before Wyatt entered them into our private database as part of his archiving project. It kept me occupied.

Betty sidled up to our table. "And how are you two this morning?"

"Grand," Christian replied, lifting his gaze and staring at her as if he'd seen a ghost.

She steered her attention back to me and patted my shoulder. "Honey, I've been worried about you. I haven't seen you around here lately. I'm glad you're doing okay."

I noticed white roots peeking through her light red hair. "How are the grandkids?"

She put her hands on her plump hips. "Where does the time go? Do I look old enough to have *great*-grandchildren? Well, now I have a third on the way. They did one of those fancy tests and found out it's a girl. Back in my day, we just had to wait to find out. I guess kids today don't like surprises."

I smiled. "This is my friend Christian."

She pulled the pen out from behind her ear and pressed the blunt end against her chin as she gave him a thorough appraisal. I waited for her reaction with bated breath. I respected Betty. She was intuitive about a person's character.

Unlike me.

I still wasn't sure about my own feelings for Christian, only that I *had* feelings that weren't appropriate for our working relationship. Maybe it was normal when partnering with someone so closely, but it didn't make sense. Christian was the opposite in looks and demeanor of men I was normally attracted to, and aside from that, he was a Vampire—the most loathsome creature imaginable. I'd spent a lot of time in the past weeks thinking it over and had finally decided to compartmentalize my feelings for Christian, keeping the affectionate ones locked up in order to keep our partnership functional and harmonious. Otherwise, it could bring consequences, and my life until recently had been one big consequence after another. In order to remain within Keystone, I had to learn to work with Christian as a team.

Christian averted his gaze from Betty and stroked his beard. "Would you have any meat and potatoes back there?"

She shifted her stance, still studying him closely. "We don't get many Irishmen. Have you been in here before?"

He scratched the back of his neck. "No. I've changed my mind. I'll have a grilled cheese, and she'll be having the same."

I narrowed my eyes. "Oh, will she now?"

"You've been staring at that menu for ten minutes," he said, taking on an imperious tone. "Are you telling me you're actually going to order something besides a hamburger and onion rings? Step out of your comfort zone and live on the wild side."

I handed her my menu. "I'll have a glass of water with that. And my *friend* will be having a glass of milk."

He held out his menu. "I'm lactose intolerant. Bring me a bottle of red."

She slowly collected our menus. "Cheese has lactose. I'll bring the milk."

I wasn't sure what to make of Betty's peculiar reaction to Christian. She was usually more bubbly and talkative, but something had shut her up.

"That was weird," I muttered, stacking one of my gloves on top of the other.

Christian gestured toward them. "I hate to inform you, but someone snipped the fingers off your mittens."

"It's easier to get to my daggers when I can grip them with my fingertips."

He pinched the whiskers on his scruffy beard. "What does Viktor have you working on? I saw him carrying files to your room."

I lifted a saltshaker and set it between us. "Cold cases."

Christian chuckled. "Ah, to be the rookie again. Sifting through old papers and given menial tasks to make you believe your opinion matters."

"It's smart of him. Maybe you guys are used to looking at something from a certain angle, and a fresh pair of eyes might see something new."

He laced his fingers together. "Pray tell, what have your fresh eyes uncovered?"

I tapped the saltshaker and accidentally tipped it over. "Why hasn't anyone pursued the case involving Vampire trafficking? The one with all the women who are promised to be newly made?"

He pinched salt between two fingers and flicked it over his shoulder. "We could never outbid anyone at a black market auction. And without victims, we have nothing. We can't even be sure if a crime is being committed. It might come as a surprise, but there happens to be a lot of women who have fantasies about being *kept* by a man. Not everyone for sale on the black market is an unwilling victim."

"Did you look at any missing-persons reports? I don't mean Breed ones, but a nationwide search in the human databases."

"Aye. But we came up with no matches based on the description. In some cases, they included a photograph."

"That means whoever's behind this is preying upon women who won't be missed. He takes them, makes them, and sells them."

Christian leaned back and draped his arms across the top of the red vinyl seat. "What makes you believe all the cases are linked? It's just an increase in Vampire trafficking. Demand affects supply."

"I don't know. Maybe it was the typo."

He furrowed his brow. "Typo?"

"Didn't anyone notice that some of the descriptions had the same typo? He didn't spell *discreet* with double *e*'s. He wrote: D-I-S-C-R-E-T-E. That doesn't have the same meaning. I also think he's an American."

Christian snorted and set his arms on the table. "You're just full of theories this morning. I hate to be the bearer of bad tidings, but there are a lot of illiterate immortals in the world. English isn't everyone's first language."

"Including yours?"

He narrowed his eyes when Betty set down our plates and glasses.

"Anything else?" she asked, her green eyes twinkling at me.

I bit my lip and hesitated on answering.

"Your slice of pie is in the warmer." She placed two straws on the table and gave me a wink before heading back to the kitchen.

Christian poked at his sandwich. "Assuming one person is behind all the trafficking, what makes you think he's an American?"

I tore the end off the paper around the straw and blew the wrapper at Christian's forehead. It bounced off and landed on his plate. "He used words that have alternate spellings in England, Canada, and all those other countries. I didn't see anything that suggested he's a foreigner."

Christian threw up his hands. "Well, for feck's sake. You've solved the case! We're after an American who can't spell, which makes everyone at table five a suspect."

I glanced over at a man who was trying to balance a spoon on his nose. "Make fun all you want. I gave Wyatt my notes, and he's adding them to the file. You never know when little things like that might come up later. You're just mad because you didn't notice it first with your ancient, dusty eyeballs."

He held up a spoon. "May I borrow yours?"

I smiled at the private joke, the one referring to our trip to Washington when a Shifter had planned to spoon my eye out.

Christian tugged on his earlobe. "Don't get too wrapped up in those files, Raven. The more obsessed you become over a dead file, the harder it is to focus on the work at hand. You need to concentrate on the open investigations. We aren't always paid for solving old crimes, and not all of them were contracted to us. Some fell in our laps, and Viktor took them on as charity cases."

"I know. It just gives me something to do."

"Well, you should have gotten a nice paycheck deposited into your account after the last case. Perhaps you should kill some time and go to the zoo."

"Why? I already live with the circus."

He cracked a smile. "Touché."

I gulped down my water and then sighed. "It's hard to get used to unsolved mysteries."

"You'll learn to live with it. It's not as if we're in a rush, and one day something might link back to those old cases and allow us to solve them. Maybe you should get out more."

"I would, but I'm without transportation."

"Last I looked, you had two strong legs."

"The walk to town is too far, so I'm saving up for some wheels. It would be a different story if the train were near the mansion." I took a bite of my sandwich, the bread so buttery I had to wipe my fingers on a napkin. "You know, I used to sleep in trains and subway stations before they started beefing up security. It was a lot safer than alleyways or abandoned buildings."

"You're just full of happy memories."

When Betty set my pie down and slipped away without a word, I peered over my shoulder to watch her. She looked back at us briefly before clearing off a table.

Vampires weren't especially frightening to look at when their fangs were receded. While their black eyes could be unnerving, they didn't stand out in a way that drew attention. Lots of people had dark eyes, and it was only when you looked close enough that you realized how bottomless they were. Betty's peculiar behavior made me even more curious about the man I was partnered with.

"*Jaysus wept.* You're not going to convince me this is cheese." He dropped his sandwich on his plate and then wiped his fingers down his black coat. "I'm suddenly reminded why I gave up eating. Cuisine just isn't what it used to be."

"I thought your aversion to food had to do with the latrine."

"That too. So, are you going to explain why you dragged me all the way into the city on such a fine morning?"

I finished half my sandwich and waited for the pregnant woman walking past us to go into the bathroom. "It's about that favor you owe me."

"You mean the favor for that inane bet where I had to abstain from sex for your amusement?"

"That's the one."

He slowly dragged the glass of milk toward him and gulped it down as if it were ale. When he finished, he held my gaze.

I struggled not to laugh at his milk mustache. "I want you to take me to see my father."

He tapped his finger against the edge of his glass. When he didn't reply, I shifted my eyes to the parking lot outside. A couple emerged from an SUV and held hands as they waddled like penguins toward the front of the diner. A few snowflakes clung to the window, and I clung to the hope that this wasn't going to erupt into an argument. Why did everything with Christian turn into such a fucking battle? He owed me a favor, and that was supposed to mean something in our world.

"Then hurry up and eat your sandwich," he finally said.

My heart skipped a beat. "I don't mean *now.*"

He leaned back. "For feck's sake, then why did you invite me out all this way?"

"I didn't want anyone overhearing our conversation, especially Viktor. You know the general opinion about cutting ties with our human life. He wouldn't approve, but this is something I need to do. When the time is right, I want to see my father without having to give you an explanation."

"What does this have to do with me? Can't you go by yourself?"

"You know why. I need a Vampire to scrub his memory when I'm done. He's already moved on with his life, so this isn't about making him feel better. If anything, it might do the opposite. I need to get some things off my chest."

"Besides your bra?" He cocked his head to the side. "Why not just go now and get it over with?"

Christian wouldn't understand. I was terrified of how my father would react when he saw me alive. Terrified that the truth might send him into cardiac arrest. Terrified that seeing him might be a mistake. Would he resent me for abandoning him? Maybe I wasn't ready for the truth that my father might be happier without me in his life. But I needed that final good-bye. That was all I really wanted—a hug from my daddy and maybe his forgiveness.

Eventually.

Just not right after my apple pie.

"Can you be available when I ask? No questions?"

Christian scratched his ear, a perturbed look on his face. "And here I thought you just wanted to share my good company. I can't be at your beck and call for the rest of eternity while you make up your mind. If you haven't called me in a fortnight, I'll drag you there myself."

I started to laugh and held it back.

He propped his elbow on the table and tucked his fist against his chin. "What's so funny?"

I averted my gaze from his milk mustache. "I just had a tickle in my throat."

"Hurry up and eat that pie. I want to get out of here before I start smelling like processed cheese and fish sticks."

"I'll tell Betty to bring the check the next time she comes by the table."

"Tell you what. I'll just leave a flat hundred on the table, and we can skip the formalities."

I took a bite of warm apple pie. "Don't be such a fanghole. She's my friend."

"She's a cocktail in an apron. You shouldn't form attachments to mortals. That's a habit your maker would have broken had he stuck around."

I shoved my plate away and leaned back in the booth. Now I'd lost my appetite. Christian was pressing my buttons on purpose.

He slapped a large bill on the table. "Let's go build a snowman."

I furrowed my brow. "Say again?"

He scooted out of his seat and stretched his arms. "We drove all this way into the city. Might as well have a little fun while we're here."

"How is building a snowman fun?"

He grinned fiendishly. "Grab the ketchup and I'll show you how Vampires have a good time."

Chapter 2

A S SOON AS WE MADE it home to Keystone mansion, I
ducked around the winged statue just inside the front
door and headed down the side hall that led to the back
of the building. After I ascended to the second floor, I moved
through a dark hall absent of windows but illuminated by a few
wall lanterns, the light of which soaked into the crevices of the
stone that arched overhead.

I should have been downstairs training with Niko, but my
head just wasn't in it today. All I could think about was my father,
and I didn't want Niko to read my color and start asking questions.

Out of nowhere, Gem flew past me from an intersecting
hallway.

"Wait!" she cried out, her roller skates skidding to a stop.
Gem circled back around, her wavy tresses curtaining her face. She
hooked her arm in mine and swept back her purple hair—a pale
shade of amethyst that matched her eyes. "Where in the world
have you been? I went by your room earlier to see if you wanted to
hang out. I've been searching all over the mansion trying to find
you."

We continued our walk down the hall, her rolling beside me.

"I went into the city with Christian to have breakfast."

She flashed me an impish grin. "That sounds mysterious."

"The only thing mysterious was his aversion to pie."

"I want to hear all the details." Gem had her eyes on Wyatt's
office just to the left and broke away to skate ahead of me through
the open door. "Visitors!" she announced in a bright voice.

I moseyed inside and noticed Shepherd lying on the black sofa to the left, an ashtray on his chest. Little flecks of grey ash were scattered across his black T-shirt. His ankles were crossed, one arm behind his head while he watched an action movie on TV.

Typical Shepherd.

Gem whirled around and finally took a good look at me. As her eyes dragged downward, she gaped at my pants. "Did you and Christian get into a fight?"

Wyatt spun around in his computer chair and looked me over. "Son of a ghost. I *knew* I should have made popcorn. What's the scoop?"

"There's no scoop." I glanced down at the red ketchup splattered on my jeans. "Suffice it to say that after building a bloody massacre of snowmen, we'll never be invited to Saint Vincent's Church again."

Wyatt flipped his beanie off, revealing a messy head of nut-brown hair. "You're going to hell in a handbasket."

I walked around him and sat on the leather stool. "I ate your chili last night. I'm already there."

He stretched his legs out and crossed them at the ankles, his boot heel propped on the stone floor. Wyatt's attitude was a lot more easygoing now that—according to him—the house was ghost-free. I hadn't caught him racing down the hallways in the wee hours of the morning, spooked by something he'd seen. "I'm looking forward to the feast *you're* cooking tonight, Julia Child."

Crap. I'd forgotten it was my week to cook. Everyone rotated chores, including cooking, laundry, trash, and general cleaning to name a few. They were spread out so that one person wasn't given both cooking and laundry on the same week. After just over a month, it was finally my turn in the kitchen. I hadn't boiled water in probably seven years. Was it possible to make ramen noodles look gourmet?

Gem glided toward a beanbag chair and plopped down. The oversized chair dwarfed her as it puffed out.

I eased my elbows on the desk behind me and faced Shepherd,

who was entertaining himself by blowing smoke rings. "Is this what you do all day?"

He took another drag, eyes still fixed on the TV. "I'm waiting on Spooky to run a file check for me."

The sound of Blue's boot heels echoing in the hallway announced her arrival before she ever set foot in the room. A falcon Shifter, Blue strutted in as cool as a cucumber and switched on the trendy floor lamp behind the couch.

"Delivery," she said, tapping Shepherd's forehead with an envelope. When she bent over the corner of the sofa to drop it in his lap, her long brown hair tickled the top of his head and made his nose twitch.

In a gravelly voice, he said, "I don't get mail." Shepherd blew out another ring of smoke.

She yanked a red pillow out from beneath his head. "You do now. A messenger dropped it off a minute ago. Better take it before I let Wyatt have the first look."

Wyatt rolled his chair across the room and reached out with grabby hands. "Gimme."

Shepherd snatched the envelope and set his ashtray on the floor. He swung his legs over the edge of the sofa, ashes scattering onto his lap. Shepherd was a lot like the furniture in some of the rooms; he might not fit in with his surroundings, but after a while, you got used to him. He ran a hand across his buzz cut, a cigarette firmly wedged between two fingers.

Wyatt used his heels to propel his chair back to his desk, where he rummaged through a drawer and retrieved a box of chocolate-covered raisins. "Well?"

Shepherd ripped open the envelope with his teeth and spit the loose paper onto the floor.

Blue picked up his ashtray and set it on the end table to the right of the sofa.

"What is it?" I asked, watching him read the letter.

He wadded the paper up in his hand. "Something I don't have time for." Shepherd stood up and showered the floor with ashes. The muscles on his arms flexed and hardened as he dusted off his clothes. Shepherd spent a lot of time doing pull-ups, and it showed with nearly every subtle move he made. He tossed the paper into the wastebasket across the room and stalked toward Wyatt, who spun out of the way so that Shepherd could grab a file off his desk. "Send me the rest when you're done."

As soon as Shepherd left the room, Wyatt nearly tipped over his chair as he dove into the trash.

"What's it say?" I whispered, sidling up next to him.

He smoothed out the crumpled paper and read it to himself. "Holy Toledo! This is an invitation from Mr. Patrick Bane."

"You mean the guy whose party we crashed?" Mr. Bane was an elite member of society who belonged to the higher authority. We'd recently attended a masquerade ball at his mansion.

Wyatt set the letter on his lap and gave a throaty chuckle. "My favorite part is where it says *Mr.* Shepherd Moon. I never thought of Shepherd as a mister *anything* but a pain-in-the-ass chain-smoker. I bet he's afraid he'll have to put on a suit."

Blue furrowed her brow. "What's the invitation for?"

"I bet Patrick wants to extend his gratitude for saving his kid, so he's inviting Shep over for dinner."

I pursed my lips, remembering how Shepherd caught the falling boy. "Does Shepherd even know how to use silverware?"

Shepherd wasn't the most affable guy, but I'd never held that against him. He didn't usually attend events that weren't work related unless they involved a glass of beer and game of darts. Better him than me. Dining with modern-day aristocrats wasn't my style.

"We should show this to Viktor," Blue said. "Whether Shepherd wants to go or not is beside the point. We have to maintain good relations with the higher authority, and this guy'll be insulted if Shepherd doesn't at least reply to the invitation."

Gem struggled to her feet and skated over, collecting the paper and thoroughly examining every word. "*Cordially* invited. Alas, I never get cordially invited to anything."

"Maybe someone should go with him," I suggested. "Just to make sure things *remain* cordial."

"Me!" Gem volunteered, raising her hand.

"Wait a second, wait a second," Wyatt interrupted. "I'm his partner. It only makes sense that I go with him."

Blue and Gem exchanged a glance and rolled their eyes.

Wyatt rose to his feet and lifted his nose in the air. "Oh ye of little faith," he said, circling around them.

Gem carefully rolled backward on her skates and then leaned against the desk. "Feel free to go. But if Mr. Bane happens to have any ghosties wandering around his great big mansion, you might end up having an argument with them at the dinner table, completely oblivious to the living people around you. Wait'll Viktor hears about *that*."

Wyatt plopped down on the couch, his eyes fixed on his skull belt buckle. "Point taken. I'm not a big fan of those intimate dinners anyhow." He lifted his head, and a smile touched his lips. "Just remember, Rollergirl, it's going to be a private dinner with a high-and-mighty political official. No studly men to admire, no dance party, and you'll be subjected to stimulating conversation about the economy."

"Point taken," she parroted back. "What about Christian?"

I chortled. "I'm not sure if Mr. Bane is prepared for asinine remarks about his décor. Plus, Christian doesn't eat, so between an imperious Vampire who eats candy and a chain-smoking caveman like Shepherd, it would be an award-winning dinner."

Blue tapped her feather earring, her eyes downcast. "Viktor should decide. Maybe it's not necessary."

"Viktor should decide what?" our fearless leader asked. Viktor's Russian accent was smoky and relaxed. Sometimes in conversation he would drift into his mother tongue, and then Gem was the only one who could understand him.

He stood at the door, his steel-grey eyes looking among us with great interest. Viktor was like a senior hipster, always making whatever he wore look like a fashion trend. His swanky loafers matched his brown chinos, and he had on a beige sweater over a button-down shirt.

The silver-haired fox stroked his short beard, his other hand in his pants pocket. "We're not keeping secrets, are we?"

Blue crossed the room and handed him the creased letter. "This came for Shepherd."

"*Spasibo.*" Viktor read the short letter and turned it over. "What an honor. I'm assuming by the condition of this paper that Shepherd has seen it."

Wyatt snorted. "Shep isn't going."

"*Nyet.* He will accept this offer. I think it best if I send one of you with him to make sure he does not insult Mr. Bane. I cannot go. If Patrick wanted me to join him, he would have included me in the invitation. He will understand why I cannot send Shepherd in alone. Too much wine, and sometimes a man can divulge more information than he is permitted."

I tied my hair back. "My vote goes to Claude."

Viktor drew in a breath through his nose and pursed his lips. "I think another male companion would send the wrong message. Why would I send another man who was not invited? If Shepherd has a female companion, it appears more casual." Viktor scratched beneath his chin and looked between us girls. "Raven, I want you to go."

"But I'm not—"

"Ah-ah," he said, wagging his finger. "No arguments. You have complained about not having enough work, so you cannot pick and choose. Everyone else has work, so you will take assignments as I give them."

"He might be insulted by the fact I'm there. I was the one who let the kid fall, remember?"

"All the more reason to make amends." Viktor left the room, Blue following behind.

"Picking Raven out of you three makes sense," Wyatt remarked, pulling his chair up to his computer.

Gem glowered. "What is *that* supposed to mean?"

Wyatt grabbed his loose beanie and pulled it over his head. "No offense, ladies, but Blue is too much of a distraction to have at the dinner table. I think Patty would lose all interest in Shepherd, and Blue would end up the center of attention."

I chortled and clapped his shoulder. "So he picked the troll. Thanks for pointing that out."

"I don't mean it that way. Blue distracts every red-blooded male with a pulse—even a stiff in a suit like Patrick." He looked at Gem. "And you're too much of a free little spirit on wheels. You're liable to leave the table and start snooping through his rooms."

A blush touched Gem's alabaster cheeks. "*Moi?* I'd never do anything inappropriate."

Gem liked snooping, and I could only imagine the temptation in a mansion like Patrick's, which we'd all admired firsthand.

Wyatt pointed at me. "So that leaves you."

I tugged at my sleeve. "Do I need to get dressed up for this?"

Wyatt chuckled. "A private dinner is rarely black-tie. Just avoid leather."

"What about Shepherd? He wears that leather coat everywhere we go."

"You can bet your bottom dollar he won't this time. Viktor will probably handpick his outfit to make sure he doesn't look fresh out of prison. I bet Viktor's quietly freaking out over all this. If Patrick starts asking questions about Keystone, change the subject. Guys like him love getting the inside scoop. It makes them feel all powerful and shit."

"Well, he's not scooping anything out of me."

"On that note, better avoid alcohol. I know how you love your wine, but—"

"No *vino*, no fun-o."

Wyatt laughed. "Be sure to take pictures."

Chapter 3

"I MUST BE CRAZY FOR LETTING Gem talk me into this." I stared up at Claude, who hovered over me with a hungry look in his eyes.

The kind of look a hairdresser gives when they see a head of long hair walk into their salon.

He continued spraying a stream of water through my hair and massaging my scalp with his other hand. It felt so good that I'd almost forgotten about the cold sink pressing against my neck. Claude had the gaze of a savage lion, his golden eyes rimmed in black. "It's about time you checked out my salon. Razor Sharp is where the magic happens."

"So this is what you do all day to fight crime?"

Claude gave a tight-lipped smile and continued the sensual massage. There was no denying the man had magic fingers.

That afternoon, Gem had decided to get a touch-up on her roots. Claude could have done her hair at home, but I gathered she liked the attention he lavished on her in front of all those women, who wanted him for themselves. I also suspected that she and Claude had ulterior motives to talk me into chopping and dying my raven-black hair.

Claude had a fascinating operation. He owned the salon and mostly booked preapproved clients. He didn't go so far as to do full background checks, but he made sure everyone was either an elite member of society or obscenely rich. At the end of the day, if he didn't hear any juicy gossip that might link to a case, at least he received a generous tip. Most people were careless enough to speak freely in his presence, assuming he was no different from hired help who kept secrets. Especially when they would invite him to their house for a private appointment. Claude said the upper class was like that, and servants were privy to some of the greatest secrets in history.

But Claude was no servant. He stood at six and a half feet tall and looked more like a cross between a Viking and Adonis, with sexy curls of blond hair and sensual lips that were made for exploring a woman's body. Whenever he'd lick those lips, women would fan themselves. Claude was as Chitah as they came, evident in the way he moved with feline grace and the way his eyes hooded when staring at people. Sometimes he growled and made other catlike sounds that could make a person's hair stand on end.

I'd seen that behavior toward him in clubs. Except here in his salon, they had to abide by his rules. So they sat obediently in their chairs, black capes fastened around their necks while they watched his every move. Claude could make combing hair look sexy.

He only hired women to work in his salon, which was clever since it never took attention away from him. That allowed him to get close to almost any customer he wanted.

I peered up. "Don't chop it all off. I know how you guys *love* to turn two inches into seven."

Claude stirred with laughter. "Actually, it's eight. But don't tell anyone."

He led me to my chair and lowered the headrest as I got situated. Then he excused himself to check on Gem, who was seated farther down to the left.

"Complete makeover or just a touch-up?"

I swung my gaze toward the man sitting to my right, his medium-length hair covered in foil at the ends. "Would you believe me if I said I just came in here to get my hair washed?"

Still staring ahead in the mirror, he replied, "Only if you believe I'm dying the tips of my hair pink."

I played with a strand of wet hair. "I'm going to a dinner at some big shot's house, so they want to polish me up."

"They?"

"My boss."

He closed his eyes. "You didn't strike me as a woman who does what she's told. Guess I was wrong."

"Do I know you?"

He chuckled quietly. "I hope your hairdresser doesn't cut off too much."

I slouched in my chair, having second thoughts about all this. It was a ridiculous idea, but my black hair was part of my identity. Chopping it off or dying it would make me feel like an imposter.

"Take my advice," he continued. "Be your own boss in life. Once you get rid of people dictating how you should live, the world is your oyster."

Claude returned and began soaking up the ends of my hair with a towel.

"I've changed my mind," I said.

He gazed at me through the mirror, a smile hovering on his lips. "Too late."

"I'm serious. I just want a trim."

He leaned over my shoulder, eyes still centered on mine. "We agreed on highlights."

I lowered my eyes, thinking about my plans to see my father. It wasn't as if a few highlights would alter my appearance entirely, but I wanted to look the way he remembered me.

"Claude, I know you can do amazing things with your hands, but I'm not ready for amazing just yet. Snip off the split ends and let's call it a day."

He shook his head, but his nostrils were twitching. Claude was trying to figure out my emotional scent, and probably the only thing he could pick up was my resolve. "Female, I wouldn't do anything but enhance the beauty that's already there."

"You gave me some layers last month. That's progress."

Claude folded his arms. "I fixed a catastrophe involving duct tape."

"Don't give me that look," I said, lacing my fingers together. "I'm not going to be guilted into something I'll regret. I've already got too many oddities going on; maybe I need something plain in my life."

Claude growled and reluctantly grabbed the comb off the counter. I should have felt guilty for wasting his time, but I kind of liked seeing him all flustered.

When I looked to my right, the customer beside me was gone.

Claude combed out my hair and sectioned off a piece. "You're going to have to do a lot of things you don't necessarily like, but that's our job."

I glanced around.

He bent down next to my ear. "No one can hear us. I usually don't allow Vampires in my shop."

"Maybe you should. Christian could use a trim."

"What Christian needs is a lawn mower from the neck up."

"I wish Viktor had chosen someone else. How am I supposed to carry on a conversation with Shepherd? The man barely grunts at me when passing in the hall."

"He grows on you." Claude snipped another section and resumed combing. "If you run out of things to talk about during dinner, rich people like to discuss travel and politics. Given you'll probably say something offensive on the latter, you might stick to asking him about Paris."

"What makes you think he's been there?"

Claude pushed my head down. "They've *all* been to Paris. Some of those European countries have a long Breed history. Most of them have old friends they like to visit."

I peeked through my hair at his reflection in the mirror. "What exactly does Patrick do?"

"He serves on the panel. The higher authority has officials in every major city, and they take turns rotating who's going to sit in on trials. They know more about what's going on in their district than anyone."

I yawned noisily. "And I have to chat with this guy for how long?"

"If Shepherd has more than four drinks, it's time to go home. Maybe if you bring up something innocuous like lager or stogies, it'll give them a topic to discuss. Shepherd isn't the most talkative male, but careful not to pick the wrong topic or he'll get on his soapbox."

"Lovely."

After a few more snips, Claude circled in front of me where I could see him. The other employees wore black button-up shirts, but not Claude. He had on a black tank top with the store logo RAZOR SHARP on the front, a pair of scissors snipping off the bottom of the *P*. His tank top showed off his amazing shoulders— the kind a man is born with and doesn't need to sculpt. Claude could ascend our rock-climbing wall faster than anyone in the group… and using only his hands.

"How are you getting along with Poe? Feeling better about Viktor's decision to pair you up?"

I shrugged. "He's okay."

Claude arched a single brow, and that's when I remembered he could smell my emotions. Lies, truths, doubt, fear—the only way to avoid Claude sniffing out the truth was to avoid answering questions.

"I noticed earlier you're still wearing that heart-shaped necklace. Didn't he give you that?"

I could almost feel the stone burning against my skin. "Don't read into it or else I'm going to have to spread rumors about all the snuggling you do with Gem."

"Gem likes my cuddles." He smirked while snipping the ends of my hair at an angle. "It's good to see you loosening up."

I furrowed my brow and shook my hair away. "What do you mean?"

Claude crossed around to the other side and trimmed a few ends. "When you first came into the house, your guard was up. It's like that for everyone. I have to admit, when I first heard about the *Shadow* killing people in Breed bars, I never imagined the ruthless killer to look like you."

I leaned my head back and grinned. "A lot of sleepless nights?"

"A few. Viktor's decision to offer you a spot took me by

surprise. I couldn't figure out why Gem liked you so much, but now I get it."

"Enlighten me. I *still* haven't figured that one out."

He combed out my tresses and held a long section straight up, a ribbon of hair falling loose as the scissors sliced together. "Blue's disciplined, hardworking, and serious. She also likes to be one of the guys. Gem is drawn to people with a sense of humor, which you have. Albeit black humor. You're not the first person I'd choose to deliver my eulogy, but you're easy to talk to."

"Thanks."

"I'm not suggesting that Blue isn't," he quickly added, "but Gem gravitates toward people who are like her in some ways."

That made me think of my odd little bond with Christian. I was already forming different connections with everyone in the house. I hadn't grown up in a big family, and even though this was work, it was probably the closest thing to family I'd ever know again.

"There. Done."

I blinked at myself in the mirror. "Already?"

He flung the scissors into an open drawer and mussed up my hair. "Regretting your decision? Because I could shave a little spot in the back—"

I slapped his hand. "Get away from me, Claude Scissorhands."

He removed the gown tied around my neck and shook it out. "I'm closing up here soon—after I finish with Gem." Claude lowered my chair using the foot pedal.

A woman handed him something, and the next thing I knew, he was wrapping a hot towel around my face, leaving just enough space in the center for me to breathe.

"Just relax and close your eyes," he said, massaging my neck.

"That's what I say to all my victims."

Something jarred me out of my nap, and it took me a second

to remember that I'd nodded off in Claude's salon, and I wasn't actually blind, but there was a towel on my face.

My hair stood on end when another pulse of energy crackled against my skin. It was stronger than a Mage flaring, like a spike in power you feel during a fight. I shot up in my seat and flung the towel to the floor. The salon was empty except for the sound of Gem and Claude talking loudly over the blow-dryer in the back. The floors were swept up, the drawers closed, and the employees gone.

The hair dryer switched off. Gem appeared, her wavy hair blown in every direction as if she'd stuck her finger in a light socket. The pale-lavender color was more vibrant and had an ombré effect that faded to silver.

"Did you feel that?" she asked, brushing her hands up her arms.

Claude's nostrils flared as he stalked toward the front door. Gem and I followed behind him. Though it wasn't completely dark outside, the lights in the parking lot had switched on. I rubbed my itchy neck and tried to dust away some of the tiny hairs.

The second Claude unlocked the door and cracked it open, he turned his head, and I watched his golden eyes morph to black.

"Claude, what's wrong?"

"He can't hear you anymore," Gem whispered. "He's flipped his switch."

The door swung open, and Claude flew out, a whirlwind of snowflakes melting as soon as they hit the floor. I didn't bother grabbing my coat. Gem and I flashed to the left to catch up with him, but I skidded out of control when I turned the corner around the side of the building.

We both stopped at the same time, staring in disbelief at Claude crouched on the hood of a car parked between his salon and another building. A thin layer of snow glistened on the concrete, but most of the parking lot was a slushy mess. The businesses were closed, so it seemed peculiar to see a car backed up against his building. A thick layer of snow covered the trunk and hood, leaving me to believe it had been out here for at least a day.

Whatever internal switch that kept him human had shut off, and what remained was a Chitah in his primal state. Still a man, but ripples of spotted patterns flashed across his arms and neck, deadly upper and lower fangs gleaming in the dim light and animalistic instincts driving his every decision.

I sharpened my light and slowly approached the car. He punched through the windshield with his fist, glass shattering in a spiral around the point of impact.

"What's he doing?" Gem asked.

Claude ripped away large chunks of the windshield. While he crawled through the opening, we hurried to the passenger side.

Gem wiped the snow off the glass so we could see inside. When Claude reached into the backseat, I noticed something.

"Claude, open the door!" I pounded on the window and jiggled the handle. "Open up!"

Gem hurried to the front of the car and circled to the driver's side. "They're all locked! Claude, you need to snap out of it. Open the door so we can help!"

She brushed away some of the glass from the hood, but I was already leaping onto the car. Without a second to lose, I crawled into the passenger seat, not even caring if he turned on me. I unlocked the door, but before I could open it for Gem, I glimpsed a woman in the backseat, fresh blood covering her hands and neck.

Claude turned to look at me, and his eyes were no longer onyx. Tears welled in them—angry tears. His lips peeled back, revealing sharp canines. "She's gone."

"What happened?"

Gem got the door halfway open and then jumped back when she saw the body. "I'll call for help."

"Don't bother," Claude said in disgust. "Just call the cleaners."

Still breathing hard, he turned around and sat in the driver's seat, his cheeks flushed. He didn't seem to notice or care that his hands were bleeding.

I got a better look at the woman. The spike in energy that I'd felt in the salon had to be related. Someone had just murdered this woman; the blood was still trickling down her neck where someone had cut her throat.

I faced forward, the frigid wind blowing through the open windshield. "Why were the doors locked?"

"The killer didn't want anyone to find her for a while. She's buried beneath clothes."

"The tall snow on the hood makes me think the car's been here for at least a day or two. Do you think she lived in here?"

"I park out front and never have a reason to come this way. Had I known a female was living in her car, I would have done something about it. Helped her."

I studied the victim, trying not to make the same mistake as I had last time by getting emotionally involved. It was hard to guess her age, but if I had to, I'd say approximately upper thirties. Frizzy black hair framed her face, and by the looks of things, she lived in her car. The space above the backseat was jam-packed full of items most people don't keep in a car. Clothes, blankets, diapers…

"She had a baby."

Claude snapped his head around. "Why do you say that?"

I jerked my thumb over my shoulder. "Diapers and bottles. The packages are open, so she wasn't pregnant and hoarding supplies. I think she's homeless. I've seen a lot of people living out of their cars. Sometimes they steal gas and move the vehicle into the Breed district, though I never paid attention if they were human or not. Nobody cares if a car sits unattended in a parking lot."

Claude shut his eyes and reclined his head. "Now I know what this is about."

"Domestic violence? Maybe she was a prostitute and her pimp didn't want her to keep the kid."

He shook his head. "Black market."

Gem stood in front of the car while talking on her phone.

"Usually when they steal the child, it's violent. The mother rarely survives."

I shivered. Babies were prized on the black market—that much I knew. "Why don't they just get a kid from the orphanage? Why go through all this?"

He rubbed his jaw. "Most orphans are discarded because something's wrong with them. They're defective in some way. I've heard stories about men killing their wives who produced an inferior child. Anyhow, orphans are tracked, and there's a screening process to adopt. The filthy ghouls who buy children aren't the type of men who would put their name on paper for adoption rights."

"Your hands are bleeding."

He turned them over and proceeded to lick his wounds. I watched, mildly fascinated as every stroke of his tongue healed the superficial cuts. When he finished, he wiped his hands on his pants to get rid of the bloodstains. "Come on. I can't sit in this car any longer."

I stepped outside, cupping my elbows and joining him at the front of the vehicle.

"They'll be here in ten minutes," Gem announced. Her lip quivered, and I remembered her story about being a child of the black market herself. Seeing this must have struck a nerve.

"Why don't you go back inside and call Viktor," I suggested. "We'll take care of everything out here."

Claude touched her shoulder and steered her away. "Go inside and get warm, female. Keep the door locked."

Once Gem disappeared around the corner, I leaned against the hood beside Claude.

"Sometimes they cut them out," Claude said on a breath.

I looked up at him in horror. "*What?*"

"If the woman is a vagabond and doesn't have anyone to protect her, she becomes an easy target. Black marketeers will stalk a woman they think is single and living alone. When she nears full term, they cut the baby out."

"That's sick. Wouldn't the baby die?"

"We're Breed. Our children are stronger than humans. They steal the baby from the womb so that no one can identify the child, not having seen nor touched it. No Chitah will have imprinted their smell, no Sensor will know their touch, and no doctor or father will recognize a birthmark or face."

I slid my jaw to the side. "Maybe I was hunting down the

wrong people all these years. Had I known *that* kind of thing was going on, I would have targeted those assholes instead. What could they want with a Chitah baby? Or a Shifter? Do they only sell them to couples? Do these parents realize that they're indirectly responsible for a mother's death?"

Claude put his arm around me—not to offer me comfort, but because it was too cold to do anything else but huddle. "The children are collected and sold regardless of who wants them, and most people bidding are not loving couples. Lucky is the child who is sold to real parents. Chitahs are excellent trackers; train them right and they'll grow up to become obedient killers. There's a dark side to our world, Raven. Even darker than you can imagine. Immortality breeds the most evil men imaginable."

The sky took on a deep sapphire hue as the day came to an end. The orange glow from a streetlamp illuminated the snowflakes, which were falling at an angle.

"A Mage did it," I said.

"How do you know?"

"Well, *she's* obviously not a Mage since they can't have babies. And back in the salon, I felt a strong flare of energy—the kind that happens during a fight when there's a lot of adrenaline going. Some guys don't know how to level down when they get excited. Gem felt it too."

He rubbed his nose. "The smell of fear burns," he said absently. "It seems to permeate through walls. The female doesn't have the characteristics of a Chitah," Claude offered. "I'll ask the cleaners to give us her identity after they search the vehicle. Wyatt can run a check on her name to see what turns up."

"Did you pick up another scent?"

He nodded. "Didn't matter. She was my priority."

I turned around and looked at the car. "You know what's bugging me? The doors were locked and the windows unbroken."

Claude frowned.

"No sign of a struggle," I pointed out. "Why does a woman, who's living in her vehicle with her baby, open the door for someone? She wouldn't have been sitting in her car with the doors unlocked."

Claude pushed off the car and strode around to the driver's side, his eyes downcast and scanning the ground. "She knew him."

"He got away fast. Maybe his energy spiked when he was driving off."

"This is the Breed district," Claude reminded me. "People who commit murders don't tarry."

I kicked the tire. Had I not snoozed in the chair with a towel on my face, would I have gotten bored and walked around outside? Would I have been close enough to help her in time? It must have happened fast.

Claude briefly stuck his nose inside the car, and when he reappeared, his mouth was open, his eyes hooded. "Stay here."

"Wait, where the hell are you going?"

"Hunting."

In a flash, he took off, leaving me alone with a dead body and no jacket.

Chapter 4

L ATER THAT EVENING, AFTER THE cleaners had shown up
and taken our statements, I headed out on foot. Claude had
returned after searching the streets in vain for the killer, his
shoes and pants soaking wet. Apparently it was much harder to run
at Chitah speed in snow and ice to catch up with a moving vehicle.
Everyone at Keystone was probably sitting around, waiting for me
to show up and cook dinner, so I used my phone to order them
a pizza. After seeing a dead woman, I didn't feel like going home,
and I sure as hell didn't feel like cooking a meal for nine people.

After a long walk, I wound up in a club called Nine Circles of
Hell, also known as Club Nine. They had nine specialty drinks,
each representing a circle of hell. Skilled Sensors, who were also
mixologists, spiked the drinks with just enough emotional flavor
to make the drink worth every penny. Treachery was green, wrath
red, limbo yellow, lust violet, gluttony orange, greed pink, heresy
blue, violence turquoise, and fraud chartreuse.

I was currently enjoying a glass of wrath. "Can I have another?"

The bartender—a sketchy-looking man named Hooper with
three lip rings and designs shaved on each side of his head—placed
his palms on the bar and forced a smile. "One specialty drink per
person. Otherwise, this place would be hell for real."

"Tequila."

While Hooper set a shot glass in front of me and filled it to
the brim, I scanned my text messages. The only one I'd received
was a Vampire emoji from Christian. Viktor didn't keep us on a
tight leash, and we were free to come and go as we pleased. Getting

out was good for my sanity, and even though Breed clubs had never been my scene, I was learning to appreciate the company of my own kind. Maybe it had something to do with not being the scavenger anymore, not fearing someone would turn me over to the law. Now I had protection, and that offered me more freedom than I'd once had.

I caught my reflection in the mirror. Claude's trendy cut was hardly noticeable amid the tousled clumps of wet hair, thanks to my standing in the snow without a hat.

Instead of knocking back the tequila, I sipped it.

"Nice hair," a man said.

I glanced to my left, and recognition sparked my memory. "You're the guy from the salon. No pink tips, huh?" The roots of his hair were dark, but a good chunk of it was bleached white and styled in every direction like an anime character. If it weren't for his alternative hairstyle, his faded jeans and button-up shirt were so ordinary that he could have easily blended into a crowd.

"Is this seat taken?"

I closed my eyes and smiled.

"I know. It's cliché." He set down his glass and made himself comfortable.

I nodded at his specialty drink. "Which one is that? I keep forgetting all the colors."

He lifted the green glass to his lips. "Treachery." Then his eyes flicked down to my tequila.

I raised it up. "Apparently I've hit my limit on wrath."

"All in good fun. This isn't my usual, but then I thought, what the hell."

I knocked back the rest of my tequila and stared absently at the bottles behind the bar.

The man beside me bit his thumbnail, and I could see in the mirror that he was watching me.

I glared at him. "What?"

"Can I have your number?"

"No."

He turned his head and looked at me in the mirror. "I didn't think it would be that easy. Just thought I'd ask."

"You don't even know me. I could be your worst nightmare."

"We're each our own worst nightmares."

"I'll drink to that."

"How is it you don't have a boyfriend?" He chuckled warmly and lifted his glass. "Just a hunch."

"I guess I'm lucky," I quipped.

"Ah. A spinster at twenty-five. Such a tragic tale. Maybe you should give me your number after all. I'd like to buy you a cat."

I snorted, still talking to him through the reflection in the mirror. "Why? So when I slip in the bathroom and hit my head, he can nibble on my remains?"

"At least he'll be well-fed."

"What makes you think I'm twenty-five?"

When he shifted to face me directly, I felt more comfortable looking into his hazel eyes than through a mirror. They were inquisitive and friendly, and his dark eyebrows sloped down in the middle just enough that it made it look like he was concentrating. "I'm an excellent guesser. When you've been around as long as I have, it comes naturally. By your manner of speech, I'm going to guess you're newly made, but you're more seasoned than most."

"You're assuming I'm a Mage?"

He propped his elbow on the bar and played with the ear stud in his left lobe. "Chitahs and Vampires are automatically ruled out. You mentioned having a boss, so that means you're not likely a Relic since they work with partners and don't waste time at social events, like the dinner you mentioned back at the salon. Most Sensors are self-employed traders. You *could* be a Shifter, or maybe something else."

"What else is there?"

He winked. "Lots of things."

Two women grinding against each other caught my attention. Their eyes scanned the bar, and it was clear they were searching for a third party to join in on the action. I was dressed down, and my body language wasn't inviting anyone over to play. So why was this guy wasting his time with me?

"You should go talk to them," I suggested.

He turned all the way around to admire the women, his elbows resting on the bar. "Eh. Same tits, different night. I never thought I'd be so sick of looking at tits."

"Maybe women aren't your thing."

"Maybe flagrant misuse of sexuality and wielding it like a toy isn't my thing. We're immortals, and look what we've become. Could you ever have imagined that men who have been around since before the Roman Empire would be doing *this* with their time?"

"Better this than bringing back gladiator fights."

He finished off his drink. "I think I'd prefer that."

When the music switched to a slower beat, I studied him for a moment. He had a friendly face. Not overly handsome or particularly ugly, just somewhere in the middle. His nose was straight and narrow, giving him a regal look that made him seem out of place in this century. Most of the time, his eyes narrowed as if he were squinting from a bright light or smiling. And for a man, what pretty lashes he had.

"What's your name?" I asked, wondering if that would shed any light on whether or not he was an ancient.

He slowly turned to face the mirror again and met my gaze in its reflection. "Let's keep it simple."

"Fine by me."

"What's your name? What do you do? Where do you live? How old are you, and what is your Breed? You'll eventually learn that none of those questions matter. Not one of them helps you to know a person better."

I gave him a sardonic smile. "How many men have you killed? What was the last crime you committed? Would you rather be good or evil?"

That must have been my drink talking.

His brows sloped down, and when he grinned, deep lines etched on the sides of his face. "Now you're getting the hang of it."

I played with the napkin in front of me. "Questions no one will answer, so we're back to square one."

"Ever want to break the rules?"

"Sometimes."

"Why do people make rules?" he asked conversationally.

I shrugged.

"Control," he answered. "And why do people need control?"

"Power?"

"Exactly."

"Rules keep us from turning into animals. If this club had no rules, no one would pay for their drinks, and the owner would go out of business because of broken bottles and rowdy customers."

The man folded his arms and tilted his head. "In Greek mythology, Chaos was the first thing to exist. Without Chaos, there would be nothing."

"That's fiction."

"Maybe you should go home and read about the chaos theory."

"You mean the butterfly effect? Bugs can't create hurricanes. I'm not buying it."

"You can't know that, and it's beside the point. Nothing in this life would ever change without chaos, and I'm not talking about revolutions and the downfall of the higher authority. Chaos isn't about good or evil; it's about unpredictability. Aren't you ever inquisitive about the effect of your actions, no matter how small?"

"My job lets me see the results of my actions."

He ticked his index finger back and forth like a pendulum on a metronome. "That's not the same. That's predictability. The same way coming in and ordering a drink is. But what if instead of drinking that glass of wrath, you left it on an empty table? Those drinks are spiked by Sensors. Maybe all someone needs to do the unexpected is a little nudge."

I chortled and looked at his empty glass. "I think that's the treachery talking."

"Why don't we give it a try?"

"Swapping someone's drink?"

He leaned in and grinned wolfishly. "Let's change destiny. Follow me if you're up for an experiment."

My brows touched my hairline as he stood up. Curious, I grabbed my coat and followed him through the crowd.

Club Nine was an enormous establishment, the main door on the front right. Upon entering a wide hall, customers found themselves in a large room mostly used for dancing. The bar ran along the front wall, the kitchen hidden behind it. Bathrooms were tucked away on the left side of the building. The unique thing about Club Nine was the lounge rooms in the back. Straight ahead, past the dance floor, an archway framed a wide hall, which was a cozy chamber unto itself. There were nine rooms, each with an arched entranceway made from brick. The lights affixed to the ceiling splashed a different color on the brick around every entrance. Four rooms on the left, four on the right, and one straight ahead. They weren't labeled since the colored lights indicated which room was which.

"Why are they separated?" I asked. "Does something different go on in each one?" If the gluttony room had a buffet table, I was all in.

My new friend turned, hands in his pockets. "The club is a perfect example of how people like order. They want to be associated with something because it gives them a sense of belonging. In some clubs, people gravitate toward their own Breed. In others, it's social status. Here, they want to commiserate and mingle with people who share common interests."

"But it's just a gimmick."

"For some it is." He disappeared behind me and suddenly stuck his head between my legs.

I hopped forward and scowled at him. "I don't know what you think is going on here—"

"Haven't you ever been to a rock concert?" He looked up at me, hands on his knees. "Ride my shoulders and switch out two of the colors."

When he moved behind me again, I didn't run off. Mostly

because it seemed like a harmless idea, and I wanted to prove to him that it was absurd.

A woman sauntered past us, paying no attention as he hoisted me up. People did crazy things in Breed clubs all the time, so I didn't concern myself with what other people might be thinking.

"Which ones?" he asked.

After he reminded me of the colors and their meaning, I pointed at the yellow and violet. They weren't the kind of bulbs that heated up, so it didn't take long to switch them out.

He set me down and studied them. "Why limbo and lust?"

I patted his shoulder and gave him a wry grin. "Lonely people need love?"

He sat down on a bench. "I would have interchanged treachery and greed."

"You mean they aren't the same?" I quipped, sitting beside him. "You wanted to prove that this has nothing to do with good or evil. If your theory has merit, then it won't matter which of the nine I selected."

"All in good fun," he replied.

After a few minutes of people coming and going, voices within the rooms grew louder. One woman stormed out of the lust room, her lips pressed tight and fists clenched. A man wandered out shortly afterward, a scarlet mark across his alabaster cheek.

Serves you right for treating her like a piece of meat, I thought.

"Feels good, doesn't it?" my partner in crime asked.

"What? Being bad?"

He leaned forward and held my gaze. "No. To be free."

"Switching a few lights hardly makes a person free."

"There's a light in every situation. You can't switch those lights when you're busy following rules."

"Are you sure you didn't drink the heresy? You seem to like anarchy."

"That would imply I enjoy negative outcomes. Believe it or not, good things can come out of chaos. Life can arise from death, just as death can arise from life." He jerked his head at the room.

"One of those lonely men in there might connect with a woman who fills the void in his life."

That was probably why I'd selected the most innocuous combination.

"That's a pretty necklace," he said. "A gift?"

I glanced down at the red heart dangling from my neck. It swung from the silver chain in a forward motion. "Not really. I needed costume jewelry for a thing I had to attend, so someone gave it to me." I stood up and put on my grey trench coat, wishing I'd worn the leather jacket instead since it was easier to carry.

"Can I have your number?" he asked again, rising to face me.

I smiled playfully. "Let's keep it simple."

He inclined his head, amusement dancing in his eyes. Then he reached out and held my pendant between his fingers. "Who gave you this heart? Someone you loved?"

"No. Just my partner."

"Your partner is a man of considerable wealth."

"It's not real."

"This is a Burmese ruby of the finest quality. It's a one of a kind and worth millions. The last time I saw it was at an auction in 1932."

My breath caught.

He winked and let go. "How's that for a little chaos? Have fun with your newfound knowledge, Butterfly."

As I watched him disappear into the crowd, I felt the heat from the ruby burning against my chest like a fiery stone.

Chapter 5

A FTER THE REVELATION REGARDING THE alleged value of my necklace, I tucked it inside my shirt. Odds were my mischievous friend was messing with my head to further his theory, and that specialty drink had done me no favors. It had altered my mood, though it wasn't so strong that I couldn't control my actions. Maybe that was why I'd participated in his game, whereas any other night I might have blown him off.

I was beginning to see the allure of all the club drinks.

After I left Club Nine and made it back to Keystone, I went into the dining room to find empty pizza boxes stacked on the table. One had leftovers inside and a note with my name taped to the box.

I lit a candle and took a seat in one of the booths along the wall between the dining and gathering rooms. Through the archway to my left, I noticed that the fire was extinguished—not a single flickering ember in the hearth. The butterscotch glow from my candle suffused against the wooden table, creating a peaceful aura amid the darkness.

Blue silently entered the room in a long red dress that looked like something out of medieval times. Her daytime attire consisted of tall boots, dark pants, and a tight shirt. In the wee hours of the morning, I occasionally caught her roaming the halls, her gown or cloak swishing against the cold floors. Blue remained an enigmatic figure in the house. On one hand, the face she showed the world was fierce. Yet within the privacy of these walls, a feminine side existed.

"You're not eating?" she asked. "We saved enough in case you came home hungry."

I waved my hand. "If you want some, it's all yours. I don't have an appetite."

She opened the box and took out a slice. "I don't think we've ever ordered pizza before. Viktor almost had a heart attack when the delivery man buzzed at the front gate."

I snickered. "I tipped him online, so I hope you guys didn't go out of your way."

She took a seat across from me and folded a slice of pizza in half. "Christian answered the door, so I don't know what he did."

"Probably said a lot of fecks."

Her eyes danced with amusement. "I think he was curious like we all were what you were going to cook."

I touched some of the hot wax dripping down the side of the candle. "I wasn't hungry after we found the body, and I really didn't feel like cooking."

She took a large bite and picked up a fallen pepper. "I thought you'd be famished."

I gave her a cold stare even though I knew she was kidding.

"Don't be ridiculous," she said. "Claude filled us in on the gory details. No one expected you to cook after that."

"Is the woman going to be our next case?"

Blue wiped her mouth, her sapphire-colored eyes focused on the pizza. "It's up to Viktor. A lot of murders happen in the Breed district; it wouldn't be the first time we've happened upon a crime scene. But we still have to get paid, so that means someone would have to hire us to solve the murder." She glanced over her shoulder at the door across from us that led down to the training room. "Shepherd was upset when he heard about it."

"Shepherd?"

She ate the pizza up to the crust and left it on the table. "After Claude described the grisly scene, Shepherd got up and left the room."

"Was Claude talking about it over dinner? No wonder."

She stroked her bottom lip. "Shepherd has an iron stomach. I once saw him eat a taco while some guy told a story about how he removed a twenty-foot tapeworm from his bowels. Gem I'd expect to leave the table, but not Shepherd."

"Maybe he had to do some more pull-ups."

Blue smiled, her cheeks glowing.

I noticed the holes in her earlobes where her feather earrings usually hung. "Don't those close up when you shift?"

"Sometimes. I could make it permanent with liquid fire, but I just pierce them again. It's no big deal."

"Can I ask you a question?"

She sat back. "Sure. But I can't guarantee you'll get an answer."

"Remember the masquerade ball? When you went with Christian to buy a wig, did you see him buying anything else?"

"Like what?"

"Jewelry or something."

Her eyes skated up. "No. He pretty much stayed in the chair and watched me try them all on. He picked out the hideous ones first so he could get a good laugh. That much I remember."

"So the guy didn't try to sell him anything else?"

"We spent about an hour picking out my wig and then loaded the costumes into the van. That was it."

I leaned back, my arms still on the table as I stared at the candle. I didn't have the best memory in the world, but I was pretty sure Christian had told me that the seller was pushing his trinkets to get him to buy something else. If that was true, wouldn't he have also bought Blue a necklace? She'd ended up wearing something Gem had lent her for the evening. Why would he lie?

I refused to believe that Chaos's statement was true, so there had to be a logical explanation.

"Is this about the necklace I've seen you wearing?" She stared at my black shirt, which concealed the stone beneath.

"I thought he mentioned buying it from that dealer, so I was going to see if he had anything else I might like. My memory isn't what it used to be," I said, hoping to throw off any suspicion.

Blue seemed satisfied with my answer and stood up, wagging

the leftover pizza crust at me. "Viktor doesn't like it when you skip meals."

"I'm half Vampire, so I'm only half hungry. I'll have a big breakfast in the morning if it makes everyone happy."

Her brows arched with subtle amusement. "Then you better be sure to cook something you like."

I smacked my forehead. "Don't we have any cereal?"

"Good night, Raven."

After Blue left the room, I glanced at the closed door that led to the training room downstairs. It was close to the exit, and I guessed that it must have once been a basement used to store food or wine. As I stood up and approached, I heard the faint sound of grunting. Either Christian had snuck in a hot date, or Shepherd was down there doing reps. I paused near the door, my ear pressed against the wood. Shepherd didn't like anyone disturbing him when he worked out, so there was no point in bothering him so late. If the man wanted to lift weights in the middle of the night, it was no business of mine, so I left the candle burning on the table for when he finally came out.

The mansion came alive at night with shadows and light reflecting on the windows. But imagined fears paled in comparison to sleeping in abandoned buildings and alleyways. Monsters under the bed didn't frighten me. The true terrors were the faces of seemingly normal men who walked the streets, concealing the darkness within them. That was why I used to hunt them down. It made more sense to get the monsters before they got me.

Once I reached the third floor, I paused before a row of windows overlooking the courtyard. Gem was floating in the heated pool, green and blue lights rippling through the still water beneath and around her. She had on a long dress or nightgown and looked so serene lying there. It must have been her form of meditation, the same way that Niko would sit for long spells down in the gym.

"Did you have a good time?"

I pivoted around on one heel, a dagger in hand.

With one finger, Christian gently moved my arm away. "Your

reflexes are quick, but you don't have to arm yourself around here. This is your home."

I blew out a breath and tucked the push dagger back in my belt holster. "Force of habit. I don't like people sneaking up on me. You need to curb all that shadow walking. Women don't like to be snuck up on."

He stood next to me and peered down at Gem through the latticed window. "She's a peculiar lass."

"We're all nuts here. Shepherd's downstairs battling it out with kettlebells."

"And I suppose you're on your way to walk on the roof?"

I strode over to a chair on the opposite wall and took a seat. "I don't know."

Christian leaned against the wall across from me, hands in his pockets. "Still thinking about the murder?"

What I really wanted to ask him about was the case of the mysterious necklace, but the longer he stared at me, the more wary I became. Was I ready to open up a can of worms, especially if Mr. Chaos had only been bluffing? Christian would love nothing more than to think that I believed he'd given me a multimillion-dollar necklace. That was the discord Chaos was trying to create, so I kept my mouth closed.

"Vampires can't read minds," he said absently.

"Someone murdered her and stole her baby. I get why they're doing it, I just don't understand it." I rubbed my temple. "This is a sick world. And I don't mean generally speaking. I mean *our* world."

"Don't give humans so much credit. They're fairly adept at wiping out entire populations and building weapons of mass destruction. Why do you think we're still in hiding?"

"I hope someone hires Viktor for this case. I'd love to catch the people behind it and give them a taste of their own medicine. Has anyone looked at the latest black market listings?"

"Wyatt's monitoring the site. It shouldn't be long before we see the auction go up. Marketeers don't like babysitting."

"If he sold the baby direct, we'll never catch him."

Christian pushed off the wall and clasped his hands behind his back. "Most immortals have trust issues and won't deal with anyone directly. If you're going to hire someone to do your dirty work, then you have to kill them when they finish the task. Loose ends are a nasty thing, so most prefer the anonymity of the black market."

"Men with money surround themselves with lackeys who do their dirty work."

"And that's their flaw. Men can't keep secrets, and money will always win over loyalty."

"That baby better show up on the black market."

"And if he doesn't?"

"Plan B."

"Plan B. Is that a pregnancy test? Your bra size?"

I crossed my legs at the ankles. "Not everyone knows who we are and what we do. Let's go to a few bars and ask around—pretend we're a couple in search of a child."

"And what if your plan results in another innocent woman's murder?"

"What if it doesn't?"

"Viktor wouldn't approve. Are you going back to your old ways, crossbreed? That's not how we do things here."

"You've never gone undercover? Don't be telling me fibs," I said in a bad Irish accent.

He paced to my right, holding the back of his neck. "If a child winds up in your arms, and it's not *that* child, you'll have to live with that for the rest of your life. Assuming you have a conscience. You'll have captured a criminal, but at the expense of another innocent life."

"But think of all the lives we'll save. Even if you think it's wrong, you can't deny the end result."

Christian stalked forward and glared at me so intensely that I blinked. "Are you langered? Because that's not a rational argument. Where did you go this evening?"

"That's a tight leash you keep on me."

"You're more combative than usual tonight. I'm just curious what's influencing such dangerous thoughts."

"I went to Club Nine."

He rocked with laughter. "Jaysus wept. No wonder. Let me guess, you drank the heresy."

"Wrath."

"No wonder you're on a mission. Let the alcohol wear off, and see how you feel in the morning. When a Sensor spikes your drink, the residual effects can last longer than you think."

"Why did Betty keep staring at you like she did?" I asked, shifting topics. It was something that had been weighing on my mind all day.

"Betty who?"

"The waitress at the diner." When just a hint of scarlet touched his cheeks and he walked off, I bolted out of my seat and followed behind him. "What are you not telling me?"

The sound of our footsteps reverberated off the stone floors, and I hurried to match his pace. When he turned a dark corner and shadow walked to get away, I flashed with a burst of energy and grabbed the back of his shirt.

Christian spun around. "What the feck is wrong with you? Can't you let a man be alone? You're always trying to stir the pot."

"You know her, don't you?"

His lips tightened, and he gave me a belligerent look.

"You might as well talk," I said coolly. "It's not as if I'm going anywhere for the next few centuries. Did you drink her blood?"

This time when he flounced off, I let him. He went out the heavy door that led to the interior balcony. It was a nice space that overlooked the front property, but I hadn't spent much time out there since the weather changed over to snow. I casually pushed open the door and saw Christian leaning forward, his arms resting on the stone railing. I crossed the distance and stood to his left where a quiet gust of wind lifted snowflakes off the ground.

Christian kept his eyes forward. "Believe it or not, Betty was a fetching girl in her youth. Fifty years ago. Maybe more."

"How did you know her?"

He shook his head, amusement in his voice. "You see so many faces in your lifetime that it's not always easy to remember the ones who have aged. Her last name is different, but not much else. I was surprised she remembered me. Well, she doesn't actually know who I am, but her uncertainty was enough to give me pause. I looked different back then. Didn't have the beard and dressed with the times."

"If you're about to tell me that you and Betty got it on, I'm not sure I want the details."

"No," he said on a long sigh. "Betty wasn't like that. She was a spirited lass with dreams about becoming an activist. She was always marching for something. Just a short little lass with fiery hair, a nice set of knockers, and a loud opinion."

I snorted. "Not much has changed. Did you love her?"

"Don't be daft. I was involved in a lot of nefarious activities back then, which I'm sure you can already guess, and I used to sit in that diner late at night and have a cup of coffee. Sometimes she'd invite herself to my table and stir up a conversation. I didn't think all these years later she'd still be there. The last I saw of her, she was betrothed to a lad who'd just joined the army. Such a tragic waste."

"Of what? It sounds like she's lived a full life."

Christian regarded me for a moment. "You don't think working in the same diner after fifty years is tragic? She could have done something more with her life than having babies and serving pie."

"She did. Betty's a lighthouse. Maybe she didn't become a social activist or whatever you saw in her, but she fed me and helped me out when things were bleak. I'm sure she didn't just sit with you because of your charming personality. She has a way of spotting lost souls. People like you are beyond her help, but she matters. People like *her* matter. Without their compassion, where would the rest of us be?"

"You shouldn't get attached to mortals."

"Humans have treated me better than any of our kind ever has. I'm sick of Breed looking down their noses at them."

He stood up straight, his breath fogging the air between us. "It's easier that way. You're too green to know what life can do to an immortal. How many people can you stand to watch go through sickness and disease, only to fade away and become nothing more than a headstone? You haven't a clue how many people I've watched go mad because they couldn't let go of the human world. Better that you forget this nonsense with seeing your father. It will only destroy you."

"He's my *father*!"

Christian's lips peeled back. "But that's not your place anymore! You don't belong there. Do you think saying good-bye makes it any easier? You have an opportunity to do something with your life. Don't be like Betty. Don't give it up for love. You can't be with your father anymore. You can't visit every Sunday and talk over tea about the latest football game, pretending that everything's normal before you head back to Keystone and plan an assassination. It doesn't work that way. Let him go."

The moment I felt the tear roll down my cheek, I hated myself for showing my emotions. "You made me a promise."

"Aye. And I'll keep that promise," he said, taking a step back. "Even if it means losing you as a partner. Do you think I didn't contemplate returning to Ireland to see if my sister was looked after? Nature has to take its course. You can't interfere. Even after I scrub your father's memory, it won't remove the emotions. They'll linger, and if he's gotten over your disappearance and death, he might end up reliving those feelings all over again without knowing why."

When Christian returned inside, my heart sank. What if he was right? What if visiting my father ended up being the catalyst that turned him back to the bottle? What right did I have to erase the peace he'd probably found after five years?

Even still, I couldn't back out.

I needed to see him.

I needed to know.

Chapter 6

"T HAT WAS THE WORST BREAKFAST in God's creation," Wyatt remarked from his office chair.

Ignoring his complaint, I stared at my file on the floor in front of me.

"I thought the jam was marvelous," Gem said from the beanbag chair.

Wyatt's laugh ended with a snort. "That's because it was the only thing she didn't burn. Toast I get. And I'll even forgive bacon. But how do you burn eggs?"

"Will you two pipe down so I can concentrate?" Shepherd grumbled. He'd taken over the sofa and surrounded himself with papers.

Since Wyatt had a lot of territory to cover with recent black market offers, he'd printed them all out for us to review while he monitored the new listings in search of a baby. The whole team was present except for Claude and Christian.

It was official. One of Viktor's contacts with the higher authority had hired Keystone to take on the case of the murdered woman and stolen child, so Viktor gave us the green light to begin as soon as possible. The team had put away their side projects to focus solely on the case.

"Is Claude still out?" I asked.

Viktor crossed his legs from his chair in the corner. "He believes the fates will deliver us the killer on a silver platter."

Claude owned the killer's scent, and he wanted to scout the area and visit some popular bars where the seedy lowlifes hung out.

Basically, he thought there was a chance he could pick up the guy's scent and solve the case.

Nothing in life came that easy.

"Is there nothing I can do to help?" Niko leaned on Wyatt's desk and gripped the edge. He'd taken two sections of his ebony hair on either side and tied them together in the back, highlighting his carved cheekbones.

Wyatt kept his eyes on the computer screen. "Sorry, buddy. I could order a braille printer and see if those work."

Niko turned his head away. "It would be an excessive waste of paper if it's just going to be discarded."

I rubbed my eyes. "What about the report I gave you a half hour ago, Wyatt?"

He spun around in his chair, a pen between his teeth. "The sellers don't always get back to you right away. He finally sent more info. Dead end. The kid was seven."

I took the last page in my pile and placed it with the others. "Well, I figured if I couldn't find the baby on the auction block, I'd make use of my time and organize the papers. Slave trade, pile one. Mage infusing, pile two. Murder for hire, pile three. And I have questions about pile four."

Wyatt held his stomach and grimaced. "What kind of questions?"

"Most of them were marked 'cemetery plots.' I was going to put them in the murder-for-hire pile but thought I'd ask first."

He leaned back. "Those aren't killers. Those people will bury your enemy alive for a long, long time. It's an archaic tradition. Gravewalkers still check cemeteries, but some of the black market traders don't necessarily bury immortals where someone can find them. At least, not until the land is bulldozed for home construction or a Walmart."

Gem shifted in the black beanbag chair to my left and squinted at him. "What's wrong with you? You're all sweaty."

"I think it was the eggs."

"Maybe it's Ebola," she suggested. "Played with any monkeys lately?"

Wyatt looked green and finally stood up to leave. I felt a twinge of guilt when he left the room holding his stomach, but in my defense, I'd never had to cook breakfast for so many people at once. Even in the years when I had an apartment—before I'd become a crossbreed—I didn't do much cooking.

"I'll make something better tonight," I promised.

Viktor shook his head. "Nyet. Not tonight."

I was about to argue until I remembered why. "Damn, we have that dinner thing to go to. Is it too late for me to back out? We've got all this work to do."

Shepherd stood up and crossed the room. He dropped a file in Wyatt's chair and locked his fingers around the back of his neck as he stretched out his muscles. "The victim's name was Jennifer Moore."

Everyone in the room stopped what they were doing and looked up.

Shepherd leaned against the long desk next to Niko. He took a cigarette from the pack on the desk and struck a match. "I combed through everything we could find on her. She was a Sensor who worked at Club Nine."

After a long puff, he shook his hand to put out the flame and dropped the matchstick on the floor.

I stood up, my back stiff. "Why was she living in her car if she had a job?"

"*Had* a job being the operative word," he said. "She used to spike their specialty drinks, but it's hard for pregnant Sensors to work, so I'm guessing they let her go when they found out."

"What does being pregnant have to do with spiking drinks?"

He blew out a cloud of smoke. "Pregnancy does strange things to a Sensor. Most can't use their sensory skills, and others have problems harnessing the right emotional energy when they have hormones fluttering about in a tiny person inside them. Those drinks have to be spiked *just so*."

"Did you find anything about a boyfriend?"

He shook his head. "The files Wyatt found on her are just

job records, her Breed alias, last-known residence, and her former banker."

"What about getting a list of all the places she's charged her card?"

His brows gathered into a frown. "Hell to the no."

"I'm not talking about her entire life. Just the past year or so. It might show a break in her pattern that's worth checking out."

"One of us should investigate the Nine Circles club," Niko said. "Her coworkers might have more information."

"You mean Nine Circles of Hell?" Gem straightened her legs and tapped the ends of her tall sneakers together. "I heard that place is for weirdos. Their theme revolves around the underworld."

"It's not that bad," I remarked. "They have good lunch specials."

Everyone silently judged me.

"What?" I sat on the couch facing the desk. "It wasn't that far from Claude's salon. It's nothing as devious as what goes on at Club Hell. Anyone ever seen *that* place? They have torture rooms and make you participate. No, thanks. That's why I used to stick to human clubs. But no, I didn't see anything weird going on at Club Nine. Their gimmick attracts people, but it's just another club."

Viktor stood up. "I want Gem and Claude to go. Find out what you can from her coworkers. Speak to the person who terminated her employment. Talk to the regulars. If anyone asks, pretend you are concerned friends looking for her whereabouts. She has a baby, and you have not heard from her lately."

Gem played with the crystal pendant around her neck. "Should I pretend I'm her cousin?"

"Nyet. If they find out you're not a Sensor, that will require further explanation. If a Chitah questions you, let Claude do all the talking. He understands how to dance around lies that would trigger a suspicious scent."

"Or Gem could go to dinner with Shepherd, and I could go to the club," I suggested. "I've already been there, so they've seen my face. I know my way around."

His eyes twinkled. "You are not escaping this dinner."

Shepherd flicked his ashes into a can of soda. "Then I'll go. Claude doesn't know the right people to talk to like I do."

Viktor glared at him. "Don't try my patience."

Shepherd smirked as he took another drag. "Doesn't hurt to ask."

When Christian strode into the room, the first thing he did was pick up the burned matchstick. He tucked it in Shepherd's shirt pocket and gave it a pat. "I couldn't help but overhear you're planning to go undercover. Need a driver?"

Viktor gestured toward the empty leather chair. "What we need is someone to watch the new auctions when Wyatt is away from the room or asleep."

Christian sat down, his legs spread wide. We were directly across from each other, and I felt a strange flutter in my stomach when our eyes briefly met.

Gem stood up and straightened out her short dress. I questioned whether it was a dress or an oversized shirt since it stopped at her upper thigh. "What do I wear to a club like that?"

"Whatever you want," I said. "I didn't see any dress codes."

She snapped her fingers. "I've got just the thing. Blue, can I borrow your long gloves? Blue?"

I glanced over at where the beanbag chairs were. Blue was facing away from everyone, her head resting against her shoulder. She had fallen asleep about a half hour ago, but no one had noticed except Shepherd and me.

"Hope it's not food poisoning," Christian quipped. "That was a remarkable meal you served us this morning. Haven't seen anything like that since the Chicago Fire of 1871."

I flashed him a look of disdain. "Maybe you should try something before you formulate an opinion on it."

He tapped his finger against one of his teeth. "Didn't want to chip a fang on the toast."

"I'll remember this when it's your week to cook."

When Wyatt appeared at the door, he looked sweaty and pale. Gravewalkers didn't contract diseases or viruses, but they were prone to stomachaches and headaches like everyone else.

Sometimes you just had to ride it out. And when he turned around and bolted, I had a feeling he was going to be riding it out for a little bit longer.

Viktor strode toward the door and pointed at the computer screen. "Keep an eye on the new auctions. Niko, come with me. We can discuss strategy for different scenarios should the baby come up for auction."

Christian walked his chair in a circle until he was facing the desk. "Tell Spooky to hurry up in the toilet. I wasn't hired to surf the Internet."

I gave Viktor a tight grin. "Maybe Christian needs some computer courses at the local college."

Christian gave me the finger. "Only if you sign up for the cooking class."

Chapter 7

A S MUCH AS I BALKED about going to a private dinner, I enjoyed the idea of having a free meal cooked by professionals. Viktor made Shepherd wear a sports jacket over his white T-shirt and jeans. He looked presentable, and there wasn't much else he could do to glam up his appearance. Shepherd was tall, tan, and tough. The two lines etched in his forehead told me he'd led a hard life, and stubble seemed to live on his face. He had intense bone structure, and the buzz cut did nothing else but draw more attention to his menacing face. At least the jacket covered the bold phoenix tattoo on his right arm and the scars on his body.

My black jeans and button-up didn't exactly complement the occasion, but the jeans didn't have holes, and my shirt didn't have bloodstains. Meeting Viktor halfway was the best I could do. Neither Shepherd nor I was putting on any airs, and this hadn't been presented as a black-tie event but an informal dinner.

The valet took the keys to Shepherd's Jeep, and another man escorted us inside to a private room.

"He'll be right with you. Have a seat, and help yourself to the wine."

I looked around the room, slightly horrified. I had imagined us in a large dining room with about fifty feet of table between us as a buffer. This was… intimate.

"Does he know I'm coming?" I asked, eyeballing the table that seated eight. "Maybe you two would rather be alone."

"You stay the fuck here," Shepherd growled, stalking past me toward the liquor table.

I folded my arms. It wasn't even an open room but one with four walls and a door. A champagne-colored tablecloth covered the table, and two candelabra adorned the center, each with five burning candles. The table sat close to a wall with a painting so massive that it spanned the length of the table itself. It depicted a foxhunt.

I bet that went over well for any guests he might have had who were fox Shifters.

"Here. This'll smooth out the rough edges."

I accepted the wine Shepherd offered. "If it dulls them, pour me another."

His glass clinked against mine in agreement, and he gulped down half the wine. "I hope this ain't one of those dinners where they bring out twelve courses."

"You better eat up and enjoy every bite. It's my week to cook, and don't expect me to order pizza every night. This might be your last chance to eat real food for the next few days."

"Nah. Your breakfast wasn't all that bad. I've had worse."

I nudged his shoulder. "So you've been to prison?"

He chuckled, and we branched apart to opposite ends of the room. Long tables lined two walls, one filled with alcohol and the other with silk flowers. Our shoes were noisy against the wood floor underfoot, though the dining table sat atop a giant gold rug. We didn't say anything, just kept walking around and admiring the décor. Shepherd hefted an empty crystal vase and tossed it up in the air before catching it and putting it back on the table. I spotted a bottle of tequila and quietly unscrewed the cap. After a quick glance over my shoulder, I took a swig and set it back down.

"I heard that," he said, amusement in his voice.

I needed something to settle my nerves, and the weak wine wasn't cutting it. Men like Patrick Bane were way out of my class. What the heck did I have in common with rich guys?

I reached through the gap in my blouse and adjusted my bra. Viktor picked the wrong girl to make an impression.

"Forgive me. I was held up with business," Patrick said as he coolly entered the room. He was a lanky man who looked around fifty, but the Mage carried himself in a manner that indicated he'd been around for a long time. He had both frown lines and laugh lines, and his fading red hair was short and nicely groomed. In his vest and dress shirt, Patrick looked every bit a politician—counterfeit smile and cocksure personality included.

He approached Shepherd first and bowed. "Patrick Bane, at your service."

"Shepherd Moon."

I almost expected Shepherd to say "not at yours," but he remained polite.

"This meeting is long overdue," Mr. Bane said in that melodic Irish accent of his. His friendly manner put me instantly at ease. "I've thought back to that night many times," he continued. "It's appalling how many of my guests made no attempt to catch the child. If you hadn't been there, it would have been a grim outcome indeed." He put his hand on Shepherd's shoulder and gave it a light squeeze. "The world could use more men like you." Then his eyes skated over to me. "I don't believe I've had the delightful pleasure of a formal introduction."

We'd met before, but I guessed this was part of the dinner dance. "Raven Black."

He glided over and took my hand. "Charmed." His lips brushed across my knuckles as he looked up at me with those green eyes.

"I'm the one your progeny tried to kill."

He coughed in surprise and straightened up. "And you have my gratitude for putting Darius away. I appreciate your candor, Miss Black. Please, have a seat."

Patrick pulled out a chair near the head of the table on the left, and when I saw Shepherd veer to the right end, I grabbed the center chair and dragged it out.

Mr. Bane quickly took hold of it and pushed it in once I was seated. "I see you found the wine."

I set my glass on the table and stared up at the painting while Patrick refilled Shepherd's glass before sitting to my left.

Patrick's eyes fixed on the candles. "I much prefer quaint gatherings, don't you?"

When Shepherd didn't say anything, I grabbed my glass. "Yep."

He better not make me do all the talking. I gave Shepherd a sharp glare as I sipped my wine. He set his phone on the table next to his plate.

Mine was in the pocket of my coat, which the doorman had taken, so I wasn't able to fake an emergency to weasel my way out of this dinner if things got awkward.

Disastrous.

As soon as the servant set the first course down, I smiled. *What's the rush?*

"Hope you like the hors d'oeuvres. I didn't think something like bruschetta would be enough to tide over a man like you," he said to Shepherd.

I picked up one of the fancy mini sandwiches and tried to shove the entire thing into my mouth, but the bread was excessively big.

"How's the kid?" Shepherd asked conversationally. He smashed his sandwich flat and ate it.

Meanwhile, my jaw was about to unhinge, so I tried the same technique.

"It was a traumatic experience. As you can imagine, he's not as trusting of strangers." Patrick cut into his sandwich with a knife. "I simply can't raise a child with that kind of fear, so I've got my work cut out for me."

I looked at the bite I'd taken out of my sandwich and noticed my burgundy lipstick smeared all over the bread. Shepherd had already scarfed down his third and final hors d'oeuvre.

"My sources tell me you're working on a new case surrounding a murder," Patrick began. He wiped his mouth with a linen napkin and proceeded to slice into a second sandwich. "Don't look alarmed. I take personal interest in those cases, and it was a topic of discussion this morning at our meeting. Have you made any progress?"

Shepherd cleared his throat. "We're not at liberty to discuss."

"Of course." Patrick sipped his wine and set it down. "I

wouldn't ask you to divulge confidential information, but I do want you to know that if there's anything I can do to assist, I'm at your service. It's the least I can do after what you've done for me."

Shepherd nodded. "I'll let Viktor know. We might take you up on that offer if you're serious."

"Criminals like these should be strung up and made an example of. That's what they would have done in my time, but now we have rules to abide by and regulations to follow. But see, that's where organizations like yours come in."

Shepherd looked up. "Meaning?"

"I think we both know what I mean. And just so you know, men like me appreciate what you do for us. Some criminals don't deserve a prison cell, and our executions are, dare I say, humane." Patrick shifted his gaze to me. "Have you ever witnessed an authorized execution?"

I gave him a nervous smile as a servant took away my plate and replaced it with a bowl of soup. "Can't say I have. Do they sell tickets somewhere?"

Patrick laughed blithely. "Our punishment is swift and certain. We carry out a sentence the moment it's given. No time for appeal. We have Regulators who perform the beheading. Friends and family can attend, although to be honest, most have none. Do you know why royalty used to have public executions? It wasn't for entertainment. Nothing instills obedience more in the hearts of men than seeing the consequences of their actions."

"It also makes a lot of people lie against their neighbor when you have a system set up that doesn't allow for appeal."

"You're a Mage," he said, steepling his fingers. "Newly made, I presume. You can't possibly imagine what life was like centuries ago and how far we've come. And yet, despite the laws we've established and restrictions on making immortals illegally, crime seems more rampant now than ever."

I gave Shepherd my best "why am I doing all the talking?" stare.

"You I haven't quite figured out," he said to Shepherd. "You don't strike me as a Shifter."

"Sensor," he replied matter-of-factly, arms folded on the table.

I lifted my napkin, and when I dragged it toward my lap, the fork fell onto the floor. "Sorry."

"I have to say I admire Viktor's vision," Patrick continued. "I've traveled across the globe and seen a few organizations like yours. Most are made up of the same Breed. I suppose it makes it easier for everyone to get along, but it's limiting, don't you think?"

I bent down to pick up the fork while they discussed Keystone. Better that they do most of the talking since I didn't want to upset Viktor by saying something I wasn't allowed to disclose. Most of it was common sense, but I never liked to make assumptions. When I lifted the tablecloth to search the floor, I blinked in surprise.

Patrick's little boy sat Indian style beneath the center of the table. It was dark down there, only a little candlelight filtering through the tablecloth. He quickly held a finger to his lips to ask for silence. I did the same to let him know I'd keep his secret. The poor little guy was probably too frightened to come out—not at all the same spirited youngster I remembered from the party. He had a black mask made of fabric over his eyes and a cape around his neck. It reminded me of a period in my youth when I wore a pair of ballerina slippers everywhere, believing they'd magically make me into a dancer. My father told me that I'd inherited both his left feet, and that was why he couldn't send me to ballet class.

I pointed at the fork. He timidly leaned forward and handed it to me.

When I sat back up in my chair, Patrick was pouring himself a second glass.

"Aye," he said. "I have a few bottles of Chartreuse left over that I bought a century ago, but it's a shame I couldn't preserve any of the ale. Nobody makes it like the monks. Are you a beer drinker, Miss Black?"

"Not really. It's okay, but if I'm going to drink, I usually want something strong."

"How's the wine?"

I lifted the glass. "Delightful."

No sense in offending our host with the truth that his wine

was so bitter that I had to bite my tongue to keep from making a face.

"Perhaps next time I'll break out the Chartreuse."

My eyes widened in horror when Shepherd lifted his spoon from the bowl and there was a whole turtle on it. He locked eyes with me for a moment before he put it back and continued eating the soup around it.

There were a lot of things I'd do in life, but eating tiny turtles wasn't one of them.

"Is something the matter?" Patrick inquired.

My stomach churned as I stared down at my bowl, knowing what lurked beneath.

Shepherd chuckled. "She's suffering from reptile dysfunction."

Patrick snapped his fingers, and on command, his servant appeared. "Bring her another plate of the sandwiches."

"Yes, sir."

And just like that, my turtle nightmare went away. I reached for one of the cheese trays between Shepherd and me and filled up a small plate.

"This work hasn't been kind to you," Patrick said, nodding at the scars on Shepherd's hands.

Shepherd continued slurping on his soup. "I handle the job just fine."

I placed a cube of cheese on my leg, and seconds later, I felt a little hand grab it away. It put a smile on my face, and I must have made a sound.

"What amuses you, Miss Black?"

"I just had a tickle in my throat."

My smile quickly waned when I saw the turtle shell appear again in Shepherd's bowl.

"Mr. Moon, would you mind if we had a private conversation after dinner? I wasn't expecting a guest, and I wanted to give you some private words of gratitude."

I looked between them. "That's fine. I can wait in the foyer."

When I pushed my chair back, Patrick stretched out his arm and placed his hand on the table.

"We've still got three more courses to go."

I felt myself turning green. "Oh, that's… perfect."

Shepherd coughed and laughed at the same time. My napkin fell to the floor, and when I bent down to pick it up, I saw the little boy had fallen asleep, his hand resting on the toe of Shepherd's boot.

The kid had the right idea. That was exactly where I would rather have been instead of stressing out about which fork to use.

I should have been the one to go to the club. Now I was stuck in the middle of a culinary nightmare that was probably karma getting revenge for what I'd done to Wyatt this morning. It made me wonder what Gem and Claude were doing.

Probably dancing and making a toast after solving the case.

Gem glanced at herself in an oval mirror as she and Claude entered the lust room at Club Nine. She was feeling radiant, her purple trumpet skirt set off by her black shirt and stockings. The spotlights above caught her hair, and she briefly admired it before moving on. Claude didn't like a uniform dye job, so there were darker shades of lavender mixed in with a gradual fade to silver at the ends. Because she usually wore it parted off-center, the overlapping colors made it luscious to look at. He hadn't taken up the length any, so her wavy locks were just where she liked them—a smidge past her shoulders. She absolutely adored Claude for all he did to make her stylish. And yet here she was, looking and feeling gorgeous, and not one man in the club had offered to buy her a soda.

Maybe it had something to do with the six-and-a-half-foot Chitah at her side.

Two men had showed interest, but they were drunk. Gem didn't drink, and a drunken man was about as attractive as a serial killer. She could have flared her energy like she was supposed to in a public place, drawing attention to herself, but all that did was attract the wrong kind of men.

She and Claude had already questioned the bartender, who

seemed like a nice guy. Hooper remembered the victim, Jennifer Moore, and said she'd quit working there a little over a year ago. He confirmed she was a Sensor who used to spike the specialty drinks. The manager had found out she was pregnant when she'd put too much violence in someone's drink and a customer almost died. They hadn't seen her in there since.

Gem and Claude were certain that some of the regulars might remember her, so Claude went to work, questioning the ones Hooper had pointed out. Gem knew the right things to ask, and Claude could smell a lie, so together they made a great team.

But after three hours, she began to lose hope that anything would come of this assignment. It was so frustrating to work on a case that led to a dead end, but it happened. That was why they kept meticulous records, just in case something ever looped back around to a previous investigation. They usually received an advance payment they would keep regardless of the outcome. Viktor was choosy with his assignments and made sure he didn't take on too many that he didn't feel they could solve. At the end of the day, Viktor wanted to make sure his team was financially secure.

Gem enjoyed spending her money on clothing and decorations to brighten her room. The rest stayed in savings. As a Mage, she would live a long time, so Viktor had advised her to save as much as she could. Gem valued the sense of belonging and doing something positive with her gifts far more than money. Born a Relic, she possessed a natural ability to understand foreign and archaic languages. It would be a waste to squander that knowledge, so Viktor allowed her to work special assignments in her private chamber. He entrusted her with secrets, and even though he could be a bit of a stiff sometimes, no one else in the house made her feel as valued for her contributions. That wasn't a feeling she'd ever known before—not even with her Creator, who was wonderful but focused heavily on refining Gem's Mage gifts more than her Relic knowledge.

The lust room was exactly as she'd imagined. Sexy red furniture, black tables, candlelight, and stone walls. You could still hear the techno music throughout the building, but it wasn't so loud that you had to scream to hold a conversation.

Claude homed in on two men hanging out in a corner and casually strode over to make conversation.

Frankly, Gem was bored with making conversation.

She plopped down in an empty chair and peeled off her long evening gloves.

"Can I get you something?" a waitress asked.

The server's brown skin carried a glow so beautiful that Gem's arms looked porcelain in comparison. All the staff wore black shorts, but their shirts were always the color of the room they worked in.

Gem glanced down and guessed the woman's high heels were probably pinching her toes. "Why don't you sit down for a minute? Those look like killer shoes."

The sassy waitress jutted her hip. "I've got to earn my tips."

Gem waved her to sit. "I'll tip extra. I wanted to ask you something about a friend of mine you might know."

The waitress arched a narrow brow and looked around. The moment she sat in the chair in front of Gem, her entire body sagged in relief. "We only have two girls to a room, so just for a minute. Who's your friend?"

Gem took out a picture of Jennifer that Wyatt had found when searching for her alias information. Most everyone had a fake driver's license. She had to be careful how to approach this. People didn't like dealing with the law or anyone affiliated with investigations, and telling the waitress that Jennifer was dead would rouse suspicion.

"Hooper said she worked here about a year ago."

"Yeah, I remember Jenny. That was back when I first started working here. She was the top spiker. It was hard finding a replacement. Did she have the baby?"

"I haven't heard from her in a few weeks, so I'm worried," Gem began, tugging on the edge of her skirt. "I thought maybe she went back with her ex. Do you know where I could find him?"

The waitress slowly shook her head. "I don't know who she was seeing. We weren't close or anything."

"I just got back in town, so I've been searching everywhere. Anything you can remember would be helpful. I've been worried about the baby; it's not like Jenny to lose touch."

"I don't think anyone here kept in contact with her."

"My name's Gem Laroux," she said, hoping that would put the waitress at ease.

"Latasha Threadgood." She flashed a bright smile and leaned against the armrest. "What did she have?"

Gem felt a flutter of panic but played it smooth. Since Latasha wasn't a Chitah, she wouldn't know a lie from the truth. "A boy. I don't know much else. She wrote me an email and invited me to come see her so we could catch up, but then I found out she moved and isn't working here anymore. That's why I thought she went back with her ex. You know how a baby can change people. I'm sure it's not easy being a single mom and trying to hold down a job, especially when it's next to impossible to find nannies."

Latasha rolled her eyes and nodded. "Someone could make a lot of money opening a daycare. More women these days are doing it alone, and I've seen a couple of girls turn to prostitution. Breed employers don't like it when you have to take off work because you can't find a babysitter. That doesn't fly, and we don't have laws to protect our rights."

So true. What little Gem knew of the human world was that employers had to go through a process to fire someone. And even then, people could collect unemployment. In the Breed world, you could simply roll your eyes at the boss and you'd be out on the street with no income.

Latasha touched her crimson hair, making sure everything was in place. There were short corkscrew curls like loose coils twisting and pointing in every direction. "I remember Jenny talking to some guy a few times right before she was fired. It sticks out because I was new on the job, and she got in trouble for ignoring her station when it happened a second time. I don't know if that helps any."

"Is he a regular?"

"We get so many faces coming through…" She waved her hand and turned a sharp eye toward a woman who set an empty glass on the floor.

"What did he look like?"

"It's been so long I don't remember. I might see him in here every day and not even know it," she said with a chuckle. "Maybe dark hair? Definitely short hair, because what I *do* remember is that he had a tattoo on the back of his neck. Some kind of design."

Gem's heart began to race. "Can you describe it?"

Latasha pulled a curl straight, and when she let go, it sprang back into position. "It's been ages, so I couldn't tell you. Why people mark their bodies up with those things, I'll never know."

Gem jotted her number down on a scrap of paper and folded a twenty-dollar bill inside. "If you remember anything else, can you give me a call? You've been so helpful."

"Sweetie, it was nothing. Duty calls." She stood up and shook off the lethargic posture she'd adopted. "If you change your mind on that drink, let me know. I hope you find her. She probably got herself a new man. Or maybe she moved. People do it all the time." Latasha winked and strutted away.

Gem had goose bumps all over.

She didn't usually like working on murder cases, but this was different. Somewhere out there was a baby wondering where his mother was. Scared. Alone. Crying. It didn't matter if he or she was too young to remember; the damage was done. Gem had been one of those children who grew up never knowing who her parents were, always wondering what her life would have been like had she not been sold on the black market. She used to believe that her mother had given her up, but after working for Keystone and seeing all the stolen children, she was certain that wasn't the case.

What fate lay ahead for that baby? Despite the rumors of hopeful couples who shopped on the black market, most of the victims were sold to nefarious criminals who wanted to brainwash those children and use them like slaves. She didn't want this baby to experience a loveless childhood filled with memories of abuse and emotional manipulation.

Claude appeared and sat in the chair across from her. He leaned forward, nostrils flaring, and held her hands in his. "What's wrong, female?"

Gem didn't talk about her past with Claude, but he sensed it from time to time when that dark cloud came over her. She quickly stood up and led him into the hall. "I have a description of someone who was seen with her."

"And?" When Claude folded his arms, his muscles pushed out.

Gem rocked on her heels. "Dark hair and a tattoo on the back of his neck."

"What kind of tattoo?" he asked flatly.

"A design," she said, making a veiled reference to Shepherd's neck tat.

Claude shook his head. "Lots of people have tattoos, Gem."

"And Shepherd is one of those people."

Claude turned in a circle, his eyes downcast. "This isn't his kind of place. And even if it was him, so what? It's not a crime to be seen with someone. He's not selling children on the black market."

"I sure hope he's not! And we're all entitled to a personal life, but I'd like to think that if we're working on a case and he recognizes the person in the photograph that he'd say something. Otherwise, it appears as though he's hiding something from us. Shepherd may be a big ol' grump, but I've always trusted him. Now I don't know what to believe."

Claude put his arm around her when a couple walked by. "Tone it down a notch. We can discuss this somewhere more private." When they reached a darker spot by the wall, he pulled out his phone.

"Who are you texting?"

The display illuminated his face. "Shepherd. I'm requesting his presence so we can settle this once and for all."

Gem shifted her weight to the other leg. "What makes you think he'll come?"

Claude flashed his butterscotch eyes at her. "Because right now he's probably praying for a meteor to hit the planet to get him out of that formal dinner."

Chapter 8

S HEPHERD SHIFTED IN HIS CHAIR, eager to get this night the hell over with. He didn't like rubbing elbows with suits, and all he could think about was getting back home, lighting up a smoke, and sharpening his knives with a whetstone.

Instead, he was on his fifth glass of alcohol.

Shortly after dinner, a familiar sound came from under the table, and that was when Shepherd realized his phone was missing. Patrick discovered his kid was hiding there the whole time... with Shepherd's phone. Shepherd had to laugh thinking about how fast that kid took off out the door, Patrick right behind him.

Mr. Bane entered the room and returned to his seat. "I'm sure your companion will find him if my servants don't. Had I known the boy was underneath the table, I would have sent him away. That's no dignified place to sit."

"He's a kid. Doesn't matter," Shepherd said, tracing his finger around the rim of his whiskey glass.

"No, but I've raised him not to steal. If he breaks your phone, I'll replace it." Patrick poured himself another glass of wine and sat back. "Never have children. It's not as easy as it looks."

"Give him up for adoption."

Made sense. After all, the kid wasn't even his. Maybe Patrick once had a thing for the kid's mom, but that didn't mean he was obligated to care for her children after she died. Then again, guys like Patrick loved that kind of shit.

Good PR.

"You make a valid point," Patrick said, leaning to one side. "But it's too late for that kind of thing now. He's grown accustomed to a certain lifestyle. I've had him since he was a wee baby. The house wouldn't be the same without him. No, sometimes a man must put aside his selfish needs and rise to the occasion. Just as you did."

Nice segue, Shepherd thought. He didn't want praise or recognition for saving the kid. He was just doing his job. A kid falls, you catch him. Period.

Patrick pulled out a cigar. "Are you a smoking man? Feel free to light up. I don't have rules about that kind of thing."

Shepherd opted for one of his cigarettes instead. Rather than wasting a match, he stood up and lit it on one of the candles. The taste was heaven. He savored the first drag that removed the flavor of turtle soup from his palate. Eating those nasty little monsters wasn't the highlight of his evening, but he'd had too much fun after seeing Raven's horrified reaction to his liking it. She wasn't normally the squeamish type, so he couldn't pass up the opportunity.

He sat down and propped his elbows on the table, tendrils of smoke climbing to the ceiling. Candles flickered between them, and his gaze distractedly dragged up to the painting on the wall to his right. He could hear Viktor's words in his head. "Make small talk."

Had this been anyone else, Shepherd would have asked him to turn on the fucking lights. Candlelight was a way of life in the Keystone mansion, but this house was wired from top to bottom.

"I want to offer you a favor of equal value. A life for a life," Patrick began. "There's only one caveat. I'm an important man, and you realize I can't have you walk away with that kind of favor to keep in your pocket. Men change over time and sometimes abuse favors that were granted them."

"What are you asking?"

Patrick puffed on his cigar and blew out a deformed ring. "I want to know your favor before you leave this room tonight."

Shepherd felt a hot coal in the pit of his stomach. "I don't need anything."

Patrick tilted his head to the side, his narrow eyes brightening. "Oh, come now. Every man has a past bountiful with enemies. Not many have the opportunity to gain a favor from someone in my position; don't be so quick to decline. I have a lot of connections." He leaned forward and gave Shepherd a pointed stare. "I'm not taking your good deed lightly, and neither should you. Whatever you ask will stay between us."

Shepherd took another drag and flicked the ashes onto his empty dessert plate. That was a lot to lay on a man.

"A life for a life," Patrick repeated before he sat back in his chair. "Would you like more cake?"

Cake? Was this guy serious? Shepherd kept staring, and before too long, Patrick rose to his feet and approached him from the left.

He set down his glass in front of Shepherd and walked off. "Just in case you need some reassurance."

Although most Sensors used their gifts to store experiences and sell them, Shepherd always wanted to be more than just someone who made a few bucks working sensory exchange for addicts. He got a high from playing detective with emotional imprints and deciphering complex emotions. It took years of practice, but he got real good with picking up trace amounts on objects that most Sensors would miss or not feel at all. He wasn't hypersensitive, only hypertrained.

Shepherd's cigarette stayed wedged between his lips as he cupped his hands around Patrick's glass. A tiny flutter of emotions tickled his fingertips, and he allowed it to move through him.

Truth. Conviction. He didn't pick up a hint of insincerity.

"I haven't always been a man of class," Patrick began, rounding the table and leaning against it as he studied the foxhunt painting. "I was born to a pauper and clawed my way out of poverty by the time I was a man of forty. And it wasn't easy," he said with a laugh. "It was years later before I was turned. Obviously I get a lot of stares from people, wondering why a man of my age was chosen, but my Creator was a visionary. In those days, Creators surrounded themselves with young men who were soldiers, but my Creator knew we were heading toward a more civilized world and leaders would be defined by the intelligent men who surrounded them, not the brave. A sharp intellect is deadlier than a sharp knife."

Patrick briskly turned and sat in his chair with a look of disgust. "What a shame that humans got ahold of him and cut off his head for treason against their mortal king. That kind of injustice would never happen now. Not just because of human laws, but because Breed finally organized a system to protect and punish our own kind. Just think of how many were lost in the witch hunts alone."

Shepherd regarded him with a smile. "You're running out of jail space."

"Humans are in love with self-condemnation. They're guilt stricken. We have better sense than that," Patrick said, tapping his head. "The more laws you create, the more jail cells you need. We can't afford to build more facilities for people who want to steal cars or do drugs. It's hard enough to keep the prisons we do have off human radar, so you have to choose your battles. What you do is admirable, but you're a smart fella. Do you really think we want them all returned alive?" He winked and set down his cigar.

"Maybe if you had smarter men, you could dismantle the black market network."

Patrick rocked with laughter. "Our hackers have shut them down numerous times, and they're always back in business within the hour. Ah, the stories I could tell…"

The conversation interested Shepherd, but not enough to distract him from Patrick's offer. And furthermore, his mind was returning to a dark place he'd spent years trying to rise out of the ashes from, just as the phoenix tattoo on his right arm and shoulder depicted. The elaborate tattoo spread from his upper chest all the way across to his back, covering his skin like a cloak.

Shepherd studied the tip of his cigarette, which had burned more than halfway down to the filter. This could be his one opportunity to avenge a death, but at what cost? How much information was he willing to hand over to Patrick?

"All I need is a name," Patrick continued. "I don't require an explanation, not unless you don't know the name."

Patrick was good at reading people, so Shepherd mashed the tip of his cigarette against the plate and ironed out his emotions.

"How do I know you won't change your mind and use this against me?"

"You don't. All I can give you is my word. If you walk out, the offer is null and void. That's the condition."

Shepherd took off his jacket and rested his forearms on the table. This was a personal offer and had nothing to do with Viktor. Even though Viktor had given Shepherd another shot at making his life worth a damn, he knew he'd never be able to move on until he permanently shut the door to his past. Maybe everyone else in the group had tucked their past into a tidy little box, but he still had nightmares that held him with a viselike grip.

Patrick kept his eyes locked on Shepherd. "Come now, every man has demons."

"I don't have a name. If I did, it would be written on a tombstone by now."

Patrick relit his cigar. "What can you tell me?"

"He's a Mage." Just saying the word aloud filled Shepherd with a cold sense of dread, as if a dark shadow were swirling within his chest. "Shoulder-length black hair, a full beard—looks like a damn pirate."

Patrick puffed on his cigar. "Any distinguishing features? Men change their looks all the time."

Shepherd thought about it. That man's eyes were seared into his memory, and he'd searched the streets for years for those same eyes. But that wasn't detailed enough. "He had a red burn on the base of his throat, coming up from his chest."

Patrick furrowed his brow. "You mean a scar."

Shepherd lifted his eyes to meet Patrick's gaze. "It wasn't a scar. It was bright red."

Recognition flashed in Patrick's eyes, and he nodded. "A firemark. I believe they call those... ah, yes. Port-wine stains. That should make him easy to find."

"Not if he's covering it up. He was wearing a high-collar shirt. I only saw it because..." Shepherd pressed his lips tight as the memories crept into his mind again. He'd noticed the birthmark while fighting for his life against another Mage who'd shocked him twice over. Once the stabbing began, the Mage with the birthmark removed his shirt, saying he didn't want to ruin it with all the blood. "He also has green eyes."

Patrick enjoyed his cigar and studied the tip for a long time before responding. "What was his crime?"

"That wasn't the deal."

"Just curious. Is he the one who put those scars on your arms?"

Shepherd leaned back. *Fuck.* Maybe this was a mistake.

Mr. Bane stood up and faced his ostentatious painting. "When was the last time you saw him? Was it here in Cognito? I need to know where to begin searching and whether enough time has elapsed that he might have changed his appearance."

"About five years ago." Shepherd stood up and walked behind his chair, resting his arms across the back. "He might be long gone by now. I spent years searching. I don't search anymore, but let's just say there isn't a place I go where I'm not looking at everyone around me to see if they have his eyes."

Patrick turned around and mirrored Shepherd's stance, his arms over the back of a chair. "I can't imagine a man crossing paths with someone like you. He'd be a fool to try. Some people are easy to run over and control, but others… You can see it in their eyes that if you do them a bad turn, they'll never let it go. That fire is a dangerous thing." He clicked his teeth together.

"I want him alive."

"That's a mighty high request. I can't add conditions to the favor, or it becomes impossible to honor without risk. I have a reputation to uphold. I can't be transporting people around."

"Yeah, but—"

"There's nothing you need to worry about, Mr. Moon. I think we've struck a fair bargain, and I'll be sure to let you know when I've held up my end of the deal. It might not be enough, but it's the best I can do."

The door squeaked open, and Raven poked her head in. "I found your phone. I'll be in the car."

After the door closed, Shepherd collected his jacket and held it in one hand. "I'd appreciate if you kept this between us."

Patrick approached him and clapped his shoulder. "Likewise. If you breathe a word of this to anyone, I'll walk away. I appreciate what you've done for me, but not at the expense of my reputation. You seem like a man I can trust. So am I, Mr. Moon. I've always been fair to those I've worked with, even my own idiot progeny who ruined every opportunity I'd given him."

Shepherd nodded, feeling Patrick's sincerity through his touch.

Patrick withdrew his hand. "I know we're only acquaintances, but if you ever want to talk about what happened, I'm a good listener. I can't profess to having any skills as a Relic to counsel you, but sometimes it's cathartic to unload on a person who won't judge you for it. Otherwise, that pain will eat away at your soul."

Shepherd's heavy breath bordered on a laugh. "You're assuming I still have one."

Chapter 9

S HORTLY AFTER SURVIVING THE DINNER from turtle hell, Shepherd and I accepted Claude's invitation and headed over to Club Nine to join them. I needed a stiff drink. The sandwiches Patrick served me were fine, but I had a feeling I was going to be having nightmares about all that slurping Shepherd had done with his soup. During dessert, a beep had sounded from beneath the table, and Shepherd noticed his phone was missing. When they lifted the tablecloth to look beneath, the little boy scampered out the door with Shepherd's phone in hand. I followed behind Patrick and decided chasing the kid would give me an excuse to stretch my legs. Mr. Bane seemed like a nice guy, but the whole dinner scene made me incredibly uncomfortable. Choosing this life meant I was going to have to be more of a social butterfly, like it or not.

And this butterfly needed a shot of tequila.

We searched the club until I spotted Gem's violet hair in the limbo room. I didn't care for limbo's ambiance. Nothing about the color scheme was remotely gold. Yellow lights splashed against the brick walls, and the upholstered furniture was a lemony color that was off-putting in such a dark club.

I approached the table by the wall and took a seat on the yellow stool. "What's shakin'?"

Claude and Gem sat across from me, plates of food in the center of the table.

"Are you done with that?"

Gem flicked her gaze down to the uneaten sliders and then up to me. "My eyes are bigger than my stomach. You can have the rest if you want, but I thought you two ate already?"

"That's a long story."

Shepherd finally swaggered up and spun a chair around before sitting to my left. A cigarette dangled from his lips, and he grinned. "I think I know what I'm cooking on my week in the kitchen." He drew his arms against his chest and made a paddling motion with his hands.

I bit into the cold burger and moaned. Greasy bacon and beef really hit the spot. Mr. Bane's sandwiches were good, but most of them had been bread and veggies, the meat shaved so thinly that a gust of wind could have blown it away.

"Good to see that appetite," Claude said. "You could use some meat on your bones."

I caught Gem nodding at someone behind me, but she was trying to be discreet about it. I glanced over my shoulder at a waitress in a red shirt who was talking to another girl in a yellow top. The staff here matched their shirt to the rooms they worked, so the girl with the red top stuck out like a sore thumb.

"Find out anything?" Shepherd asked.

Claude propped his elbows on the table. "Dead end." He took another swig from his beer and set it down.

Shepherd reached out and grabbed the bottle. "You mind?"

Gem's eyes flicked behind me again. When I peered over my shoulder, the waitress looked at Shepherd and shook her head.

Shepherd guzzled the entire bottle and then stared at it. "What the hell are you lying to me about?"

Claude snatched his bottle away. "Since when did you start reading my emotions?"

He delivered a stony glare. "Since I tasted your beer and felt a fucking lie on my fingertips. What's going on?"

Gem held her crystal pendant in one hand and shared a look with Claude. "Let's tell them."

I took off my coat and let it drape to the floor. "Tell them what?"

Gem fiddled with her hair. "The waitress saw a suspicious guy talking to Jennifer before she was fired, and he had a tattoo on the back of his neck."

Shepherd's jaw set. "So you thought *I* had something to do with this? *Jesus.* I need something stronger." He launched to his feet and stalked off.

"Wait! It's not—" Gem touched her upper lip, a look of uncertainty on her face.

I tugged on my fingerless gloves. The material was thin enough to be comfortable inside. "Did Jennifer know the guy, or was it an ex?"

Gem shrugged and put her hands in her lap. "A waitress said she got in trouble for talking to him a few times and ignoring her customers. She didn't remember what kind of design was on his neck. Claude and I just thought…"

I laughed. "I've seen a dozen guys with tats on the back of their neck, and you go and accuse Shepherd. Maybe we should take our drinks over to the treachery room and finish this conversation."

"He doesn't have to be such a grump about it," she declared. "If someone had described her talking to a girl with violet eyes, I'm sure Shepherd would have suspected me."

I pushed the plate away, suddenly full. "Well, a neck tattoo narrows it down. Something we can keep an eye out for. If he's been in here more than once, he might be a regular. Did she remember anything else about him?"

Gem shrugged. "She sees a hundred faces a night; I'm surprised she remembered that much. Alas, we're back to square one."

Claude scratched his chin. "Her whole life was in that car, and the Regulators didn't find anything useful. All we can do is hope the baby turns up," he said, hinting toward the black market offers that Wyatt was researching.

"How are we going to link that person to the one who broke into her car?"

He bent forward, menace flickering in his eyes. "Because I own his scent."

Gem leaned against Claude, and it seemed to pacify him. She was a girl with a small frame, her features so unique that she looked like a fairy who'd stepped out of a storybook. Around her dark lashes, her skin sparkled with flecks of silver glitter. When she smiled, her cheeks glowed. And while she had a small mouth, her lips were full with the subtlest Cupid's bow.

Claude put his arm around her and tilted his head down. "Are you ready to go home? I think we're done here."

I snorted. "So you just invited us over to get the waitress to ID Shepherd?"

"I'm never living this down, am I?" Gem scooted out of her seat. "Never, never! I'm going to hear about this for the next fifty years."

Claude stood up and stretched. "Join the club. I still have to hear about the time I streaked through a supermarket."

Gem chortled. "That wasn't the funny part."

He speared her with a hot glare as he put on his jacket.

"Tell me," I said.

She poked her tongue between her teeth, a wide grin on her face. "He shielded his manlies with a box of Trix cereal."

"They're definitely not for kids," he added. "Do you want a ride home?"

"Shepherd's already hammered. I can't leave him with the Jeep, so I'm the designated driver."

"Don't let him drink too much. See you at home."

After they left, I switched seats to face the room and sent Christian a message.

> **Raven**: Want to meet up for drinks?
> **Christian**: The last time we drank, I lost a bet.
> **Raven**: You're missing out. Gem accused Shepherd of being the killer.
> **Christian**: Better I stay at my bar and you stay at yours.

I wanted to tell him Shepherd was acting weird, but I let the conversation end.

My thoughts drifted back to dinner. That little kid was a good hider. I'd used my Mage ability to track down his energy, even though it was faint since he wasn't a Mage. But he sparkled. Those intense emotions of happiness fluttered in the air like particles of light falling off a sparkler. He'd figured out how to take pictures, because he snapped one of me. I made a mental note to remind Shepherd to erase that picture.

And speaking of the devil, I watched Shepherd stumble to the table with half a bottle of whiskey and two glasses. He filled each one, and even though I wasn't a whiskey drinker, I accepted the offer.

"What's on your mind?" I asked, noticing his change in demeanor. "Did you and Mr. Bane have a stimulating conversation tonight?"

He downed his entire glass and immediately refilled it. Shepherd was a big guy, just over six feet tall, and I was willing to bet I could bounce quarters off his biceps. He kept rubbing his hand across his short hair, his eyes squinty and not fixed on any one thing.

Shepherd gave me a refill and held up his glass. "To demons."

Our glasses clinked together, and I took a small sip. "Is something bothering you?"

He lit up a cigarette and stared up at the wall behind me. "No matter what you do, the past always catches up with you. You wake up, brush your teeth, do heroic shit, make a sandwich, day after day after fucking day. Then all of a sudden, bam!" His fist slammed against the table and made me jump. "Resolve whatever shit you've got to resolve while you're young."

I set down my glass. "Easier said than done."

He pointed at me, pupils dilated. "Truer words were never spoken."

Shepherd's speech was slurring more than usual. He liked drinking, but I'd never seen him this inebriated before. I wasn't sure if something had triggered his drinking episode or if the alcohol had caused an old wound to reopen, but I knew that look. I'd been in that dark place where the only way to survive was to ignore or dull the pain.

Shepherd refilled his glass. "I used to be a nice guy. I could have been that guy." He pointed at a table where a couple was sitting. "Guys like that don't have a fucking clue what they have right in front of them. They just wake up and think their life is perfect."

I remained quiet so he could have a moment to ramble. Even if his thoughts weren't cohesive, he clearly needed to get something off his chest.

"Happiness is an optical illusion."

"Maybe we should go home, where we can drink for free," I suggested. "Give me your keys."

He slowly shook his head. "Nobody drives my Jeep. I don't need anyone stripping the gears. Paid good money."

"Well, I could always call Viktor to come pick you up."

A look of resignation crossed his face. Shepherd's hands disappeared beneath the table as he leaned to the left, then to the right. He furrowed his brow. "I just had them on me."

I searched around the table and on the floor. "Where did you go earlier?"

He pointed left, then right, then made a circle in the air.

While Shepherd filled up his glass and continued rambling about demons, I sent a message to Gem. She quickly replied and said Claude had to take another route because of an accident, so I decided not to trouble them. They were close to home and probably tired after a long night of questioning people in the bar. Christian was being antisocial, Niko was blind, and I wasn't sure if Blue could drive. So I messaged Wyatt since he was Shepherd's partner.

Wyatt gladly accepted, obviously eager to get out of the house. When I finished our conversation, I looked up, and Shepherd was gone.

Voices overlapped, and techno music thumped from the main room by the bar. I scanned the room. When I saw a neck tattoo, I stood up to go get him, but as I neared, I realized it wasn't a lover's knot like the one Shepherd had on the back of his neck. I turned in a circle, and my eyes widened when I spotted Shepherd sitting at a table, his arm around the man he'd pointed out just moments ago in his drunken stupor. Across from them was a very confused woman.

As I neared, their conversation became audible.

"You need to worship the ground she walks on," Shepherd said, his anger barely quelled. "Men like you don't deserve what you've got. Are you going to make her pay for her own drink? Are you one of those assholes?"

"I think you need to take a walk," the man said. Thankfully he wasn't a Vampire or Mage, but was insulted nonetheless.

I put my hands on Shepherd's shoulders and gave them a light squeeze. "Let's go. Wyatt's coming to hang out with us. Maybe we should check out the gluttony room and order sandwiches. Or would you rather have turtle soup?"

Shepherd ignored my quips and tightened his arm around the man's neck. "Infidelity isn't your worst nightmare, brother."

The young man wrenched away, and his chair legs scraped against the floor as he stood up. Fire burned in his eyes as he gave Shepherd a scathing glance. He was nowhere near the same size—just a young man with prescription glasses and a blue tie. Probably a Relic or Shifter if I had to guess, though glasses were less common among Shifters since most Breeds didn't suffer the same degenerative afflictions as humans.

But Relics did, and that made me concerned. A guy like Shepherd could do a lot of damage to a Relic.

"Come on, Trudy. Let's go somewhere private," the man said.

Shepherd rose to his feet. "Aren't you going to buy her dinner? Did you just want to get her liquored up so you could stick your plug in her socket?"

I grabbed the back of Shepherd's shirt. "Let it go, Shepherd. You don't even know these people. Where he sticks his plug is none of your business."

Trudy was a petite girl with a round figure and wearing a blue dress. She was as pretty as a doll but looked terrified of the situation.

When the man took Trudy's hand, Shepherd grabbed him

by the collar and yanked him back. I wrapped my arms around Shepherd's waist and hauled him away until he collapsed on top of me. My back hit the floor with a thud, knocking the wind out of my lungs. Over two hundred pounds of muscle on top of me wasn't helping my breathing situation either.

"What the hell is wrong with you?" I spat.

Shepherd rolled off me and knocked into the table, tipping over a glass. With his lips pressed tight, he sat up and appeared more placid. In fact, something completely switched off behind those dark-brown eyes. The fire extinguished, replaced by a tide of hopelessness.

I scooted next to him. "What happened tonight? You didn't say anything mean about Patrick's kid stealing your phone, did you? Did Patrick threaten you?"

Even if Shepherd had said something vulgar or offensive, Patrick had no right. Especially after what Shepherd had done for him.

"Why the fuck am I here?" he murmured.

I patted his leg, searching for the right words, but I had none. "You know what? Let's just sit here for a while. I'll get the bottle and glasses, and we'll have a drink under the table. No more talking. Sound good?"

He nodded.

While I didn't have words of wisdom that someone like Niko could have offered, I had years of experience. My father was a recovering alcoholic, and I'd learned early on how to talk to a drunk by reading their body language and listening. What to say, what not to say, what they needed. My father wasn't an angry drunk, but he had his moments where his emotional outbursts became intolerable. He used to take me to the bar and spend hours there, so this wasn't my first time at the rodeo. But it was the first time I'd shared a drink and understood what it meant to have demons of my own.

An hour later, Shepherd had finally given up the booze and

was working on his first cup of coffee. He hadn't said much, but I'd gotten him off the floor and into a booth, so that was progress.

Limbo had a different vibe. Most people were low-key and not as boisterous as in other rooms. They were lost souls who wanted to either connect with others or be left alone. Maybe Shepherd and I fit right in.

Near the door, the crowd parted, granting passage to a man strolling in. Wyatt had swagger, and when he walked, people noticed—black cowboy boots, army-green jacket, and all. He wasn't overly handsome or especially tall, but his charisma and charming smile made up for any shortcomings.

He flattened his palms on the table so I could see all the letters tattooed on his fingers. "I'm here to save the day."

Shepherd sipped his coffee and stared listlessly at the cup.

"Where are your keys, Shep?"

"Someone stole them."

Wyatt slid in beside him, directly across from me. "Your Jeep is still outside. Why would someone steal your keys and not your car? You misplaced them, you drunken bastard."

"I already searched the club," I said. "No one's turned them in, but the waitresses are keeping an eye out."

"Buttercup, the only thing those ladies are looking for are tips." Wyatt propped his elbows on the table and tapped his fists together. "How did dinner with Mr. Fancy Pants go?"

I pointed my finger at him. "Next time we do anything like that, *you're* going."

Wyatt regarded Shepherd for a moment with a concerned look.

"I'm going to close the tab," I announced. "Meet me by the bar."

"Hold up." Wyatt shot out of his seat and fell into step beside me, his voice low. "What's up with him?"

"I don't know. Has he ever been this way before?"

"Cantankerous?"

"No, drunk for no reason."

We both stopped and looked back at Shepherd, who was pouring sugar into his coffee.

"He's pretty tanked," Wyatt said. "Nothing unusual happened tonight that set him off?"

I shrugged. "After cake, I left them alone to talk privately. His whole mood changed when we got here. Maybe it was Gem and Claude accusing him of murder."

Wyatt shook me by the shoulders and laughed. "You guys really know how to make a guy feel loved. Run along while I do some damage control. We need to get back so I can monitor the, uh... listings." His gaze darted around.

"No one is watching? What if someone puts him up?"

"Hold your horses, Calamity Jane. Blue's my backup, but I don't want to leave her alone too long. Christian better get his butt home. He's supposed to take over the night shift while I sleep." Wyatt glanced back at the table and rubbed his chin. "I just hope Shepherd doesn't put up a fight. Sometimes he gets too comfortable hanging out in these places."

I poked his shoulder. "Drag him if you have to. Let's go."

I strode down the wide hall, passing each circle of hell. Red light illuminated one wall, blue on another. The music grew louder as I entered the main room, people dancing all around. I'd brought sufficient cash tucked in my front pocket—a habit from my old life—and closed out the tab. Afterward, I pulled my fingerless gloves out of my back pockets and realized I wasn't wearing my coat.

"Dammit," I whispered.

Hopefully one of the guys had noticed and grabbed it on the way out. Just in case, I decided to send Wyatt a quick message. But before I could reach for my phone, a guy across the room caught my attention.

I stood frozen, observing a man and woman standing beneath a red light. The woman had her back to a pillar and appeared uncertain as the man kept talking. He had a tattoo on the back of his neck, and I remembered him from earlier. Sure, lots of guys had tattoos, but now that we had a vague description of someone in this club who had been talking to our victim, it was enough for me to pay attention.

He touched her shoulder, still talking a mile a minute while she listened, her eyes downcast. The whole conversation felt off, as if he were trying to talk her into something. Maybe he was just hitting on her and she didn't know how to let him down, but it didn't appear as innocuous as that.

I squinted, trying to make out what his tattoo was. Nothing identifiable like a panther or someone's name—just a strange design.

Someone bumped into me, and I stumbled forward. A bevy of women moved between us, and when the tatted guy headed toward the door, I cut through the crowd and followed behind him.

"Excuse me!" I yelled out, hoping to ask him if he knew Jennifer.

He glanced over his shoulder and kept walking. He didn't react the way most men would if they saw a woman chasing after them.

I quickened my pace, and when he looked back and finally noticed me, he picked up speed. I shoved my way through a sea of people who made little or no attempt to move aside when they saw me coming.

"Raven!" Wyatt yelled from behind.

I looked back and spied him through a gap. He held up his arms as if asking "What gives?" and I pointed frantically toward the door, hoping he could read the expression on my face.

When I turned around, the main door down the hall was closing. I bolted toward it, weaving around a woman who shrieked when I bumped her glass and splashed red wine all over her dress.

The moment I emerged outside, a burst of frosty air burned against my skin. My silk blouse was as good as wearing nothing at all for all the warmth it provided. I scanned the pockets of people who were gathered together for a smoke or a chat.

"Sneaky little bastard," I whispered, racing around to the parking lot on the right side of the building.

Footprints were everywhere, and I couldn't sense his energy among so many other Breed. He was probably long gone.

Before I could turn around, I heard an engine throttling and tires skidding on slush. A car gunned toward me—headlights off—

and the man in the driver's seat was the guy from inside. He almost flew past me until a group of people crossed in front of his path and forced him to slam on his brakes.

I rushed up to the door and pulled the handle.

As if it would be that easy.

When our eyes met, my adrenaline skyrocketed. I was a predator chasing prey, and that old familiar rush felt exhilarating.

Just like old times.

As the slow-moving crowd dispersed, I had seconds to decide if I was going to let him go or stay on his tail.

One thing was for certain: innocent men don't run.

Chapter 10

I PUNCHED THE PASSENGER-SIDE WINDOW. NOTHING broke except maybe a small bone in my middle finger. The car lurched forward, and I flashed after him, spotting Wyatt and Shepherd out of the corner of my eye as they raced to the Mini Cooper parked by the main street.

"Follow him!" I yelled.

I caught up with the car and touched the trunk just as he sped onto the main street. My Mage energy would only carry me so far. Seeing that he was nearing the on-ramp to the freeway, I surged forward, stepped onto the bumper, ran up the back window, and threw myself on top of the roof. He jerked the steering wheel left and right, trying to throw me off.

I grabbed the rack rails on either side, which were like raised handles, praying they wouldn't break off.

When my phone rang, I looked down incredulously, my cheek pressed against the blistering-cold roof. The fishtailing had stopped, so I reached in my pants pocket.

"Hello?"

Christian sounded amused. "A little bird told me you're hitchhiking."

I raised my knee and anchored my foot against the other rail since the phone was in my hand. "I'm a little busy!"

"So I heard. If he slows down, I want you to jump. It's not worth your life."

My life wasn't about to end on the turnpike.

The wind blasted me in the face, making it impossible to hear, so I stuffed the phone back in my pocket without ending the call and held on. My shirt inflated with air and ballooned out, and I suddenly felt like a sail on a boat. As we approached the highway, the car slowed down to turn onto the ramp.

A cartoonish horn sounded from behind—Wyatt was closing in on us. I peered back, wondering if I could jump onto his hood, but I was reluctant to let go. We might never find this guy again. It was possible he didn't have anything to do with Jennifer's murder, but now he was just pissing me off with his erratic driving.

He made a sharp turn, and I slid to the left as we merged onto the expressway.

I growled between clenched teeth, my body going into a state of shock from the icy wind. Since the rest of me was plastered against the roof, I kept my head down to shield my face.

Great thinking, Raven. Leave your coat behind in winter and go car surfing.

Thankfully my gloves helped me keep a firm grip on the rails since they protected the palms of my hands from the cold.

Wyatt's incessant beeping stopped, and I looked over my left shoulder behind me to see what was going on. His little red car looked like an angry hornet coming after us. Wyatt's steering wheel was on the opposite side, so it took me a second to realize that Shepherd wasn't the one driving. He sat to the right with one hand over his face, probably regretting his drinking binge by now.

Because of the weather and late hour, the roads weren't active— just a few semis and sanding trucks. When my guy suddenly jerked the car into the left lane to pass an eighteen-wheeler, I almost rolled off. We were nearing the Five Level Interchange, and my stomach dropped when he took the northbound ramp. The car slowed down a little, but not enough for me to make any bold moves. We climbed the overpass, veering left, and my eyes widened when I noticed a man standing on the ledge of the road above us, his arms wide.

It was Christian. His black coat flapped behind him like a cape as he leapt off and crashed onto the hood. The car jolted.

"Hold on!" he shouted.

Christian reached back and then punched through the windshield. The car sideswiped the wall and offered me a glimpse of the underpass far below. Christian climbed in until all I saw were his legs. A struggle ensued—probably a fight for the wheel. Panic set in when the vehicle hit a patch of ice and lost control.

Oh my God, we're going to roll over!

I scrambled to my feet as best as I could and jumped off the moving vehicle just as it skidded onto its side. A loud explosion of metal sounded behind me, but I was too busy doing a rollover of my own. I cradled my head and came to a jarring stop when I slammed against the concrete wall.

Headlights popped into view about fifty feet away. Wyatt hit the brakes, then he and Shepherd got out and broke into a run.

My arm screamed with pain, as well as my leg and shoulder. Dizzy, I managed to stand up. The car was upside down, smoke rising from the engine. I limped toward it, ignoring the pain.

The man emerged from the broken window and staggered away from the car, blood streaming down his face from a gash on his head. A flare of Mage energy rippled through the air, and he looked at me long and hard. I returned the same menacing glare as I continued my zombielike advance. I couldn't flash in my condition, but I was ready to fight. With my good arm, I reached for my belt and pulled out a push dagger.

When he pivoted around, I threw the dagger in frustration, and it bounced off the concrete as the Mage vanished into the night.

"You asshole!" I fell to my knees.

The front end of the car lifted up a few feet before Christian crawled out from beneath. He stood up and spat out a mouthful of blood. His left wrist and fingers looked like a grotesque nightmare the way they were dangling in the wrong directions, the bones shattered. He held his hand upright and stared at it for a few seconds before the fingers began wiggling normally again. Because he hadn't lost any blood, his healing abilities worked much faster than when he got shot.

I, on the other hand, wasn't healing as quickly.

Christian's fangs were out, and he balled up his hands into fists. "I had the bastard. Had him right in my hands!"

Wyatt jogged up, wheezing and out of breath. "Son of a ghost. That was the craziest thing I've ever seen!"

I glanced back. Shepherd ambled toward us like the walking dead, and he looked green.

Christian ripped the license plate off the vehicle and flung it at Wyatt. "Look that up in your database. See if the shitebag is registered."

Snowflakes eddied around us from the changing wind direction, and a few caught in Christian's dark hair and beard. He turned away to retrieve my dagger.

"Are you okay?" Wyatt asked, his eyes scanning my body in disbelief. "For a minute there, I thought you were going to be my new haunt."

Still in shock and denial that I might have internal bleeding, I summoned a smile. "Just a scratch."

What I couldn't figure out was why the Mage hadn't tried to kill us. If he was hiding something, wouldn't he have taken the opportunity to do us in? That was what I would have done in his shoes.

Wyatt twirled the license plate and pointed it at me. "Stay here, Evel Knievel, while I get the car."

He spun on his heel and hurried toward Shepherd.

Christian swaggered up, my dagger in hand.

"Why didn't you kill him?" I asked.

"On what grounds? Assholery? If that's the case, then more men must die." Christian handed me my dagger and touched my cheek. "*Jaysus.* You're like ice." He shucked off his coat and then stripped off his sweater, putting it over my head.

I tried to lift my right arm, but pain shot down every nerve ending. His body heat was still in the threads, and I sighed a little when he put his coat around my shoulders. I knew he was right about killing the guy. Viktor had hired me for my instincts and bravery, but part of the deal meant controlling my impulse to kill. It was like teaching a hunter how to capture and release.

Christian held my gaze for a moment and tapped my chin. "You'll live."

"I can't feel my face."

He suddenly snapped his gaze up at the overpass. Before I could utter a word, Christian hauled me off the ground with one arm and spun around. The world moved in slow motion as a thunderclap of metal and concrete drew my eyes skyward. My jaw slackened when a large truck plummeted off the overpass above us.

With me in one arm, Christian bolted toward the wall and dove to the ground. The truck crashed on top of the car, smashing it to pieces just feet away from us. The back end broke apart, releasing an explosion of small boxes. They hit the road, some cascading over the ledge. Individual packages had burst free, showering the pavement with plastic-wrapped chocolate.

Wyatt jogged onto the scene and fell to his knees, a mountain of MoonPies surrounding him. "Jackpot!"

Christian pushed away from me and stood up.

I stared at the open driver's side door and empty cab. "That bastard came all the way back to kill us with sugar."

A tire rolled off the truck and zipped past Shepherd. He stopped short and surveyed the carnage. Wyatt had jammed a MoonPie into his mouth while stacking the undamaged boxes.

Christian offered me his hand and helped me up. We stood amid twisted metal, chocolate, and an open gas line spilling fuel onto the road.

Shepherd kicked one of the packages with the tip of his boot and stuffed his hands into his pockets. "This looks like something we'll have to deny later."

I stared bleary-eyed across the room, keeping my focus on Blue to distract myself from the pain. She was sitting at Wyatt's desk, focusing her attention on dual monitors. I'd been lying on the sofa for a half hour in the exact same position.

"Where's Shepherd?" Blue asked, expanding a window on one of the monitors.

Wyatt hauled another MoonPie box into the room and shoved it under his desk. "Probably hugging the toilet and regretting his life choices. Boy, you really missed out. You should have *seen* Raven riding on the roof of that car. It was out of sight."

"Is that so?" she said flatly.

Wyatt bounced on his heels while admiring the smaller snack cartons on the floor. "I'm too wired to sleep. After I run a check on these plates, I'll take over and relieve you of your duties."

"That's a sugar high you're feeling," she pointed out. "Don't count on it lasting all night. I've got this until Christian takes over. How many of those things did you eat?"

Wyatt put his hands on his hips. "I don't think I like your judgmental tone."

"File a complaint."

Since we didn't have any bodies to clean up at the accident scene on the highway, we'd skipped out. Christian said our Mage must have had second thoughts about issuing us a warning, so he hijacked a truck and ran it off the road to drive his point home.

The only thing that drove home were all those MoonPies.

Wyatt had stuffed as many as he could cram into his tiny trunk and the floorboards, and we each had cartons on our laps. Shepherd balked about it, but since Wyatt was the one driving and offered to leave any complainers behind, we quit arguing and got the hell out of there before someone called the state troopers.

Niko entered the room, Christian following close behind. He stopped for a moment and appeared to be looking around.

Christian leaned against the doorjamb. "She's over there on the sofa. Refusing anyone's help."

Niko's bare foot kicked one of the cartons, and it skidded across the floor. Without breaking stride, he approached the couch. I couldn't help but notice his drop-crotch pants. They were baggy all around except at the ankles and not something I usually saw him wearing. Given he was sans shirt and his hair was uncharacteristically messy, Christian must have dragged him out of bed, and that made me feel a little bit guilty.

Niko looked me over. "I almost didn't recognize your energy." He knelt down. "I heard you tested the theory of gravity tonight."

I conjured a mirthless grin. "It's my elbow. I'm just waiting it out until morning."

"Is it cut?"

"No. I think it's broken. I banged it up pretty good."

Niko put his hand on my hip and felt around until he located my arm. "This one?"

"Yep."

"Can you remove your coat?"

"My arm and leg hurt most from hitting the wall. I've got some scrapes and bruises, but—"

"You can draw light in the morning, but it's better to fix breaks right away. Sometimes if a bone starts to set in the wrong position, it has to be rebroken."

That thought didn't sound pleasant, so without sitting up, I let Niko help me free my arm from the sleeve. I growled when I had to bend it, the pain intolerable.

"Apologies. Just a quick touch of light to set the bone."

Warm heat penetrated my skin like liquid, and before I saw the flash of light, the pain in my elbow vanished. I still ached in other places, but nothing unbearable.

"Better?" he asked.

I sighed, grateful for his kindness. "Thanks, Niko. You always save the day."

"Just be sure to draw light first thing in the morning. If it's overcast again, come see me, but only if it's something serious... like internal injuries."

"I'm just a little banged up, that's all."

"I hope your suffering was worth the effort."

"We got a license plate," Wyatt said around a mouthful of chocolate, marshmallow, and graham cracker. He sat down in a leather chair and switched on a laptop. "Suspect numero uno."

"If this doesn't turn out to be the right guy," I began, "I still want to know his name and address."

Wyatt began typing. "What are you going to do, give him a speeding ticket?"

Christian came up behind Blue and put his hands on her shoulders. "How's the search going, lass?"

"Only one bid came up for a minor—a twelve-year-old."

The room fell silent.

"Can't we bid on him?" I asked.

Christian turned. "You can't save them all. We don't have unlimited funds."

"But you'll have rescued the kid."

"Aye. And if we're lucky enough to catch the seller, we might not have enough evidence against him. We can't prove they were the kidnapper, and we can't link them to a murder. It would be the decent thing to do, but it would also put us out of business. Sometimes there *is* no child. Here we have an opportunity to capture the person on the front end. Whether he's the actual seller is irrelevant; he's the man who does the dirty work. If we catch him, we can save a lot more lives."

Niko rubbed his eyes and stood up. "If my services are no longer required, I'll bid you all a good night."

"Hey, Niko," I quickly said.

He half turned.

"I owe you a training session."

"Tomorrow. One hour before breakfast, we'll work on balance."

After Niko left the room, Christian strolled over to the sofa and looked me over. "You should lie down."

"That's what I'm doing."

"Viktor might have plans for us tomorrow once we fill him in. Better you get some rest in a proper bed."

Without warning, he bent down and scooped me into his arms. I grimaced when a dull ache spread across my shoulder, but I didn't complain. My leg was fine as long as I didn't walk on it.

We moved into the hall, which was illuminated by a few lanterns on the walls. Christian hadn't put on a shirt since arriving home, and unlike me, he was buzzing with energy. He had the look of a person after they get off a roller coaster. Even the smirk beneath his scruffy beard told me his spirits were high.

"Why are you in such a good mood?" I finally asked.

"I thought Blue was a daredevil, but I don't think I've ever met a woman as fearless as you."

I smiled lazily. "My daddy's a biker. It's in my blood."

"Were you this brazen before you were turned?"

"I once went train surfing at night."

"Surprised it wasn't on an airplane."

"Couldn't afford the ticket."

He ascended a wide staircase that gently curved to the left.

"Where were you at tonight?" I asked.

"Just having a pint."

"You got to the bridge pretty fast."

"It wasn't that far off. I shadow walked most of the way. Had to leave behind the Honda."

"Maybe you'll get lucky and someone will steal it."

"Now is that any way to talk about my girl? She's a classy one. Reliable, fast, warms my arse."

"She's also not your type."

"And how would you know what my type is?"

"Guys like you don't do practical. Why are you trying to be someone you're not? The bike is definitely you, so why not get a car that's more your style?"

"And what would that be?"

"I don't know. Something dark, dangerous, and rough around the edges."

He pushed my door open with his shoulder. "My Honda makes me a respectable man."

"Since when does a man who has sex with women in public care about respect?"

"Touché."

He placed me on my bed and strode over to the window. I could barely make him out in the inky darkness.

I sat up and took Christian's coat off before scooting to the right side. "Would you mind lighting a candle? I can't see as well as you can."

His voice neared. "Don't make ordering me around into a habit."

He struck a match, the flame engulfing the end, and lit three candles. Instead of placing them on the tables beside the bed, he walked to the wall opposite the bed and set them on the hearth before using one of them to light up the kindling. I tossed his coat on the foot of the bed and propped two pillows behind me. Because the bed was low to the ground, I could lie down at night and watch the fire across the room.

"What made you chase him?" he asked, opening the flue.

"The mark on his neck. Gem said a waitress remembered a guy with a neck tattoo talking to Jennifer shortly before they fired her. Most criminals have stomping grounds. They're creatures of habit and stick to places where they feel in control. They know who works there, what the regulars are like, and where all the exits are located. Anyhow, I noticed him talking to a woman, and it didn't seem like casual flirting."

"Was she pregnant?"

My brows knitted together. "I don't think so."

The log succumbed to the flames and glowed in the hearth. Flecks of orange and gold twinkled against the darkness. I hadn't done much to my room in terms of decorating aside from a picture, a rug, and new bedding. On my left was the door, and in the corner to the right of it the standing mirror. All my clothes fit perfectly in the armoire to the left of the door. Honestly, I didn't have enough personal belongings to warrant buying a shelf or even a bigger desk. The scarlet-red bedspread kept me warm at night, especially with a fur blanket and a fire going. My chamber was a palace compared to living on the streets. And as of late, it was finally beginning to feel like home.

Christian set the candle on the bedside table, moving the faux roses out of the way before they went up in flames. He sat down next to me, his back straight against the headboard.

"Thanks for coming tonight," I said. "You looked like Batman jumping off that bridge."

"All in a day's work. Now I'm beginning to understand why all your trousers have holes. I thought you bought 'em that way."

I glanced down and noticed the blood and grit on my jeans from the accident. Then I poked my finger through the hole in his sweater, which I was still wearing. "Do I want to know how you got *this*?"

He peered over. "Probably not."

We both chuckled.

Firelight danced on the ceiling and walls, spreading across the bed like a river of orange light. I sat up to remove the sweater.

Christian helped me. "What's your da like?"

The sweater came over my head and messed my hair up. I swept it away from my face and sat back. "I can best describe my father in one story. I wasn't one of the popular girls in high school, so I didn't go out a lot. When I was fifteen, the high school quarterback asked me to a dance." I nestled against the pillows and kept my eyes on the fireplace. "I was so damn excited that someone had finally noticed me. My father took me to a dress shop and spent a good amount of money on this blue dress. Chiffon. That was a big deal because we bought most of my clothes at the thrift store. But I kept telling him it was a formal dance and the most important thing in the world."

"Ah, to be fifteen again."

"I was too embarrassed for Kyle to pick me up at the trailer, so I told him I'd wait by the main road. Crush—my daddy—wasn't happy about it one bit. So I waited and waited, watching one car after the next drive by as the sun went down. Then Kyle's yellow Mustang appeared at the end of the road. When it slowed to a stop, a girl in the passenger seat stared daggers at me. A couple of his buddies were crammed in the back, and that's when I realized the whole thing was a joke."

Christian scooted down the bed and began taking off my shoes. "Is that all?"

"They were laughing at me. He asked if I had really thought

someone like him would take a loser like me to the dance. Then they called me trailer trash, and one of the girls made a remark about my dress being secondhand."

"Shitebags."

The second shoe dropped to the floor, and then he removed my socks.

"Yep. They turned around and yelled a few more nasty remarks before speeding off. So I went home crying like a little kid. Crush asked what happened, but I think he knew. I lived in the worst area of the city, but lucky me, we were just within the limits to go to that school. Most of the kids there were rich."

Christian finally covered my legs with a fur blanket and sat back. "That's a sad tale, Raven Black."

I snickered. "That's not even the beginning. Crush was pissed, and you didn't get on his bad side without paying the price. I just wanted to go to my room and shut myself away, but he grabbed my makeup bag, called a few of his friends, and put me on his motorcycle."

"For what?"

"Well, the first thing he did was call a good buddy of his with an eighteen-year-old son. Switch was a good-looking kid with long hair and a tattoo on his arm. Girls wanted to date him, and guys wanted to be him. I'd met him a few times at parties and picnics, but most of my father's friends were like family, so I always thought of him as a cousin. He met us up at the school and walked in as my date. In retrospect, Crush did the right thing. He taught me to stand up for myself and give the world the middle finger. But at the time, I was still mortified and afraid to look those kids in the eye. They were popular, and I was just the girl from the wrong side of the tracks." My eyes closed. "I thought the date was real. It's not like I didn't have friends, and Kyle was in my English class and sometimes smiled at me."

"Kids are petty little bastards. If they don't find one thing, they'll find something else to single out others."

"Well, every head turned when I walked in with Switch. I'd only ever seen him in jeans and muscle shirts, so when he showed up in a suit, my jaw hit the floor. Crush insisted that I point Kyle out to him, and I did on the condition that they left the building. Switch spoiled me. They must have paid him good money to be nice, because he was getting me punch and even dancing."

"Your da's a good man."

I shifted my gaze and looked up. "But wait, there's more. While I was inside, having the time of my life, Crush was up to no good. I spent two hours getting pictures and feeling like a princess, but when the dance was over, we walked outside and saw a row of bikers with their arms folded. That's when I knew the night wasn't over."

Christian sputtered with laughter. "Did they beat up the little numpty? Jaysus."

"No, as much as I'm sure he would have liked to, they were grown men and knew better than that. They showed up to support me and make sure that nothing happened after the dance. They might have also covered Kyle's car with dog shit."

Both of us erupted with laughter. It was the first time I'd ever seen Christian lose himself, and at one point, he went completely silent with his mouth open and eyes shut, tears streaming down his face.

"I can't even begin to imagine where they got that much dog shit," I continued, trying to catch my breath. "But he had trouble finding his precious yellow car in the parking lot. His friends bailed on him, and his car smelled like manure for the rest of the semester." I laughed so hard that pain lanced down my shoulder. "God, I needed that laugh."

Christian wiped his eyes as we settled down. "Now I see where you get your attitude from."

I turned my attention to the fire. "My father wanted to show him what it felt like to be humiliated. I don't know if it made a difference in the person he became, but it sure did with me. Crush taught me to be a strong woman and to never let anyone get the best of me. He didn't want me to be ashamed of where I came from, and I struggled with that for years. That's why I don't make apologies for who I am now. It's too bad I didn't figure all that out until I got killed."

Christian tilted his head to the side. "Some people still haven't figured that out. Hate me all you want, but I make no apologies for who I am."

"I never said I hated you."

He laced his fingers across his chest. "What happened after that?"

"We drove home with an escort of about fifty bikers. I guess Crush was afraid I'd go back to my room and sulk, so we had a cookout. Barbecue, music, a few games of dominos on the picnic table. All the guys and their old ladies told me how pretty I looked."

"And Switch?"

I gave him a one-sided grin without reply.

Christian rolled over and caged me with his arms. "You can't leave me hanging. Did old Switch steal your virginity and make it a night to remember?"

I shoved at his bare shoulders. "You're a pig."

He waggled his brows. But when the playful look waned and his gaze traveled down to my lips, my body roared with tingles I hadn't felt in a long time. My heart quickened, and he must have heard it, because he settled his body on top of mine.

Something electric was transpiring between us—an unstoppable force like a runaway train. I reached up and cradled his neck, my fingers tunneling beneath his dark hair. When my nails scored his nape, his eyes smoldered.

What am I doing? I need to stop before it goes too far.

"You have a cut on your head," he pointed out. "And your cheek is scraped."

The weight of him was sublime and familiar, as if we were right back in that motel room in Washington. I'd tried to forget about the blood sharing, but sometimes I thought about the taste of him—the sweet, decadent, enigmatic flavor of Christian Poe.

Did all Vampires taste as sinfully divine?

"What are you thinking?" he asked.

I wasn't thinking. My body was humming with desire, craving

a man's touch. A little voice was also reminding me that Christian was my partner, and if I craved a man's touch, I needed to head over to the bar and find someone else.

His lips grazed the shell of my ear. "Do you want my blood?"

I felt myself trembling beneath him. Was that all it took to make me wet? To make my body flush with need?

"A few drops should patch you right up," he continued.

Which deflated my balloon. Was this all in my head? Christian's offer was to heal me. Otherwise, he would have kissed me by now.

"Get off," I whispered.

He rolled to the left and stood up. "It's going to snow in the morning. It's not good for you to take so much light from Niko. It might create an addiction."

I arched an eyebrow. "And your blood won't?" I began to unbutton my shirt with my left hand. "Why don't you go check on Shepherd?"

"Exactly what happened tonight to get him so langered?"

"I don't know, but maybe he'll talk to you since you're drinking buddies."

Christian folded his arms and sighed. "Do you think men sit around and share their innermost secrets over a glass of ale?"

"Don't you?"

"We talk about which nipples are the most beautiful and which knives are the most effective when severing a head."

"So which are best?"

He circled his fingers around his chest. "I'm partial to the larger ones that aren't too dark or too pink. It depends on the size of the breast. If they're too small, a large nipple will only—"

"I meant the knives."

Christian stuffed his hands in his pockets. "I can't seem to recall beheadings in your file."

"I'm just curious. Maybe someday I'll get over that squeamishness."

He leaned forward on one foot and gave me a pointed stare. "*No one* gets over the squeamishness. It's the best way to kill an immortal, to be sure, but it's a brutal act that requires a man to reach deep down inside himself and shut off his emotions. Leave the dirty work to the men."

"Maybe you need my help since there seems to be an abundance of male criminals to behead."

"What are you saying? That women are incapable of evil? Take my word when I tell you there are women out there who are as cold and heartless as a serial killer, with just an empty chamber of darkness for a soul. And rest assured that there is nothing more dangerous than a woman who's lost touch with her emotions."

"Is that going to be us in a thousand years?"

I stripped away my shirt and winced, several bruises showing up on my ribs and upper arm. I was lean but had a toned body. I glanced down at my bra and smiled, wondering what Christian would think of my nipples. Too big? Too small?

Christian dodged the opportunity to gape at me and turned on his heel to face the armoire.

"It's too late to be gallant," I said. "It's nothing you haven't seen before."

"Maybe I don't like reruns."

I sat on the edge of the bed and unzipped my pants. "We were *so* close tonight. We almost had him."

"And then what? He confesses all his crimes?"

"No, but you could have charmed information out of him."

"Along with a few teeth," he ground out. Christian peered over his shoulder and closed the distance between us. "Let me do that." He gripped the waistband of my jeans and winked at me. "I'm quite talented at removing women's clothing."

I leaned on my good arm and lifted my hips as he pulled my jeans down, revealing my black panties and the Keystone tattoo on the right side, below my navel.

When I caught his eyes lingering on the tattoo, I sat up. "That's enough. I can do the rest."

He stepped back a few paces. "Switch lost out on his chance. He's probably an old fat bastard by now."

I kicked off my pants. "Not that old. Just in his thirties."

"Potbelly, seven kids, a part-time job at the gas station, probably a criminal record. I bet when he buys his carton of smokes and drives home in his El Camino, he thinks back with regret and wonders why he didn't flatten you in the back of his Chevy."

"Ford, actually. And that's the takeaway you got from my story? Nothing about loyalty or teaching a woman to conquer her fears?"

He shrugged and strode toward the door. "Just an observation. Poor Switch. I'll be sure to remember him in my prayers tonight."

I fell back on the bed and laughed. "If you ever put your hands together to pray, you'll probably turn into a pile of ash."

He opened the door. "Be sure to sweep up my remains. You know how I hate littering."

"I'll collect your ashes and sprinkle them around your favorite bar," I quipped.

"Maybe you should sprinkle them in your favorite bottle of wine. Then you can enjoy tasting me for the next century. Sleep well, Precious."

Chapter 11

"ANYONE WANT SECONDS?" I ASKED, eyeing a bowl of spaghetti.

A few people gave me quiet glares except for Christian, whose plate was empty as usual.

Maybe spaghetti for breakfast wasn't the greatest idea, but it was the easiest thing to make. I was still sore from Niko's training session where he had me balance on one leg while he tried to tip me over. Besides, inappropriate meals were part of my master plan to botch up my cooking week so badly that they'd never want me to do my rotation again.

Viktor shoved his plate away. "Do they not teach young girls domestic skills?"

I gulped down my water. "Sorry, Viktor. They just teach us how to be doctors, lawyers, and politicians."

Gem pulled both feet up on her chair and stared at the floral print on her leggings. "Shepherd's been reclusive this morning. I thought it was a hangover, but when I passed him in the hall earlier, he barely acknowledged me."

Blue rested her chin in her palm. "Should we take him some food?"

Christian's lips twitched. "Nothing goes with a hangover like noodles."

Viktor stroked his beard and gave me a critical look. "Are you sure there's nothing else you want to tell me about last night?"

"I told you everything that happened. Maybe the turtle didn't sit well with him. They talked while I chased the kid around. I'm not keeping anything from you. If I was going to keep secrets, I would have left out the part where I climbed onto a Mage's car and rode down the freeway."

Gem gave an elfin smile. "I would have loved to have seen that. Raven flying like a bird."

"We should have stayed behind," Claude growled, tossing his fork down. "Then *I* would have been the one to give chase, not Raven. She could have been killed."

"It doesn't matter if it was you or me who jumped on that car," I pointed out. "Gender has nothing to do with—"

"Bravado?" he finished.

"I was going to say aptitude. I didn't chase after him because there wasn't a man there who couldn't or wouldn't. I did it because it's my job."

He pressed his finger against the table. "You could have been hurt."

Christian pushed away his empty plate. "You should quit while you're ahead."

"I wouldn't say he's ahead," Blue added, a smile hovering on her lips. "Seems like Raven is leading by a point."

"It's too bad the license plate didn't link to a name," Gem said absently, putting a stop to the playful banter.

She was right. That guy probably wasn't going back to Club Nine anytime soon, and he was our only lead.

Viktor steepled his fingers. "Shepherd is in no condition to leave the house. Someone must go back to the club and look for his keys. I have much work to do. Any volunteers?"

"I'll go," I said, raising a finger. "Maybe one of the waitresses on the morning shift will know something about that guy."

Gem snapped her fingers and put her feet on the ground. "Smart thinking. I'll go with you since I had luck with getting information from one of them."

"Nyet. You have a paper to translate for me. I need it by noon for my contact."

Her shoulders sagged. "Not even for a few hours? I promise I'll—"

Niko launched to his feet and knocked his chair over. "Something's wrong."

Christian slowly rose. "It's Shepherd."

Viktor sat back. "What's going on?"

We looked up at Christian, whose brow furrowed as he cocked his head to the side. "I can't make out anything intelligible."

Gem swept her hands down her arms, and that was when I felt it. Energy prickled against my skin like tiny rivulets of static. That was something we'd normally feel with another Mage, but sometimes rage could produce a similar effect. It was faint, but Shepherd's room was also on the other side of the mansion.

Claude's nostrils flared, and he rose to his feet, shoulders squared. Everyone immediately bolted out the door. Shepherd's room was on the first level, past the stairs and down the main hall that ran along the right side of the mansion. Just before reaching the back, we turned left down a hall that had rooms on either side. Claude was in the lead with Christian bringing up the rear. Wyatt was already standing there with his hands on his hips.

"What's going on?" Claude boomed.

Wyatt backed up a few steps, hands in the air. "I didn't do anything. He locked the door."

Claude tested the knob, but it didn't open.

Blue stood next to him and knocked loudly. "Shepherd, open the door."

"He's quieted down," Wyatt said, stating the obvious.

Claude pinched his nose as if something was burning it.

Niko weaved past me and stopped short of the door. "Someone needs to get in there and find out what has him so distraught," he whispered. "His energy is leaking through the walls, and it's foul."

Everyone turned to Christian.

He shook his head. "Only if the repairs come out of your pocket, not mine."

"Do not break my doors," Viktor said calmly. "Wyatt, what did you say to him?"

Wyatt wiped a hand across his mouth. "I just came down to show him the good news." He caught Gem glaring at the metal whistle hanging around his neck. "Okay, *maybe* I also wanted to see if he still had a hangover. I checked to see if there were any street cameras in the area since the guy we were chasing was on foot after the wreck. There's one set up on the freeway heading eastbound, but it was too grainy and only showed him waving down the snack truck. He blasted the driver with a shot of energy and hijacked the vehicle. The camera caught him flashing back after the accident, but it's just a blur on film."

"This is news?" Viktor asked.

Wyatt flipped up the ends of his beanie. "City cameras I can hack into; the private ones are another story. I didn't think he'd run all the way home in this weather, so I figured he might have gone into one of the gas stations. A buddy of mine did me a favor and checked all his sources. He located footage right around that time, and it's a match."

"How do you know it was him?" I asked.

"This guy walked in without a car, talked on the phone without buying anything, and waited for someone to pick him up. He wasn't wearing a coat and had a tattoo on the back of his neck. I'm pretty sure it's him unless we have doppelgängers around the city. Anyhow, I just got the footage and printed out a close-up shot. At least we have a face to work with."

"Where is it?" I asked.

He pressed his finger against Shepherd's door. "When I showed it to him, he lost his shit."

I jiggled the locked doorknob. "Why didn't you question him?"

He snorted. "You've obviously never seen his armoire."

Viktor waved his hand. "Come, everyone. Let us leave Shepherd to calm down. If he needs to be alone, we should respect that. I'll speak to him when he's ready to come out. Perhaps next time you should monitor how much he drinks."

Claude turned on his heel. "I'm not his mother. If a man wants to nurse the bottle, that's his prerogative."

I stared at the door, riddled with guilt. Maybe I shouldn't have sat down and let Shepherd get tanked before trying to sober him up. Some people are angry drunks, some introspective, and others happy. I'd seen Shepherd with a few drinks in him, but this time I feared he might be a danger to others if we didn't ride it out. What if he was in the middle of a psychotic break?

I jumped when Viktor put his arm around my shoulder, coaxing me away.

"Come, Raven. There is nothing you can do for a man when his door is closed."

Shepherd sat on the floor, his knees drawn up and arms draped over them. The photograph on the floor taunted him.

Those eyes.

Wyatt handing him that photo had reawakened raw, visceral pain. Shepherd then lashed out, smashing a wooden chair against a wall. Uncertain where that anger might direct itself, he'd thrown Wyatt out of the room and locked the door. After the storm passed, Shepherd slumped down on the floor across from his bed and surveyed the damage.

There wasn't much *to* destroy. He'd flipped the mattress onto the floor but had the good sense not to destroy the frame. His clothes were scattered from where he normally folded them on a bench by his bed, but that was all the damage he could do without breaking apart the only two things he loved: his weapons and his desk. He leaned his right shoulder against the armoire and stared at his desk by the door. By candlelight, he would quietly sit there and clean his weapons or review case files. His centrally located room didn't have a fireplace. Didn't need one. Stone surrounded him from all angles, and he preferred that type of environment. The bathroom entryway was across from the door. In front of it, a large green-and-gold carpet where he did his meditation and calisthenics when he wasn't down in the gym.

Keeping his body in shape was a religion. That was how he'd begun to rebuild his life again, one push-up at a time. It kept him focused. Maybe he couldn't control all the bullshit around him, but he could manipulate the strength of his body, the tone of his muscles, the definition of his abs, and the deadliness of his weapons.

Shepherd continued staring at the photo on the floor between his legs. The Mage had cut his hair and changed his beard to a goatee, but it was the same guy. Those electric-green eyes had haunted him for years, and he wasn't even the man who'd almost stabbed Shepherd to death in a savage attack. That Mage had already met his maker when Shepherd spotted him a couple of years ago outside a hotel. He'd followed the man into a dark parking lot and tried to get information on the other Mage, but the man refused to talk. Enraged, Shepherd unleashed hell, shoving a stunner into his back and stabbing him repeatedly before severing his head.

It wasn't until Shepherd had hit rock bottom that Viktor had approached him with an offer to join Keystone. It was a chance for a fresh start, but the agreement required him to walk away from his past. Shepherd left behind everything. His clothes, his memories—even his name.

The walls around him evaporated as he slipped back to a time when he used to go by the name Samuel. He looked like a Samuel. Soft in the belly, clean-shaven… even had a charismatic smile that made all the women giddy. He used to work a desk job for the Sensor Council, lifting emotional imprints off weapons collected from crime scenes. That was how he'd become familiar with weapons; he handled them on a daily basis. One day the Council reassigned him to work as a security guard at the local hospital. It was a lateral move with no pay increase, but one of their insiders had quit, and they needed an immediate replacement. Time diluted emotional imprints, which was why analyzing weapons had never bothered him. But in a human hospital, the emotions were fresh and saturated everything. He was careful not to inadvertently touch anything a patient or grieving family member might have come into contact with, but accidents happened.

All the time.

If anything, working around humans had taught him how to separate himself from emotions.

Shepherd's job was to pose as a security guard and monitor

everyone admitted, including and especially morgue duty. It wasn't uncommon for Breed to wind up in a hospital with injuries so severe that they were either unconscious or paralyzed by a weapon. Shepherd kept an eye out for nonhumans and reported any persons—living or dead—to his contact. They sent in Regulators to collect and move the patient before doctors or pathologists got their hands on them. A Vampire usually accompanied them to erase memories, records, and video.

It was in the hospital cafeteria that Shepherd met with destiny. Maggie was the most stunningly awkward woman he'd ever encountered. She wore large, square glasses with black frames, but it was her wavy blond hair that he noticed first. She had it pulled up in a messy knot, and there was a pencil dangling from the back as if she'd forgotten about it hours ago. He stood behind her at the register, and when the pencil slipped out and dropped to the floor, he picked it up and felt her emotional imprint on his fingertips. That was how he discovered she was Breed, like him.

Shepherd rubbed his face and wondered if the fates were punishing him for striking a deal with Patrick. He had two choices. He could hand over the photograph to Patrick and let him honor his end of the deal, or he could take matters into his own hands and risk losing his position with Keystone.

Either way, that green-eyed Mage was going in the ground. It wouldn't bring back Maggie, but maybe her soul would rest in peace. As Shepherd stared at the candle across the room, his thoughts drifted back to that fateful night, and his stone-cold heart ached for the first time in years. If someone had pushed him into the ocean, he would have sunk to the bottom from the weight of his sorrow.

The doorknob jiggled, snapping him out of his thoughts. The hinges creaked, and a slim figure tiptoed in, a sheer duster floating behind her. The candle on the desk illuminated Gem's small frame, and his eyes drifted down to her floral leggings that she sometimes wore with her crazy-ass sneakers.

Gem approached him as she might a wild animal. Without a word, she squatted in front of him, her knees against her chest.

She held up the photograph to catch the light from the desk behind her. "You know him, don't you?"

He gestured toward the door. "I should have never taught you to do that."

She tucked the bobby pin back into her hair, and a long stretch of silence elapsed before she finally spoke. "Keystone wouldn't be the same without you. We need you. Viktor needs you. I know you don't take me seriously half the time, but I'm a good listener. Niko's the one with all the good advice, but if you ever want to bend my ear, I'm always around the corner. Viktor probably knows more about you than I do, but nobody wants to dump their feelings onto their boss's lap." She set the picture back on the floor. "If you know this guy's name or how to find him, I can help come up with a plan so they won't know where we got the information, and you won't have to deal with questions."

"I don't know his name," Shepherd said, barely recognizing his own voice.

She touched his hand. "The fates brought him back into your life for a reason. Maybe it's so you can get your revenge, but maybe it's not. We still have a little baby out there whose life depends on us."

That brought Shepherd down to earth.

Gem rested her head across his arm and smiled at him. She batted her lashes in that endearing and playful way that was all Gem. "Please help us find the baby."

Shepherd nodded, suddenly feeling embarrassed about his outburst. He didn't like people thinking he didn't have things under control. "If anyone asks, just tell them I was mad I missed breakfast."

She patted his hand and stood up. "There's *plenty* left over. I'll just tell Raven to heat up the sauce."

His lips twitched. "Sauce?"

Chapter 12

NIKO PINNED ME AGAINST THE mat. "You're losing focus."

Exhausted, I simply lay there while he stood up and wiped his face and chest with a towel. After Shepherd's meltdown, I had decided to extend my morning session with Niko. I enjoyed our time together even if we spent most of it knocking each other down. When working out, he had me focusing on upper-arm strength by climbing the rope or doing pull-ups. But during our one-on-one sessions, he taught me how to fight. It wasn't that I didn't know how to protect myself, but I fought dirty. Niko wanted to demonstrate actual maneuvers, which would probably take me centuries to perfect. He said that relying heavily on Mage energy could be a weakness, and only a true warrior could fight without it.

He tossed me a bottle of water, and I caught it in my hand before sitting up.

"What was that about upstairs?" I asked, unscrewing the lid.

"Do you mean with Shepherd?" Niko heaved a sigh and hiked up his loose black pants so he could sit down in front of me. "He's never spoken about his past or personal life. I've never known him to lose control."

"How are we supposed to help him if he won't let us in?"

Niko swept back a wayward piece of hair and tucked it through the elastic band holding his hair in a knot. "We must leave it up to Viktor. If he's too unstable to work on this case, Viktor will pull him out."

I gulped my water down and set the bottle aside. "Has this ever happened before?"

Niko's blue eyes looked through me. "Shepherd has always been emotionally stable, and I'm good at reading energy. He has a unique relationship with Wyatt because they're partners, but he's always gotten along better with Christian. Perhaps they enjoy each other's company because they are more alike than not."

I leaned on my arm. "Maybe Viktor's taking a big risk hiring a team of secret agents who have the kind of criminal record we do."

"If Viktor didn't give us a chance, who would? He's giving us an opportunity to start over. Where would you be now if he hadn't come along? Here we can forget our past and rebuild our lives."

I stood up and straightened my tank top. "We might be done with the past, but the past isn't done with us. Ever think of that? Maybe the only way to move forward isn't to shove all our skeletons into a closet and pretend they never existed. The closet's still there, Niko. And the next time you open it, all that shit's going to fall on top of you."

He slowly rose to his feet and cocked his head to the side. "You're not talking about Viktor anymore. What are you contemplating?"

"Nothing."

He narrowed his eyes, and I knew he could read my lie.

My father was an unresolved issue, and no matter how perfect my new life seemed, if I didn't close that door once and for all, it was going to haunt me worse than any of Wyatt's spooks. I might end up like Shepherd with mood swings and outbursts of rage.

I turned on my heel and headed toward the door. "I need to shower."

"Raven!"

He followed behind me, and when I realized he wasn't going to let it go, I flashed up the stairs and across the mansion.

After several flights of stairs, I reached my room on the third floor and closed the heavy door behind me. I liked Niko, but not enough to confide something that could make me look bad in front of Viktor. While we each shared the same tattoo, Niko was loyal to Viktor first and foremost. My plans had nothing to do with Keystone, and no one had any right interfering.

I'd stripped out of my shorts and was grabbing a clean pair of panties and some clothes from my armoire when all of a sudden, Niko burst into the room.

"Why did you run from me?" The door closed behind him, and his gaze followed my energy trail until he found me by the bed.

I stood there in nothing but a pair of panties. Could he see my nudity? My guess was no when he didn't flinch or look away.

His eyebrows sank into an angry slash. "Everyone has secrets, but if you're planning to do something that'll hurt this organization, I can't allow that to happen. Your energy flickered back there. *Guilt.*" He closed the distance between us. "It is not my job to protect you. Everyone must make their own decisions. But don't waste our time. If you have a choice, then you need to make the right one."

"Like you ignoring those guys who follow you around?"

His jaw set.

"You're good at reading people's light. Don't tell me you haven't spotted them once or twice when we've gone out. They sure as hell noticed you. And whoever that guy is, he's not going anywhere. Ignore the past all you want, Niko, but eventually it's going to make you pay attention. Why not face it on your own terms instead of waiting for it to destroy you? Don't misinterpret my actions. I want to stay here. I want to start a new life and be a better person, whatever that means."

Niko shook his head. "Keystone isn't about angels and sinners. We help people, but your hands won't be clean. Sometimes we have to turn a blind eye, and sometimes we have to kill. If you imagined yourself a monster before, don't assume getting paid will change anything."

"I thought that was the whole point of joining Keystone. To clean up our act."

He took a few steps toward me. "It's easy to lose yourself when you're alone. Viktor uses our talents and keeps us from crossing the line. Otherwise, we would become no different from the men we hunt. We're ideal for this job because we have nothing to lose, but that also makes us a danger to ourselves."

"Viktor can't control our lives."

When I veered left to go through the open doorway to my bathroom, I felt his fingers swipe my bare back as if he were grabbing for my shirt.

Niko inclined his head when he realized I was naked. "Apologies."

I sighed, not at all upset with him. "If Shepherd's gone off the deep end and he does something to bring this organization down, then I'm with you. But… I also think we're entitled to free will when it comes to personal matters. What I want isn't going to hurt Viktor or the team."

He turned away and strolled toward the window. "It's not just about what could bring down Keystone. Viktor's rules also protect us. Desire makes you weak, whether that desire is for love, revenge, or material things." Niko moved around to the desk, feeling some of the objects on it. "It would be a shame to lose you, Raven. I've come to enjoy our private conversations."

"That's not a threat, is it?"

"You needn't worry. This conversation is between us. But like Christian and Shepherd, I can see you're still struggling with letting go. Those men who follow me are inconsequential. I have the power to walk away, whereas before Keystone, I didn't. This is my life now, and I no longer entertain ghosts." He furrowed his brow and held up the stainless-steel box. "Did you solve this yet?"

I shook my head. "It's a cube for decoration. It has neat little etchings on the sides. Can you feel them?"

It danced on the tips of his fingers. "It's a puzzle box. Didn't you know?"

I strode around the bed and looked at it. "Gem translated the symbols, but she didn't say it was… What exactly is a puzzle box?"

He began attempting to twist and push at it. "They're a novelty. Usually there's a hidden compartment, and the only way to access it is by solving the puzzle. You press the pieces or slide them in a specific order." He finally held it out for me to take. "I'm afraid it's not mine to solve."

I gripped the cube and set it on the bed. "Are we good? I don't want you to leave on a bad note. I'm not planning anything devious to undermine Viktor. It's—"

"Personal," he finished. "The most difficult decision you'll ever make is to let go of the thing you want most. If this is a test, the fates will punish you for making the wrong choice, even if it might seem like the right one."

"The fates gave up on me the day I was made. They don't care about me anymore. Please don't mention this to Viktor. I don't want him doubting my intentions."

Niko bowed. "As you wish." When he reached the door, he stood still for a frozen moment. "I won't enter your room again without knocking. I had no right to disrespect your privacy."

I laughed. "You're the only person in this house I don't mind seeing me naked."

"That's because I'm blind."

"Exactly."

"Some blessings are a curse," he said, quietly leaving the room.

Since Shepherd was still unfit for public appearances, Christian and I volunteered to head over to Club Nine and search for his keys. If we couldn't find them, Christian knew a locksmith. I could probably start the car with a little Mage power, but I'd never done it before and didn't want to risk blowing up his engine.

It was late afternoon, and the snowfall was finally tapering off. I peered inside my trench coat while Christian turned into the parking lot.

"That's the third time you've looked in there," he said. "Did you lose your breasts?"

"No. I'm just wondering if I can hide a few daggers in here. I've always had to carry the big one strapped to my leg, but that's not practical when I'm wearing jeans. The push daggers are fine; I like them close to my body for easy access."

"When Shepherd comes out of his cave, maybe he'll take a look. He's clever with modifications."

I put my foot on his dash and retied my shoelaces. "What do you think is wrong with him?"

Christian removed his sunglasses and squinted at the bright snow. "Probably what's wrong with all of us. We're fecking loons. Get your foot off my dash."

I dropped my leg and unbuckled my seat belt. "I thought you guys were best buddies."

"I'm not having this discussion again. Now quit flapping your gums, and let's get this over with."

"Enjoy your reprieve," I said playfully. "When you get back, you'll be staring at a computer screen for the rest of the night."

He shut off the engine. "On that note, there are some sick bastards in this world."

I got out of the car and met up with him next to the building. "Why? What did you see?"

"Last night, there were pets going up for sale."

"Pets?"

"Aye. Some of those humans you love so much have an infatuation with Shifters. They volunteer to become their pets. Leather collars and everything."

I snorted. "Do they wear a leash?"

"The higher authority frowns upon that kind of thing, but it's entirely legal. The demand for pets is higher than the supply, so some of them coordinate with marketeers to find the highest bidder. That way the human gets a little something out of it in addition to fulfilling whatever sexual fantasy they're searching for."

"So it's a sex thing?"

We rounded the corner.

"It makes some Shifters feel empowered to have dominion over a human pet. Shifters were once slaves within our world. I guess freedom isn't enough for some and they want a taste of that power. A pet is a servant."

"A servant with a collar. Sounds more like a slave. Do they care which animal bids on them? Wolf? Panther? Sheep?" When Christian ignored my remarks, I egged him on. "What about a cow? Do they get to milk them?"

He held the door open and gave me a scathing glance. "My deepest condolences to the woman who dropped you on your head."

I reached in my pocket and tossed a receipt onto the floor. Without looking back, I knew he'd bent down to pick it up. Just as we reached the bar, I tossed something else from my pocket onto the ground.

Christian slammed his hand on the bar with the scraps of paper beneath it. "Now you're just goading me."

Hooper turned and gave Christian a look of annoyance. He licked one of his lip rings and ambled toward us. "Is there something I can get for you?"

Christian lifted his hand, revealing the wadded-up papers. "She'll be having a trash can."

"He'll have world peace," I said. "Could we trouble you for a minute? A friend of ours left his keys here last night, so we thought we'd come in and look around. Has anyone turned anything in?"

He looked between my mismatched eyes. "I remember you now. Is the car still out there?" he asked with a smile.

"Yep."

"Must be a jalopy. Most of the keys lost in here never get found, and neither do the cars."

Theft wasn't a crime that could land a man in Breed jail, so what would deter someone from taking the Jeep? "Would you mind looking around? Maybe one of the waitresses placed them behind the bar or something and didn't relay the message. My friend here will check the men's room." I patted Christian on the shoulder and he wrenched away, heading toward the restrooms. He didn't look angry. In fact, his stoic expression made me want to try harder to get a reaction. "Check every stall!" I yelled out.

Hooper winked. "Be right back."

After he disappeared behind the bar, I plopped down on a

stool and spun around to face the club. A few people were hanging out, but it wasn't as busy as the evening hours. When I crossed my legs, an attractive man with long hair winked at me. He must have liked the no-makeup-and-crazy-hair look.

A familiar face strode by on his way out. "Careful, Butterfly. That one's a Vampire."

I stared at the man's bleached hair and hopped off my stool. "Hey, Chaos. Your little ruse didn't work."

"Oh?" he said, not turning around or slowing his pace. "And what trick would that be?"

I followed him out the main door. "My necklace isn't real. But I can appreciate how much fun that must have been to instigate a fight between me and my partner."

The man laughed and stopped by the corner, his eyes bright with humor. He had on a grey coat with a high collar, and his hair was messier than I last remembered. Out in the light, I could see a few tiny dark moles on his face. They stood out because it didn't look like he got much sun.

"Why were you chasing that man last night?" he asked.

"Do you live here?"

He traced a dark eyebrow with his finger. "Your jumping on top of a car seems far more interesting than how often I frequent the club. Was he one of your targets? Or did he make the mistake of asking for your phone number? I might get jealous if you gave it to him."

I crossed my arms and decided to head back inside where it was warm. "Maybe I'll see you around."

"I thought you might want to know that man's name, but seeing as you're in a hurry, I'll bid you a good evening."

I blinked in surprise as he strode around the corner. "Wait!" I seized his cuff. "What do you know about him?"

His brows arched to his hairline. "I assumed you knew already."

"What can you tell me?"

"I shouldn't get involved."

"Please?"

He reached in his pocket and took out a pen. "Give me your hand."

I peeled off my fingerless glove. The felt-tip pen tickled my palm as he began scribbling something.

"It's a dangerous side of the city. I wouldn't advise going there after dark."

Maybe getting to know regulars in the clubs wasn't such a bad idea. I watched my new friend taking his time with his penmanship. His amiable personality made it seem as if we'd known each other for years. Sometimes you just meet people in life who are on the same wavelength.

"What's your Breed?" I asked.

He let go of my hand and put the cap back on his pen. "I'm like you."

"A Mage then." I read the address on my hand. "How do you know where he lives?"

"I know many things."

My shoulders sagged when I realized that nothing came free. "What do you want in return?"

He leaned in, his mouth close to my ear. "Your fealty."

I took two steps back. Maybe he was one of those weirdoes who owned people pets.

A smile touched his lips. "See you when I see you."

I headed back, stoked that I had a lead. Once inside, Hooper shook his head to indicate he hadn't found our keys. With Christian nowhere in sight, I ventured to the limbo room and tried to retrace Shepherd's steps as best as I could imagine. I searched beneath the chairs, inside the seat cushions, and especially around the table where we had sat.

Nothing.

Then I crawled on my hands and knees, because maybe they got kicked around and landed somewhere else. I grimaced when I bumped into a familiar pair of legs.

Christian anchored his hands on his hips and looked down at me with a wolfish grin. "Now *that's* where I think you belong."

I stood up and straightened my coat. "Find anything in the potty room?"

"Besides dirty arses? Afraid not. I better call the locksmith."

When he reached for the phone in his pocket, I gripped his arm. "Wait."

His eyes flashed up. "That's a look I've seen before. Trouble."

"Forget the keys. I know where to find our guy."

He barked out a laugh. "I was away for ten minutes, and you've solved the fecking case?"

I held my hand in front of his face.

He turned it sideways and read the address. "Where did you get this?"

I lowered my hand. "The fates. They want us to find the baby."

"I suppose the heavenly angels came down and gave you his address? How convenient."

"A friend of mine. He's a regular here and recognized the guy. Saw me chasing after him."

"And what did he want in return?"

"Nothing." I moved past Christian and into the main hall.

"Nobody gives away something for nothing," he said, following close behind. "How do you know this isn't a trap? You're a fine-looking Mage, Raven. A lot of men would like a taste of that."

I rolled my eyes even though he couldn't see. "If he wanted some of this, he could have easily gotten it already."

"I'm not even going to ask what that's supposed to mean."

I stopped near the bar and turned to face him. "So, are you up for a little danger? Or would you rather go back to Keystone and babysit the computer while Wyatt's out buying two sacks of fries?"

His eyes narrowed. "Did you consume one of the specialty drinks? Should I be concerned about your sudden agenda change?"

"This idea is not drink induced. You should know me better than that. So, what'll it be?" I rocked on my heels, eager for an adventure.

He put his arm around me and led us to the door. "I can't let you have all the fun, now can I?" Christian came to a halt. "*Jaysus.* I should have known."

"What are you talking about?"

He gave me a scathing glance and pointed at a ring of shiny keys sitting on a nearby table.

"If you wanted to get me out of the house, you could have just asked me out on a date."

"I didn't swipe Shepherd's keys as a master plan to get you out of the house. It's fate. We're supposed to take his Jeep to search for the Mage." When I approached the table and held up the keys for a closer inspection, I recognized the house key. Yep. They were Shepherd's.

Christian swiped the keys from my hand. "Maybe the fates want us to take the car home. Why do I have the feeling I'm going to regret this?"

I smirked. "Is that what Viktor said before he hired you?"

"That's what your husband is going to say before reciting his vows."

"That's what every woman says before they have sex with you."

Christian swaggered toward the door, swinging the keys around his finger. "That's what I'm going to say before you serve our dinner tonight."

Chapter 13

THE ENGINE REVVED AS CHRISTIAN plowed through a patch of ice. He flashed me a wolfish grin. "She handles like an experienced whore. I might have to get me one of these."

As much as I hated taking Shepherd's Jeep Wrangler without permission, Christian had insisted we needed a vehicle with traction to maneuver the slick roads. It wasn't the smaller model but a special edition four-door with a hardtop and extended cab.

He could literally run over Wyatt's car with this machine.

"What happens when we get there?" I asked.

Christian's fangs lengthened. "Let me do all the talking."

I yanked a few loose threads from a hole in my jeans. "Should we tell Viktor what we're up to?"

"He created teams for a reason. We don't even know if this Mage is the same man who murdered the poor lass."

"He ran from me."

"Maybe he just caught a whiff of your perfume and the desperate look in your eyes."

As soon as we pulled up to a light, the engine died. Christian turned the key, and it started up only briefly before dying again.

"Oh, for feck's sake. We're out of petrol."

"Are you sure?"

"These new cars have too many gadgets, but I know the sound of an empty tank."

I sighed and stared at the road ahead. Maybe it was a sign.

"How's your leg?" he asked.

"Better. We had about fifteen minutes of sunshine this morning. I didn't want to run downstairs and miss it, so I climbed out a window and healed myself."

Christian turned a few switches and finally pulled out the keys. "We're walking from here." He gave me a scrutinizing look before searching the console and glove compartment. He tossed one of Wyatt's hats on my lap. "Put your hair in that."

"Why?"

"You've never been to the Bricks?"

I looked around at the empty streets. "Is that a bar?"

"No. It's a place rife with danger and out of the higher authority's jurisdiction. Put on the hat and look unassuming."

"I'm not sure if that's possible."

When we got out of the Jeep, Christian locked the doors and patted the hood. "Nice knowing you."

"No one's going to steal it without gas," I pointed out.

He unwrapped a lollipop as we crossed to the sidewalk and stuck it in his mouth. "They'll strip her down like a two-dollar hooker. There's nothing we can do about it now."

"So why am I wearing a hat? Is that the law in Munchkinland?"

"Because you look like a girl."

I chuckled. "So without a hat on, I don't? That's quite a compliment, Mr. Poe."

He pulled the stick out of his mouth after biting off the candy and tossed it into a trash can. "You have a tough look for a woman. The coat hides your breasts and—"

"Vagina?"

"Don't be daft." After yanking the oversized hat down and covering my eyebrows, he lifted the collar of my coat to shield my face. "Keep your head down. If you think juicers are a problem in the parking lots, you haven't seen anything yet. This neighborhood isn't used to beautiful women outside of the powerful untouchables."

"You think I'm beautiful?"

He finished tucking away the loose strands of my black hair. "They'd love nothing more than getting their hands on a woman so they could bind with her."

I shivered. Juicing was stealing a Mage's light for an energy high. Binding was an intimate act of sharing sexual light between couples. Having a Mage do that against a person's will was the equivalent of rape. A rogue I could handle, but I started imagining gangs of men descending upon me like vultures. Christian was a skilled fighter, but impalement wood could immobilize him. I set my mouth in a grim line and tried walking like a man.

Christian laughed. "Strut like you've got a pair between your legs, not like you need to take a shite."

"I've never had a pair between my legs."

"Is that so?"

I shoved him hard enough that he lost his balance and stumbled into the gutter. "If these black marketeers live on the shanty side of town, maybe the higher authority should do a raid and clean up the riffraff."

We turned a corner, and Christian pointed at a pile of rubble across the street. "Do you think they haven't tried? That's why they call it the Bricks. You'll see plenty more piles of them scattered throughout. Over the years, some of the buildings were destroyed in Breed battles. No one rebuilds out here."

"Don't the humans notice?"

"We have insiders who work to keep city officials out."

"So we're protecting the criminals?"

"Aye. Depraved men who would love nothing more than to start a war with mankind. Better the humans keep out. The higher authority can't control these men, so there's an unspoken agreement that we'll turn a blind eye so long as they don't call attention to themselves."

We walked by a vagrant leaning against a building, and I pulled my lips in even tighter. I must have looked like a feral Chihuahua, but Christian had me paranoid, so I tried to look as crazy as possible.

After we passed the guy, Christian quietly said, "Don't look back." Then he released a boisterous laugh and patted me on the shoulder.

I glanced at a pile of rubble that was once a wall. "This place looks like a tornado ripped through it. Why would anyone want to live like this?"

"Some people thrive amid disaster."

"There are better sides of town to live in," I said, kicking aside a paper bag.

"They have freedom out here, and freedom means power. Some are illegally made immortals, but most are ancient. They rejected the higher authority and local Councils when they were established. Not everyone wanted to abide by rules. You'll find something like the Bricks in every city."

"What about small towns?"

"They congregate in the woods."

"Like you?"

"That's my home away from home."

"That's not a home; that's a hideout. What are you hiding from?"

"Your cooking."

I dodged his gaze. Christian had won that round.

In the blue haze of twilight, I mentally counted my weapons. Small blade in the heel of my boot, a push dagger disguised as a buckle, and another hooked to my belt on the side. I unbuttoned my coat for easy access. Only one of them was a stunner, so I needed to make sure that this time I didn't miss.

"Do you know anyone who sells good weapons?" I asked. "There weren't any that caught my eye at Pawn of the Dead."

"What are you looking for?"

"Something I can carry on my arm or beneath my shirt that's easily concealed. I also wouldn't mind a few impalement stakes."

He gave me a cross look.

"Aw, don't look so glum," I said, hooking my arm in his. "I'd only use it against you on special occasions."

"I can find you a weapon, but if you're looking for something specific or need sizing adjustments, you'll want to talk to Shepherd. Old Mother Hubbard has nothing on *his* cupboard."

I dropped my arm to my side when we passed a raucous bar.

"What are you looking at?" a man snarled. "You got a problem?"

Christian kept his head high and his eyes fixed on the sidewalk ahead. I didn't look back, but my ears perked up. Christian had better hearing, and based on his cool stride, he didn't seem concerned that the man would follow us.

He pointed toward a red building on the right. "That's the one. Do me a favor and try not to kill anyone. All we're doing is following a lead."

"Now where's the fun in that?"

When we reached the entrance, the doors were locked. We needed either a key or someone inside to buzz us in.

I folded my arms. "Now what?"

Christian selected a random button.

"Yeah?" a surly man answered.

"Pizza delivery."

"I didn't order no pizza."

"I'm freezing my arse off out here. Two pepperonis and one supreme, already paid for. What's the problem?"

I laughed in disbelief when the man buzzed us in.

Once inside, Christian ran his fingers through his disheveled hair. "Never underestimate the stupidity of men when it comes to food and sex."

When we reached the sixth floor, I looked down the hall in both directions, making note of where all the exits and stairwells were. It was an old building with peeling paint, wainscoting, tubular lights along the ceiling, and black doors inside small recesses in the wall. I concealed my light so as not to tip him or anyone else on the floor off that a Mage was lurking about. Christian gave me a light push to stand away from the peephole. He took off my hat and pulled it over his head, as if somehow that magically changed his appearance.

I pulled my stunner out of its sheath and gripped it firmly, the blade protruding between my middle and ring finger. I gave Christian an impatient look, wondering if he was going to stand there all day or get this show on the road. He pinched his chin, studying the door, and finally rapped his knuckles against it.

"Who's there?" a voice boomed.

Christian cleared his throat and took on an American accent. "Al's Wrecker service. We found your vehicle. We can't scrap it until you sign release papers. Unless you'd rather I leave it outside. Either way, I need your signature."

I nodded. Quick thinking and believable.

"Goddammit," the man grumbled.

"There's also a fee for cleanup," Christian added.

I kicked him in the leg. No need to push it. If this guy was cheap, he might keep the door locked. I stayed out of view as the latch clattered against the wood.

The moment the door cracked open, Christian wedged his foot inside, his arm leaning against the doorjamb. "Didn't think you'd see me again, did you?"

When the man tried to close the door, Christian flung it open.

"Oh, for feck's sake. Put the weapon down, you dolt."

I wedged past Christian and stepped to the left. The Mage glared at us, a small piece of impalement wood in his hand, no bigger than a pencil. I quickly noticed his appearance now that I had a good close-up look. Dark hair shaved on the sides and long on top. When I noticed he had shoes on, I guessed by his rumpled hair that he must have recently woken up and was planning to go out soon. No sign of any weapons on his person outside of the wood in his hand, so we'd definitely caught him off guard.

His apartment was bright, spacious, and unremarkable. It lacked curtains and furniture that one might acquire over a lifetime. The door on the right presumably led to a bedroom. Straight ahead, a turquoise sofa faced an old television set, and the wooden coffee table in front of it was littered with notebooks and soda cans. I noticed a cheap desk on the left-hand wall and something blinking on the computer monitor. The narrow kitchen to our immediate left was dark and empty except for a bowl of cereal and carton of milk on the bar.

The Mage didn't bother to wipe the milk stain off his goatee as he held up his weapon in self-defense, which made it all the more comical. "Get out of my space, fanghole."

Christian slammed the door shut with the heel of his boot

and inched forward, his gaze sharpening on the man, who quickly broke eye contact. "You want to tell me why you ran from us?"

"None of your business, *Vamp*."

Christian glowered. "What do you know about Jennifer Moore?"

The Mage winced. It was so subtle it could have been mistaken for a casual blink, but I'd caught enough men in a lie to spot the tells. He reached in his pocket and palmed what looked like a smart key for a car. When he pressed the clicker, two large speakers on his desk illuminated blue around the edges, and "Walk Like an Egyptian" started up full blast.

Christian and I exchanged a glance, silently agreeing that this search had just hit level weird.

The man sneered. In a quick motion, he drew back his arm and flicked his wrist, the impalement stake spiraling through the air toward Christian, who dodged it. The stick would never have gone through Christian's coat, so the Mage was stalling.

I flashed toward him with my stunner in hand just as the door crashed open behind me. I didn't have time to look. When I shoved the Mage to knock him off-balance, he spun to the side and sent me careening straight toward the wall. I quickly turned and swiped my blade in a crisscross motion, now aware of the drama ensuing by the door.

A Vampire had burst into the room and attacked Christian. Their fangs were out, and it looked like one of those late-night paranormal movies—minus all the hissing. Christian threw the other Vamp against the wall, leaving behind a large crack.

When the Mage ran past me, I caught the back of his shirt and slashed at his arm. He spun around and punched me in the nose, blood immediately spraying the floor and gushing down my face. A hot flash of pain stunned me for a second, and then I noticed an odd red mark on his upper chest where the buttons had popped off his shirt.

Did I do that?

I flashed around him and attempted to drive the stunner into his back, but he twisted and bellowed in pain when it sliced him across the side instead. The Mage bent my wrist at a painful angle, forcing me to drop the dagger. Before I could pick it up, he kicked it across the room.

His eyes darted left toward the window, giving away his intent. Before he made a move, I delivered a high kick and struck him in the chest. He pirouetted toward the wall and crashed into a floor lamp, which he grabbed and swung at me. The brass clipped my shoulder seconds before I flashed out of the way.

Where's my dagger!

I glimpsed it across the apartment, but I didn't dare go after it, or this guy would get away. Fighting wasn't his priority so much as jumping out the damn window right behind me. My coat was becoming a hindrance, restricting movement, so I quickly took it off and flicked it aside.

Meanwhile, the Bangles were singing about waitresses bringing more drinks, and it made me notice the wine bottle on the bar. I grabbed it just as the Vampire slammed Christian across the sink, pinning him with a choke hold. Christian frantically swung his arm around in search of a weapon, so I put a potato scrubber in his hand. He gave me a scathing glance before I spun around and flashed after my Mage, who was halfway out the window. I gripped the waistband of his pants and yanked him inside, smashing the bottle across his head. Shards of glass fell to the floor, and white wine splashed across his back.

He spun around and swung his arm, but I dodged his punch. My best chance to incapacitate him was to bite an artery and drain him, but I couldn't get close enough.

I grabbed his ankle and yanked it, but he held on to the end of the bar and shook me off. When he caught sight of my fangs, his eyes rounded. I was used to that reaction, and it made me smile a little wider and lick them for show.

Meanwhile, I glimpsed Christian impaling his attacker with a piece of wood. Panting, he stood up—a pizza cutter in one hand and a cheese grater in the other. "Pick your method of execution, you short-fanged, beady-eyed little numpty. Your onion breath is more offensive than your fighting ability."

The Mage flung open a narrow closet door and grabbed a long sword, which he started brandishing. I jumped back, assuming he was going to swing at my neck. Instead, he suddenly threw it like a spear. I flashed backward and fell, my eyes wide as the sword sliced the air two inches above my nose before clattering across the floor behind me.

When I sat up, the Mage briefly glanced at his speakers and then fled out the window.

Christian torpedoed across the room and yanked me up by the arm. "Get the feck out!"

"Wait. Where's my stunner?"

"We don't have time," he snapped, dragging me to the window.

"Why not?"

"The music is a countdown."

My jaw slackened. "To what?" I climbed onto the fire escape.

"Hurry!" he yelled, shoving me ahead of him.

I bounded down the first flight of stairs. Just as I jumped onto the landing, a bomb exploded, sending a fireball through the windows and raining glass and bricks. I shielded my head, the Mage already a few floors below us.

I recoiled when another set of explosions went off, bricks knocking against the fire escape and more flames licking the cold air just above us. When the Mage reached the bottom and took off down the alley, I swung my legs over the railing, held on for a second, and then let go. It was a one-story drop.

Christian's boots hit the ground next to me as he landed solidly. Debris covered the concrete, and a few people were looking out their windows as we fled the scene.

I flashed to keep up with the Mage, slippery patches of ice and street corners slowing me down. Christian couldn't shadow walk since it wasn't dark enough, so he tried his best to keep up. When we reached a dead end, I thought we had our guy until he scaled a wall and vanished. Not one to give up the chase, I stepped on a wooden crate and scrambled onto the garbage bin. Christian came up from behind and boosted me over the wall.

"He's heading toward the subway station!" I shouted, remembering the layout of the neighborhood.

The Mage flashed in spurts to conserve energy, so I ran at human speed since I didn't have as much power to waste. This guy probably didn't work out as often as I did, so it wouldn't be long before he ran out of steam. He periodically stopped to catch his breath and then flashed to put distance between us.

He scaled a chain-link fence and crossed a field, the train station just ahead. With renewed vigor, I scrambled up the fence and jumped off, picking up speed as I followed his tracks.

We descended a stairwell that led to the underground station. The pungent smell of illegal Breed drugs hit me first, followed by the sight of vagrants sleeping on the concrete as I weaved through the crowd. I leapt over the turnstiles and realized people lived down here—tents and desks were set up as if they were businesses.

The Mage ducked behind pillars, and I kept losing sight of him. I jogged alongside the platform as he vanished into the mouth of the tunnel.

Christian jogged a few paces ahead and looked both ways before jumping onto the tracks. "Well, are you coming?"

I shook my head, out of breath. "The train."

"It's an abandoned station. The train hasn't stopped here since you were a babe in nappies. But pay attention if the tunnel splits, lest we have to scrape you off the tracks."

"Perish the thought," I muttered, taking his hand and leaping off the platform. Even though he assured me the train didn't come this way anymore, entering that tunnel gave me the shivers.

He stole a quick glance behind us. "There's nowhere for him to go for at least a mile, and he won't be flashing on these tracks for long."

Darkness swallowed us whole, and a blanket of dread came over me. We were on this guy's turf, and that gave him an advantage. What if he was waiting around the corner with a sickle? It was far too grainy for me to see in total darkness.

"Can you see him?" I asked, slowing to a stop.

"Worry not, lass. You're in capable hands."

A draft blew past me, and when I reached out into the void,

Christian was gone. I just *knew* that fanghole would run ahead and leave me behind!

I flashed but quickly stumbled, unable to see. Suddenly, an idea sprang to mind. With a simple shift in concentration, I channeled my energy to my fingertips. Blue light leaked out like tiny cobwebs caught in a breeze. It provided enough light for me to see a raised platform on the right. The Mage probably took this route to flash, and if so, there was a chance he was long gone by now. I climbed on and created a steady stop-and-go pace. It worked well enough that I finally caught sight of Christian standing at a fork in the tracks where the tunnels split.

"Shhh," he said, cocking his head and walking to the right-hand tunnel. "I can't hear the bastard."

"He knows a Vampire is following him."

"Even if he stopped, I'd be able to hear him panting like a dog."

"Maybe he's holding his breath." I jumped down, and when my feet hit the tracks, I pointed to the right. "He went that way."

"You can't even see which way that is."

"No, but I can feel his energy."

Christian seized my hand and moved so fast that I had to flash to keep up. Vampires could slip through shadows like liquid, and at some point, we'd ended up on the platform to the right.

"Stop! You're making me dizzy."

When he let go, I lost my balance and tipped backward. Christian locked his arm around my waist, and I clutched his neck and pulled myself tight against him. He slowly moved me away from the edge, and my cheeks heated from the intimacy of that small act.

"He's that way," I said, pointing at a door.

Christian released me. In a split second, he ripped the door off the hinges and it landed on the tracks. Artificial light pierced the veil of darkness, and we ascended a short stairwell.

Out of breath and falling behind, I realized the Mage's energy was waning as the distance between us grew.

Christian reached another door and flung it open.

Once outside, my legs gave out like jelly trying to hold up a horse. I fell in the snow, my side aching and lungs burning. Tiny flakes of snow swirled overhead, and I blinked up at trees, which led me to believe we were in a park.

"See him?" I asked, out of breath.

"Footprints," he said. "Get up. He'll be heading where there isn't any snow."

"This wasn't in the brochure." When I stood up, I wiped my mouth, which was still wet from my nosebleed. The bones in my nose were probably shattered, and the last drop of light from the sun, which I could have used for healing, was now gone.

Once again, destiny screws me over.

Because of the lampposts, Christian wasn't able to shadow walk. I had to hand it to the Mage—he was smart. He could have run off into the darkness, but his tracks were right beneath the light, which would slow Christian down and keep him off his tail. I'd used up too much of my core light with not enough in reserve to continue flashing.

I straightened my nose and winced from the sharp pain. "Who bombs their own apartment?"

"Someone who's hiding something," he said, not out of breath in the least. Christian strode forward, his eyes alert. "If you're going to blow up your house to '80s music, at least pick a song like "Burning Down the House" to put on your playlist."

"Maybe that would have been too obvious."

"The shitebag who broke in was his partner, to be sure. And you can saunter on for giving me a scrubbing brush as a weapon."

I laughed and weaved around a park bench. "It was either that or a spoon."

Christian leapt onto the wall that served as the entrance to the park. He turned in a circle, his eyes narrowing as he cocked his head to the side.

I remained absolutely still so as not to make a sound, though my beating heart was probably a marching band in his ears.

Christian finally sat down on the highest part of the wall. "He's long gone."

I scaled the short part of the wall and up to where he was sitting. "What makes you say that?"

"Tracks disappear by the main road, and we wouldn't be able to differentiate his from the others. The clubs are in full swing, so better we stay away from the night crowd."

"Why? Don't I blend in now?"

He glared up at me. "You look like a bloodsicle. I'm sure every Vampire would line up for a lick."

I kicked the snow off the ledge and sat beside him, our feet dangling ten feet off the ground. "Viktor's going to kill me."

"Why's that?"

"My phone's in my coat pocket."

He looked down at me. "Where's your coat?"

"In the apartment. I liked that coat too."

He sighed. "You won't be alone in the flogging. My phone fell out of my pocket during the scuffle."

I swept back my tangled hair. When I noticed the bloodstains on my fingertips, I wiped my hands on my jeans. "Now what?"

Christian leapt off the wall and looked up at me. "We find a place to lie low for the night."

"My vote is for calling a cab."

He laughed darkly and turned in a circle, arms wide. "Do you really think cabs come out to the Bricks at night? If you want to stay alive, we need to find shelter."

I scooted off the ledge, and he caught me, lowering me to the ground. "Let's go back to the subway."

"We weren't alone in those tunnels."

Now *there* was a creepy thought.

Christian's brows knitted as he held a distant look in his eyes. "I only saw one motel… but we're interlopers. We'll attract attention. People around here are curious when they see a new face, and the welcoming committee isn't so receptive."

"Maybe I don't know the Bricks, but I know the streets." I smiled and took his hand in mine. "Come with me if you want to live."

Chapter 14

WE WALKED ALONGSIDE A DILAPIDATED fence behind a row of buildings, careful not to attract attention. What we needed was a way to climb up to one of those rooftops without having to enter the building. Christian hadn't exaggerated about how dangerous the Bricks were. We'd witnessed a murder not fifteen minutes after leaving the park.

Our pace slowed as we approached an unoccupied building that looked like a casualty of war. The back wall on the third floor was blown open, leaving a cavity that allowed us to see the desolation within. I pointed up at the hole.

Christian gestured toward the first-floor window, and I shook my head.

"And why not?" he asked. "The entire building is as barren as your womb."

I gave him a cursory glance. "We have a better chance of escaping or defending ourselves up there if someone decides to drop in. The third floor buys us time, whereas on the first floor we're just sitting ducks. Why do you think I spent so many nights on rooftops?" Before he could open his mouth with a retort, I jumped up to reach for the fire escape. "Can you give me a hand?"

Christian climbed on top of a trash bin and pulled down an old metal ladder. I cringed at the racket it made but decided there was no better security alarm. While I climbed up to the third floor, Christian pulled the ladder back into place and continued his ascent.

I crawled over the crumbling brick wall.

"Watch your step," he said. "There might be holes in the floor." Once he reached the top of the ladder, he jumped inside and walked ahead of me.

The roof was still intact, but most of the back wall was blown out. Twisted pieces of rebar stuck out from the broken chunks of the wall. It could have also been a Vampire fight that caused it. Or a meteor. Snow dusted the floor near the gap, so we moved toward the center and looked around.

"All clear," Christian said. He disappeared behind a pillar and moved around in the darkness. He finally strode toward me and wearily scratched his jaw. "One staircase is blocked with debris, and suffice it to say that no one will be taking the elevator."

I felt better knowing the ladder was the only way in or out. With my teeth chattering, I scoped out the room for the safest spot that would get me the hell out of the open. A large row of filing cabinets in the back looked accommodating, so I checked out the space behind them. The nook would shield us from the bitter wind, but it was too easy for someone to corner us.

"Christian, can you pull the cabinets away from the wall so there's a gap?"

Without argument, he began pulling the first sectional, which was about five feet tall. I closed some of the open drawers until they clicked shut while Christian dragged the second one to meet up with the first. Dirty papers littered the floor, but they were adequate protection against the cold concrete.

My foot slipped from beneath me when I sat, and I came down hard. Not that it mattered. My body was aching with exhaustion, and my depleted core light made me shiver with unwanted cold. Leaning against the wall, I drew up one leg and kept the other straight.

Dried clumps of blood were stuck to my chin and lip. I glanced up at Christian. "You wouldn't happen to have a handkerchief, would you?"

He removed his black coat and draped it over my legs. Then I watched him rip a large piece away from his shirt before kneeling next to me. "Let me have a look."

"I think there's a big clot in my nostril. Do you think it's okay to blow it out?"

"Are you sure it's not your brains jammed up in there?" He licked the material and gently wiped at my cheeks and upper lip. "A broken nose is a good look on you. It fills in your face."

I reclined my head and closed my eyes. "We didn't even get his name. I'm not sure if that pisses me off more or that we lost him twice. Why didn't you tell me there was a bomb? Maybe if I'd known that, I would have stolen his computer."

His hands deftly cleaned my chin. "I didn't know until he looked at the speakers before jumping out the window. I'd guessed the music was a way to tip off his Vampire friend that there was trouble, but he was damn determined to dive out that window instead of fighting a woman."

"There you go again, assuming a man can beat me because he has a penis between his legs."

A smile touched his lips. "It's not what *I* think that matters. That's how most men think, and most wouldn't run from a woman. Something lit a fire under his arse."

I winced when he touched a sore spot near my nose. "Yep. Dynamite. Do you think the Vampire's dead?"

"Unless someone pulled him out, a fire that intense would kill him, to be sure."

"I didn't think fire hurt Vampires."

He stopped cleaning my face, his eyes downcast. "Aye. We burn like everyone else. It takes more to kill us than a Mage since we regenerate, but a burning building is the last place I want to be. It's an incinerator. You're a crossbreed, so there's no way to know your limitations without testing them. Best you remember that."

"Have you ever been burned?"

Christian set the cloth in my lap and leaned back against the cabinets across from me, his knees bent.

"What happened?"

He reclined his head and looked up at the wall above me. "There was an apartment fire, and I was foolish enough to think I could play fireman. Singed the skin right off my arms."

I grimaced.

"It healed up… eventually."

"What was worth risking your life?"

He shook his head as if ashamed. "The sound of children screaming. Humans standing around doing nothing. I saw a wee lass, and it made me think about my sister. Do you see why mortal ties are dangerous? They make you do foolish things."

I pulled his coat up to my waist. "And did you save anyone?"

"An old woman. She couldn't walk, so I lifted her out of her bed and carried her to the hall. Humans were rushing down the stairs and trampling each other. I kept climbing up, looking at closed doors and listening. I heard a child's cry and saw the flames. The fire started on the lower level, eating its way up and spreading fast. Smoke poured through the closed door, so I kicked it open. Half the floor was gone."

His story gave me chills as it hit close to home. "Did the children die?"

"There was only one child. A little girl crying for her mum. There was no way to get to her room without setting myself on fire. I'd turned away to leave, when I heard her cry, 'Please come get me.' Fecking hell, I couldn't just walk away. So I kicked down the door and gave her my coat to protect her from the flames. I had to walk through fire to get us out of there, and after I handed her over to someone in the hall, I headed up to the next level to knock on doors and warn everyone that the fire was spreading. When I reached the roof, I climbed down the escape and spent the next two days in hell. Burns like that don't heal quickly—not without Vampire blood."

As he told the story, shock overwhelmed me, and tears streamed down my cheeks.

"Jaysus wept. If I'd known you were that hormonal, I wouldn't have told the story."

"How old was the girl?"

"I don't know. Five? Six?"

Christian didn't realize.

He couldn't possibly.

That wasn't just any little girl he was talking about; that child was me.

All this time, it was Christian. *He* was the one who'd broken down my door and collected me in his arms after shielding me with his coat. Now, looking back, all the pieces fell into place. His dark hair, the glimpse of a beard as I saw him turn the corner at the top of the stairs. I still remembered the stench of his burning flesh.

Before I knew it, Christian was beside me with his arm around my shoulders. "You shouldn't have flashed as much as you did. Now you're nothing but a drained battery with leaky faucets."

"You don't understand," I choked out. "It can't be true."

"What are you going on about?"

I looked up at him, barely able to comprehend the truth of it all. "That was me, Christian. When I was five, my building caught fire. My mother died, and I almost did too until a man rescued me from my bedroom. He threw his coat over me and carried me through fire."

Christian recoiled, his face aghast. "You're fibbing."

All those memories of my mother came flooding back. The funeral. My life changing in an instant. A father unable to console a little girl who cried herself to sleep every night.

"It can't be," he whispered. "She had hair like yours, but I don't remember her eyes."

"You didn't see them when I looked at you through the glass?"

He covered his mouth. "Jaysus. That *was* you."

"My mother. What happened to my mother? Why didn't you save her?"

He looked down as if searching his memories. "There was smoke and flames. The only door I saw was to the right. It was half-open, but there was a giant hole in front of it with fire climbing in."

I covered my face. *Oh my God.* My mother had died a horrific death trying to save me when I woke up crying for her. I'd somehow convinced myself that the smoke had overcome her, because it was the easiest way to think about her death.

Christian took me in his arms, his embrace so familiar that

it was as if we'd always known each other. "She didn't suffer," he assured me. "The fall would have been quick, to be sure. You were the only living soul in the apartment."

What I began to internalize in that moment wasn't my mother's death, which I'd learned to live with for most of my life. It was the realization that Christian had saved my life. If it hadn't been for him, I would have perished in that fire. I owed my life to him—my human life.

"Why me? Why did I live?" I drew back and wiped the blood from my face, which was wet again from my tears. "So I could become *this*?"

He rubbed the lines in his forehead.

When our eyes met, I searched for an answer. "What does this mean?"

"I don't know," he said, his voice somber. "The fates are at play, and we are their pawns."

I pulled my knees up to my chest and wrapped the coat around me.

"Is that why you have nightmares?" he asked. "Because of the fire?"

Christian could never understand that he was the reason why I *didn't* have nightmares about that fire. My night terrors had nothing to do with the events of my childhood.

"No," I said but didn't elaborate. Beneath his coat, I gripped my heart-shaped necklace and squeezed it in the palm of my hand.

"If you want to sleep, Raven, I'll watch over you."

A draft snuck through the gap by the wall, and Christian secured the coat over my right shoulder. "Are you mad it was me?"

I nestled against him, my feelings conflicted. "No. I'm just… confused."

Christian had always been the antithesis of what I considered an honorable man, and yet little by little, he kept proving me wrong. After this new revelation, my feelings shifted toward him, though I wasn't sure how. But I trusted him more than I had five minutes ago. Vampire or not, the man had pulled me from certain death without thought to his own life. Finding out Christian had endured severe burns made it clear that the only motivation that could have been behind it was his heart.

But why had fate brought us together again?

"Is that why you hate humans so much?" I asked. "Because you almost died saving one?"

"I've learned over the years to grow more detached in my feelings about mortals. I cursed my decision. I wondered if it was all for naught when that little girl would probably grow up in abject poverty and not amount to anything in life. And now... here you are."

"Sorry to disappoint."

Christian leaned around and met my eyes. "Just have a look at you. A crossbreed. Who could have imagined that one day you'd become an immortal like the world has never seen? Perhaps I don't feel so regretful about the pain I went through to pluck you from the flames." He reclined back. "Had I kept walking that evening, I wouldn't have anyone to torment me with her dark humor and horrendous cooking."

"You didn't even try my food."

"I think I've built up an appetite. Perhaps next time."

The wind rustled a few papers around us, and I watched them scatter across the dirty floor.

"Why don't I charm someone out of their car and get us home?"

I chuckled. "Where's your sense of adventure? I'm too tired to move. Let's just lie here until morning. You said yourself the streets are too dangerous and cabs don't come out here."

He clasped his hands together. "Now that we're getting to know each other, do you want to tell me about your Creator? About how you were made? I think you at least owe me that."

And I did.

As much as I'd wanted to bury that part of my life and forget it ever happened, I owed Christian the truth. He had given me a second chance in life, and maybe he needed to understand what exactly that meant.

"Promise to let me finish? No jokes?"

"I don't wish to quarrel."

I drew in a deep breath and began. "Well, I already told you about my Vampire maker and how we met. He wanted to make my death believable, all the way down to admitting me to the morgue. He drained me close to death after a blood exchange, but I don't think he finished the process. I don't really know how that works." Just speaking about it sent terror through me, as if recounting the memories would make them real again.

"It's magic," Christian said. "Somewhat. It's a careful exchange of blood. We give you just enough of our magic to keep you regenerative but not quite alive."

"I woke up in a morgue. My maker was supposed to come get me, but he never came. The man in the room didn't seem surprised when I rose from the dead."

Christian inched back enough to look at me. "Was he Breed?"

I scooted away from him, finding it difficult to snuggle up to anyone while telling this story. "A Mage. He took me away. I was too weak to do anything, and I thought he was helping me."

"What happened?"

"He gave me my first spark. I'm guessing that wouldn't have normally worked on someone who was turned by a Vamp, but here I am." After a moment's pause, I added the most important fact of all. "He was a juicer."

Christian cursed under his breath.

"I didn't know anything about the rest of the Breed world. I made the decision to become a Vampire on a whim, so I didn't realize what was happening to me."

"Creators are the worst of the lot. Did you get his name?"

I averted my gaze. "He kept me for seven long months, Christian. Do you think I didn't get his name?"

"Then we have to find him. Bring him to justice."

I shook my head.

"Raven, you can't protect him. If he did it once, he'll do it again."

"I can't. I'm afraid of him." I clenched my fists at the admission. I'd hunted down all types of nefarious men. But my own Creator, I couldn't bring myself to go after. "He brought me to a place where

I felt less than human—like a possession or an animal. I can't. You don't understand what it's like. He's got some kind of power over me."

"His light is inside you. I understand a little about that. It's not much different from how blood ties you to your Vampire maker. There will always be a connection you can't deny, but that doesn't mean he owns you."

I sat Indian style and leaned forward. "My brain tells me that. But there's a voice inside me that warns me not to open that door again. As much as I want him dead, I'm not ready to revisit that place in my life. If it doesn't kill me, it'll take what's left of my soul. It took me *years* of struggle to become the person you know. Maybe that's not saying much, but if you saw who I was then…"

My lip quivered, and I turned my head away. I'd successfully switched off my emotions these past few years—that was why I was impervious to fear—but now the floodgates were opening, and it made me furious. "I guess now you think I'm an emotional basket case."

"Tears don't make you weak," he said. "Fear does. Weep all you want over what happened to you; that's your right. But never give someone your fear. That's power. That's control."

I wiped my nose and grimaced from the pain. "You're always telling me to leave the past behind, and now you want me to dig it up? That's not what Viktor would want me to do."

I turned to look, and Christian's jaw set.

"I'll keep watch," he said, finally standing up. "With all this chattering, someone's liable to hear us."

I ignored the old me for just ten seconds and stood up, turning Christian around so we were facing each other. My hands rested on his straight shoulders, and our breath clouded the air between us. "Thank you for saving me," I whispered.

His warm fingertips touched my cheeks as he held my gaze. The old me would have looked away from his penetrating Vampire eyes, but Christian and I were caught in a thread of time where the past and present overlapped. I wasn't looking at a Vampire or even my partner. I was looking at the man who'd stolen me from the arms of death.

There was nothing more intimate.

He leaned in and kissed the corner of my mouth, and my breath caught.

"Déjà vu," I said, puzzled by the emotions ripening in me like a familiar fruit I'd tasted once before.

A forbidden fruit.

Christian's scruffy beard brushed against my chin, and he held that torturous position for longer than I could bear. There was a softness to his lips, the way they touched mine without kissing, and his smell was intoxicating. Maybe Vampires didn't have a unique scent to Chitahs, but there were subtle nuances. It was as if I could smell his blood. When my fangs slid down, he cradled my neck possessively, and I leaned into him.

Dark hunger burned in his eyes, but what I was feeling was so powerful that it went beyond lust. I'd come full circle, finally face-to-face with the man I'd kept on a pedestal my entire life. And yet Christian had turned out to be the very Breed I loathed—the part of me I shunned.

We didn't kiss, and yet that "almost" kiss was the most passionate I'd ever known.

"I'm a different man," he said, still holding my gaze. "Colder. But if you asked me to do it all again, knowing what I know now… I would."

Chapter 15

FTER RUNNING THE FULL GAMUT of emotions and expending all my Mage energy, I'd fallen asleep. I woke up bone-cold, lying amid rotted papers stained with my blood.

Yet…

"Your face was a mess," Christian said from the opposite side of the filing cabinets, his arms folded. "It was only a drop."

I touched my nose and ran my fingers down the straight bone. There was still blood clotted in my nostrils, but it wasn't swollen or broken that I could tell. "You force-fed me your blood?"

"That would imply against your will."

"I was unconscious."

"Oh, for feck's sake. I didn't play with your fanny in the night. A few drops of my blood on your tongue was all it took to heal your face. You barely stirred in your sleep. For what it's worth, the sun didn't come out this morning, so you might want to thank me."

I rubbed my stiff neck, deciding to let it slide. I felt much better than I did six hours ago, aside from the fact I probably looked like one of Wyatt's ghosties.

After staggering to my feet, I rubbed my eyes and stretched. Even though I'd fallen asleep on the concrete, I vividly remembered waking up with my head on Christian's lap. He must have also put his coat all the way on me since I didn't recall doing it myself. I tucked my hands inside the pockets and fished around until I found a piece of candy to remove the taste of blood in my mouth.

And not *my* blood.

I popped the mint in my mouth and crunched on it. When I shook out my hair, particles of dust and dirt floated to the ground. "What are we going to tell Shepherd about his Jeep?"

Christian strode over to the opening in the wall and turned away from it. "I don't give a shite what he says. Assuming it's still there, we're heading back to get my sunglasses before walking home."

Ugh. The idea of walking back to Keystone in the snow after all that had happened left me bitter. But I soldiered on and followed Christian down the ladder and through the alley, the wind at our backs and fresh snow having covered our tracks from the previous night. He didn't ask for his coat, and I didn't offer. But it felt good to be moving again, and it generated some much-needed body heat.

This time no one we passed gave me a second glance. I blended into the scenery with my scuffed shoes, dirty coat, rumpled hair, bloodstains, and sour look. Even with my nose healed, I could only imagine what my face must look like.

It was overcast with a light flurry, but the world seemed too bright to admire. We passed by a shirtless Vampire sitting on top of a broken intersection light, watching us with keen interest. His long black hair rippled in the wind, whereas the rest of him appeared as lifeless as a statue.

"Do they sleep outside?" I asked.

"Some of us don't require sleep." Christian rubbed a few flakes off his beard. "You'd be surprised what some of the buildings look like inside. A few rich bastards remodeled them into castles fit for a king. Some are in ruins but livable, others abandoned. It's impossible to tell from the outside who's making all the money. If Viktor hadn't taken you in, this is likely where you would have ended up."

"What about you?"

"I lived here a short while. But that was some years back."

"You lived here?"

That offered me a new perspective. I'd seen Christian gleefully torture and murder men as part of our job, but it made me wonder what kind of man he was before Keystone to wind up in a place like this.

My stomach growled as we continued our march.

"Sounds like a wild boar in there," he remarked. "We better get home while there's still time for breakfast."

I groaned. "This rotation thing isn't working out."

"Perhaps you can cater again," he quipped.

"I would if I had my phone."

After what must have been an hour, we reached the intersection where we'd abandoned Shepherd's Jeep. I didn't think anyone would steal it since it had an empty tank, and as we approached, the only thing different about it was a layer of snow on the hood and roof.

Christian slowed to a stop. "Are you seeing what I'm seeing?" He approached the vehicle and circled it, eyes brimming with disbelief. "They didn't even take the tires!"

Even more astonishing was that the door was unlocked and nothing was stolen from the vehicle. I climbed inside to warm up and take a breather before we continued our walk.

Christian sat in the driver's seat, and after he retrieved his sunglasses, he stared at the console. "If the battery's still alive, maybe we can walk to a gas station and get enough fuel to move this thing out of here."

"Sign me up for that plan."

When he turned the ignition, the Jeep started up. It didn't just turn on, it roared.

"Feck me." He thumped his finger against the panel in front of him. "It says a full tank. Hand to God, it was empty when we left."

"Maybe Shepherd needs to take it into the shop and get the needle checked. Sometimes they get stuck, or maybe it froze in the cold weather."

Christian rubbed the back of his neck. "If I were a man who believed in fairies, I'd think one was playing tricks on us."

That made me chuckle. "Maybe it was a leprechaun."

He waved his hand. "Don't start with the Irish jokes."

"Did you bring your lucky clover?"

Christian gave me a cursory glance before turning the Jeep around. When I switched on Shepherd's music, the chorus chanted: Let the bodies hit the floor.

"Now there's some uplifting music," Christian remarked, changing the station over to classical.

"Air on the G String," I said, remembering it from music class back in high school. "I didn't take you for a Bach man."

"It's easier on a Vampire's ears. Be thankful you don't have to suffer hearing every sound magnified."

I slowly took off my gloves, staring at Christian's profile. Sometimes when he was thinking, he would draw in his lower lip and lightly scrape his teeth against it. I noticed his scruffy hair covering the top of his ear and had a strange urge to tuck it back.

"Is it like that all the time?" I asked. "Hearing everything. Does it hurt?"

"When it comes to bright light, I've got these," he said, tapping his finger against the sunglasses. "But filtering sound takes practice. A Vampire learns to block out noise, and I'm quite good at it. I don't hear the engine running, but I can hear a cat howling in the alleyway. If I wanted to, I could silence every sound in the world but the breath in your lungs."

My face flushed, and I turned my attention out the window to two men fighting in the street. One Mage blasted the other man with energy, and in a split second, the tall man's eyes rolled from yellow to black.

"Chitah," I said, locking my door. Once they went primal, they targeted anyone who looked like a threat.

The Chitah took on a predatory stance, flashing his upper and lower fangs as he circled the Mage. They were worthy adversaries. A Chitah could kill a Mage with his bite, and a Mage could take down a Chitah with enough energy blasts.

If he could get close enough.

The Chitah rushed the Mage, and they rolled end over end

across the snow. As Christian drove past them, I turned in my seat to steal a final glance of the violent ending.

A lawless society terrified and intrigued me. The appeal of a place like the Bricks was undeniable, even to the most honorable man. I'd lived in fear of the Mageri for many years. As an illegally made and undocumented immortal, our laws supported my execution. And yet criminals were given a safe haven in a place like this.

During the ride back to the club to pick up Christian's car, we didn't speak. The silence wasn't awkward, and for the first time, it felt like we were two partners out on a ride.

By the time we made it back to Keystone, everyone had already eaten. I felt guilty that Viktor had to cook breakfast on my week, but I trudged upstairs and decided to worry about it later—after I took a hot shower.

With my hair still wet, I put on a workout hoodie, jeans, and thick socks. I used cotton swabs to clean out the dried blood from inside my nose, and once I finished that delightful task, I felt like myself again. My blue eye was a little puffy from rubbing it, but no one would ever know to look at me that I'd fought a Mage, dodged a sword attack, escaped an explosion, gone on a subway chase, traipsed around the Bricks, and slept on Christian's lap.

When I knocked on the door to Wyatt's office, no one answered. The lights were out, which was unusual.

"That's a first," I muttered, heading to the staircase. Why wasn't anyone monitoring the black market website?

When I reached the first floor, I steered toward the dining room to see if maybe they were eating. Voices overlapped from the adjacent gathering room, and a log crackled and snapped within the hearth on the wall opposite the entryway.

"Hold your ponies!" Wyatt said, clearly flustered. "I have to put in the right amount. Don't break my concentration."

As I entered the room, I glanced up at the massive window

on the left, admiring the way it sprayed colors onto the floor. The fireplace glowed, Niko sitting beside it with his back to the wall and one leg drawn up. I stepped behind Gem's chair and faced the group. The long wall to my right dividing the gathering room and dining room had small archways in the middle that allowed those sitting in the booths to peer into the room. The couch was against it, Blue sitting next to Wyatt, who had a MoonPie in his mouth, laptop on his legs, and was wearing a grey T-shirt that said: NO BONES ABOUT IT and depicted a skull and crossbones.

I leaned against the back of Gem's chair, Viktor sitting in the chair that faced the sofa. "What's going on?"

Gem and Viktor were in the middle of a conversation, only I didn't understand a word of it. Gem had an arcane knowledge of ancient languages, but that didn't exclude everything in between, including Russian. When he swung his gaze up and said something, I shook my head.

"In *English*," Gem said.

He cleared his throat. "The baby is on the auction block."

"How do you know it's the same one we're looking for?"

"The child is a Sensor and of the same age. Babies don't go up on the market every day."

Gem peered up at me with wide, expressive eyes. "There's a bidding war going on."

My gaze darted around the room. Christian was on the far end with a glass of alcohol in his hand, Claude nowhere to be seen.

"Where's Shepherd?"

Viktor stroked his beard. "Resting."

"He can rest on my fist," Christian muttered from a distance.

Viktor wagged his finger at him. "Remember what we talked about."

"He *knows* something," Christian bit out. "I'd stake my life on it."

I stayed quiet, uncertain how much Christian had revealed about our night in the Bricks. Wyatt folded his arms, his eyes centered on the screen.

I sauntered over to the liquor cabinet in front of the stained glass windows where Christian was isolating himself. "What did you tell them about last night?" I whispered.

"Viktor knows," he said, implying they'd had a private conversation.

I ran my hands through my damp hair and thought about Christian's remark. Shepherd's meltdown happened after Wyatt showed him the picture. If he knew something about our guy, then why wasn't he helping?

"You should eat something," Christian suggested.

"I'm fine."

His dark eyes lingered on me for a moment.

"Blast!" Wyatt kicked the table in front of him.

"Another five," Viktor said calmly. "Small increments. The bidder will try to raise it high in the end, so let's not push it too early."

Blue stroked one of her grey feather earrings, eyes glued to the screen.

I nodded at Christian's empty glass. "Isn't it a little early for alcohol?"

"It wasn't too early for Shepherd."

"Did something happen between you two?"

"I haven't seen him yet, so the jury's out. But mark my words, that man is keeping something from us." Christian leaned against the table, hair slicked back from a recent shower. The sleeves of his charcoal shirt were pushed up, and it fit his body so snugly that I could see the outline of his abs and chest.

"Something catch your eye?" he said, amusement in his voice.

Before I could retort, Shepherd moved into the room.

Covered in sweat.

He hiked up his grey sweatpants, which left nothing to the imagination, and wiped his face off with a wadded-up T-shirt. He lingered by the doorway and watched with trepidation. "What's going on?"

Christian rocketed forward and ate up the distance between them. "You're going to tell us the name of your friend," he barked out, pointing his finger. "That's what's going on."

Both Viktor and Niko rose to their feet, but Christian veered left and shoved Gem's chair a foot before lunging at Shepherd.

When they began throwing punches, I jogged across the room for a closer look.

Shepherd circled around Viktor's chair. "Lay off," he snarled.

Christian ignored the obstacles in his way. "Do you want to know where Raven and I spent last night? After going to pick up your car, we chased down the Mage in the photograph."

Shepherd blanched and stepped back, Niko wedging himself between them.

Christian restrained himself when Viktor grabbed his shoulders. "That's right. And we almost got blown to smithereens. I'm sure you wouldn't have shed a tear for a Vampire like me, but you would have had to use a spade to scrape Raven off the floor. Whatever secret you're keeping almost cost us our lives."

Energy crackled in the room, raising the tiny hairs on my arms.

Gem appeared as curious as I was to see what might happen next. Blue and Wyatt were too engaged with the ongoing auction to steer their attention away. I tugged on the drawstrings of my hoodie, noticing the guilt on Shepherd's face. Guilt was a look I was quite familiar with from my former line of work, and he wore it like a mask.

"Start talking," Christian ordered. "Or I'll charm it out of you."

"Don't you fucking threaten me!" Shepherd spat.

Niko put his arm in front of Shepherd, holding him back.

I edged closer for a better look. "If we lose the auction, we lose the baby. Maybe that doesn't matter to you, but this guy will keep doing it again and again. We need something to go on. I have his face, but we need his name. Do you want to support his murderous rampage on women?"

Shepherd turned away and planted his hands against the fireplace.

As the tension dissipated, Viktor exchanged private words with Christian, who reluctantly backed down and scooted Gem's chair back in place.

"Sorry about that, lass."

"No sweat. That was better than a soap opera."

Viktor smoothed out his silvery hair, trying to regain his composure. "If everyone has calmed down, let's focus on business. You and Raven will have new phones this evening. I just need Wyatt to program them, and that means you'll need to sit with Blue and help me with the bidding."

Then the strangest thing happened. Niko rested his hands on Shepherd's shoulders as if consoling him. Christian took notice but remained apathetic. Gem, however, looked like a woman who knew a secret.

"Her name was Maggie." Shepherd's choked words made everyone look up. He moved away from the hearth and wiped his face with the T-shirt he picked up off the floor. When he sat down in Viktor's chair, I rested my arms on top of a chair facing Gem.

Shepherd hunched over, hands in his lap. "Years ago, I used to work for the higher authority in the evidence room. On short notice, they transferred me to a security job at a hospital—not the most ideal job for a Sensor. I kept an eye out for immortals in the morgue and emergency room. It wasn't so bad. You pick up a lot of useful shit by watching what goes on there, like how to stitch wounds and perform basic medical care. I finally got to practice some of that knowledge on you guys."

Shepherd held everyone's rapt attention.

"Maggie worked at the hospital. She was a Relic who specialized in human medicine, so she didn't work directly with Breed. She loved her damn job, even though most people looked down on her for helping humans. I wasn't allowed to fraternize with anyone at work, and neither was she. So we had to keep our relationship a secret. She also had a strict family who was all about keeping the bloodline pure, if you know what I mean. They would have disowned her."

We all nodded. A lot of folks didn't like interbreeding. If children could be conceived, they were often born defective—devoid of all the inherent knowledge or abilities that are unique to one Breed or the other. Not every mixed couple could even have kids, so a person risked losing their family, status, and even their job.

Shepherd took a deep breath and sank in his chair. "I didn't like keeping it a secret, but I also didn't want to do anything to hurt her. Maggie was the best woman I ever had. Smart, funny, beautiful—I can still remember her laugh."

My gaze drifted up to the large stained glass image behind Gem. The colorful display depicted wolves and people living in harmony, surrounded by flowers and greenery. It seemed a stark contrast to the reality of our world.

"What happened?" Blue asked when he fell silent.

His hands were shaking when he reached up to rub his eyes. "Working at that hospital taught me how to shut off the emotional pathway. I became unaffected by pain and suffering so it wouldn't ruin me. That job gets to a lot of people no matter what your Breed is, but it's especially tough for Sensors. You see a lot of suffering in those places. Anyhow, we couldn't hang out at work, so sometimes we'd meet up at my place or go on a date." He wiped his hand across his mouth as if struggling with his emotions.

"You don't have to talk about this," Viktor said. "They know enough."

"No," Shepherd said tersely, swinging his brown eyes up. "They don't know shit. If I'm telling the story, I'm telling the whole fucking thing." He cracked his knuckles before continuing. "She was supposed to meet me at the coffee shop one night. I sat around and waited, then I got worried. She didn't call, so I knew it wasn't work related. I thought maybe she was sick or hurt. Relics can catch the flu and all that, so I headed to her house to check on her. I noticed an unfamiliar car parked nearby. Didn't think much of it then. When I neared the door, something was off. There was a strange emotional print on the knob. I peered in through the window and saw a light coming from the hall, so I went inside. The door wasn't locked. That's when I heard a muffled scream." Shepherd launched to his feet and paced behind his chair.

I had a feeling I knew where this story was heading: a one-way ticket to Traumaville.

He lifted the fireplace poker out of the tool rack and jabbed the log in the hearth until the flames were roaring even higher. "They were killing her. I tried to get in the room, but a man guarding the door knocked me down and took out a knife. I didn't feel anything when he began stabbing me. I kept trying to get to Maggie. The next thing I knew, I was lying on the floor in the hallway. My attacker was a Mage, and he'd blasted me with enough energy to put down a horse. I could barely move, but I could still see her on the bed. I held up my arms to block the knife attack, but—" Shepherd's voice cracked. "I watched the second man murder my woman."

When I heard a quiet gasp, I realized he was crying.

"That green-eyed bastard you tracked down is the one who killed her. That maniac destroyed the only thing in this world that mattered to me, and he savored it. That fucking animal put on a show."

Shepherd's face reddened, the lines deepening in his forehead as he mentally relived what must have been the most horrific experience of his life.

Gem's eyes glittered with tears, and she shielded her face with one hand.

"That's not the worst of it," he continued.

Viktor strode to the window and put his hands in his pockets.

The iron poker made a loud clang when Shepherd tossed it to the floor. "She was nine months pregnant."

A thunderstruck silence followed.

Stone-faced, Shepherd stood as tears slipped from his eyes like raindrops down a window. "I was bleeding out, unable to move. After he stabbed her through the heart, he... cut her open. Then I realized he wasn't just killing her; he was killing our baby." Shepherd sat down on the hearth, knees bent as he stroked the Celtic tattoo on the back of his neck. "They left me for dead. I woke up in a hospital, but not the same one I worked at. It took the higher authority three days before they realized I was missing. They transferred me to a clinic where two Relics healed me."

I looked down at his scarred fingers, hands, and arms. The ones on the back of his left hand were worse than the right, but most of them were defensive wounds—from blocking the dagger that had left scars on his chest and back. Jesus. I figured he picked them up over the years doing criminal work; I couldn't have imagined that they were all from one attack.

"Did the baby survive?" Gem asked through sniffles.

"Nothing could have survived that." He wiped his face wearily. "They buried Maggie before the Relics released me from their care. The higher authority discharged me, said I was neurotic and incapable of performing my duties. They didn't like my involvement in the case, and when they didn't have enough information to go on, they dropped it... just like that," he said, snapping his fingers. "She wasn't important enough in their eyes to waste time on. I spent years on the streets looking for that man. Viktor saved my life. If he hadn't come along, I'd probably be dead or living in the Bricks." His eyes shifted to Viktor, who remained facing the window. "I want him dead. He deserves nothing less than what he inflicted on my woman and child. I gotta be fucking honest about it—if we can't catch him, I don't know if I can work here anymore. He's become my white whale, and there's nothing else right now that matters. I don't have his name or anything else that will help you find him. What I do have is fifty-three scars. The Relics said it was a miracle I survived, but it feels more like a curse. I'm here for a reason... and now I know what that reason is."

Viktor turned to face him. "We cannot kill for revenge. Until we find out this man's name and whether or not he's a declared outlaw, we cannot murder him in cold blood."

Shepherd rose to his feet. "Speak for yourself."

Chapter 16

VIKTOR WASN'T SURE HOW LONG the auction would last. To prepare, he sent three of us into the city. That way if the auction closed early and there was a drop-off location, we would be first on the scene. The lucky candidates were Christian, Claude, and yours truly. Christian and I received new phones, and Viktor instructed us to stay in close contact.

Claude followed us to Ruby's Diner so we could establish a base camp. I'd spent so many years going there that I knew the staff's schedules better than they did. Betty was ending her shift soon, but she made a point to check on us even though we had another waitress. The lunch crowd had already dispersed, and we lounged in my favorite booth while Claude amused the staff with his bottomless pit of a stomach.

I finished the last bite of grilled cheese and licked my fingers. "Shepherd's a liability."

"She's right," Christian said. "I'd be willing to wager that Shepherd's sharpening all the knives in his drawers. Better we find this Mage before he does."

"What does it matter who kills him?" Claude asked with a mouthful of fries.

"The higher authority assigned us the case, you dolt," Christian reminded him. "They're invested, and they're not going to pay unless we provide enough evidence and facts to support a murder. Unless they say they want him dead or alive, Viktor has to follow protocol."

I pushed my plate forward. "What protocol?"

"The one that forbids us from dismembering suspects. If our lives are at stake or all hell breaks loose during a raid, they're more likely to turn a blind eye. But if Shepherd picks him up, drives him out to a cornfield, and feeds him to the crows, that might not work in our favor. Especially if the Mage turns out to be someone important or is proven innocent."

I played with the straw in my glass. "Shepherd's going to murder him. I know all about that kind of hate."

Claude finally sat back and heaved a sigh.

I chuckled softly. "You're going to ruin your figure with that appetite."

He patted his stomach. "Someone should have told me about this place before now. I haven't had a milkshake that delicious in decades."

I studied him for a moment. "Exactly how old are you?"

He winked. "Centuries."

Claude was a good five or six inches taller than Christian, towering over most men like a giant. I'd seen Chitahs over seven feet before. They usually stood out when mingling with people of normal height, which was pretty much anyone outside of their Breed. One brunette had walked to the bathroom twice just to get his attention, and Claude gave it to her. He was suave and flirty without being obvious or egotistical. The magic was in his smile and the way he'd lean back and use his body language to convey interest.

Claude Valentine was so handsome that he didn't need to flirt. He could put french fries up his nose and still attract women with his sexy hair and kissable lips. He possessed the perfect male form with a V-shaped torso and strong collarbones. Not muscular like Shepherd, but I'd seen him climb the rope in our training room with Gem on his back.

Personality-wise, Claude was too sweet for my taste. I'm not sure what that said about me, but I didn't feel chemistry when I looked at him—not the way other women did.

I slid my leather jacket over my lap and searched the pocket.

"Put your money away. I'll take care of this," Christian offered, setting his wallet on the table.

I pulled my hood over my head and tugged on the drawstrings. "Do you think they'll really bring the baby?"

Christian studied the label on the ketchup bottle. "Assuming we win the auction, there's a chance."

"Depends on how much money he wants," Claude pointed out. "Sometimes they set up a few fake transactions to collect money and then sell the baby later. That way they get more."

"That's risky," I said. "Someone could show up and kill him."

Christian set the bottle down. "Something tells me the Vampire back at his apartment was his lackey and delivered the goods. With him out of the picture, I'd be surprised if the Mage has a second right-hand man he would trust with such a task."

I put on my fingerless gloves before sliding my arms through my jacket and zipping it up. "If he's got the baby, where do you think it is?"

Christian scratched his cheek. "If he's a professional, then he's smart enough to keep incriminating evidence as far away as he can manage. He didn't set up the bomb as a weapon; he wanted to destroy anything in that apartment that linked him to a crime."

"Can I get you another milkshake before I end my shift?" Betty asked, offering Claude a warm smile. She'd liked him right from the start and even gave me a playful wink. I wondered what she thought of my parading all these men around her since joining Keystone.

"Three is my limit," Claude replied.

"Next time try the banana shake."

He tilted his head to the side and looked at her name tag. "Only if you make it, Betty."

She laughed. "You betcha. Are you ready for the bill?"

I nodded, and she collected our plates.

"Nice lady," Claude said, watching her return to the kitchen. "Humans are so eager to make people happy. You don't see many older females waitressing where we live."

"I don't see many older women period," I said.

Claude grinned. "You don't come in the salon enough. Older Chitahs have no interest in hanging out in bars or dance clubs."

Christian tugged on his beard. "Speaking of bars, I'd like to go back to Nine and find out who Raven's little birdy is."

"Birdy?" Claude's eyebrows drew together.

"Aye. The one who told her where our Mage lives. If he knows that much, he might know more."

"He was in your salon the night the woman was murdered," I added. "Remember? Bleached hair, had the foil things in it."

"Maybe. Clients come and go." Claude put on his stylish leather jacket and stood up. "I'll wait outside so I can warm up the car."

When I got up to leave, Christian remained seated. I tapped my black fingernail on the table. "Aren't you coming?"

"Give me a minute."

As I slowly headed to the back door, I glimpsed Christian placing more hundreds on the table than I could count. Curious, I walked at a snail's pace to the van, my eyes fixed on the window as Betty came into view and sat down in front of him. He leaned in a little and did all the talking.

"What's that about?" Claude said from his rolled-down window.

"I don't know." I leaned against his red Porsche and hugged my body from the cold. "I wish I'd taken something from the Mage's apartment for you to sniff. Can you really make a positive ID from a pillow or a sock?"

Claude's lower canines grew in length and made him look like a tiger. His voice lowered an octave, rumbling in the back of his throat. "I *own* his scent. Do you know what that means to a Chitah? It's burned in my memory forever. We imprint the ones we love and our enemies. That means we never forget."

"But he's not really *your* enemy."

"Any male who slays a female is my enemy."

We watched Christian emerge from the diner, his breath clouding the frosty air. Claude revved the engine of his red sports car and sped off.

"Change your mind on that pie?" I asked.

Christian approached the van and opened the door on the passenger side. Once I climbed in, I blocked the door to keep him from shutting it. "I changed my mind."

He tilted his head to the side. "About?"

"Seeing my father. After witnessing Shepherd's meltdown, I don't want that to be me someday because I reopened a door to my past. It might make things worse, and I'm not sure if I could live with that."

"Does it feel like the right thing to do?"

I swung my gaze back to the diner. I wasn't sure how to answer that. I'd been so convinced that seeing my father would help me move on, but after watching one of the toughest guys in the house threaten to defy Viktor and lose everything he'd worked hard for, I began to wonder. What if seeing my father devastated me in ways I'd never recover from?

"I'm not sure what the right thing even means, Christian."

"Then hold that favor in your pocket. Just don't use it to make me take over your cooking rotation. I'm not a chef."

I laughed. "I thought cooking potatoes was in the *How to Be an Irishman* manual."

He stared vacantly at the diner and chewed on his bottom lip. "Betty won't be giving me the evil eye anymore."

My smile withered. "What do you mean?"

"I did what I should have done a long time ago. I scrubbed her past memories of me as best I could—of every time I could remember that we'd talked. Of every Irishman she'd ever spoken to so that my accent won't trigger something in her mind."

"Even today?"

"Only our private conversation we had just now, but not the dinner. That would be confusing if you mentioned me around her." He chuckled and shook his head.

"That's funny to you?"

Christian gripped the doorframe. "She thinks we're an item."

I blinked in surprise. "What did she say?"

"That she liked your Asian friend better. I still left her the thousand-dollar tip."

He shut the door and slowly strolled around the van.

"You're not such a bad guy after all. For a Vampire," I said quietly.

Christian flicked a glance at me, but I didn't look away. I'd meant for him to hear the compliment.

And he deserved to hear it.

Claude arrived at Nine Circles of Hell ahead of us and claimed a table in a private area of the main room. The vibe was different with rap and sexy dance songs playing. Women were misbehaving on the dance floor with their high heels, skintight dresses, and enough sexuality to set the club on fire. In the Breed world, people had no real concept of time. Many were wealthy and didn't have jobs, and Vampires never slept.

I carefully studied every face I passed. Chitahs, Vampires, men with hair down to their waist, others with shaved heads. But none had the signature blond hair of my friend Chaos. Christian nodded for me to look in all the rooms, so I weaved through the crowd, staring at one unfamiliar face after another. One man tried to put his arm around me, and when I shoved him away, a Chitah took that as his cue to jump in and instigate a fight.

That was in the wrath room.

Men were less aggressive in the lust room, but one of them actually looked back and forth at my mismatched eyes and flinched before turning away.

Idiot.

"Well?" Claude asked, stretching his right arm across the empty space beside him in the booth.

I looked across the table at Christian, who mirrored Claude's body language down to the amount of space he left for me to sit. "I didn't see him."

"Have a seat," Christian offered, patting the back of the booth.

"I prefer to stand."

Claude gestured to the open space next to him. "Come and sit, female. We might be waiting a long time."

I put my hands in my coat pockets. "I know a bet when I see one, so if that's what's happening here, I want whatever you two wagered."

When Christian rested his elbows on the table with a look of annoyance, I sat next to Claude.

"So what did I win?"

Claude locked his hands behind his neck, showing off his muscles. "The next beer is on us."

"I'll take a rain check. We need to stay sober until we hear from Viktor. Any news?"

Claude checked his phone messages. "Nothing yet."

I looked at the long bar to my right, colored lights matching the theme splashed against the bottles and glasses along the back wall. Hooper was polishing a glass and talking to a man who wore a tribal tattoo on his right arm. When the man got up to leave, one of the waitresses winked at him as she briskly walked behind the bar to mix a drink. She swirled the glass in her hand, a red glow appearing from her fingertips and lighting up the glass.

"Why don't they just spike the bottles of alcohol instead of each individual order?" I asked.

Christian followed the direction of my gaze. "Just imagine a row of bottles spiked by Sensors. You don't think that would be tempting to thieves? One can only guess how much they'd go for on the black market. A bottle of wrath could make an otherwise sane man do terrible things. Imagine what it might do to a man who's already insane. Imagine serving them to members of the higher authority at a banquet."

"Okay, I see your point." My gaze traveled across the room. "I see something interesting."

"A plate of onion rings?"

I kicked him under the table. "No. But remember that woman our Mage was talking to before he ran off? Well, there she is."

Claude craned his neck. "Are you sure it's the same woman?"

"Pretty sure, unless blond hair with black bangs is the latest trend in your salon this season."

"You slay me."

When I rose from my seat, Christian snatched my arm. "You're certain it's her?"

I nodded.

He regarded Claude for a moment and discreetly pointed at his own eyes. Claude gave a curt nod and stood up, ambling over to the bar and turning to face the crowd.

Christian quickened his pace when the woman steered toward the dance floor. I fell back a few steps and let him take the reins.

"I've had enough of this nonsense," he said to her, irritation in his voice.

The woman looked warily at him, as did I. That was certainly a way to get a woman's attention, but not the route I would have chosen.

"I was sitting across the way and noticed you standing alone." He looked at her with smoldering eyes and turned on the charm, his voice sticky-sweet. "I've not seen eyes that lovely in a hundred years."

I snickered. "Do you say that affirmation to yourself in the mirror every morning?"

Christian heard me but was putting on a performance. He seemed quite adept at playing a role to get what he wanted in almost any given situation. He'd left his jacket in the car, and he had on one of those threadbare T-shirts with a wide V-neck that showed off his chest. He placed his hand on a pillar and leaned against it, forcing her to take notice of him.

"I'm not interested in a drink," she said.

"A lovely lass such as yourself deserves more than a drink. What you need is a luxury car. That's how *I* treat a lady." As he spoke, it dawned on me that his eyes never looked away. He was drawing her under his spell but making the conversation appear innocuous to the crowd around us should anyone be listening. "Would you like to know what the inside of a Porsche feels like?"

She nodded, and that's when I closed in on them.

Christian petted her cheek and slowly pulled her into his arms. "I'll keep you warm. How do you feel?"

"I'm hungry," she said.

As they moved toward the door, she remained under his influence. He looked away briefly to signal me to open the door for them, and once outside, he instructed her to follow him. Only then did he look away.

"We need to make this quick," he said to me.

I peered over my shoulder at the woman following. Her puffy beige coat was unzipped, snowflakes sticking to her blouse. She looked like a pale-faced zombie with all that dark mascara and eyeliner.

When we reached the van, he opened up the back. "It's warmer in here. Would you like to get warm?"

She took his hand and climbed into the back.

Once inside, Christian shut the back door and made her sit down on one of the benches along the side. He squatted in front of her to maintain eye contact, and I sat across from them.

"What's your name?" he asked.

"Amber Warren."

"Were you here a couple of nights ago?"

"The night of the sixteenth," I added.

She nodded, her face expressionless.

"Do you remember talking to a Mage?" Christian asked. "Dark hair, a tattoo on the back of his neck, green eyes…"

She nodded adamantly. "Cristo."

I jerked my neck back. "Crisco?"

Christian peered over at me. "*Cristo*. We're not looking for cooking oil, unless you plan on baking brownies."

"What kind of name is that?"

"Do I look like a fecking census taker?"

"He didn't have an accent, and his name sounds foreign. That's the only point I was making."

"His Creator could have been Spanish. Now will you shut your gob and let me carry on?"

I gave him an impish grin. "Dazzle me."

Christian faced Amber, his feathers ruffled. "Does Cristo have a last name?"

She shrugged.

"How do you know him?"

"He pays me to watch them," she said in a monotone voice.

"Watch who?"

"The children."

I jumped out of my seat and sat beside her. "Where's the baby?"

She continued gazing into Christian's obsidian eyes.

He narrowed them. "Has Cristo asked you to watch any babies in the past week?"

She nodded.

"Can you show me?"

Amber shook her head. "I don't have him anymore. Cristo took him away this morning."

"Where?"

"I don't know. The baby cried a lot. I've never taken care of a baby that little before. He always brings me kids."

"Why would he trust her?" I asked Christian.

"It's easier that way. Men like him prey on weak women. They distance themselves from the merchandise, and that baby would be a lottery ticket in the Bricks. And like I said before, it also keeps his hands clean if something goes wrong."

I nudged the woman. "Where did he take the baby?"

Christian clucked his tongue. "It doesn't usually work like that. Most of the time, they only listen to the one who's charming them." He patted Amber's hand. "Can you tell me where they went or his phone number? Anything?"

She robotically shook her head. "He calls me. He goes to the club; that's where we met. I left the baby alone the other night to find him and tell him I didn't want to do this job. He got mad. Told me I needed to go back home and stay there until he called."

Christian tugged on his earlobe, his gaze drifting off. "At least we have his name. Uncommon names make them easier to track."

"Assuming it's his real name." I stood up and sat on the opposite bench.

"Did he pick up the baby in a car?" Christian asked. "Can you describe it?"

"White," she quickly said. "I almost didn't open the door when

I saw it through the curtains. I don't know anyone with a white car."

"Was he alone?"

She shrugged.

"That's good, Amber. I enjoyed our friendly conversation. Taking care of those children must have been frightening. Men like Cristo are dangerous, and they'll creep into your house in the middle of the night and slit your throat."

I kicked him in the ass. "Why are you scaring her?"

"You want to turn over a new leaf," he continued, ignoring me. "What are you good at?"

"Sex."

I belted out a laugh. "You two have fun. I'm just going to wait outside."

"Stay right where you are. I want you to see this."

"Why?"

He shifted around to look at me, the intensity in his gaze making the hairs on my neck stand on end. "Because you need to see with your own eyes what it's like when I scrub memories."

I swallowed hard. The idea that a Vampire could tiptoe around in someone's head and erase things was disconcerting. I couldn't imagine walking around with a piece of myself missing. But I knew why he wanted me to watch. This was what I was asking him to do to my father.

Christian locked eyes with Amber. "Remember when I first approached you in the bar? Do you recall the moment I spoke and when you looked up and saw my face?"

She nodded.

"That never happened," he said, his voice smooth and suggestive. "We never spoke, and you've never seen the woman sitting behind me. You never walked outside in the snow to a black van and got inside. You never revealed any information about the baby or Cristo. When you walked away from the bar earlier, you sat down and watched people dancing. I'm going to take you to that table where you've been sitting for the past fifteen minutes. You'll be warm, a little thirsty, and thinking about changing your life and getting a job. You've never seen my face before, and if you see it again, you won't even notice me."

I watched Christian get out of the van and lead her toward the front of the building. Then he stopped and whispered something in her ear, and she headed around the corner alone.

I shuddered.

A flurry of laughter erupted when four people abruptly rounded the corner and walked toward the parking lot. Christian casually propped his back against the wall, his head down. I rocked on my heels and pretended to look around as if waiting for someone. When the small group flashed toward two cars several rows down, I collected my thoughts about what we'd just discovered.

Wyatt couldn't help us research this newfound information since he was busy trying to buy a baby. We also couldn't go traipsing across the city when Viktor might need us at a moment's notice.

I approached Christian. "Now what?"

He reached underneath my jacket and pulled out my hood. "We have a name. If Viktor wins the bid, we have a witness that links him to previous crimes. If Viktor loses the bid, we'll have a lot of work to do."

"So we have a name and we have to sit on it."

"Smart as a whip." He secured the hood over my head and tucked my hair inside. "You should wear a warmer coat."

"It blew up in the fire, remember? Anyhow, a few flurries don't bother me so much."

"Liar."

I chuckled and matched his stride as we headed back to the door. "When I lived on the streets, I got used to the cold. Now I'm spoiled because of a warm bed and a hot meal every day."

"I'll have to rectify that. Remind me to put your bed on the roof when we get home."

"And what would you do if I froze?"

"Bury you in Greenland. Worry not, lass. I promise to come get you before archaeologists in the future discover your body in a cryogenic state."

"You'll still owe me a beer."

Chapter 17

AMBER SAT LISTLESSLY AT A table near the front hall, watching people dancing and having a good time. She'd been in a haze since Christian wiped her memory, and thirty minutes later, she finally snapped out of her stupor and checked her phone.

"How's the um… bargain hunting going?" I asked Claude, trying to be discreet about the black market trading.

He scooted down in his seat, still reading a text message from Gem. "It's intense. Sometimes these things can go on for days."

I gave Christian a lethal glare. "I'm not sitting in here for *days*."

Impervious to my harsh tone, he crunched on his candy. "Would you rather we go bowling? I'm afraid there aren't many options. Here we have food, drink, comfortable seats, and lovely breasts," he said, admiring the buxom waitress who approached our table, her shirt thin and tight.

Leaning against the booth, she flashed a smile that was signed, sealed, and delivered to Claude. "I do love me a tall drink of water. Can I get you something to nibble on?"

I smiled, unable to help myself. "He's *starving*. Do you have any steak and fries?"

Claude lowered his head ashamedly. After devouring half the menu at Ruby's, his tank was full and the look of regret in his eyes never more evident.

Apparently not wanting to insult the waitress, he slid a predatory gaze up to her and purred, "I'm in need of nothing at the moment, female. I'm just fine."

"Yes. Yes, you are," she agreed. "I'll bring a pitcher of water and a few glasses."

She sauntered off, and Claude admired her, but not in a lecherous way. Claude looked at women differently than most men, as if he admired their power and spirit more than their assets.

If what Claude said about auctions was right, we might wind up sitting around for a long time. Club owners didn't care how long patrons stayed. Hours, days… just so long as they kept ordering off the menu. Vampires don't require sleep, and not everyone needs a job. Old money offers the luxury of a sedentary lifestyle.

Regardless, I wasn't comfortable with the idea of staying in a place like this for longer than needed. The thought lingered in the back of my mind that one of those Vamps I'd staked years earlier might show up and recognize me.

I put my hands on the seat, and my pinky brushed against Christian's. When he hooked his finger over mine, I snapped my arm away.

Was he just trying to rile me up to see if I was attracted to him?

If so, he was right.

I'd grown up fascinated by clean-cut men because I perceived that as signifying a better life. Those were men of money or ambition—people who didn't aspire to live in a trailer home. To be attracted to a Vampire who didn't shave, wore shirts with holes, and owned a shack in the woods made no sense. But something about Christian's brooding personality and dry humor appealed to me.

I squirmed in my seat when he gave me a roguish grin.

He also had smoldering eyes, and sometimes he licked his lips and did this thing where he gently scraped his teeth over his bottom lip as if he were in the midst of a sexual fantasy. The more feelings I developed for him, the more skeptical I became. Did his blood have residual influence over me? If so, then did mine have any power over him? Was part of him still inside me? It sometimes felt like none of the men I'd drunk from had left my body, so maybe having a little of Christian wasn't such a bad thing.

And then there was the revelation of him being the hero of

my past. I hadn't been able to shake that out of my head all day. Neither of us had brought it up since, but the scene kept replaying in my mind like an old movie stuck on a loop. When he folded his arms on the table, I stared at them, imagining what his burned body had looked like after the fire and the pain he must have endured while healing.

All for me.

I might have won a silly bet for a favor, but in reality, I was the one who owed Christian.

"Something vexes you," he said quietly. "Your heart rate is accelerating."

"Stop doing that. You can't read into everything."

He propped his elbows on the table, his fingers laced together in a prayerlike gesture. He had his thumbs straight out and chin resting on them. When I caught the direction of his gaze, I realized he was staring at my necklace.

I reached inside my leather jacket and zipped my hoodie all the way to my neck.

The waitress finally appeared with a pitcher of ice water and three glasses. While she poured, Claude put his phone away. After she left, we each took a long sip and stared aimlessly around the bar. When I peered over at Christian again, his fangs were visible.

The expression on his face was so comical that I pushed my finger against a fang to snap him out of his trance. "If you're hungry, we can stop by the blood bank," I teased.

"Shhh."

Then I noticed the angle of his head and realized he was listening in on a conversation. Claude and I exchanged a glance but remained silent.

Christian turned slowly, like a predator, and glared over his shoulder. "She's going to meet up with him. I just overheard their phone call. He said he needs her to watch the baby for two hours while he finishes up a business deal."

The adrenaline in my blood spiked.

Claude stood up and swiped the keys to the van. "I'll drive."

We discreetly followed Amber out the door, staying a good ten paces behind her. She wouldn't recognize us, so it wasn't likely she was going to speed off. We took our time getting into the van and watched her cross the parking lot and unlock the door to a silver car.

Since Christian had claimed the passenger seat, I was forced to sit in the back. Claude's red car would stand out like a sore thumb trailing behind her. Aside from that, it was always better to stick together on a job.

"We have a lead," Claude said into his phone. "Right into the lion's den. Let me talk to Viktor."

I gripped the bench when Claude backed over something and then hit the gas.

"Viktor, I wanted to let you know we've got a strong lead. She's taking us to the Mage."

"Cristo. That's his name," Christian added.

Claude looked at him, phone still to his ear. "His name is Cristo. We might be able to take him by surprise. He's handing over the baby to the woman, so we're going to sit tight. I'm not putting the child in danger. … I agree. … Okay, I'll let them know." When he hung up the phone, he relayed the message. "Viktor doesn't want us going after Cristo. We follow the woman, sit tight, and wait until she has the baby. When Cristo or his man is gone, we move in. Viktor thinks Cristo will keep the auction going even if we steal the child. At least then we won't have to worry about the baby getting hurt and we can focus on hunting him down."

"I'm on board with that plan," Christian agreed. "Fall back another car length. She won't recognize me, but I don't want her getting spooked because of a black van on her bumper."

The streets weren't busy, so Claude slowed down. Snow between Amber's car and ours obscured visibility. The treacherous roads made it easy to keep up with her since she was driving carefully.

Christian turned in his seat and gave me a pensive stare. "It looks like we're heading back to the Bricks."

I concealed my light so Cristo couldn't detect me. As much as I wanted to drain the bastard, this was a better plan. Save the baby first, and then set a trap. Otherwise, we could put the baby's life in danger by gunning after Cristo.

Christian turned on the radio and said something to Claude. While there weren't windows I could see out of, I had a feeling we'd reached the Bricks since Christian was trying to cloak his conversation with obnoxious music.

"Slow down," he said to Claude. "Park right here."

I made sure the laces on my black boots were tight in case we had to get out and run. *What the heck are we going to do with a baby?* Our van wasn't exactly equipped with child seats.

"Here he comes," Claude said.

The suspense was killing me. I wanted to peer between them, but Christian turned off the radio and began texting someone. He was probably trying to listen to their conversation, but I wasn't certain he could hear anything at this distance unless they were talking loudly.

The engine rumbled, and the van began moving again.

"She's turning," Christian said. "She'll probably make a left up ahead. That road leads out."

I peered around Christian's seat and watched the car in front of us make a right turn.

"Where the feck is she going?" Christian asked, not expecting an answer.

A cold feeling of dread washed over me when we turned down another empty street. "Something's not right," I said. "Claude, turn around."

"She's got the baby," he growled. "I'm not letting her go."

My heart raced at a wicked beat.

Christian suddenly grabbed the wheel. "She's right. Stop the van!"

Claude hit the brakes, and we watched Amber's taillights flash as her car came to a stop. I looked ahead of her and realized we'd reached a dead end.

"Turn around!" I shouted. "Quick!"

Instead, Claude put the van in park and got out.

I rushed between the seats to look. "What the hell's he doing?"

Claude ran Chitah speed toward the car and pried open the door. He reached in, and when he stood up, he was holding a doll in his hand.

His gaze drifted upward to the buildings above the van, and in a flash, he disappeared.

Gunfire erupted.

Christian dove into the back and threw himself on top of me. Each bullet pierced through the metal wall and roof with a sharp explosion. He cradled my head with both arms while gunfire rained upon us like a hailstorm. A bullet ripped through my calf, and another grazed my arm. I quickly pulled my limbs in tight so that Christian became my shield, but his body provided no relief from the unmitigated pain where the bullets had struck.

Just as suddenly as it began, the attack ceased. My ears were ringing, making it impossible to focus. When Christian raised his head, the strained look on his face told the story. I'd seen that same look before when he'd taken too many bullets.

I threw my bleeding arm in front of his mouth. "Hurry up and drink!"

Without argument, he punched his fangs out and bit into my arm. Christian drew blood until I heard bullets popping out of his body and hitting the floor. Once he'd taken enough to heal, he licked my wound and sat up with a look of murder in his eyes.

"Ready yourself," he said, shaking out of his coat. "They're coming to kill us."

"They? How many are there?"

Christian's eyes scanned my body, and it didn't take long for him to notice the gunshot wound on my leg. He crouched over me and shoved his wrist into my mouth. "Bite!"

I shook my head, stunned by the offering.

"Listen to me, and listen good," he began, still holding his wrist against my mouth. "You won't be able to run far with that leg gushing blood. But we both know you have temporary strength when you drink my blood, and you're going to need all the strength you can get. Take my vein, Raven. Heal yourself."

Regardless of what my mind told me, my Vampire instinct

knew exactly what it wanted. I resisted at first, afraid of that savage side of me that felt disconnected from my humanity. But when Christian's decadent blood filled my mouth, my taste buds awakened, invigorated by his adrenaline and thirst to kill. The emotions ripened as they mixed with my own blood. Which were his emotions, and which were mine? Was I the one who wanted to kill mercilessly, tasting the blood of my victims? He retracted his arm before I could get a second swallow, but one was all I needed to heal.

Christian and I faced the back of the van.

When the door burst open, my instincts kicked in.

Fight or die.

Chapter 18

S HEPHERD PACED THE HALLS OF the expansive mansion
that was closing in on him like solitary confinement. He'd
obeyed Viktor's orders to stay behind while Christian,
Claude, and Raven were on the front lines. Viktor was probably
afraid Shepherd would do something unpredictable.

Maybe he was right.

Shepherd paused at the end of a hall and gazed up at the
keystone on the archway of the first floor. It was bad enough he was
on lockdown, but on top of that, Niko had been shadowing him
around the mansion. He was stealthy, always lurking just around
the corner, but he wasn't smooth enough to get past Shepherd.
Niko could shield his energy and silence his footsteps all he wanted,
but his emotional imprints were everywhere.

The heavy tread of Shepherd's boots bounced off the walls as
he headed toward the back of the mansion and up the stairs. His
partner was busy trying to close a deal on a baby auction. Shepherd
had nothing to occupy his time. He'd already polished his weapons
before heading into the training room, but hours had passed since
then.

He was restless.

Agitated.

All he could think about was that man's face. Shepherd might
not have recognized him had it not been for those piercing eyes—
the last thing Maggie ever saw. Maybe that was what burned him
the most. It hadn't been Shepherd's eyes she saw while she took her
last breath. He hadn't gotten to hold her hand and tell her it would

be okay, even if the words were lies to ease her suffering. He'd spent years thinking about what he could have given Maggie in her final moments. Words of comfort she never received, a tender kiss, the touch of his hand. And most of all, his ability to erase the pain. Sensors could make a man forget they were dying. He could have eased her suffering if only he'd been close enough to touch her. And maybe with a miracle, he could have healed her. Just maybe.

Shepherd reached in the front pocket of his loose jeans and pulled out a box of smokes. He stopped at the corner of the stairs by a statue and struck a match against its face, lighting the end of his cigarette and drawing in that wonderful first taste. Sensors didn't have to worry about bullshit diseases like lung cancer or emphysema, so a man could truly enjoy his vices with no guilt. Smoking wasn't something he'd done much around Maggie; she didn't like the taste on his breath or the smell on his clothes. But Shepherd indulged in smoking because it brought him comfort and pleasure the way a familiar blanket might to anyone else. A good cigarette was the one thing he could count on in stressful times. It topped off a great meal or complemented a strong drink.

It also calmed him the fuck down in moments like these.

He passed one tall window after the next until he reached one of the central halls, which was where Wyatt's game room was located. Instead of going in, he leaned against the wall by the open door and listened to the conversations overlapping inside.

Blue's voice sounded surprised. "What do you mean it's over?"

"Just what I said," Wyatt replied. "It's gone… as in poof."

"Gone. I do not understand gone. Did we lose the bid?" Viktor asked.

"It didn't close," Wyatt said, frustration edging his voice. "The auctions always end with either a winner or the seller closing the curtain if the price doesn't meet their requirements. But it's just gone, like he took it down. I hit refresh, and I'm trying to see if maybe it's a server issue. Just give me a minute."

It sounded as if Viktor was pacing back and forth. Wyatt would be sitting, and Blue's boot heels made a distinctive click against the floor. Shepherd tucked his left hand in his pocket and stared at a crack in the wall.

Someone's phone vibrated. "What's happening?" Viktor asked. After a minute of choppy conversation, he breathed out a heavy sigh. "Claude has a lead on our Mage."

Shepherd looked toward the doorway.

"Is that why he canceled the auction?" Wyatt asked.

"Nyet. The Mage is not aware they're tracking him down. They're following a woman, and they plan to rescue the infant. This is good if we can separate him from the child. Keep searching for bids; perhaps he wanted higher offers or was testing the waters to see how many fish would bite."

"Who's the woman?" Blue asked.

"Claude did not say. But we have a name for our Mage. Cristo."

Shepherd stepped closer.

"Last name?" Wyatt pressed.

"That is all I have."

And that was all Shepherd needed. As he pivoted on his heel to head to a quiet room, he ran into Niko.

"Going somewhere?" Niko asked, tilting his head to one side.

"You're one nosy Chinaman."

Niko smiled impatiently. "I'm not Chinese, and you're trying to instigate something so I'll leave you alone. Viktor gave us orders to remain here until summoned."

Niko knew him all too well. Shepherd never made derogatory remarks about his team, but he needed Niko to back off so he could make a call. He also needed to stay calm since Niko could read his energy, so he took a long drag off his cigarette, smoke tingling on his tongue as he drew in a deep breath.

"If it's all the same to you, I'd like some privacy. Sit in the hall if you want to play watchman, but I'm going into that study, and I'm going to shut the door and smoke my cigarette. Obviously nobody around here needs my help."

Regret flickered in Niko's blue eyes. "Your contributions are valued."

"Viktor's afraid I'll flip. I get it. Look, we each have a tattoo that binds us like brothers, and brothers have each other's backs. Think about that the next time you're in a tight spot with Viktor and need someone to lean on."

He clapped his hand on Niko's shoulder and walked past him into an empty room. After closing the soundproof door, he struck a match and lit one of the lanterns on the wall. Because there were so many rooms in the mansion, most of them weren't used. Some were bereft of furniture, and others were storage spaces for antiques that had come with the estate. With the cigarette between his lips, Shepherd swiped his finger across his phone and called Patrick.

"Give me just a moment," Patrick answered, putting Shepherd on hold. After a minute, his voice came back on. "I'm sorry for that; I was in a meeting."

Shepherd blew out a breath of smoke. "I have a name."

"Grand."

"It's Cristo."

There was a short pause. "C-r-i-s-t-o?"

"I didn't win the spelling bee," Shepherd retorted. "But here's the deal: I want him. Give me whatever information you can, and we'll be square. I need it fast, and I need it now."

"If that's what you desire. I have to make another call."

"I'll be here."

Shepherd paced. He wanted to get a jump on this while Wyatt was still preoccupied with the auction fiasco.

After five minutes, his phone vibrated. "Yeah?"

"I'll have what you need this evening. I'm sorry, but that's the best I can do. I can only go as fast as the men who work for me. Will an address suffice?"

"So long as it isn't an apartment on the corner of Morningstar. Dead end."

No sense in visiting an apartment blown to pieces. Shepherd needed new information, and chances were this guy owned a second residence. Smart criminals didn't box themselves in with only one car and one house. Cristo had been doing this long enough that by now he'd learned how to keep his hands clean.

Patrick's voice took on a more pleasant cadence. "I can assure you that we'll have this resolved by the evening. But I want to be clear that the information I give you will absolve me from any further debt owed, regardless of the outcome. Obtaining this information puts me in a precarious situation, so I hope you understand. Otherwise, I'm more than happy to pursue this individual at my own speed."

"I'll wait for your call."

"Very well, Mr. Moon."

Shepherd stubbed the butt of his cigarette in a marble ashtray. After putting out the lantern, he stepped into the hall and immediately noticed something was off. Hurried footfalls sounded from around the corner, and Niko was nowhere to be seen. Shepherd rounded the corner and caught sight of Blue's long brown hair flapping behind her like a ribbon in the wind as she ran toward the stairs and disappeared. When he reached Wyatt's room, he peered inside. The lights were on, a half-eaten MoonPie was on the keyboard, and the laptop displayed an auction room.

But not a soul remained.

Chapter 19

WHEN THE REAR DOOR TO the van swung open, the long-haired Vampire from our previous visit greeted us with a sardonic smile.

Cristo stood several paces back and looked genuinely stunned that we weren't incapacitated and bleeding out. The gunshots wouldn't have killed us, but they would have taken us by surprise. Guns were noisy, required bullets, and not a favorite weapon for most Breed.

Except in the Bricks, where apparently everyone carried a semiautomatic.

The Vampire slowly licked his lips, his eyes soaking in the blood on my arm and leg. "I can't wait to taste that juicy vein."

Christian edged in front of me.

"Watch out for the woman," Cristo warned. "She's a mutant."

I narrowed my eyes.

Christian torpedoed out of the van and lunged at the Vampire. Their colossal fistfight made the ground quake. I'd never seen him fight like that. So calculated and swift, each countermove followed by an offensive blow. He elbowed the Vampire in the jaw with enough force that it knocked him out of sight. Who was this guy? Jean-Claude Van Poe?

Lightning quick, I drew my push dagger and jumped out of the van.

Someone fired at me, so I flashed to the right. Before I could attack one of Cristo's men, Claude dropped from the rooftop above and crashed onto him. He was in primal mode, all four incisors out and a savage look in his eyes. He sank his teeth into the man's neck, and a scream poured out—the scream of a Mage powerless against the deadly poison of a Chitah.

A shooter on the rooftop fired. Since I was out in the open, I flashed back to the van.

"Fecking hell!" Christian roared as the bullets pinged against the concrete all around him.

The long-haired Vampire gracefully jumped on top of the van and climbed up an inactive intersection light as if he were an acrobat.

Cristo looked like a maestro as he watched from the middle of the street. He was in the safest place possible with gunmen protecting him from above. That dickless bastard wasn't going to make a move until I got shot.

His eyes widened in surprise when I flashed toward him, dagger in hand.

I crashed into him, my fangs scraping his neck as I went for his jugular. He flailed, and we went rolling across the snow as sporadic gunshots went off.

"What the fuck are you?" he growled, shoving my face away as I went for his neck again.

"Your worst nightmare."

I grasped his hands and pulled just enough of his core light to make him tremble with terror. He blanched and scurried back on his elbows, realizing that as a Stealer, I could end his reign of terror by stripping away his immortal light.

Cristo brandished a long dagger that made mine pale in comparison, and I sprang to my feet. While stunners didn't affect me, the way he twirled the blade in his hand proved he was skilled with a knife. Cristo was a big guy and had probably taken a head or two, so I backed up a step. He waved his hand, gesturing for someone to join him.

Claude scaled the building, chasing after the second gunman, but that wasn't who Cristo was summoning.

"They're all yours," he said, backing away.

Several goons emerged from the surrounding buildings. I

counted seven, one of them a Chitah by the looks of his light hair and eyes.

Christian shook the intersection light pole, trying to get the fanghole—who was laughing maniacally—down.

When Cristo flashed away, I chased after him. Snow crunched beneath my boots as I closed in on him. He suddenly stopped, placing a parked car between us. "How long do you think he'll last on his own?" he asked, jerking his chin at Christian.

I risked a glance over my shoulder. Two men surrounded Christian, one of them holding an impalement stake.

Three onlookers descended upon them like hyenas.

I slammed my fists against the parked car. "Fight me!"

"Satisfying my ego isn't worth the risk."

"Then why lure us here? So other people can do your dirty work for you?"

"Bingo. I just make the money, honey."

When I moved to the right, he inched left. "A real man fights his own battles."

Cristo laughed haughtily. "Real men are only real until they're dead. You're just a blip on the radar. Nice knowing you, blue eye." Cristo fled, flashing down the street in the opposite direction from the van.

Oh, no you don't!

When I caught up with him, I grabbed the back of his shirt and swiped my dagger. It pierced his shoulder, but Cristo didn't stay still long enough for the blade to sink in. He pivoted, ducked, and tried to escape as I kept a firm grip of the fabric. I finally just dropped the blade and punched him in the face. He flew back several feet, reminding me that Christian's blood had given me temporary strength.

Invigorated with Vampire blood, I lunged, but he raised his feet and slammed them against my chest. The wind whooshed from my lungs as I fell to my side and coughed up blood.

In the blink of an eye, Cristo scrambled up and flashed off. Still coughing, I staggered to my feet, pants wet from the snow, and harnessed my energy. The instinct to go after him was powerful, but something held me back.

I looked over my shoulder at Christian fighting off a number of men. I couldn't leave my partner behind. Without a second thought, I flashed down the street just as a Chitah came up behind him with an impalement stake. I blasted the attacker with energy, and when he flew onto the concrete, he hit his head on the curb and fell unconscious. Christian and I stood with our backs together as the men circled us. I hefted a trash can and hurled it at a beetle-browed man in a blue coat.

I sharpened my light, throwing myself at one of them and blasting him in the chest. He convulsed, overpowered by the energy. When he involuntarily shifted into a mountain lion, I blasted him once more, taking no chances.

I couldn't keep this up. The flashing had depleted my Mage energy as it was, and I didn't have enough in reserve to fight all the men coming out of the woodwork. Not to mention it wouldn't even work on Vampires. Still filled with residual Vampire power from Christian, I fought my next assailant hand to hand. I grabbed his beard and gave it a hard yank before kneeing him in the groin. His Mage energy rippled against my skin, so I drove my stunner into his chest to the hilt.

More gunshots blazed overhead, and I slipped on ice as I rushed to the other side of the van. When someone tried to grab me, I quickly slid beneath the vehicle on my stomach. Toward the front, a man fell, blood spraying the white snow. Claude's familiar sneakers strode by. When a second set came up behind him, a struggle ensued.

I did a belly crawl until I reached the front of the van and stood up. To my horror, more men were advancing in our direction. The Vampire perched on the intersection pole overhead watched with a look of amusement.

This was how people in the Bricks entertained themselves.

While I'd taken down a number of men in controlled environments, nothing had prepared me for what was essentially a street battle.

"We're outnumbered!" I shouted.

"Damn right you are," a man growled from behind me as he snaked his arm around my midsection.

I lifted my knee and pulled out the small dagger hidden in the heel of my boot. He swung me around, and my head slammed against the front of the van. Without looking, I reached up and swiped my blade several times until he made a gurgling sound.

I stumbled forward, my breath heavy and the cold air burning my lungs and throat. Claude was nowhere in sight, and Christian was fighting five men at once. His eyes were so bottomless that you could almost see the pit of hell in them.

I gripped my tiny blade and wanted to laugh. Was this how my life would end? In the middle of a snowy street, surrounded by bored men who didn't even know who they were fighting or why?

When a horn blared in the distance, everyone turned.

At the end of the street, a black sedan faced us. I breathed a sigh of relief as Viktor emerged from the passenger side. He ran toward us and gracefully shifted into his grey wolf, his clothes falling away as he lunged at a man and tore at his arms.

Next came Niko, and he was armed to the teeth with a katana in each hand. His long hair rippled behind him like a shadow in flight as he charged toward us, slicing his blade through a man on his left without breaking stride.

I winced when a bullet struck my hand. Hearing someone coming up behind me, I kicked my leg back and knocked him in the chest.

My thoughts crystallized. Though the man was taller and fifty pounds heavier, we fought like equals. I punched him in the throat, jaw, and probably the nipple—anywhere my fist would land. He took a swing, but I dodged his fist and flashed behind him. Sensing his Mage energy, I realized the only way to take him down was by physical force. I pounced on his back and locked my arm around his neck, squeezing the breath out of him and cutting off circulation to his head.

"Die, you squirmy little bastard!" I growled.

He flailed in a pathetic attempt to throw me off, but I held on like a cowboy at a rodeo, ignoring the pain radiating across my back when he slammed me against the side of the van.

"Lights out," I growled in his ear.

Applause sounded from above as the Vampire watched on.

The man stumbled, his face purple and eyes half open, and finally hit the ground. I held on, just in case he was faking. Niko's spinning swords sliced at another man who had a blade of his own.

The idiot didn't stand a chance. Niko was on form.

Blood tainted the streets, attracting even more onlookers.

The second I stood up, I jumped back with a start when a ball of light flew past me and exploded in a crowd of men. The energy wave ripped through the air like a meteor, prickling against my skin like tiny spikes. A pile of men lay in the snow, their skin blackened and the stench of burning flesh wafting in the air.

I turned on my heel, my mouth agape at Gem, who stood at the far end of the street with her arms extended. To the left, Blue was swinging her tomahawk like a warrior. Despite her long legs, shapely breasts, lush lips, and hair like silk, Blue wasn't a woman who used her beauty in battle. She was fierce, relentless, and spattered with blood.

I blasted a man with energy while running toward the van. When I reached the driver's side, I jumped in and slammed the door. The keys were still in the ignition. As soon as the engine started up, I hit the gas and crashed into Amber's car, knocking it forward a few feet. She had bailed from the scene the moment the fight started.

I was turning the wheel left to do a U-turn when someone jumped into the back.

"Claude's hurt," Christian said. "Get us the feck out of here!"

"Shut the door!" I steered over the sidewalk and clipped a guy before skidding back onto the street.

"Niko!" he shouted. "Get in!"

I glanced in the mirror and saw Christian helping Niko in the back.

"Hang on!" I hit the gas, and the van torpedoed through the crowd like a juggernaut. They fell away like bowling pins, but one

Vampire suddenly punched through my window and gripped the wheel. I slammed on the brakes, hoping to throw him off, but he held on with fierce determination.

"Get away from her, you shitebag!" Christian leaned across me and broke the Vamp's arm before throwing him out. "Get up. I'm taking over."

We switched places, and I stepped into the back of the van just as Christian hit the gas. I gripped the passenger seat to keep from falling and assessed our situation. Claude lay unconscious, and Niko was opening one of the back doors.

"Blue!" he shouted. "Blue!"

The van slowed.

"Take my axe!" She reached inside and handed him her tomahawk before shifting. Her falcon ascended out of sight just as an explosion rocked the van.

I stumbled to the bench, my heart racing. "Was that Gem?"

I looked to Niko. Staring into chaos, he held on to the end of the closed door.

My eyes drifted down to Claude, and I realized how grave his condition was. I had initially thought someone knocked him out, but blood pooled on the carpet beneath him in ghastly quantities.

I crouched beside him. "Claude, can you hear me?" I pulled his eyelids back, searching for signs of life. "He's hurt bad. He's not waking up."

The van jerked to the left, and my back hit the bench.

"Hang on," Christian shouted before slamming on the brakes.

Niko reached out and pulled Gem inside. Wyatt jumped in behind her, out of breath. Niko's sharp whistle summoned Viktor's wolf, who charged inside and onto a bench. Niko slammed the back door, and we took off.

I looked around. "Where's Shepherd?"

Wyatt stepped over Claude and led Viktor's wolf to the front passenger seat. "He didn't come. Holy Toledo, get the hell out of here, Christian. The freshies are everywhere!"

When Gem saw Claude on the floor, her eyes rounded, and

she crawled next to him. She stroked his hair, tears wetting her cheeks. "Niko, you need to help him."

"Won't he heal?" I asked. "He's a Chitah."

Niko stumbled as he tried to find a place to sit. "Not if he's lost too much blood. Chitahs are good healers, but his light is dim, and we don't have Shepherd here to stitch him up. I need everyone to stand back."

Gem reluctantly scooted away, her crystal pendant swinging from her neck as she leaned over to watch. I collapsed on the bench and peeled out of my leather jacket. I was actually sweating. Blood dripped from my hand, so I pressed the wound against my jeans to stanch the bleeding. While Niko knelt beside Claude and used his X-ray vision to look at whatever energy Claude was putting out, I turned to Christian since I was sitting right behind the driver's seat.

"Are we safe?"

"Aye. For the moment. Unless there's someone on the roof."

"There's a freshy up there, clinging to the van like a sock from a dryer," Wyatt informed us. He widened his legs and stared at me from the opposite bench. "If he comes home with us after all I went through to clean the specters out of the house, I'm demanding a raise."

"Will you be quiet?" Gem spat. "Claude… Can you hear me? Blink if you can hear me."

We turned our attention back to our Chitah. His leather jacket was open in the front, revealing holes and bloodstains in his white undershirt. I counted three. I'd always assumed Chitahs were resilient, but I was learning that everyone had limitations.

Claude suddenly coughed, blood ejecting from his mouth and spattering on his face and shirt. My heart sank. His ashen skin and bluish lips told the story.

Niko assessed him carefully. "I can't heal them all," he finally said. "His energy is dark around his chest. I'll do what I can." Niko's hand hovered as if he was searching for the wound.

Claude's eyes fluttered and then opened.

Gem cupped his face in her hands, staring at him upside down.

He struggled to smile. "Don't cry, female. I'm not worth the tears."

Wyatt leaned over. "Stop trying to out-die us. You're not going anywhere. I don't want to have to deal with staring at your handsome ghost for all eternity. You hear me? You'll give me an inferiority complex."

Claude's lips twitched as Gem wiped away droplets of blood that were on his cheeks.

Niko placed his hand across one of the bullet holes, and after a moment, I squinted from the flash of light that cracked like a whip. Claude sighed. Watching Niko heal someone else besides me allowed me to see the magnitude of how much energy it required from him. Despite his hooded eyes and lethargic movements, he continued. Gem let go just as Niko healed another wound.

When he finished, his eyes didn't carry that spark of light they usually held.

"Niko, maybe you should stop."

Out of breath, he fell back against the bench. "How many more does he have?"

Gem pulled Claude's jacket away and lifted his shirt. "One on his shoulder and I think his leg." She rose up on her knees for a closer look. "It's too dark in here; I can't see."

Niko's beautiful brown skin now had a greyish hue. The graver the wound, the more of his gift it required. He probably could have kept going, but the quality of his light would have diminished, assuming he could stay conscious after repeated energy depletion.

Claude rolled to his side. "I'm good."

Gem helped him to sit. "Are you sure? You don't look good."

He smiled weakly. "I always look good."

Wyatt sighed and took off his beanie, rumpling his hair with one hand as he looked at Christian. "When you called for backup, I thought maybe you were outnumbered by two or three guys. Four tops. Half a city? Now that's a twist I didn't see coming."

I leaned back and shut my eyes, trying to ignore the throbbing pain in my hand, my sore jaw, and my aching muscles.

"Why the feck did you bring my car?" Christian spat.

Wyatt snickered. "Because you drew the short straw. Plus, we couldn't all fit in mine. It's not as if we had time to contemplate anything. We hauled ass to get here."

"Grand. Now what are the odds that I'll never see it again?"

Claude gripped my right arm. "Let me see your other hand."

I held it up, a bullet having pierced through the palm. "Sorry, but this is one injury you won't be licking. Lie back and rest. It sucks to be a Mage in winter, but I'll find a drop of sun if it kills me."

Niko chuckled. "Apologies. I'm laughing at the truth of it."

Some of the bullet holes around the van let in narrow strips of light, but it wasn't the direct sunlight that I needed to heal.

It didn't matter anyhow. We were almost home.

Chapter 20

E VERY LANTERN AND CANDLE IN my bathroom was aglow, bathing the stone walls with an ethereal light. I had a magnificent bathroom located in the room behind my bed. There wasn't a door, and as you walked in and turned left, you faced a standing shower and small window farther ahead. Lanterns were affixed to the left wall on each side of the oval mirror above the sink. Next to it, a toilet. The best part about the bathroom was that against the opposite wall sat the most glorious claw-foot tub. It was large and tucked inside the partially recessed wall. There was even a nice ledge in the wall where I could set my candles or toiletries.

I stood inside the dry tub with every intention of drawing a hot bath, but I ended up sitting down with my clothes still on. Exhausted, I reclined back, my injured left hand hanging out of the tub and my knees drawn up.

Sometimes it just felt good to slow down and gather my thoughts. As crazy as things had gotten in the Bricks, it was a good thing I hadn't killed Cristo. Working for Keystone meant curbing my impulsive instincts, and we still had a baby to rescue.

"That's an interesting way to wash up," Christian remarked.

I glanced left where he was standing in the doorway, arms folded. "Did you have fun today?"

Christian swaggered to the mirror, where he proceeded to admire his dark beard. He raised his chin, studying the rogue hairs that grew below his jawline.

"There's a razor if you want to give it a whirl." I gestured toward a plastic one on the sink.

"I don't mess with perfection."

"How's Claude?"

"Receiving affection from all the ladies in the house. Is that what it takes to get dinner in bed?"

I reclined my head, my thoughts nebulous. "This guy is really pissing me off. How could he have known we were following that woman if you scrubbed her memory?"

Christian pivoted around and stepped inside the tub, making himself comfortable at the opposite end by mirroring my position. "She must have been a Blocker."

"I thought that was a Mage gift."

"Never assume. A Mage Blocker can thwart other Mage gifts. But there are those in the Breed world who also have a natural blocking ability against other Breed gifts. There aren't many out there, and most of them don't want others to know their secret."

"I'm guessing that means Vampire gifts don't work against her."

"In her case, no."

"Why didn't she just lie about Cristo?"

"Because I was looking her in the eyes, and she knew I would have caught her lying. Afterward, she sent a text. He could have sent a message back and told her to leave, but I bet he had a grand time conceiving a plan to do away with us by staging an attack. Criminals in the Bricks look at murder as a recreational activity."

"Swell."

"How's your hand?"

I held it up and turned it so he could see both sides. "Have you ever had a ripped cuticle? Imagine that times a thousand."

"What about Niko?"

"He's tapped out. Poor guy. He went straight to bed and probably won't wake up for hours. That was really something he did for Claude." A quiet moment passed as I reflected on how selfless Niko was. He could have kept his gift a secret when he joined Keystone and let every man fend for himself. "We might need to think about relocating to Florida. Isn't that the Sunshine State?"

"Just be glad we don't live in Washington."

I shuddered at the thought. Even when it snowed, the sun in Cognito poked out from the clouds every so often, so I couldn't complain. It just required patience. I was fortunate to have learned how to heal from sunlight. For years, I'd had to hide until my body healed naturally.

Then again, I wasn't exactly getting shot up and attacked by forty men back then.

Christian began unlacing my boots and pulled them off one at a time. "We need to keep the blood sharing a secret," he said quietly. "If Viktor knew what we were doing, he'd break us apart."

"Maybe he's right."

"And maybe not." Christian peeled off my socks and tossed them over the edge of the tub. "It's what makes you and me a force to be reckoned with. I couldn't have fought off that many men had you not healed me."

"With my blood," I added, staring at the bloodstains on my pants as I drew my knees up even closer. "Blood is addictive, and you said yourself that Vampires shouldn't be sharing it."

Christian licked his lips. "Rest assured, I don't crave you in the wee hours of the night."

I flicked a glance up at the same time he looked at me, and butterflies tickled my stomach. "Nothing whets your appetite?"

He smirked darkly. "I wouldn't go that far, Precious. But the things I crave have nothing to do with blood. I haven't had bloodlust since I was a youngling."

"When you gave me your blood, I could taste your desire. You don't need to lie."

He bent his arm and leaned his head against his index finger. Light played on his shadowy face, and he averted his eyes. "Yours doesn't taste like other Vampire blood. Maybe it has to do with your being mixed, but it has a unique flavor I've never known before." He waggled his brows. "Worry not. I'm a man who can control my urges."

I snorted. "Except for sex."

"Haven't had much of that lately either."

I tucked my hair behind one ear. "What was she like?"

"Who?"

"The woman you previously worked for. The one who… didn't need your services anymore. I'm good at reading between the lines."

He pursed his lips and tilted his head to one side. "She found herself a big pussy to latch on to."

I quirked a brow.

Christian straightened his arm and drummed his fingers on the edge of the tub. "She mated with a Chitah. And I didn't love her, for feck's sake. I just… She just reminded me of that connection. Maybe it was her drinking my blood that brought out those feelings."

"Is that something you normally do with your clients?" I smiled impishly and bumped legs with him. "You probably didn't have many women hire you to protect them, so the whole caveman instinct kicked in. I think it's understandable, but you can stop playing bodyguard when we're out on a job. I'm not a client."

Christian barked out a laugh. "You're an entirely different woman, comparable to none. Especially being as new as you are. Rarely have I seen someone not born into our world acclimate so well. You're tough, fearless—"

"Pretty? I bet *she* was pretty."

"Aye, she had a soft face. Her hair wasn't as black as yours, but her skin was simply flawless. She had the complexion of a Vampire even though—"

"She wasn't a Vampire?"

"Mage."

"So much for sticking to your own kind, Mr. Poe. Good to know. Anyhow, it doesn't sound like she was your type."

"And what type is that?"

"B negative?"

We both chuckled.

"She wanted to be tough, but she wasn't born that way."

I pulled my arms inside the tub and put them on my lap. "So

you want a tough girl? Someone to bend you over her knee and give you a spanking? What a naughty boy you are."

His cheeks flushed. "Put a cork in it. I don't want a relationship. She just reminded me of my humanity."

"Ah. The pesky thing you keep trying to kill. You act as if caring about someone will ruin your reputation."

He pinched his beard, deep in thought. "I've seen too many men lose their lives for a four-letter word. If the fates gave us immortality, it wasn't for us to waste on such a frivolous emotion. That's not the Vampire way."

Christian's hand stroking my ankle belied his words. He clearly craved physical affection. Maybe that was why he engaged in debauchery—to have that connection with another person. The same craving I felt whenever he touched me so tenderly.

"Didn't mean to bring up a sore subject," I said.

"Doesn't matter. She wasn't the biggest mistake in my life."

Were the women he had sex with a means to make him forget that he actually had a heart and had made the mistake of listening to it once or twice? Thinking about what went on inside Christian's head had become not only a pastime of mine, but a means of torture.

"Should I cook dinner?" I offered.

He gave me a crooked smile. "If you enjoy the suffering of others, by all means."

"Don't you ever get hungry, even for blood?"

"No."

"So you just live in a state of nothingness? Never hungry, never full."

He scratched his scruff, a sign he was hiding something.

"What?" I nudged him with my foot. "Tell me."

"We didn't have exotic fruits in Ireland. When I came here, you ate whatever was local. It wasn't until years later that I began noticing strange fruit. Watermelon fascinated me. Such a hard exterior with ugly markings, and yet when you sliced it open, it was gorgeous. Juicy and bright red." He licked his lips. "I'd never tasted anything like it. Every so often, I crave watermelon."

A smile touched my lips. "Am I strange fruit?"

When his smoldering eyes latched onto mine, a sexual heat pooled low in my body. At first I thought the blood exchange was making me feel that way, or the fact that he was the man who'd rescued me from the fire. The worst part was that I couldn't stop analyzing my feelings about him and what they meant, because I'd never felt such an unyielding attraction to anyone before.

"You're strange indeed," he murmured. "Did you come in here to hide away like a little mouse?"

I shrugged. "I like to be alone when I'm hurt."

Christian abruptly leaned forward. "Let me see your hand." He took my injured palm and turned it over, running his finger over the partially sealed wound. "You need to fix this. There are twenty-seven bones in the human hand, and I'll wager the bullet shattered at least one."

"I can't keep drinking your blood," I said, retracting my arm.

Christian gripped the edge of the tub and slowly put his knees down, forcing me to open my legs. "There's nothing wrong with what we're doing. You're my partner. You came in here to hide like a wounded animal because that's what you're used to doing. You're not alone, Raven. Together we're stronger than any of them," he said, nodding toward the door. "Don't think I haven't figured you out."

I blinked in surprise. "What do you mean by that?"

He took a lock of my hair between his fingers and looked at it for a moment. "I know why you hate Vampires. Your Mage Creator was a cruel man. Most people despise their tormentor, but you hate your Vampire maker because he's the one who abandoned you to evil. He was your hope—your salvation. You trusted him, and he betrayed you. The Mage side of you is the only part you understood—no matter how vile or terrible, it made sense. You never learned what it is to be a Vampire. It's as simple as that." Christian hovered as if he might lie on top of me. "I won't abandon you. I won't betray you."

I trembled when he stretched out his neck before me, his artery pulsing with healing blood.

"Drink," he whispered, his neck brushing against my lips. "Don't fight it."

Everything about his offering was so sensual that my fangs extended. I wanted to fight against my Vampire nature—against the very idea of consuming blood from another person—but I couldn't. The scent of him, the feel of his warm neck, his willingness to give himself to me—it called to my Vampire heart, and I cradled his neck in my hands. My body hummed with desire, and I hadn't even tasted him yet.

I wasn't even sure I wanted to.

I pressed a kiss below his jaw—completely unnecessary when drawing a vein closer to the surface.

But I couldn't help myself.

Christian wrapped one arm around me, holding me close as my lips locked over his neck. I felt the low rumble deep in his throat when my fangs barely touched his skin. As I began to suck on his neck, renegade pleasure raced through me, and I pulled him even closer. My teeth hadn't even broken the skin, and already this bathtub was getting much too small.

The moment my fangs pierced his flesh, Christian sat up with me in his arms so I was straddling him. Ancient blood filled my mouth—the lifeline of generations of Vampires who came before him, all woven together. My hips rocked against his, stroking against the granite-hard erection beneath his trousers. His arms were everywhere around me, but he was careful not to pull too tight, not to squeeze too hard and shatter my bones. There was nothing deadlier than being within a Vampire's grip.

I finished swallowing a mouthful and licked the wound to seal it, but I couldn't stop tasting him, kissing him, sucking on his skin.

Damn. Christian was everything my body craved, and I wanted him to kiss me back, to carry me to bed. He reached under my shirt and cupped my breast, his thumb circling the rounded tip of my hardened nipple beneath my bra.

I moaned, pressing my body into his touch. My lips dragged their way up his scruffy jaw, across his cheek, and down to his mouth. Just before our lips met, he turned his head away.

"What's wrong?" I asked in confusion.

"We're not supposed to feel this way," he said on a jagged breath. "Don't get your heart attached to me, Precious. I'm not a thing to love."

"Who said anything about love?"

He sharpened his gaze at me. "You're not the type to have casual sex."

"How do you know what type I am?"

He stroked my stomach as he withdrew his hand from beneath my shirt, causing me to shiver. "Because I know. You're hungry for a man's touch, and I just happen to be within proximity."

I jerked my neck back. "You make it sound like I'm desperate."

He grinned as if proud of pushing my buttons. "Who's grinding who?"

I rocked my hips, his erection stroking me between the legs. Christian moaned as if he were in pain, his eyes hooding. "I can't stroke what isn't there, and it seems like you feel a whole lot more for me than you're admitting to." I sighed and got out of the tub, putting distance between us. "Let's see what's going on downstairs."

He glared up at me with a look of reservation and doubt. "You're not mad?"

I turned on the faucet and washed my bloody hand. "Maybe you're used to women who spring tears from their eyes and flounce out of a room, but that's not me."

Christian rose to his feet and stepped out of the tub. He strode over to the doorway and then casually leaned against the wall. By the expression on his face, he looked as if he was trying to figure me out. "I think we'll work well together if you just stop trying to get in my trousers. I know the eye candy must be torture, but fecking control yourself."

I stripped out of my shirt, and when his eyes drifted down to the red satin bra that held my breasts firmly in place, I gave him a smug grin. I splashed water on my chest. "Anything you say, Vamp."

His eyes narrowed. "You keep using that word and seem to forget that you're only *half* a spark plug."

"Yep, but I'm not as offended by the word as you are. I've been called a lot of things in my life, and Vamp is the least insulting." I rinsed my hair beneath the running water and then washed the blood off my arms, clavicles, and face. "The past is history. You spend a lot of time getting offended over trivial things," I said, drying my face with a towel.

"You're not old enough to appreciate the prejudices we've endured as a race."

I slipped on a tank top and then removed my bra. "No, a crossbreed wouldn't understand anything about prejudice. Now quit trying to piss me off. It's not working."

Christian took a moment to visually acknowledge my hardened nipples pressing against the fabric of my tank top. Then he took a step forward and gazed down at me with those bottomless eyes. "I love the way you smell when you're wet."

I blinked up at him in surprise. "You can smell me when I'm turned on?"

His grin widened. "I meant when you're clean, but that does raise a curious question."

I'm not going to get flustered and storm out.
I'm not going to get flustered and storm out.

I stroked my hand over his cock, which was still hard. "Yes, it certainly does." Then I patted his shoulder and walked out of the room.

Since everyone's schedule was thrown off, I didn't bother cooking. Blue and Viktor had already prepared something in the kitchen for Claude, who was upstairs healing. According to Gem, Shepherd had dressed some of his wounds and then quietly left the room without a word. Wyatt went back to his office to keep an eye on the black market website.

I decided to pay Claude a quick visit to see how he was doing. His bedroom was located on the second floor in a separate hall from Gem.

Now I could appreciate why.

I stood in the doorway and laughed when I took a gander at the bed on the right-hand wall. Gem was curled up beside Claude, who was giving his best impersonation of a hibernating bear.

"I thought that was a chain saw."

Gem sat up and gave an elfin smile. "He snores." When she turned to poke him, he stopped and made a purring sound before rolling onto his side.

"Mind if I come in?"

She gestured toward the chair on the right, which faced the bed. A candle flickered on the bedside table from the draft of her movement.

"Nice place," I said, admiring his abode.

Everyone's bedroom reflected their personality. Claude's private chamber was laid out the same as mine with the fireplace on the left wall and bath in an adjoining room behind the bed. But instead of arched windows opposite the door, he had a massive circular window with a clock design. I'd seen it from the outside of the mansion, never realizing it was his bedroom. Though it was too dark to see, I knew the glass was stained blue with black Roman numerals. The lanterns affixed to every wall weren't lit, so the only candles burning were one in the entranceway to the bathroom and another on his bedside table. He didn't have a small bed like mine. Claude was much too tall for one of those.

What surprised me most? I'd expected the room to be lavishly decorated in gold because that seemed fitting of Claude's regal personality. However, that was not the case.

"So, Claude's a leather man," I remarked, looking between the leather headboard and leather bench at the foot of the bed.

Across the room, the window sat within an alcove. Two leather couches faced each other on the opposite walls, a white shag rug between them.

I noticed the fireplace across from the bed had a large, rectangular mirror with a black frame above it. I stepped inside the room and turned around to admire his black armoire beside the door. I imagined him sitting on the leather stool while putting on his shoes and socks. There were only two chairs in the room. One was plush with a wide seat by the fireplace—a great place to doze off with a good book on a winter's night. I sat down in the other one next to the bedside table. It was small, stiff, and smelled a lot like Claude. There were creases in the arms and a few imperfections.

"How's he doing?" I asked.

"Better." Gem's legs dangled off the bed comically. "Shepherd had some special medicine that'll help his wounds heal faster. He'll be back to himself in no time, but he needs rest. Niko's drained, and Claude refuses to accept any more help from him."

I glanced at my hand, guilty that I couldn't have done the same and just healed on my own.

Gem reached up and tied her hair into a messy knot. Her baggy grey sleep shorts and shirt indicated she was foregoing her usual nightly swim.

"Should we light a fire?" I asked, staring at the cold hearth.

"No. Claude gets hot when he sleeps. He usually doesn't light it unless it's for *ambiance*," she said, dramatically emphasizing the last word.

I watched her picking at the chipped polish on her short nails. "That was really something you did back there with the light show."

Her brows knitted together for a moment before she looked at her hands. "Oh. *That*."

"I know you're smart and all, but maybe Viktor worries for no reason when putting you on the front line. Seems like you can take care of yourself."

She rubbed her fingertips together, and a tiny ball the size of a marble formed. It was composed of blue light and quickly dissipated when she smashed it in the palm of her hand with a tight fist. "I only get a few good shots, and there's always a chance something could go wrong. That's what Viktor's afraid of since it requires concentration and control. It depletes my energy. If I use too much, sometimes I can't flash for a day. Every gift has a drawback."

"That's some gift, though. Is it a rare one?"

She fell over on the pillow next to her and curled up in the fetal position. "Some rare gifts are rarer than others. My Creator told me there aren't many who can do what I do."

"What do they call it?"

I knew Gem was a Blocker who had the ability to block many Mage gifts, such as those from Mentalists or Charmers, but she hadn't detailed everything about her powers, and it wasn't my business. Now that the cat was out of the bag, it didn't seem rude to ask about it.

"When there isn't an official name, we give it one. The Mageri recorded my gifts when they measured me, but they didn't mention a name for it. Wyatt wanted to call me a ball buster. I just call it wielding, so I guess that makes me a Wielder."

Man, Gem was one lucky girl. Every Mage was different in not only what rare ability they possessed but also how many. Some had just one gift, while others had several. Niko had informed me that some didn't discover hidden abilities until years later, that the gifts would lie dormant until accidentally revealed.

"I'm just a Stealer," I said.

"Just a Stealer. No biggie. You're also a Vampire *and* a Mage who doesn't turn into a floppy doll when someone puts a stunner in you. Not to mention you're immune to Chitah venom. If this is a contest, you win."

I buried a laugh when Claude let out a sudden snort. "No wonder he's still single."

Gem's eyes twinkled with amusement. "Every perfect man has a flaw."

"Does that mean that every flawed man has something perfect about him?"

"Food for thought."

I stood up and cleared my throat. "Are you sleeping in here?"

She nodded as if there was no other answer.

"But you're just partners."

She swung her legs over the edge and hopped off the bed. "I could use something to drink. Let's walk."

After she closed the door and we paced away from the room,

Gem folded her arms. She smiled at the sudden height difference between us. Just four inches, but I could tell she didn't like looking up at people.

"I should have put on my slippers," she remarked before turning to face me. "You haven't formed a special bond with Christian yet? That concerns me."

"It's just work."

"True, but when you work closely with someone—when you put your life in their hands—the relationship becomes like one of my energy balls."

"Deadly?" I said with a snort.

"Well, once you learn each other's weaknesses and strengths, yes. But I meant powerful. I like everyone in this house, but Claude gets me. He doesn't know everything about my past, but we're there for each other. We trust each other completely. And even though Shepherd is going through some kind of a mid-immortal crisis, Wyatt's there for him. I just thought that you and Christian were finally getting along. He's going to be your partner for a long time."

We continued our pace and turned a corner.

"I love Claude," she said. "We butted heads a little in the beginning, but we found common ground and forged a friendship. He doesn't show his real side to everyone, but he's such a giving man."

"Sorry, it's none of my business."

"But it is. I don't want you to think because I spend the night in his room that there's something going on between us. People are a lot like languages. We each speak with a different vocabulary and dialect, and our job is to try to understand one another. I regret that you don't have that kind of closeness with Christian. It must be hard to feel forced into a partnership you don't care about." She gripped my wrist as we walked. "I'm still here. If you can't talk to Christian about stuff, just come see me."

"Thanks, Gem. I think Christian and I are getting along a little better. At least we're not trying to kill each other as often," I said, thinking about our near-sexual encounter in the bathtub.

Not to mention our blood sharing.

And grinding.

And almost-kissing.

I studied her as we walked. "Aren't you afraid you might mix up those chummy feelings and accidentally sleep with him?"

She blurted out a laugh and let go of my hand. "I'm not sure what you mean. I've never had accidental sex before. And feeling close to someone doesn't automatically mean I'm going to share bodily fluids with them."

I scratched the back of my head. "That's one way to put it. Look, I didn't mean to offend you or anything. I'm still trying to work on my people skills. I lived alone on the streets for a long time. That's no excuse, but I lost my filter somewhere along the way."

She worried her lip, her violet eyes wide and doe-like. "Can I say something?"

"Sure."

"Don't take this the wrong way, but if you're... you know... lonely, maybe you should fill those needs outside the house. I don't think that you and Christian will be doing the naughty, but if you're afraid to get close to him because you might accidentally sleep together, then maybe another man isn't such a bad idea. *He* certainly does. With women, I mean."

"Is that what you do?"

Her cheeks turned bright red. "I'm too busy working to dwell on physical relationships. I'm not suggesting you should sleep around, but sometimes when people have trouble separating their emotions from physical needs, they don't make the best decisions."

I looked over my shoulder, uncertain how to respond.

She shrugged. "I just thought you might be dealing with something like that since you assumed I could accidentally sleep with Claude."

Gem was smarter than I gave her credit for, and sometimes I forgot that despite her youthful appearance, she was over fifty years old. No matter how innocent she came across, Gem had acquired some wisdom in those years.

Nothing awkward about this conversation. Nothing at all.

I steered down the hall that led to Wyatt's office. "Do you hear that?"

Our leisurely walk turned into a quick jog as we headed toward what sounded like a heated argument brewing.

"You just *left* me," Shepherd growled.

We reached the doorway and stood just inside. Shepherd glared down at Wyatt, who was seated in his leather chair with a box of MoonPies on his lap.

"It's not like it was a conspiracy," Wyatt retorted. "We had to run—literally—and Viktor said we didn't have time to find you."

"Bullshit. Niko knew where I was."

"I ain't gonna sit here and argue with you. Viktor's the one who calls the shots." Wyatt tossed his phone on the desk behind him. "He's on his way up. I'll let *him* do the explaining. Meanwhile, don't take out all your hostilities on me. Rollergirl bailed just like everyone else did. Why don't you yell at her?"

"Don't encourage him," Gem said, sauntering into the room barefoot. She sat on his desk and crossed her legs at the ankles. "Shepherd, it didn't make sense to bring you along. You're volatile."

"What is this all about?" Viktor said, weaving around me and approaching Shepherd.

I tried not to laugh. Viktor had on men's pajamas. Just seeing him in silk pajama bottoms with an open robe showed me a side of him I wasn't ready to see.

A sexy one. For an older gentleman, he had a nice torso and abs. Viktor looked like he belonged in a men's catalog with a glass of brandy in one hand and a pipe in the other.

Gem was right…

I might actually stop ogling everyone in the house if I got laid.

Shepherd wiped his hand slowly down his black T-shirt. He locked eyes with Viktor and spoke, his voice calmer. "I know where to find Cristo."

"How did you—"

"I overheard the call. Just so you know, I could have taken this information and gone by myself to finish it. But Maggie wouldn't have wanted that. She would have said I've got a good thing here, but maybe I'm not so sure how good this thing is." He folded his arms, pushing out his biceps. "If you can't trust me enough to include me in a search, then I don't belong here. I have medical experience. I could have helped Claude and Raven so it wasn't all on Niko. And what if he'd gotten knocked out or some shit and wasn't able to heal anyone? I thought we were a team, but you took off without me."

Silence filled the room. Shepherd was right. You couldn't punish a man for what he might do. Had Viktor pulled a stunt like that with me, I would have been tempted to quit. On the flip side, I understood Viktor's reservations, but maybe they should have discussed it beforehand.

I felt Christian come up behind me. How I knew it was him, I couldn't say.

Viktor clasped his hands behind his back, eyes locked on Shepherd. "You say you know where to find Cristo. Do you want to tell me how it is you came across new information when not even our computer genius could find anything?"

Shepherd squared his shoulders. "I can't say. Are you with me? I'm leaving tonight. This might be the only opportunity we have."

"He's right," Wyatt said, swiveling in his chair. "Nothing's come up on the auction. I've done some preliminary searches on his name, but we don't have any leads."

Shepherd widened his stance. "Are we a team or not?"

Viktor rested his hands on Shepherd's shoulders, his expression somber. "You have placed more trust in me than I have in you. It shouldn't be that way. I apologize for excluding you on such an important mission."

Shepherd averted his gaze. "I know why you did it. I just… I need you to have my back and let me have yours. Deal?"

Viktor searched the walls for a clock. "How much time do we have?"

Shepherd pinched his chin. "We should leave within the hour."

"I need weapons," I said.

Shepherd jerked his chin toward the door. "Come with me."

We walked at a brisk pace down to the first level. Usually we rotated the job of lighting certain candles down the main hallways, but with everything going on, some of the halls were pitch-black.

"Claude can't go. Not in his condition," Shepherd said as he pushed open his bedroom door. He struck a match and lit a bright lantern. "Hold this."

"Claude's not going to like us leaving him behind."

"Yeah, but he'll understand. He's injured, and we don't put an injured man in danger. It puts not only him at risk, but everyone else, including his partner. He's also dead asleep thanks to pain meds." Shepherd strode up to his armoire, and when he opened it, my jaw dropped.

"Holy shit."

He looked over his shoulder at me and essayed a smile. "What do you think armoires were originally used for?"

Shepherd's cabinet was filled to the brim with weapons. There were mounts on the inside of the doors holding all kinds of daggers and knives. I gaped at the guns, impalement stakes, and even a crossbow. He pulled open the bottom drawers, revealing boxes of bullets and miscellaneous weapons such as throwing stars and concealable spikes.

He stepped aside. "Pick your poison."

"Do you have something I could strap to my arm beneath a long-sleeved shirt? I want to hide my daggers where I can reach them. The leg harness I have is fine for when I'm wearing dresses, but that's not often."

He reached inside and handed me a few. "Try these. The blades are sharpened."

I gave him the lantern and secured one of the straps on my arm.

"Those are fine if you're not trying to bulk up," he said. "But they're not comfortable. You might think about one of these." Shepherd held up a larger harness with a sheath. "This one hooks around your shoulders, so you can wear it beneath a button-up or jacket. No one will know."

I looked at the large blade hanging from it. "That one's too big for me."

He nodded. "You like the push daggers and small blades. Nothing wrong with that. They get the job done just fine, especially if they're stunners." He handed me three small daggers and two arm straps. "On the house. Next time you run low, I charge a fee. These are some of the best weapons money can buy. Some are mine, others are for the team. So don't get it in your head to help yourself."

"Thanks." I stepped forward, my voice low. "Did Mr. Bane give you the information? Don't worry, I won't say anything. I got to thinking that maybe he offered you some kind of favor for saving his kid."

"We're even now." Shepherd closed the cabinet drawers and turned to face me. "That's why I need to make this count."

"If Viktor wants to take him in alive, are you going to be able to do that?"

The lantern flickered against his strict features. "I can't make any promises."

Chapter 21

I POKED MY FINGER IN A bullet hole on the van wall. "Well, at least we can see outside now."

Christian glared down at my tank top and button-up shirt. "Where the feck's your coat?"

"It's restricting."

"Like the bra?"

I smiled. "You noticed. Where's *your* coat?"

He pinched his tight T-shirt and gave me a smug look. "It's restricting," he parroted. "Wouldn't want to deny the ladies a glimpse of my chiseled pectorals."

"Exactly what ladies are we talking about?" I gripped the bench when we hit another bump.

He winked. "The ones I'll be seeing after we finish the job. A man needs to unwind."

"A man also needs to trim his nose hairs."

I stifled a laugh when Christian leaned away and subtly pinched his nose. He didn't have any nose hairs that I'd noticed, but nothing pleased me more than pointing out his arrogance by means of finding his insecurities. Our verbal banter had become a form of stress relief, and neither of us ever took it personally.

"Turn that shit off," Shepherd growled toward the front of the van.

Viktor was driving, but Wyatt had dominion over the radio.

"Don't start," Wyatt said. "You know how I feel about Air Supply."

Shepherd rolled his eyes to the chorus of "Making Love Out of Nothing at All."

"You'll get along famously with the man we're hunting," I said. "He loves eighties music."

"I didn't say I liked eighties music," Wyatt countered, leaning around his seat. "Air Supply just speaks to my soul."

"Your soul is dead," Shepherd grumbled.

"Lay off. That's the year I got my first computer. It's nostalgic."

I laughed. "How old are you again?"

Shepherd folded his arms. "He lost his virginity to 'Oh! Susanna.'"

Everyone snickered.

Wyatt stared daggers at him. "Whatever, Dirty Harry. And I wasn't *that* old when I lost it."

"Why is he here?" I whispered to Christian. "I thought Viktor didn't want him coming on dangerous missions."

"We'll need someone in the driver's seat in case we need to make a quick escape. Wyatt's also the liaison who'll contact the Regulators, and that'll depend on what we find."

Shepherd relaxed his posture on the opposite bench, just as cool as a cucumber. Niko possessed a look I'd seen many times in the training room when he was getting into his zone, and Gem was sandwiched between them. I glanced at Blue on my left, who was sending a text message to Claude. He replied back telling her to make sure we females were careful, and that made me chuckle.

Niko drew his hood over his head. "We have a good chance of succeeding. Cristo paid men on the street to take you down. I suspect he operates alone."

"He also likes bombs," I mentioned.

Shepherd crushed his cigarette beneath his boot. "She's right. If he doesn't have anyone there protecting him, he might have laid out some traps. Keep your eyes open. And Gem, stay *inside* the van. Not on top of it."

She launched to her feet. "Stay in the van. Stay in the van. You didn't witness my epic fireworks show earlier. And you shouldn't put your cigarettes out on the carpet!"

"We're going to have to replace the whole damn thing anyhow," he retorted.

"Well, it's a filthy habit and—"

The van shuddered when we hit a bump. Gem fell forward, and Niko swiftly caught her with one arm.

"Careful, braveheart. We need you in one piece." He turned and sat her down in his place before moving up front to speak with Viktor.

"Why am I even here?" she asked herself. "To babysit Wyatt?"

Gem didn't seem to like going on jobs that involved crime scenes and dead bodies, but I found it interesting that she was eager to partake in a raid.

"You are here as protection," Viktor answered from the front. "If he escapes to the street, we need you to track him. You are our eyes and ears."

Gem crossed her legs, satisfied with that responsibility, but I could see she was still on a high after helping us with her energy balls. I surmised that Gem didn't get to practice her wielding ability too often, so I understood the danger if one of us was standing in the line of fire. That made me nervous, especially after seeing how charred those men had been. But having her topside wasn't a bad idea in case Cristo tried to escape. Given his track record, I wouldn't put it past him.

The van finally stopped, and the engine turned off, but the music kept playing—probably to block out some of the conversation still going on up front. Blue scooted all the way down to the rear doors.

When Viktor got out, Wyatt hopped over to the driver's seat.

"Let's roll," Shepherd said, opening the back door and jumping out.

Niko and Blue followed behind him.

As I stood up, Christian caught my wrist. "Are you armed?"

I showed him my new bracelet. "That's some armoire Shepherd has in his bedroom. At what point does a hobby become a fetish?"

"If he starts wearing a leather thong with a concealed dagger, you'll have your answer."

The team was more jittery than usual, and maybe part of that had to do with the fact that we hadn't yet rescued the baby. What would a desperate man be willing to do to escape? My thoughts drifted back to when Darius had thrown that little boy over the ledge so he could flee, and I imagined Cristo was brazen enough to pull a stunt like that.

My boots hit freshly fallen snow as I stepped onto the curb and looked around. The buildings in the immediate area appeared uninhabited and partially demolished, in much worse condition than the other parts of the Bricks I'd seen.

I stepped closer to Viktor. "Are we near his building? I don't think walking out in the open is such a good idea."

"Nyet." He brought us into a huddle. "The address Shepherd provided belongs to a residence underground. Tunnels run below the city, constructed many years ago by Breed who were not given permission to live topside. It is an elaborate maze, and the tunnels lead to underground dwellings. I've been here once before. Do not speak to anyone, and do not let yourselves become distracted."

Shepherd unzipped his jacket and stared at the pothole in the center of our circle. "Are there rats down there? I don't like rats."

Viktor raised the collar of his long grey coat. "Let's not be dramatic. Blend in."

We all exchanged glances. *Blend in with rats?*

One at a time, we descended the iron rungs. Christian was the last one in and moved the cover back in place. I was surprised there were working lights affixed to the walls. This wasn't at all like crawling around in the sewers. The tunnels were tall so that you didn't have to hunch over. There was even a sign on the wall in front of us with arrows pointing both ways, a series of numbers below them.

"This way," Viktor said, leading us to the right. "Spread apart so we don't look suspicious."

I fell back with Christian. "Okay, now this is getting weird."

"You haven't seen anything yet, lass."

Without wind, the temperature underground was tolerable. In front of us, Niko made no attempt to conceal his two katanas beneath his black coat like he usually did. He wore them affixed to his back. Blue kept pace with him, her midnight-blue cloak covering the tops of her tall boots. She'd drawn the hood over her head to conceal her long hair, probably for the best. Christian and I were in the rear, with Viktor and Shepherd up front.

"Did you live down here or topside?" I asked.

Christian glanced behind us before answering. "Both. Neither offered privacy, which is why I have a little house in the woods."

"You mean cellblock eight?" I quipped.

He suddenly grabbed my sleeve and pulled me to a stop. "Keep your eyes low."

"Superstitious immortals?"

"Not just that. In our line of work, you always want to avoid anything that makes you stand out in a crowd. Think about when we first met in the bar and how later it took you a minute to recognize me. People tend to ignore hair and clothing, because those are things you can change. Down here, people pay attention to eyes, tattoos, and scars. If we run into a tangle with any of these shitebags, you don't want them putting a bounty on your head. And a girl with a blue eye and a brown one isn't so hard to find. Make yourself forgettable."

"What about Niko? He's got a distinctive eye color for his race."

"He's also learned a lot in his long life. Notice how he always keeps his eyes low. It's a submissive gesture."

I snorted. "A man with two swords isn't exactly the submissive type."

"Most people arm themselves down here; they'll just assume he carries them for show."

"Maybe I should have worn contacts if it's such a big deal."

"Ever been punched in the eye while wearing a contact lens? There's a reason most of us don't wear those." Christian tucked my necklace beneath my shirt. As if my hair wasn't disheveled enough, he ran his fingers through it and scrunched it up. "Don't smile at anyone."

"Afraid they'll see my fangs?" I punched them out just for effect.

Christian's eyes hooded, and he stepped closer. "And don't do that either."

We stared at each other for a long moment, the air between us a degree warmer.

"Hurry up," Blue shouted.

Christian turned on his heel, and we picked up the pace. When the tunnel branched, we turned right.

"Are there women down here?" I asked.

"Aye. Powerful women. So careful not to start any catfights."

I nudged him. "Don't act like you wouldn't watch."

"Make no mistake, Raven. The Vampires down here kill for sport. You look at someone the wrong way and they'll cut your throat. Not everyone down here is a maniac, but laws don't exist. No one will come to your rescue. Remember that."

We reached the end of the tunnel and entered a wide elevator with a caged wall. Viktor switched a lever, and the mechanical parts slowly began to turn. The wall just outside the rusty bars moved upward, and when it disappeared, I gawked at the view below. It wasn't just a maze of underground tunnels; it was a world. We were in an enormous cavern, stories high, that served as a gateway to numerous tunnels built into the walls. Some were above us and others below. Bridges made from wooden planks and ropes connected a few openings on opposite sides of the massive room. I pressed my forehead against the bars and gaped down at a river.

A Chitah scaled the wall with astonishing grace as he climbed to a higher tunnel. My hair stood on end when a wolf howled, the sound reverberating off the walls around us.

"Careful what you say," Christian murmured. "Vampires down here use information to their advantage." He lifted my chin with the crook of his finger. "Are you listening? Don't get swept away by all this."

The elevator came to a hard stop. I turned around to the opening to see a man lighting a pipe just outside. He ignored us as we circled around to the other side and approached one of those rickety bridges.

A man guarding the bridge held up his hand.

"*Privet.* We are here to see an old friend," Viktor said.

The black-bearded man smiled. "Russian?"

"*Tak tochno.*"

"I thought as much. A fellow countryman."

They immediately conversed in Russian, and I wished Gem were around to fill me in on what they were saying. Viktor showed the man his watch, and they spoke further. It looked like there was some bartering going on, though Viktor had cash in his wallet. Did money not matter in this place?

After Viktor gave him the watch, they shared a laugh, and the man let us pass. I picked my way across one plank at a time—some of them broken—holding on to the ropes for dear life as I stared past the large gaps in the wood. When my foot slipped through a loose board, Christian snaked his arm around my waist.

"I got it," I said, my heart racing. Heights I had no problem with; water was another story.

Niko gripped the ropes, guided by Blue, who was talking him through each and every step.

Once we reached the other side, Viktor and Shepherd led the way through a tunnel carved from natural rock, and we all put distance between us again. Lanterns were affixed to the walls, light flickering on the uneven rock and water dripping from several crevices.

"Do people have jobs down here?" I asked.

Christian tucked his shirt in where it had come out in the front. "Some. The bridge watchers know almost everyone, and they're not too keen on letting strangers pass."

"Well, it looks like all men can be bribed."

"Just be lucky he didn't take a fancy to one of you girls."

I nudged him in the ribs. "Or one of you boys."

"Over my rotting corpse."

After ten minutes, we climbed a short ladder to an upper level. There weren't as many people passing by, and it was eerily dark. This one looked more man-made, judging from the large slabs of stone and rock. When we reached a fork, Viktor gathered us in a tight huddle.

"We separate from here. We must approach him from all sides."

"What's his address?" Christian asked.

Viktor locked eyes with him. "12 U-B."

Christian grimaced and pinched the bridge of his nose. "That's an abandoned section. It's a large amount of space, Viktor. He'll have the advantage if he's set traps. Time to escape. I don't know all the connecting tunnels; hardly anyone goes in there except for the crazies."

I swung my eyes up. "Crazies?"

His black eyes met mine. "Just an affectionate term for Vampires who gave in to their bloodlust. Juicers also like to hide in those spaces, and I don't mean your casual energy sippers, but the ones who'll drain you until your heart stops. It's where the savages go. They hide in the shadows, and no one can catch them."

Niko reached over his shoulders and touched the handles of his katanas. "Then we should divide ourselves by who can see in the dark. Christian, you go with Blue. I'll stay with Viktor, and Raven go with Shepherd."

I wondered at first why Blue and Niko didn't stay paired since they were partners, but Niko could see energy in a way that none of us could, and we needed him to protect our leader.

A candle flickered in the distance.

Viktor lowered his voice. "Does everyone know the way?"

Christian and Shepherd nodded.

"Be careful. Eyes and ears." Viktor and Niko disappeared into the inky shadows of one tunnel.

Christian took Blue's arm and led her to a metal ladder. "This way, lass."

She glared up at the opening. "Are you sure?"

"Have I ever lied to you before?"

She narrowed her eyes. "When you said you didn't wash my red dress with all my whites."

"Okay, *that* wasn't my fault."

After they climbed the ladder and were out of sight, I followed Shepherd down an adjacent tunnel, staying a pace behind and focusing my Vampire eyes on shadowy corners. The smell changed from an earthy scent to stale air and mold. The walls glistened with a clear residue that looked like the slime trails that slugs leave behind. Shepherd stopped at a metal door marked 12. He placed his fingers on the door, tracing them down to the knob.

"Nothing," he said. "You sense anything?"

I shook my head.

"Why does that make me nervous?" He took a deep breath and gripped the handle. "Do me a favor and stand back for a minute."

I stepped aside. To have quick access to my weapons, I removed the button-up shirt I wore over my tank top.

The hinges made a terrible screech as Shepherd pushed open the door. With heart-stopping speed, he suddenly dropped to the ground. I jumped back a step when something whistled by me. A crack sounded, and on the wall opposite the door, a steel arrow had split the stone in two.

Shepherd, still on his back, locked eyes with me. "Booby trap."

I held out my hand and pulled him up. "Maybe you should let me go first since I'm the immortal."

He wiped the sweat off his brow. "This place is a deathtrap. Watch out for floor levers. The firing mechanisms might release anything from a landmine to an arrow."

I peered inside to see what he'd stepped on, and all it looked like was a broken section in the cement floor. The expansive room had pillars, and pieces of rubble were piled in places where the ceiling or walls had partially collapsed.

Shepherd moved stealthily, a serrated knife in his hand. His leather jacket not only held weapons but offered some measure of protection against knife attacks. We veered farther right before he began walking a straight line. A broken wall beside us revealed another room, but it was small, and after poking our heads in, we continued toward the back where the tunnel light couldn't reach.

My Vampire eyes didn't work as well as a pureblood's, but I could see just enough to keep from falling. I noticed Shepherd struggling in the dark, his hand extended, so I stepped in front of him as a guide. He pinched a loop on the back of my jeans and followed my lead.

I came to a stop.

"What's wrong?" he asked.

"I don't know," I said, staring at the floor ahead of me. "I thought I saw something."

"What did it look like?"

I backed up a step and crouched before standing up again. "Like a straight line that goes across the room."

"This is a clusterfuck," he muttered. "Does it look like a trip wire?"

"I don't know, Shepherd. I've never seen a trip wire before."

"Don't be a smartass. How high is it?"

"Oh, about to my waist."

"We'll crawl."

Shepherd got down on his hands and knees, putting the blade between his teeth as he flattened himself out and propped himself up on his elbows.

I knelt to do the same thing but suddenly grabbed his belt. "Stop!"

He froze.

When I got a little lower, I saw it. "There's another one close to the ground. We can't crawl."

On his elbows still, he scooted himself backward and stood up. "I'm guessing this isn't the way he comes in every day. Does it go all the way across the room?"

I leaned back and squinted. "Looks like it."

"Anything we can stand on to jump over?"

"Nope."

"Lead me to the wall on the right."

We walked a short distance and stopped.

"Is the floor clear of debris?" he asked.

"Yes."

He felt the wall all the way down to the floor. "Anything on the other side… like a pillar?"

"No."

He continued, his questions rapid-fire. "Any holes in the floor?"

"Exactly what's your plan?"

"Lead me a foot from the wires."

I did as he asked, convinced we would be forced to retreat and search for another way inside.

Shepherd locked his fingers together and bent over. "Put your foot in there. I'm going to hoist you over."

Without questioning his plan, I put my foot in his makeshift stirrup and flattened my hands on his shoulders.

His body tensed. "Are you ready? One… two… Geronimo!"

Shepherd lifted his arms, and I sailed over the wires and slammed against the concrete with a thud.

I wiped the dirt off my face and sat up. "Geronimo? Whatever happened to three?" After giving the room a quick scan, I stood up and rubbed my sore shoulder. "And how the hell are *you* getting over here?"

Shepherd placed both hands on the wall and then took large strides backward at an angle. "On a wing and a prayer." He slid his knife across the floor, and it skidded past me.

My eyes widened when he charged toward the wall. Once his hand made contact, his legs rotated as if he were doing a cartwheel. Shepherd spun right over the wire, defying gravity as he hit the ground and rolled to safety.

I stared down at him in disbelief. "You are one crazy-ass Sensor with a death wish."

Without a word, he found his knife and stood up. We continued at a slower pace so I could focus on possible traps. When we reached the far end, I slowed down.

"Door," I whispered, wondering what this place had originally been used for.

"How many?"

I examined the long wall in front of us. "Just one."

He cursed under his breath and moved around me. "How much can you see?"

"Very little. It's too grainy, and I can only make out shapes."

Shepherd inspected the door, pushing his fingers beneath

the crack at the bottom and feeling all around. "Well, here goes nothing." With a hard jerk, he shoved the door open and flew back.

We both stood with our backs against the wall, waiting for something to blow up or fire at us.

Nothing.

"What if it's a room full of spiders?" I said quietly.

"You're not helping."

I peered inside and then took his arm. "It's clear." The moment I stepped inside, I felt myself falling.

Shepherd caught my arm at the elbow, and I almost slipped through his fingers. With my legs suspended in midair, I stared down and into the abyss. It was a hole in the floor, and God only knows how far it went.

"Pull me up!" I shrieked. "Back away!"

He stumbled backward and dragged me to safety. "What the hell?"

I panted hard, my arms now wrapped around his thigh. "There's no floor. It's a big hole."

"Why don't you unglue yourself from my crotch and I'll check it out."

I crawled to safety and then stood up. Meanwhile, Shepherd lifted a rock and tossed it into the hole. When it never hit the bottom, I shuddered.

He kept tossing pebbles all around until they tapped on the concrete. Finally, he tucked his knife back in its sheath. "Five feet."

"Don't bother locking your fingers together. I'm not jumping over that hole. We should head back and follow behind Viktor."

"Son of a bitch. If the door opened the other way, I'd take it off the hinges and throw it over the hole."

That was an interesting idea, assuming he had a screwdriver on him.

He tossed more pebbles to the left and right. "Looks like it's only in front of the doorway." Shepherd gripped the top of the door with his left hand, held the knob, and then kicked off so it swung inward with him hanging on.

I poked my head through the opening and watched him drop safely to the floor on the far left.

"You're next," he said.

"Wait a second. You spend all day doing pull-ups. And besides, I can't reach the top of the door."

He stood up and dusted off his pants. "Improvise."

My jaw set as the door swung toward me. "Improvise, he says. Fall into a bottomless hole that goes straight to hell. It's probably filled with spiders. Sounds like a plan."

"Will you quit talking about spiders? You're going to give me fucking nightmares."

Tempted to jump to reach the top of the door and hang on, I opted against it. No sense in accidentally falling into a portal to hell. Could I jump the distance? And if so, was the ground on the other side stable? It wasn't worth the risk.

So, as Shepherd suggested, I improvised. I squatted down and grabbed the doorknob on each side with both hands. Once I had a firm grip, I clamped my thighs shut with the edge of the door between them and kicked off, the door swinging in his direction.

"Catch me!" My eyes widened in horror when Shepherd blindly waved his arms, assuming I was higher up.

"Down here!" I squeaked.

He quickly reached down, hooked his hands beneath my arms, and hauled me to safety.

Instant relief came over me, but it didn't last long. I stood up and looked around. "Let's go. I can see something up ahead."

At the far end of the room, which was similar to the last, was a slice of light that could only be coming from the bottom of a closed door.

An explosion rocked in the distance, shaking the ground beneath our feet. Dirt and small bits from the ceiling sifted down, and I covered my mouth.

Once there was enough light to see, we finally stopped by a spray-painted pillar. "What now?" I asked quietly.

He wiped the sweat from his brow. By the way his eyes shifted around, it looked like he could see a little as well. "Let me take over from here."

"You can't go in there alone, and I didn't come all this way to wait outside." My breath caught when a shadow moved behind him.

Shepherd didn't speak. He studied my face and mouthed, "Mage?"

I shook my head. No energy licked against my skin, and I couldn't even sense the presence of a non-Mage, which left only one possibility.

Vampire.

Maybe Shepherd had deduced the same, because he retrieved an impalement stake from inside his jacket. It had what looked like a metal weight in the center. He gripped his fingers around that metal and held it like a spear. Instead of turning to look, he watched my eyes.

I studied the darkness, making small talk. "Maybe we should knock on the door and see if he answers."

"Yeah. Sounds like a plan," Shepherd said flatly, still focused on my eyes.

I caught a shadow to the left and flicked my eyes in that direction. With lightning speed, Shepherd spun around and threw the stake. It whistled through the air before striking the shadow.

I flashed over and flipped the man onto his back. Even though my fangs had appeared, I was reluctant to bite a Vampire without knowing the effect his blood would have on me. The stake had punctured his chest, and I shoved it in farther for peace of mind. Then I searched his pockets for weapons or...

"Keys," I whispered.

"Give 'em here."

Shepherd briefly inspected them before silently approaching the door. He knelt down, peered beneath the crack, and then touched the knob for a moment.

"It's clear," he said, testing the key in the locks. "That must be one of his guards. Pussies always hire Vampires to do all their dirty work. I don't think there'll be any traps inside unless they're alarms. Think fast and move fast. Got it?"

As soon as the door opened, fluorescent light pierced my eyes. It looked like a small security room for lazy guards. To the right, a red chair and ottoman. Magazines were scattered all over the floor, and someone had tossed an empty bag of potato chips in the corner.

Shepherd freed two knives from their sheaths and twirled them in his hands. "Get ready to move fast."

We neared the door directly in front of us. When I turned the handle, we rushed inside a long hallway. Passing a few vacant rooms, I ran as far as it went. Energy spiked against my skin, and I heard the unmistakable sound of swords clashing. The end of the hall diverged, so I followed the sounds and flashed to the right. Having left Shepherd behind, I burst into a dark room lit by computer screens. Niko was in a clinch with a man whose sword was impressively long.

"Other room," Niko grunted. "I have this." He shoved the man off-balance before hopping back and putting distance between them.

Disregarding the two men, Shepherd plowed right past me and through an open door on the opposite side of the room. When Niko advanced on his attacker, they engaged in one hell of a swordfight. I wanted to sit and watch, but instead I flashed to the other side to avoid getting sliced in two.

I ended up in a hall and followed the sound of Shepherd's heavy footfalls going left. The hallways were reminiscent of an ancient prison, complete with decrepit walls, pipes running along them, and dirty floors. The only modern thing was the overhead lights. The temperature was noticeably warmer.

I slowed my pace when a loud commotion sounded from a room Shepherd had entered.

On the floor, Christian was straddling Cristo, his hand firmly wrapped around the Mage's throat. "Where is the baby?" His eyes never left Cristo's for a moment.

"Safe," Cristo replied tersely.

Viktor encroached on them, a streak of blood across his face and his clothes ragged and torn. There weren't overhead lights in this room, just a pool table and lanterns on the walls.

Shepherd loomed over the man, his knives in hand with the pointy tips tapping impatiently against his thighs.

Blue appeared in the doorway, out of breath. The hood of her cloak had fallen away from her head. "He's not here. I checked all the rooms."

I pointed at Cristo.

"No. I meant the baby."

"Are there any more goons?" I asked.

She shook her head, eyes on Christian. "Niko's taking care of the only guard we found inside."

"There might be more outside. We ran into a Vamp."

She nodded. "Us too. Vampire guards are popular since they're mostly undetectable. That's why I brought these." She opened her cloak. In addition to her tomahawk were two impalement stakes, but all I noticed was the blood dripping down the handle of her axe.

"Where's the baby?" Christian pressed.

"Safe," Cristo replied.

"Safe where?"

"Safe."

Shepherd removed his leather jacket and it dropped to the floor. "Let me ask him. I promise I'll be nice."

Niko came up beside Blue, his hair askew and swords back in their scabbards.

"Where the hell is the baby?" Christian growled.

"Safe," Cristo repeated.

"Why is it not working?" Viktor asked. "Is he a Blocker?"

Blue drifted into the room and stood beside Viktor. "I think he means a safe. Ask him."

Christian leaned in so tight their noses touched. "Is the baby inside of a safe?"

"Yes."

"Oh, for feck's sake, why didn't you just say so, you poor excuse for a spark plug?"

I turned to Niko. "Can you see the baby's energy?"

He entered the room and scanned it. "Not behind walls."

Christian slapped the Mage. "Where's the safe?"

"Upstairs."

"What's the code to open it?"

"Six one six, nine five nine."

Christian stood up and kicked him hard. "There's a special jail cell for men like you. One with hungry rats and broken toilets."

Cristo coughed and rolled to his side. "No jail can hold me."

Shepherd slowly circled around him and knelt down.

Cristo glared up at him, his nose bloodied. "What the fuck are you looking at?"

Shepherd tapped the tip of his blade against his own chin. "Remember me?"

"I don't know you."

"But I know *you*." Shepherd held out his arms to show him the scars and then sliced open the front of his shirt, revealing more.

"Is that supposed to mean something?" Cristo, still lying on his side, stared daggers at him.

Shepherd gave him a mirthless smile. "Five years ago, an acquaintance of yours tried to stab me to death while you murdered a woman in her own bed."

Recognition sparked in Cristo's eyes. "Oh, yeah. That was back when I ran with a partner. I knew he should have cut off your head."

"Your buddy cried like a baby when I killed him."

Cristo rolled onto his back and gave him a crooked smile, blood smeared across his face from a broken nose. "That was years ago when I was new at the game. Taking on a partner was a mistake, so you did me a favor. We could tell you weren't a Mage or Vampire, but he should have taken your head anyway. Joe was always sloppy. Sorry bastard almost got me killed."

With lightning speed, Shepherd stabbed Cristo through the palm, pinning his hand to the floor. Cristo bellowed in pain, and before he could even think about blasting Shepherd with his free hand, I flashed over and stepped on it.

Shepherd twisted the knife slowly. "You killed my woman. You killed my future. And you killed… my… baby."

A slow chuckle rose in Cristo's chest until he rocked with laughter.

Shepherd wrenched the knife free and chopped off Cristo's fingers. The Mage's green eyes bulged, and he clutched his bleeding hand to his chest.

Shepherd held the blade against Cristo's neck, and a rivulet of blood trickled out. "You held its lifeless body by the leg as if it were nothing but garbage! I've waited for this moment for years, but before I make you suffer, I want to know why."

Cristo stared at the ceiling, his eyes watery and bloodshot from the pain he must have felt in his hand. Yet despite his obvious agony, he looked at Shepherd with amusement. "You really don't get it, do you? Why would I kill a baby? They're worth more alive than dead."

Shepherd blanched, and I stepped on Cristo's hand even harder until he whimpered and tried to jerk it free.

"Do you think that was my first cesarean?" he continued. "That's not how I run my business anymore; it was too messy. But I can bring a baby into this world better than any Relic can. I remember that job. Accidentally cut his face when my knife went in. Thought I killed it. I only got paid half for damaging the merchandise."

Cristo continued laughing maniacally, and I stepped on his hand even harder until I felt the bones crack beneath my boot.

"Fucking bitch," he snarled.

Incensed, I fell on top of him and clasped my hands over his. With every ounce of power I had within me, I drew out his core light. It happened so fast that his eyes widened with shock. With the last drop, a white flash pulsed between our hands, followed by an audible snap.

"Give it back!" he shouted, realizing I'd stolen his immortality. "Give it back!"

His filthy light coursed through my body like a plague, and I instantly wanted to vomit. Instead, I stood up and wiped the blood off my hand.

"It's not so funny when someone takes something from *you*, is it?"

With Cristo now a human and easier to subdue, Viktor led everyone out. Shepherd, however, stayed behind with the ex-Mage. When Viktor closed the door, he stood with his back to it, arms folded as a scream erupted from inside the room.

Not the scream of certain death. The scream of horrors untold.

Chapter 22

I FOLLOWED BLUE AND CHRISTIAN DOWN a narrow hall. Niko remained with Viktor to gather evidence while we searched for the baby.

Christian stopped beneath a metal ladder that went through a round hole in the ceiling. Blue went first. I followed close behind and, once I reached the top, looked around at a kitchen with stainless-steel appliances.

"Who pays the electric bill?" I wondered aloud, not even certain how they managed to get electricity down here.

Christian emerged and stepped off the ladder. "Lucifer. Now let's get to work. There are only three rooms up here. A bedroom, kitchen, and a study. I can't hear anything, so I'll check in here while you two figure out the rest." He turned on his heel and began pulling at cabinets.

Blue gave me a curt nod. "Let's go." She cruised through the study and went straight into the bedroom. The doorways all faced each other, so you could walk straight through each room.

I entered the study, which had books filling the built-in shelves, and headed toward the wall on the right. I didn't know what a hidden safe looked like, but I remembered the one at Darius's home and what had triggered it to open. Books flew off the shelves as I littered the floor with the classics. None of the shelves or lower cabinets activated a secret door when I pushed and pulled on them, though I still wasn't certain if the safe was a room or an actual safe. I ripped the TV out of its cubby and smashed it on the floor.

"In here!" Blue shouted. "Hurry!"

I raced into the room and gripped a wooden post on Cristo's four-poster bed. He had some nerve tucking himself away in a room surrounded by wood paneling, gaudy paintings, satin sheets, and a liquor cabinet. Meanwhile, children were ripped away from their mothers and sold as slaves—all so this man could have a flat-screen TV. Where had all the money gone from his crimes? Had he blown it on vacations and prostitutes? Truth be told, I didn't care. I'd tracked down criminals for years, and most of them either hoarded their money or wasted it on expensive restaurants and extravagant cars.

Blue yanked on a brass picture frame to the left of the bed. "Nobody bolts an ugly painting of a bridge to a wall. He doesn't have any other paintings in the house but in here. Can you help me?"

When she dragged the nightstand away, the table lamp fell to the floor.

"Try pushing on it," I said. "It's probably a simple trick."

Christian walked into the room, his stride purposeful. "Let me have a look." He gripped the frame and effortlessly flung it across the room.

"Show-off," I muttered.

We stared at a keypad on the wall, a handle to the right of it.

Blue swept her hair back and leaned in. "Six one six, nine five nine."

Christian took his time pressing each number carefully. When finished, three beeps sounded, and a mechanism clicked behind the wall.

"That was too easy," he muttered.

When the door opened, we slowly walked inside. A battery-operated lantern hung from a hook by the entrance, casting light on the mint-green walls and mahogany floor. To the left, a single-size bed and white blanket. Across from the door, a toy box overflowing with dollies, blankets, and stuffed animals. Crayons and drawings were scattered on the child-size table in the corner—the ghostly remnants of children.

Blue hurried to the crib on the right and peered in. I watched with bated breath as she bent over and reached inside. A foul stench burned my nose from the open trash can to the right, dirty diapers wide open inside. No wonder he'd hired someone to watch the children. He was completely incapable of caring for another individual. Just knowing he'd shut up some kids in here—no toilet or fresh air to breathe—made me want to haul ass back to that room and drive a dagger through his mortal heart.

Blue turned around, angry tears glittering in her sapphire eyes. She cradled the baby in her arms and gently rocked him as he stared listlessly. His dark golden skin lacked a healthy glow, and the only thing he had on was a baggy diaper.

"The mattress is soaking wet," she said, her jaw clenched. "I bet he's been crying for hours in here… all alone."

The little guy made a dramatic grimace and began to wail. It broke my heart because I knew he was crying for his mother. Blue set him down on the bed and found a clean diaper.

The safe room was essentially a prison cell. Cristo must have used this room as a temporary holding tank until his female friend took the children off his hands.

Christian tapped his finger against the wall. "He soundproofed the walls."

My eyes fell to the handle on the door. "Christian, why is there a keypad on the inside?"

"Perhaps he was afraid one of the children would shut him in."

"The handle's too high for a child to reach."

"You're going to be fine," Blue said, her voice motherly and soothing. "Shh, shh. Everything's all better now."

The keypad suddenly began beeping, and a red light flashed. Christian stepped out of the room and punched a series of numbers. When the beeps drew closer together until they were a flutter of sound, a chill ran up my spine.

The lights in the building shut off. Seconds later, red lights popped on in each room.

Blue stood up with the baby in her arms. "What's happening?"

"Feck me," Christian growled. "Get out!"

Blue went out first. As I followed behind her, I noticed the panel above the keypad had digital numbers that were changing.

"What the hell is that?"

His nostrils flared. "A countdown."

According to the numbers, we had less than five minutes to escape.

As they ran through the study, I pulled out my phone.

"Raven!" Christian's black silhouette turned in my direction.

Viktor needed to know what was happening, and I didn't have time to send a text to the team. I called him, and he answered immediately. "It's a bomb, Viktor! We have four minutes before this place blows up. Get everyone out!"

My heart raced as I jogged toward Christian. Instead of descending the ladder, he opened a heavy door to the left, revealing an outside tunnel.

The baby screeched as Blue jostled him with each step. She cradled his head to reduce the bouncing, and when we reached the end of the hall, she stopped and tucked him inside her coat.

"Be quiet, sweet baby," she said, putting a pacifier into his mouth.

"Is this how you guys came in? Are there any traps?" I asked Christian.

He pulled the collar of his shirt aside and showed me a stain of blood on his chest, the wound healed. "I took one for the team. Left is a dead end. To the right is an open room, but it's black as night."

"Sounds familiar. Any pillars?"

"None straight ahead. But there's an opening in the floor in two places. Traps to the left and right, so we'll have to jump over the holes."

I swallowed hard. "How far of a jump?"

"Christian, I can't jump with the baby," Blue said. "It was hard enough by myself."

He reached out. "Give him to me."

She recoiled.

"For feck's sake, I'm not going to drop him."

When Christian collected the baby in his strong arms, my nonfunctioning ovaries sprang to life. He held the infant as if he'd held one a million times. When he brushed his thumb tenderly across the little guy's cheek, that protective image made my heart clench.

"I'll go first," he said. "Follow behind me, and keep running until I say otherwise."

We followed his lead, and the heavy door behind us eventually closed, immersing us in darkness. I could vaguely make out the grainy image of his shape in front of me.

"Stop!" he shouted, and then silence when he jumped. Christian landed with ease, the soles of his shoes sliding across the dirty floor only a fraction. "It's fifteen feet in front of you. There are traps on either side, so there's no way around it. Raven, you go first."

The hole in the floor looked like an inky pool of water.

"Time's ticking, lass."

I pushed down my fears and ran to the edge before jumping. I was suspended in the air for only a second or two before my boots hit the ground and I rolled over my shoulder.

"Tell me when," Blue said. She surged forward, her cloak flapping behind her.

"Jump!" Christian shouted.

She sailed over the hole, and when she landed on the other side, she stumbled and fell flat on her face. "Thank the fates," she breathed.

"Maybe you should shift and fly over the holes," I suggested.

She rose to her feet, her eyes wide in the darkness. "I don't shift until I have to. The tunnels are too dangerous, and I could be captured."

We continued running until Christian shouted out again, signaling the next hole. This time when Christian vaulted over the hole, the baby wailed, his voice raspy. It was a terrible sound—one of fear. Christian clutched him to his chest, cradling his head with one hand.

"Are you sure there isn't another way?" I asked, looking left and right. The rest of the room appeared passable.

"I can see better in the dark than you can. Trip wires everywhere." As he spoke, he swayed his body to calm the baby.

I made it safely across, though my nerves were even more rattled than the last time. Blue began her attempt, and when she jumped, it was a foot too soon. I could already see she wasn't going to make it. She hit the edge of the floor with her chest and clawed desperately as she began slipping into the hole. Though her animal was a bird, Blue's falcon wouldn't be able to fly in the dark.

I reached behind her arms and pulled as hard as I could, but the floor had no traction, and my shoes slid across slippery dust. "Christian, I can't hold her!"

He walked up and bent over, the baby cradled in his left arm. "Take my hand."

A worried look crossed her face.

"We don't have time to argue," he said. "You're not going to fall."

As soon as she reached out with her left hand, she slipped. Christian caught her wrist just as I lost my grip, and Blue dangled over the abyss. Her eyes grew wide, legs kicking at the void.

He lifted his arm up and stepped back until she was on solid ground again.

I'd seen Christian display his strength numerous times, but it never ceased to amaze me how effortless it was for him, especially with a baby in his arms. Though I didn't care for my Vampire nature, a small part of me envied him for those gifts. Why couldn't I have been given what all Vampires had when it came to strength and perfect sight?

Blue collected the infant and quickly wrapped her cloak around her body to conceal him.

"Hurry! We don't have much time." Christian shadow walked out of sight.

I flashed forward and suddenly slammed on the brakes when a door came into sight. While he held it open, I peered into an empty hallway. There were dim lanterns along the rock walls and puddles of water on the floor.

Blue finally caught up and positioned herself between us, Christian in the lead. We had an unspoken plan to protect the person carrying the baby.

A rumble sounded, followed by a loud explosion.

The bomb.

My eyes widened when I looked back. A fireball erupted from the doorway, heading straight for us.

"Run!" I shouted, fire licking at my heels.

We took a sharp right into another hallway, and the flames roared past us and quickly dissipated.

I reached for my phone.

Christian turned on his heel and kept going. "We don't have time. There's an elevator up ahead."

My phone suddenly rang, and I fumbled with it while jogging. "Yeah?"

"It's Niko. I've fallen out of touch with Viktor. Where are you?"

"In the tunnels," I panted. "We've got the baby, and we're heading to the elevators."

"Single body?" he asked.

"Huh?"

"Tell him yes," Christian shouted from up ahead.

"Yes."

"Who has the baby?"

"Blue."

"It'll take me time to get out. I'll call Wyatt and tell him the exit location has changed."

"Do you know where we are? *I* don't even know where we are." I slowed down when Christian stopped in front of a metal box affixed to the wall.

"I rarely get lost. See you soon."

I gaped at the narrowest door I'd ever seen. It was rusty and had no knob. "What the hell is that?"

Christian knocked his knuckles against it. "The elevator. Most prefer not to take it for the obvious reason."

"And what reason is that?"

When the metal panel opened, I stared inside at a small cylinder just big enough for one person.

"Single body," he said as Blue stepped inside. When he pushed a button, the door closed. "Someone built it a few years ago as an emergency escape."

I laughed. "A skinny woman?"

Christian folded his arms. "Perhaps. You won't find Shepherd squeezing himself in there. The ascent is slow, and there aren't any lights."

I bent over, hands on my knees as I took a moment to catch my breath. Sucking out Cristo's dark energy was the worst decision, but I also had no idea we'd be dodging more traps and running for our lives. A cold sweat came over me as that murky light mixed with my own. "I think I'm going to be sick."

"Why did you do that back there? Pop his cork and render him human."

"I was afraid Viktor was going to stop Shepherd," I admitted. "Who's to say if Cristo would have gotten the death penalty? They don't keep people locked away for all eternity. Maybe I didn't want to give him the opportunity of a possible parole in five hundred years. I'd rather he grow old behind bars and wither away until nothing remains but a dried-up husk of a man, but maybe cutting off his head is the better idea."

Christian's eyebrow arched. "I think it's safe to say you won't be winning any congeniality awards this year."

"Bummer."

His eyes flicked behind me. "Trouble's coming. They must have heard the explosion."

"Who?"

He gripped the back of my neck and led me away. "Men who don't like trouble in their territory."

"How many?" I asked, looking back at the empty hall.

He quickened his pace, his hand still behind my neck. "More than three."

"What Breed?"

"Definitely not Mage, or they'd be flashing."

The tramping sound of footsteps sent chills up my spine, and when I glanced over my shoulder, five men were barreling toward us. They looked as if they'd lived their entire lives underground. Their alabaster skin made their black eyes appear demonic, and every one of them had ebony hair.

"*Jaysus wept.* Vampires. The lot of them. *Run!*"

I flashed and left Christian in the dust. Maybe he could fight off Vamps, but I sure as hell couldn't. They didn't react to Mage energy, and I didn't have any impalement stakes on me. When I reached an intersecting tunnel, I stopped, uncertain of which way to go.

"Left!" Christian shouted, his fists pumping hard as he gathered speed behind me. His lips peeled back, his expression fierce.

I flashed to the left, but as the crowd thickened, I had to weave around them and run normal speed. Despite how sick it made me feel, Cristo's light had given me a boost of extra energy that I might not have had otherwise.

The hall widened, and I skidded to a stop in front of a vendor with a rock display on his table.

"Care for a trade?" the old man asked. "Every stone has a power."

I laughed in disbelief, still out of breath. "Got any fireballs in there?"

"Trade me that pretty necklace, and you can have anything you want."

I glanced down and tucked my pendant back inside my tank top. "Not for sale. Sorry, I don't have any money."

Christian finally came into view at the far end of the tunnel, as did the men chasing behind him.

The old man leaned over to follow the direction of my gaze. "Looks like you need some Vampire repellent."

I snorted. "Does that come in a spray bottle?"

He held up a round stone the size of a grapefruit. "This will solve all your problems. Those are some nice shoes. Yes, yes they are."

I glanced down at my lace-up boots.

"You don't have much time," he said. "I bet you can run just as fast without those shoes, little Mage. I'm not so sure about your friend. This stone is guaranteed to fight off Vampires. *Guaranteed.* Yes, indeed."

I flicked my eyes at him and then bent down. "I can't believe I'm doing this," I muttered while unlacing my boots. I could almost hear Christian mocking me. But hey, I had enough money to buy a new pair of shoes, and this old man in his raggedy clothes could probably use some business.

I tossed them onto the table. "What do I do with it?"

He carefully set the stone in my hands. "Throw it at them. Careful not to drop it."

My jaw set. "I gave you my boots so I could throw a rock?"

He lifted my shoes and cackled as he set them into a cardboard box and sang, "Fair and square. Fair and square. The boots are mine, and they're in there."

I stared down at my socks. This just added a new level of fuckery to the situation. Stone in hand, I turned on my heel and flashed until I reached another intersection.

People were staring, genuinely intrigued. I could hear Christian's words in my head, reminding me to blend in and avoid eye contact. Strangers moved around me, scrutinizing me with their gaze.

Christian passed the old man and glanced at him before finally reaching me and skidding to a stop.

"Now which way?" I asked.

He glared at my rock, and I could hear the profanities firing off in his head. But all he said was, "This way."

I ran at normal speed as we cleared from the crowd and descended a spiral staircase. My blood ran cold at the idea of Vampires tearing me apart, limb from limb.

Christian smashed in a door without wasting time to open it. He sprinted down a dark hall that traveled in a continual curve to the right.

My lungs were on fire, and even after flashing ahead of him, I needed to stop and breathe. "I can't keep going."

He raked his fingers through his hair from back to front. "I can't fight off all of them. Maybe three, but *not* five."

"Pussy."

His eyes narrowed. "And what are you going to do? Throw a rock? I can't believe you fell for a hustler."

"Have a little faith. Maybe there's something to it."

"I bet he has a penthouse suite somewhere in here. You're so gullible."

Vampires appeared, coming at us like a plague of demons. I shoved the stone at Christian since he was stronger. "Throw it!"

He swung his arm back like a baseball pitcher and hurled it at them. It rolled across the floor before coming to a stop.

"Brilliant," he said tersely.

The men didn't break stride, but just as soon as they reached the stone, it exploded.

Christian and I fell to the floor as the air whistled around us, pinging off the walls.

When I sat up, all five of the Vampires were immobile on the floor. There was nothing left of the rock but a pile of pebbles and a small plume of smoke.

I spied a tiny spike of wood on the ground next to me and pinched it between two fingers. It was larger than a toothpick and looked like the same wood used for impalement stakes. The size of the wood didn't matter much, but people preferred larger pieces. If you're going to get close to a Vampire, you don't want your stick snapping in two as soon as it hits their jacket.

I stood up, and that was when I saw those wooden splinters all over the place, some of them sticking out of the men's heads, arms, and backs.

Next to me, Christian was lying facedown. I nudged him with my foot. "It's over. Get up."

My eyes traveled down his body until they stopped at a cluster of sticks in his ass. I laughed and knelt down, giving his backside a nice little pat with my hand. "I always knew I was a pain in your ass." One at a time, I plucked them free.

Christian rolled over to all fours and stood up. While stroking his beard, he studied the fallen men. "Okay. I was wrong, you were right. Let's not speak of this again."

"Maybe we should go back and buy something else. I could use a pet rock."

"I'm sorry to inform you that we're running for our lives and don't have time to do any Christmas shopping."

"I can make time," I quipped, holding a wooden stick between my fingers. "Is this really all it takes?"

"Some wood works better than others. The smaller ones are useless unless there are a lot of them or they go deep. Good luck if they can get someone to retrieve those sticks from inside their body."

There was a gruesome thought.

A man strode toward us from up ahead, followed by another. He looked down at the fallen Vampires and then swung his gaze up, fists clenched.

When he bared his fangs, I damn near tripped over my own feet as I spun around and took off.

Christian jogged past me. "You ever watch those animal kingdom shows about the lions chasing prey?"

I kept running, my heart pounding against my chest like a drum.

"We're the gazelle," he said, huffing as we weaved around people in a crowded tunnel. "Sometimes predators don't need a reason. They just want to chase."

"So this is for fun?" I glanced over my shoulder at the two men not far behind. "Why don't we just kick some ass?"

"Rule number one: Always know when you're outnumbered."

I glanced over my shoulder again. "But there are only two."

"Not down here, lass. They multiply like chicken pox."

When we reached the rickety bridge, I grabbed the ropes and scuttled across the planks.

"Faster," he shouted from behind.

I hopped over a hole. *Faster, my ass.*

Halfway across, I slowed down at the sight of three men guarding the other side. Maybe they were waiting to cross, but their black eyes and hair made me turn around. The two men behind us were blocking the other end of the bridge, and one of them made a slicing motion with his hand across his neck. He looked to his buddy on the other side and gave him a curt nod.

"Hurry up!" Christian snarled.

I gave him a grievous stare. "I don't think we're going anywhere."

He looked both ways, and the gravity of our situation sank in. In a quiet voice, he asked, "Do you trust me?"

I frowned when he took my hand. Christian gestured toward the water below, and I vehemently shook my head. "I *can't*."

"We have no choice."

"I'm not a good swimmer."

A smile touched his lips. "It's not as if you'll drown."

I tried to pull my hand away, but his grip shackled me to him. "I played in the kiddie pool as a child, Christian. I can't swim for real."

He peered at the river below. "I was never a fan of heights, but sometimes you have to tell your fears to piss off. Hold my hand, Raven. I won't let you go."

"Do you promise?"

He lifted my chin with the crook of his finger. "My word is my bond."

The bridge rocked when the Vampires descended upon us from both sides.

"Turn around," he instructed. "Put your back to the rope."

I gripped his hand tightly when I realized we were about to flip ourselves backward over a suspension bridge. "I can't—"

Before I finished the sentence, he leaned back and took me with him. The world turned upside down as we plummeted toward the river below.

With my heart in my throat, I tightened my grip on his hand, the rush of wind blowing my hair in front of my face.

Our feet hit the water with an explosion of sound, quickly

followed by the muted roar of the river. In seconds, my entire body was encapsulated in ice water. The world of air and sky vanished, and the depths were infinite, black, and cold.

Still holding Christian's hand, I opened my eyes. His hair floated angelically around his head, and his features were softer. A few bubbles came out of his nose as he guided my hand to his belt. When I latched on, he turned around and swam.

We remained underwater, and I tried kicking my feet to propel us even faster. I didn't know if those men were following, and I also didn't know what kind of Breed lived on the banks of an underground river.

The light dimmed as we distanced ourselves from the bridge. When my lungs began to hurt, I released small breaths to relieve the pressure, but it only worsened. Finally, the need to breathe gripped me like nothing else. I let go of him and panicked.

Christian appeared and cradled my head in his hands. Seconds away from gulping in air, I signaled him with my eyes that I couldn't go on.

He suddenly put his mouth on mine, and my lungs filled with sweet oxygen.

I stared at him in disbelief as the water held us in suspension. He drew back and nodded as if to ask if I was okay. I nodded back.

Christian turned, and I gripped his belt as he swam hard, never tiring or slowing down. Determined to overcome my fear, I let go with one arm and mirrored his moves. Maybe an immortal couldn't die from drowning, but I was certain I'd fall unconscious, and then I'd be nothing but dead weight.

Christian swam upward, and when I hit the surface, I gasped for air. I accidentally inhaled water and went into a coughing fit. His hand came about my waist, and we treaded water. Maybe I was going into hypothermia, because I wasn't as cold as when we'd first jumped in.

I held onto his neck and looked around at the tunnel. It had a cavernous look, minus the high ceilings. "Please tell me this isn't the sewer."

When we reached shore, he pushed me out of the water. I

rolled onto my back, heavy with exhaustion. Every breath felt like fire in my lungs, and Cristo's light slithered its way through my body like a parasite.

"Are they following us?" I asked between coughs.

"No," he said, still in the water. "They probably didn't want to get their hair wet."

"How did you do that trick with your breath?"

He climbed up next to me, his wet hair dripping down his face. "A Vampire can do a great many things." He looked over his shoulder. "We're safe now."

I sat up and squeezed out the ends of my wet hair. "Do you think those men we took out were their friends? They looked like they were part of some gothic Vampire club. Only black-haired douchebags need apply."

He chuckled softly and stood up. "Perhaps *you* should have applied."

I took his hand, a little unsteady on my feet. "You're not my friend anymore."

"I'll remember that next time you're hanging on to my crotch for dear life. Let's get out of here before they change their minds."

I dragged my feet, one of my socks missing and the other flopping around. I reached down and tossed it into the water. "I always thought underground rivers were something in the movies."

"Where do you think spring water comes from? Subterranean rivers are a real thing, Raven. The world is bigger than you imagine it to be."

I shivered. "So I'm learning."

We continued at a sedate pace, Christian impervious to the biting chill. His teeth weren't chattering like mine were, and he made no effort to squeeze the ends of his drenched T-shirt. The walkway bordered one side of the river, and the light in the distance glittered off the murky water like fireflies in the dark.

Christian slicked his hair back. "In Xanadu did Kubla Khan, a stately pleasure-dome decree: Where Alph, the sacred river, ran through caverns measureless to man, down to a sunless sea."

"That's pretty. What's it from?"

"Samuel Taylor Coleridge. Jaysus, didn't your schools teach literature?"

"We read Shakespeare and learned the anatomy of oysters. I guess it wasn't in the budget. Do you think he was talking about this place?"

Christian wiped the droplets of water off his beard. "He wrote it while high on opium. Chances are slim to none."

I touched my chest, relieved my necklace hadn't fallen off. "Can we sit down? Just for a minute?"

He looked in both directions. "Aye. Just for a moment." Christian led me to a stone slab within a recessed wall.

"I changed my mind," I said, collapsing onto the rock.

"For feck's sake. We just sat down."

"Not about that. About my father." I shivered hard when the cold air licked over my skin.

"Are you sure?"

"I don't want to end up like Shepherd with unresolved issues. At first, he was the poster boy for closing the door to my past. But I can't. It's eating away at me. My father won't live forever, and it'll be the biggest regret of my life if I don't see him one last time."

"Even if it means him despising what you've become?"

I squeezed the end of my wet tank top. "Even if it means him not loving me anymore. I never got the chance to say good-bye. I need him to know that I didn't seek out to hurt him. He deserves to know how great of a father he was and how ungrateful of a daughter I was."

Tears welled in my eyes but easily blended in on my wet face.

Christian put his arm around me. "Did you know penguins huddle for warmth?"

I laughed against his shoulder. "You spend too much time reading encyclopedias."

"Every man needs a hobby."

"Is that where you learned your mating technique?"

"You're one to talk, praying mantis."

"The men I lured into bathrooms weren't prospective lovers."

He reached around and squeezed the ends of my wet hair in

front. "Neither are the women I bed. They're just… recreational. Lover is a serious word. It implies commitment and devotion."

"I thought that was marriage."

"That's an archaic tradition for humans. Some Breeds mate or bond, but that requires exclusivity."

"Lovers aren't exclusive?"

His thumb traced across my clavicle. "Haven't you ever taken a lover?"

The air between us crackled.

I no longer had the fear of him charming me and stared deep into his bottomless eyes. Maybe it was foolish to trust a Vampire, but I couldn't bring myself to look away. His dark lashes matched his hair, and serious eyebrows framed his black eyes. Despite being a Vampire, he had wolfish characteristics. I tried to imagine how handsome his blue eyes must have been against his roguish features, but I couldn't. Black eyes were the only color that seemed fitting for Christian, and there wasn't anything wrong with that. They had a luster and mystery to them all their own.

"Will you take me to see him?"

"Aye, Precious. I'll make good on my promise."

My voice fell to a whisper. "Why do you have this effect on me?"

The pad of his thumb smoothed over my lips, and he looked upon me with fascination. "Your lips are soft."

I got up and walked away. "We can't do this."

Christian appeared out of nowhere and pinned me to the wall, dark hunger simmering in his gaze. "You are torturously beautiful. I need to taste you."

I flattened my back against the wall as he loomed even closer. "You can't have my blood."

He leaned in, his voice silken. "That's not what I want to taste."

The water lifted a scent off him that I couldn't get enough of. He gazed at me like a predator until our lips touched…

And melted me where I stood.

Christian didn't kiss me tenderly, but with fire. He cupped my nape and stepped closer until our bodies joined.

When our tongues met, I quivered with need. Best of all, I could touch him without the fear of my sexual energy knocking him out. No sparks that came from my fingertips compared to the electricity I felt when wrapped in his arms. Christian tasted just as I'd imagined.

And *oh God*, how I'd imagined it.

His lips were soft but insistent, like a man who knew when to take what he wanted and yet savored the hunt. I moaned, clawing at his shirt as if we were still in that river. He gripped the corner of the wall, and the rock crumbled beneath his fingertips, reminding me of his incredible power. Yet he held me like an ordinary man.

When I nibbled on his bottom lip, Christian grabbed my ass and pulled me against him, his erection demanding and hard against my belly. He was several inches taller than me, even more since I didn't have my shoes on. I stood on my tiptoes—one leg hooked around his—and as he deepened the kiss, something came over me.

Déjà vu.

My fangs elongated, and he stroked one of them with the tip of his tongue.

I drew back to catch my breath. "It's your blood, isn't it? That's what's making me feel this way."

The sound of rushing water drowned out my racing heart.

Christian stroked my cheek, his lips still swollen from my kiss. "It's not the blood."

"Then why is this so familiar? Why does it feel like I've tasted your kiss before?"

He drew in a deep breath. "Because you have."

I searched his eyes.

Christian inclined his head, his hands on my shoulders. "I can't lie to you anymore. You made me promise, but it was an unfair thing to do. I'm going back on a favor because it's not right."

"What's not right?" I asked warily.

"We kissed before. Intimately. Passionately."

I shook my head slowly. "No, we haven't."

"Aye, we have." He cupped my head in his hands, and his gaze reeled me in. "Remember everything, Raven. The wall is coming down. *Oceans.*"

The moment he said the word "oceans" without breaking eye contact, a flood of memories filled my mind. Restored memories. The training room, throwing myself at Christian… Our kiss. That sensual, erotic kiss where he pinned me to the wall and I wanted him to take me. I'd never known that kind of insatiable desire. The kiss hadn't been as slow burning and shattering as the one we'd just shared; it was chaotic and consumed with primal need. We'd crashed into each other like two comets in the night. I remembered the argument afterward and asking him to scrub my memory of the kiss. It would have been impossible for me to work beside a man that I'd felt that measure of lust for, but his scrubbing my memory of the kiss never erased my desire for him as I'd hoped. It was always there, simmering beneath the surface. Only now did I realize that it wasn't our kiss that had made me want him—it was my wanting him that led to the kiss.

My heart constricted, filled with the sting of deceit. "How can I ever trust you?" I shoved him away. "I feel like such a fool!"

"No, Raven. I'm the fool for agreeing to such a request."

"Then why did you do it?"

"Because if I hadn't, you would have walked away from Keystone."

I tilted my head to one side. "Isn't that what you wanted all along? So you did this out of the goodness of your own heart? That's bullshit. You didn't like me back then, and I'm still not really sure what *this* is," I said, motioning between us. "What else did you erase?"

He held up his hands. "That's all. I swear on my immortal soul."

I covered my eyes and threw my head back. "We can't keep doing this. I don't think I can handle a casual relationship with my partner."

"Define casual."

I dropped my arms. "Making out. Sharing blood. Cuddling. Sitting in the bathtub together. *Casual.*"

"Afraid it'll crush your dreams of becoming a do-gooder? A respectable member of society? Would you really leave Keystone over something so trivial?"

I pressed my finger against his chest. "That's exactly what I'm talking about. You're stringing my emotions along, and I should know better than to feel anything for a man who treats love like a venereal disease."

He gently took my arm and stepped close. "And what exactly do you feel for me?"

I wrenched away. "That's not fair."

And it wasn't. Christian couldn't expect me to disclose my emotions for his own amusement. Vampires used the truth against people. Now my feelings about him were a tangled mess. I wasn't foolish enough to expect him to reciprocate, but in that moment—when I felt the most betrayed—I realized by the clenching of my heart and tightening in my chest that I really *did* love him. That silent admission made me curse my stupidity for falling for a guy who would mock me for it.

What the hell is wrong with me?

Maybe I was caught in a vicious cycle of repeating my parents' mistake of loving someone who couldn't give themselves completely. That was all I knew about love.

He reached out to touch my face. "Raven—"

"Don't make me say something we'll both regret. Look, I appreciate you restoring my memory. I know I'm the one who asked you for the favor, but I can't help it. I feel violated. I trusted you would never do something like that to me. Why didn't you talk me out of it?"

His lips tightened, and he took a step back. "I can't make it right. It won't happen again, on my word. Even if you throw your naked body against mine and grind me like a cat in heat, I'll make you remember every embarrassing detail."

I flounced off. That was exactly the kind of thing I expected Christian to say. He was like Jekyll and Hyde, and I wasn't sure which man was the real Christian Poe.

Nor was I certain which man I loved.

Because even as I stormed off alongside the river, it didn't change a damn thing about what I felt for him.

I loved Christian, and somehow I was going to have to live with that ugly truth if I wanted to remain with Keystone. This was more than a job but a chance to have a makeshift family. I couldn't allow my feelings to compromise what truly mattered. I already had a million reasons to hate Christian.

But somehow they weren't enough.

Chapter 23

CHRISTIAN AND I DIDN'T HAVE to walk for long topside before Wyatt found us. He'd first picked up Blue and Niko, who had quickly located each other after Blue made it up the elevator. We eventually drove back to the spot where we'd originally parked and waited for a long time in silence. No one had heard from Viktor or Shepherd, and our worst fears were taking root in our imaginations. Would Keystone continue without our leader?

Wyatt and Christian sat up front and kept watch. Gem peered over Blue's shoulder at the baby until Blue finally handed her the sleeping bundle.

Blue stood up. "I'm going to search for Viktor."

Niko blocked her from leaving the van. "We're safer here."

"He might be injured."

"Needn't worry about Viktor. He's a cunning man with a better chance of escaping the underground than the rest of us. He'll come back here, so we wait."

Wyatt turned in his seat. "The good news is I don't see any freshies. Shep wouldn't miss the chance to come back and haunt me before leaving."

Wyatt's jokes belied his doleful expression.

"Is the baby warm enough?" Niko asked, removing his coat. "Wrap this over him."

Blue reluctantly took the coat and sat down next to Gem, placing the blanket over the already-swaddled baby, who was sleeping.

"We need to get some food," Gem said. "He's probably hungry and too weak to cry."

"First stop as soon as Shep comes back," Wyatt promised, tapping his fingers on the steering wheel. "Maybe I should turn on the lights."

"Don't run down the battery," Christian muttered. "I'll take a walk and see if I hear anything." He opened the van door and got out.

I leaned forward and looked at the baby. He was a couple of months old if I had to guess. "What are we going to do with him?"

Niko sat down to my left. "We hand him over to the authorities. They'll place him in an orphanage until someone adopts him."

"Is there a high demand for Sensor babies?"

"The orphanages prefer to place children in homes who are the same Breed. It's not always easy. Many couples don't like the stigma of handicapped children."

"He looks perfectly healthy to me."

"Yes, but I'm referring to Breed gifts. Children with defective gifts aren't desirable. Our powers and unique gifts are what make us strong. Without a history of the parents, there's no way to tell with an infant this small if his abilities are sufficient. But who knows. There might be a couple out there who doesn't care about such things."

Gem kissed the baby's forehead. "I think he's perfect just the way he is. I just love the way babies smell, don't you? Here, smell his head," she said, lifting him up to Blue.

Blue merely looked at the child before collecting Niko's coat from the floor. "Don't get attached; he's not a puppy. Like it or not, we have to turn him in."

Gem cradled the baby and smiled. "I know that. But look at his little nose. And those sweet little lips. Want to hold him, Niko?"

"Best not to wake him," he replied, his hands clasped together.

"Oh, come on. How often will you ever get to hold a real baby?"

"Blue's right. You shouldn't get attached. Emotions make people do foolish things."

She laughed. "Do you think I'm going to steal him?"

"The thought might enter your mind when it comes time to hand him over to the Regulators. Perhaps you should give him back to Blue."

She pouted. "No. I want to hold him. He likes me. He's all snuggly and warm."

The baby began to squirm, and a few seconds later, a wail poured out of him.

"Shhh. Don't cry, baby." She bounced him a little in her arms and handled him with inexperience. He cried even harder. "I'm not doing anything."

Blue reached over. "I'll take him."

Gem looked flustered as she passed the baby off and then quickly stood up. She was the only one who could stand all the way up without having to stoop because of the ceiling.

Niko looked up, his tone compassionate. "Gem, you did nothing wrong. Babies cry. He no doubt misses his mother."

She pressed her palm against the side of her head and made a plaintive sound. "He doesn't like me. Why doesn't he like me?"

The baby calmed as Blue gently rocked him in her arms and hummed a lullaby. That sight seemed to have a negative effect on Gem, whose bottom lip quivered.

I patted the bench to my right. "Come sit down. I'm not good with kids either. I think it's my resting bitch face."

A smile touched her lips, and she reluctantly took a seat beside me. "Where are your shoes?"

I straightened my legs and stared at my bare feet. "Long story. They were old anyhow."

Blue stood up and carefully made her way to the passenger seat. "I'm going to sit up here for the ride home. It's not safe bouncing around in the back with a baby in my arms. Not the way you drive."

Wyatt leaned over for a look. "He's a pudgy little burrito."

Gem couldn't seem to keep herself away from the baby. She got up and squatted between them while Wyatt fiddled with the radio.

"You smell like the river," Niko said absently. "That must have been a long fall."

Neither Christian nor I had mentioned our bridge dive.

"Nothing gets past you, does it?"

"Sighted people tend to ignore their other senses." Niko's wispy long hair slipped in front of his face when he lowered his head. "My apologies for the way I spoke to you in your bedroom. I care for you, and I care for Keystone. But you must make your own choices, or you'll never learn from your mistakes."

"Not every choice is a mistake."

"True. But every mistake is a choice."

"Do you think Viktor made a mistake by leaving Shepherd alone with Cristo? We could have done it by the book and taken him in."

"I don't know. The fates placed that Mage in our path for a reason. Perhaps Shepherd will no longer have a dark shadow looming over his light."

I lowered my voice. "We haven't known each other very long, but I wouldn't do anything to hurt or betray this organization. This is all I've got in this shitty world. But I'm still figuring stuff out, you know? I don't have a millennium of experience. I'm just out here winging it as best I can and trying to make decisions that won't haunt me for the rest of my life. Maybe we owed Shepherd the benefit of the doubt. We're all here because we're each a little fucked up in some way. But we have to trust each other until we give people a reason not to trust us."

"I agree. We shouldn't have left Shepherd behind."

"I know it wasn't your decision," I said. "We can't punish someone for what they *might* do. It's like that movie where they can see into the future and catch criminals before the crime. And no, what I'm thinking about doing isn't a crime. It's personal."

He placed his hand over mine. "Should you need me for anything, just say the word."

"Now that you mention it, my feet are kind of cold. Mind if I borrow your shoes?"

Niko's eyes curved like crescent moons when he gave a tight-lipped smile. "As you wish." After unlacing his boots, he set them in front of me.

The residual heat felt toasty warm. "I never noticed you had such big feet."

"You know what they say about big feet."

My brows arched, and I sat back.

Niko nudged me. "Big shoes."

I laughed. "I don't think that's how it goes."

"Tell me something."

"Sure."

He rubbed his hand over his mouth. "I understand what it means when something sucks. But why is it when something blows, it means the same thing? The words are opposite."

I smiled. Niko was well-spoken and had a good grasp of the English language. Maybe he didn't watch enough television to understand slang. "I don't know, Niko."

"Sometimes wordplay like that confuses me."

"What brought that up?"

He moved to the bench across from me. "I heard conversations in the tunnels."

I tucked my stringy hair behind my ears. "I never knew places like that existed."

He laced his fingers together. "How are you feeling?"

My stomach churned. "Cristo was an evil man. Let's just leave it at that." When I noticed a conflicted look in his expression, I decided to let him off the hook. "Don't worry. I'm not asking you to take out his light. It'll go away once I sleep it off. It was different the last time; I was injured and couldn't handle the additional stress."

What I didn't tell him was how dark light slithered like insects, devouring me from the inside out. I could taste it, smell it, and feel the evil deeds as if their ghosts were all around me. The adrenaline from running and jumping off the bridge had numbed me for a little while, but the sickness was quickly taking hold. Pulling Cristo's core light had been my decision, so I needed to suck it up.

My heart flip-flopped when the back door suddenly opened.

Viktor's grey wolf leaped inside, his paws wet and dirt all over his coat. He smelled everyone—especially the baby.

Christian rocked the van when he jumped inside and sat next to me without a word.

Realizing we were a man short, my stomach knotted. "Where's Shepherd?"

"Miss me already?" Shepherd said in a gravelly voice as he climbed in the van, his pants shredded and face spattered with blood. He tossed his leather coat on the bench, his shirt ripped down the front and hanging on him like a vest.

"Everyone thought you were dead," Wyatt informed him.

Shepherd sat down across from us and wearily stretched out his legs. "If I were dead, I'd come back to haunt your ass."

Wyatt put on his hat. "See? I told you guys."

It didn't take long for Niko to notice that Shepherd was hurt. "You need my help."

"All I need is a cigarette." Shepherd used his shirt to wipe the blood off his face, which continued dripping from the gash on his head.

Christian crossed his ankles. "Don't trouble yourself, Niko. I'm sure Claude will give him a tongue bath when we get home."

Shepherd flicked his gaze between them. "Fine. Just the gash on my head. It needs stitches, and I don't trust any of you boneheads enough to thread a needle."

The shakes came over me.

"Cold?" Christian asked.

While Niko began working his healing magic on Shepherd, Wyatt started up the van and headed home.

I wrung my hands. "No. It's not that."

"Can't you force it out?"

"It doesn't work like that. Can we stop talking about it?"

"Aye. Lean against me." Christian draped his arm around my shoulder. "I see you found a nice pair of shoes."

"I feel like a wet sock that just came out of the washer."

Viktor's wolf wedged himself between us and rested his head on the bench.

I stroked his soft ear. "What happened back there?"

Shepherd peeled off his bloodstained shirt and tossed it on the floor. There was no need to guess whose blood that was. "We got out alive."

"And Cristo?"

A long silence filled in all the blanks. Killing Cristo wouldn't bring back his woman or change what had happened, but at least no one else would suffer at the hands of that deranged lunatic.

My eyelids dropped like anchors, and I sighed against Christian's chest.

He spoke quietly so no one else could hear. "When do you want to see your da?"

"Tomorrow," I whispered back.

"Daddy?"

"Maybe another night you can call me that. Quiet now. I'm carrying you back to bed." The familiar Irish accent snapped me out of my slumber.

I'd somehow lost myself in my dreams, going back to a time when I was a child and my father would carry me to bed after I'd fallen asleep watching TV. It only took me a few seconds to fast-forward and realize I wasn't that little girl anymore.

I opened my eyes. Beautiful stained glass windows drifted by, open candles flickering against the wall as Christian floated past them.

"How's Claude?" I mumbled.

"You shouldn't worry about that pussy. He's got Gem bringing him food on a silver platter."

"I thought Chitahs didn't like women serving them."

"He's learned to pick his battles with Gem."

I suddenly convulsed when the urge to vomit came over me. Though my stomach was empty, my body was searching for ways to purge Cristo's light even though it would leak out on its own in due time.

"I need to go to bed," I rasped.

Christian kept a firm hold of me. "We have a family meeting upstairs."

Cold sweat touched my brow, and I wiggled my legs. "Then put me down."

"We'll get there faster if I carry you."

"Please, Christian. I need to walk."

He set my feet on the ground and held my arms until I found my balance. I reminded myself that the sickness would only last another day. In my old life, I would have slept it off. But if Viktor wanted a meeting, then dammit, I wasn't going to sit it out.

"What floor are we on?"

"The second. We're going to Wyatt's World."

I bit down my laughter. "That makes it sound like an amusement park."

"It's the closest thing we have to one. An office, game room, and television all supervised by a clown."

"How's your ass?"

"Firm."

"Any more splinters?"

"Perhaps you should give me a thorough examination after the meeting."

"I'll pass."

"Any second thoughts about going to the family reunion tomorrow? You look like the dead."

"Just let me sleep in. And tell Viktor I'm not up to cooking breakfast."

"All part of the master plan?"

"Yep. I deliberately drank all that dark light just to get out of scrambling eggs."

Claude appeared in the distance and looked as bad as I felt. Gem was trying to be his crutch, but Claude wasn't about to lean on a woman. Especially a petite one half his size. His arm was in a sling, his shoulder bandaged, and he had a noticeable limp.

When we locked eyes, his brows drew together. "Are you hurt, female?"

"She has a raging bout of diarrhea," Christian announced. "It's grisly. Perhaps someone should bring a chamber pot and air freshener in case the meeting goes on too long."

I glared up at him. "Are you sure you aren't an escaped mental patient?"

As we entered the room, Wyatt was clearing trash off his long desk. Niko held up the wall by the door, his eyes closed and arms crossed. I let Claude and Gem take the couch and decided to sit down in one of the beanbag chairs so I'd have a direct view of the doorway. I half expected Viktor's wolf to trot in, tail wagging. But instead, Viktor swaggered in wearing a dark robe tied at the waist and pajama bottoms underneath. He pulled out a leather computer chair and sat facing the room. Gem switched on the floor lamp beside the sofa to give us more light.

Wyatt shoved the overflowing wastebasket under the desk.

Viktor gave him a peevish look. "This is stolen property."

"Found," Wyatt corrected, crossing his ankle over his knee.

Viktor stroked his beard and didn't bother arguing the details. "I want them returned tomorrow."

"You want me to just walk into a store and give them a box? It doesn't work like that."

"Nyet. I want you to locate the company from whence they came and leave them on the property."

"Better do as he says," Gem piped in. "You're starting to grow a tire around your waist."

He winked. "A woman needs something to grab on to."

Christian sat on a roller stool next to Wyatt. "I'll handle breakfast in the morning," he announced.

A few eyes darted my way, but no one said anything.

"Sorry I'm late." Blue strode in, the baby cradled in one arm and a bottle in the other hand. "I had to give him a quick bath."

Claude reached out. "Let me feed him."

She looked at him warily. "Hold him gently. Have you ever fed a baby before?"

Claude took the baby in his good arm. The moment the baby started to cry, Claude released a purr that was more felt than heard.

The vocalization was different from previous ones he'd made, and it delivered the same comforting embrace of a mother or father's hug. The baby instantly shushed, delighted by the sound as he gripped one of Claude's long fingers. Blue rubbed the nipple against the baby's lips, and when he opened his mouth and began sucking on the bottle, Claude took over.

I studied Christian, curious where the bottle and formula had come from. "Did we stop for baby supplies, or do you guys just have that stuff lying around?"

Wyatt answered for him while unwrapping a MoonPie. "You sleep like the dead."

"From what I hear, the dead don't sleep."

He pointed at me and winked. "Now you're catching on."

Shepherd appeared in the doorway, looking like a man who'd survived an explosion by the skin of his teeth. He hadn't changed out of his shredded pants, so I could see the cuts on his legs, probably from escaping the bomb. Though his face and hair were rinsed, he hadn't done anything to clean the dried blood off his chest. He took a seat on the short end of the L-shaped sofa that faced me and tossed a pillow on the floor.

Viktor pinched the bridge of his nose. "Now that we're all here, I'll give you an update. After speaking with the higher authority about tonight's events, the case is officially closed. Final payment will appear in my account in the morning, and I will distribute it to everyone by tomorrow evening."

The baby suckling the bottle drew our attention away.

Blue tilted the end of the bottle higher. "Hold it like that so he doesn't swallow air. This isn't one of those fancy bottles."

Claude was lost in the smell of a new baby. His nostrils twitched when he leaned over and sniffed his head. Unlike others in the house, Claude didn't appear uncomfortable with holding him.

Viktor yawned. "I've requested the Regulators come by in the morning to collect the infant. Tonight he should rest and eat plenty while in our care."

Wyatt yawned dramatically. "That goes for the rest of us too. Do we need to give statements, or can I sleep until noon?"

"I want to commend all of you," Viktor continued. "The child is safe, and the threat is contained."

I unstrapped the knife holster from my arm and set it on my lap. "What do we tell the Regulators about what happened to Cristo?"

Viktor centered his eyes on mine. "That he perished in the explosion. They will not send anyone down to scrape up what remains of him. Our confirmation will be sufficient."

"Is that what really happened?"

He tilted his head to the side. "Did you see anything otherwise?"

"Nope."

Viktor rose to his feet. "Tomorrow we rest. Christian, come with me. I need your help with a cradle upstairs."

"You can put it in my room," Blue said. "I'll go light a fire. Does anyone want to make bottles? I'm not sure how often he eats, but it's a long walk to the kitchen, and I could use the help when he wakes up hungry."

Gem raised her hand. "I can."

Blue jerked her head toward the door. "Come on. I'll show you how. Claude, are you okay with him?"

Claude was in another world. He pulled the bottle out of the sleeping baby's mouth and bent him forward, lightly patting his back until a burp slipped out. "Go on. He's in good hands. Aren't you, little one? No one's ever going to hurt you again."

When the little guy spit up, Claude lifted his own shirt and wiped the baby's chin dry.

"There's just one more thing," Viktor said before Blue stepped out of the room.

Wyatt's chair squeaked when he spun it around. "There's always a catch."

"No catch." Viktor strode toward the door. "Just an invitation."

"To what?" Shepherd asked gruffly.

"A charity ball hosted by Patrick Bane."

Wyatt snickered. "This guy has more balls than a golf course."

"I was going to respectfully decline, but after tonight, I have decided to donate my share of the money to the orphanage. Specifically, the orphanage that will be caring for this child. I think it is important that each of you attend and learn more about the politics involved. Our case ends, but it doesn't really end. Perhaps with more of us there, we can persuade others to donate. Most people do not get to see where their money is going as we do," he said, gesturing to the baby. "We have saved him from the black market. Let us see if we can save him from an underfunded system. Or else one day he might end up on our list of outlaws."

Chapter 24

I T WAS A ROUGH NIGHT. I'd thought a hot bath might help to relax me, but the water felt like toxic sludge lapping against my sensitive skin. It was all in my head, but that knowledge didn't remove the vileness within me. Dark light always pressed upon my own, leaving me with an irrational fear that it might never leave, like a dirty fingerprint left behind.

After throwing on a T-shirt, I pulled a blanket over me and curled up in the fetal position. There were moments I drifted off and saw those Vampires chasing after me. Only, in the dream, they gained on us and the rock didn't explode. My blood-curdling screams reverberated off the tunnel walls as my limbs were torn from my body.

"Raven… Raven, wake up."

The voice echoed in my head, and my eyes snapped open. It sounded like Christian, but when I turned over, no one was there. Shadows moved about the dark room, and my eyes closed again.

The cycle repeated for hours until I drew the covers over my head and shut out the world.

"Raven, wake up."

Someone pulled the cover away from my eyes, and I squinted at the bright window.

"It's late afternoon." Christian set a silver thermos next to the bed and took a seat in my chair. "Thought you could use the caffeine."

I propped the pillow behind me and scooted up, my head

pounding. After blowing the steam from the opening on the lip, I sipped the aromatic coffee. "It's good."

"No cream. No sugar. Maybe a drop of blood."

"You're not funny. Is the baby gone?"

"Aye. Regulators came by this morning and spoke with Viktor before collecting the evidence. They had no interest in questioning the rest of us."

"The baby being the evidence." I gazed up at the window and yawned. "What time is it?"

Christian turned around and looked at my desk. After shoving a few things around, he gave me a peculiar look. "Wait a minute. Why the feck am I looking for a clock? You're half Mage. What happened to your internal clock?"

"I hit the snooze button. It's just that I have to wait until my father gets home from work before we go. I also want to give him time to eat his dinner, because he hates being interrupted when he's eating."

"And my job is to sit around while you have a talk-show moment, and then I scrub his memories? Sounds like a fruitless task."

"You owe me a favor. And I'll buy you a box of gum on the way home. How's that sound?"

He crossed his legs. "Grand. And do you plan on telling him the whole story? The whole of the whole? Fangs, magical light, your history as a serial killer…"

"I don't know. I'm just going to wing it and see what happens."

He chuckled. "This might be interesting after all."

My hands were steady, so that was a good sign that Cristo's light was finally draining. Caffeine made me feel normal again, but I still had no appetite.

The susurration of snowflakes blowing against the window drew my attention away. "How bad is the weather?"

"It's a mess out there. I asked Wyatt to check the forecast on his computer, but I don't need a fancy computer to tell me the weather. The snow will stop by nightfall."

I combed my fingers through my rumpled hair and took a last

sip of the coffee before setting it on the nightstand. "Do I look okay?"

He stared at me unblinking. "You'll not be winning any beauty competitions this evening."

"I just meant do I have dark circles or look… not human?"

"Run a comb through your hair and put on that blood-red lipstick if you like. That might help with your corpse-like appearance."

"Maybe I should paint my nails. The black polish is chipping."

"I can promise you that the last thing your da is going to be shocked by when he sees his dead daughter standing in his doorway is the state of your cuticles."

"Do you think Viktor will ask where we're going?"

Christian stood up. "I'm taking my partner out for a drink. Don't forget to wear a jacket. I wouldn't want your da thinking I'm an irresponsible friend."

I laughed and stood up. "Irresponsible is the least of your worries."

"And what's that supposed to mean?"

I crossed the room and reached into the armoire for my favorite ripped jeans. "Nothing. Just that my daddy doesn't like your kind."

Christian strode over and leaned against my blood-red armoire. "Handsome? Well endowed? Or is it the Irish part?"

"Cocky. He can smell an asshole a mile away."

"Perhaps prison is where he belongs."

I decided to keep my long black T-shirt on and reached for socks and a pair of shoes. When I sat on the bed, nerves tightened in my stomach like a coil. "You know what my worst fear is?"

He arched an eyebrow.

"That he's gotten over me."

"I thought that's what you wanted, lass."

I pulled the laces tight on my black-and-white sneakers. "I do."

"And you think I'm the one with issues." He turned around and ambled toward the door.

I grabbed my leather coat and attached a push dagger to the

waistband of my pants. "Stop trying to understand women. It's not your strong suit. Are we taking the Honda?"

He held open the door. "Unless you'd rather we take the motorbike. Wouldn't that impress the old man?"

I zipped up my coat and chuckled. "If you're looking to impress my father with stupidity, then riding a bike in the snow would be the way."

I spit my stale gum into a silver wrapper. "I'm surprised this thing is in one piece," I said, referring to the Honda we'd left behind in the Bricks during the ambush.

"I only had to replace four tires," he remarked. "And she'll need a new paint job, but she still runs like a dream. Those fecking shitebags."

Christian had recovered his car earlier that day. Four flat tires, busted taillights, and someone had spray-painted a giant penis on the hood.

I wiped the condensation off the window with my sleeve. "How do you think Cristo found all those single moms and pregnant women?"

Christian turned down the volume on the car radio. "Men like Cristo sniff them out. They pay people on the outside to find single women in desperate times. It's not hard to do. It sounds like early in his career, he stole babies from the womb. It takes a certain kind of animal to do something so vile. It probably didn't take him long to figure out that stealing children was easier, and the older ones probably easier to take care of than a newborn."

"All that for what? A few homes in the Bricks? He wasn't exactly living in the lap of luxury."

"He's a hoarder. Immortality is a terrifying thing for men who don't have a trade. There comes a time when you realize you're going to either work until the end of time, or you need to hoard as much money as you can to sustain you in the centuries to come. The room we found him in had a hidden safe in the kitchen."

"Which he blew up."

"He probably has a little everywhere he resides. Not everyone trusts the bankers, and I've known a few men to bury gold bars in the woods. You lived on the streets for enough years to know that no man wants that life forever, and an eternity is a long time to live. Not everyone commits crimes to feed an addiction or live on a yacht. Some of them are frightened mice who fear what the future holds for them."

I opened the visor, and light illuminated the vanity mirror. "Maybe black eyeliner was a bad idea. I look like the walking dead."

"You *are* half Dracula. A bloodsucker. A shark of the night. A parasite."

"All right. I get your point."

"Maybe it's easier if he doesn't see the little girl he once knew." Christian made a right turn. "Exactly how many times are we going to circle the area? We're practically plowing the snow."

I stared up at the stars. Like Christian predicted, the snow had tapered off just after sunset. It was a beautiful night—stars glittering against the inky sky like flecks of ice suspended in midair. These were *my* stars, the ones above my trailer park that I'd gazed up at a million times.

"I guess I'm ready," I said. "He might be asleep by now. Maybe we should come back another time."

Christian jerked the wheel and made a hard left down the road that led to my father's place. It was a single-wide mobile home with one bedroom, an older model and considerably small. There was a decent amount of land surrounding each trailer since the park was on the outskirts of the city—good land to build a house on if a person had enough money.

"Let me guess. The mailbox with the red flames is yours?"

I didn't disagree. Christian made a left turn and slowed the car to a stop.

"Switch off the lights or he'll come out here with a gun," I said.

Christian shut off the engine, and we stared at the trailer. It wasn't the first time I'd dropped by in recent years. I snuck out here now and again when I needed to feel connected to something.

Crush owned a green trailer with a small porch and four steps on the right that led up to it. I gazed at the picnic table, and a landslide of memories came back. Playing dolls, barbecues, Fourth of July fireworks. His bikes must have been in the garage, because I only saw the beat-up truck out front.

"Outlaw?" Christian asked.

I followed his gaze to the decal on the back of Crush's truck window. "He's not a man who believes in the system."

Christian unbuckled his seat belt. "Now I'm beginning to see where you get your rebellious nature from. I feel like I'm about to learn a lot about the infamous Raven Black."

I nervously tugged at my fingerless gloves, the air in the car quickly cooling down. "The lights are still on. That means he's watching TV."

Christian shifted in his seat and gave me a pointed stare. "You're taking this too seriously. Remember the story about the man who traveled with the ghost to visit his past?"

"Scrooge? Are you comparing me to Scrooge?"

"You're just passing through this life, Raven. It's not real anymore because you're no longer a part of it. I don't see how this is going to accomplish anything but mess with your head. You're a fecking lunatic if you think this is going to bring you any resolution. I'm here, I'll do as you ask, but it's not your life anymore. It's like when you end a relationship with someone and they pay you a visit years later. It feels familiar, and that makes you think you can have it all back. But you can't. You're a ghost to those memories."

"Someday a ghost is going to knock on your door, and we'll see if you have the balls to slam it shut. Now quit getting all philosophical; you're making me nervous."

"As nervous as the man on the porch with a shotgun?"

My eyes widened when I looked up. "Oh, shit."

"Who's out there?" Crush bellowed. "Get the fuck off my land."

I opened the door and put my hands up. "Don't shoot."

"What do you want? Did your car break down? Tell your friend to get back in that pussy-ass car of his."

"Christian," I hissed. "Stay there."

"Your da's a real charmer," he said quietly, resting his arms over the roof of the car.

"That's the pot calling the kettle black."

I slowly approached the trailer, my hands still up. The gun was obscuring Crush's face, and the light on the porch turned him into a silhouette.

"Daddy, it's me."

When he lowered the gun a little, I took a few paces forward. He slowly descended the steps, shotgun still pointed. The closer he got, the better I could see his blue eyes aimed straight at me.

I finally wasn't a ghost anymore. I was real, and he saw me. The closer he came, the more he lowered the gun until he was staring at me stone-faced. Crush had a hard look on his weathered face. He still had the grey mustache and long goatee I remembered from most of my life. His hair wasn't tied back like usual, and the wind blew some of it around. Neither of us spoke. I stood frozen in fear, my hands trembling, my breathing so rapid that I began to feel light-headed.

Crush drew in a deep breath, and when he released it, a cloud of frosty white air filled the space between us. His inscrutable expression gave away nothing. When he dropped the gun in the snow, I couldn't move fast enough. Crush surged forward and pulled me into a tight bear hug.

Then he smelled my hair.

"It really *is* you, Cookie."

I burst into tears like a little girl, crying right into his whiskery neck. He squeezed me so hard I couldn't breathe, but it was the realest thing I'd felt in a long time.

"I'm so sorry, Daddy," I whispered, caught in a maelstrom of emotions.

I'd missed his voice, his bear hugs, and even that awful cologne.

He finally let go and drew back, his eyes shining. "I knew they'd lied to me. You always were a tough cookie."

I wiped my face. "We need to talk. I can't stay long."

His eyes flicked back to Christian and then returned to me. "What kind of trouble are you in? Is he mafia?"

"Yep."

The two-fanged mafia.

Crush knew my sass, but he still looked like a man in shock. "I think you better come inside." He picked up his gun and led the way, Christian tailing behind in his black trench coat and looking like… the mafia.

I mentally sighed as I climbed the steps and then lifted my foot to remove my wet shoes.

Crush captured my wrist and jerked me inside. "Forget it. I don't care if you throw mud all over my floor; get your ass inside."

"Same old bulldog," I said.

He leaned against the divider wall between the living room and kitchen. "Same old smack-talker. Who's your friend?"

Christian shut the door behind us and stayed quiet in the background, like a plastic plant.

"A friend." I gestured to the table on the left. "Can we sit?"

Crush ambled into the living room to the right and muted the TV.

"I see you still have that same ratty old recliner."

He chuckled. "My boys are going to bury me in that. Might as well be comfortable in the afterlife." Crush returned to the kitchen in front of us and switched on the light.

I took a seat at the table by the door and watched him make a cup of cocoa. He kept peering at me suspiciously but didn't say a word. Crush looked exactly the way I remembered him. Black jeans, a skull T-shirt that was too tight for him, and biker boots. He didn't have on all the skull rings and other jewelry he often wore, so I guessed he must have been getting ready for bed.

"How's business at the garage?" I asked.

He set the cocoa in front of me and took a seat to my right. "You don't get to ask me irrelevant shit like that until you tell me where you've been. I *buried* you."

My palms began to sweat, so I peeled off my gloves. "I never meant to hurt you."

Crush waited with immeasurable patience as I stuffed the gloves into my pockets and then sipped my cocoa.

He jerked his chin toward my cup. "Three tiny marshmallows, just the way you like."

"You hate marshmallows."

"I couldn't bring myself to get rid of the bag. Damn, they're probably stale."

I set the glass down. "They're great. They're perfect." My attention wandered around the room. Same wooden cabinets, even the same shag rug in the living room. I kept searching for something new, but it was as if no time had passed. It even smelled the same.

Crush reached across the table and grasped my hand. He started to say something and then covered his face, wiping his red eyes. "It's just so damn good to see you. Where have you been all this time? Why didn't you call? Are you in some kind of trouble? I got friends, Raven. You know that. They can make problems go away."

"I don't have problems."

"That's a nice blade on your belt. Think I didn't notice it?"

I pulled away and sat back.

Crush wiped his face and tugged on his goatee as he studied me real hard. "You look different."

"I am different."

He jerked his chin up. "Does he have something to do with it?"

"He's part of my life now. But he's not the reason I left."

Crush stared daggers at Christian. "Go stand outside. This is family business."

It hardly mattered with Christian's Vampire hearing, but I gave him a look to go anyhow.

When the door closed, I rested my elbow on the table. "I don't know where to start."

He scooted forward. "From the beginning. I'm not going anywhere."

"You know how aimless I was years ago. It was a confusing time for me, and I was busy trying to find myself. Someone offered me a better life, but I couldn't come back to this one. That was part of the deal."

"What deal? You're not making sense. Did you sell yourself into prostitution? I've seen some hard shit in my day, Cookie. Nothing will shock me."

I rubbed my face. Was I really going to do this? What the hell did it matter? Christian was going to erase his memory, but now I realized that my daddy was going to think I'd been locked up in a loony bin. "The world isn't what you think it is. I can't explain the hows and whys; all I can tell you is that someone offered me a chance to be an immortal. I stupidly listened to them and wound up in a morgue. Someone else took me in—a bad man. But even when I escaped, I couldn't come back to this life. That's the deal. I'm… I'm not human anymore, Daddy. I'm a monster."

He sighed. "Maybe I know a little something about demons. There's a hardness in your eyes that wasn't there before; I've seen that look. I never thought I'd see it in my own little girl." He wiped his eyes, fighting back the emotions. "I tried to protect you from that. Tried to teach you."

I reached out and took his rough hand, still stained with oil and grease from the shop. "It's not your fault. I came here because this is the last time I'll get to see you. I'm not even supposed to be here, but I had to come back. I needed to tell you…"

"Tell me what?"

My lip quivered as I stared into his blue eyes. The lines on his face told a story of a million bike rides and living life to the fullest. "How much I love you. How you were a good father and I was an ungrateful little shit who never should have left home."

Crush got out of his chair and pulled me into a tight hug. "There's nothing you could have done that'll make me not love you. Do you hear me?" He jerked back and firmly held my head between his hands. "Do you hear me, Raven? Nothing."

"I've killed people."

His jaw clenched. "Did they have it coming?"

"That's not the point."

"It doesn't matter what you've done." He pressed his finger against my forehead. "I know your heart. I know that piece inside you that you never let anyone else see. You always tried to be the tough girl—Daddy's girl—but I wanted a better life for you. Not to live in some shithole trailer park and marry a no-good loser who spends too much time at the bar and thinks he can put his hands on you. I thought if you worked in my garage I could pass it down to you someday and you'd have your own business, but maybe my version of a better life and yours were never on the same level. We fought, but that's because I wasn't ready to let go of my baby girl. I knew you wanted to meet different people and have a nice job—it was the letting go part I couldn't deal with. Once you got a taste of the good life, I wouldn't have a place in it anymore."

"I wasn't too good to work in your shop. I was stupid."

He sat me down and then took the chair in front of me. "You never belonged in a garage. You're better than that. My princess deserves a mansion."

Thinking about Keystone, I offered him a fragile smile. "I have a good life now—a nice place to live. I'm not living on the streets and struggling to survive anymore."

"You could have come home anytime. You've always had a place here."

"I know you feel that way, but I don't belong here anymore." Without dragging out the explanation, I let him see my fangs.

Crush sat back and got real quiet.

Embarrassed, I retracted them and warmed my hands on the mug. "How did you bury me without a body?"

He folded his arms, eyes downcast. "They had one, but it was badly burned. I couldn't give a positive ID. I had your dental records, and they said it matched."

"They lied. That's what they do to protect their own." I closed my eyes, knowing my Creator had staged the elaborate fiction. "He made you believe I died in a fire?"

Of all things—it was the one cause of death that would have devastated my father, who had lost my mother the same way.

"I buried you. Tried to forget for a while. But I don't know. Sometimes I could feel you," he said, closing a fist over his heart. "It was easier to imagine you found a new life than to think it was you in that coffin. I'd be okay with living alone if it meant your happiness. You're my heart." His voice cracked, and he tightened his lips.

I bent forward with my head in my hands. "This is *so hard*. This is so much harder than I thought it would be." I quietly sobbed, my teardrops falling to the linoleum floor.

Crush got out of his seat and disappeared down the hall. I untucked my T-shirt from the front of my pants and wiped my face on it. What I'd been seeking all along wasn't resolution or even an explanation; I wanted permission.

Permission to live my life. Permission to leave him. Permission to be happy.

Crush's heavy gait pulled me out of my thoughts. He set a familiar keepsake on the table. "I thought you might want it back. It was broken when you left it here, but I tinkered around and..."

When he lifted the lid to the jewelry box, I admired the pink satin lining. A sweet melody played as a ballerina in a white skirt twirled in front of a mirror. I smiled through tears as I touched the empty holders.

"I gave away your jewelry to Ren's little girl. Remember her? She was a few years younger, and her momma never bought her anything in the way of trinkets. Hope you don't mind."

I shook my head.

"Your clothes too," he added. "Not just to her, but a few of the guys saw me packing them up a year ago and asked if their kids could look through them. I guess it's kind of nice seeing a part of you on them."

"Can I keep this?"

"It's all yours, Cookie. Your leather cuff bracelet is in the bottom drawer. One of the studs fell off, but I couldn't bring myself to get rid of it. You practically wore it every damn day when you were fifteen. You can keep it or throw it away."

I closed the lid and took a deep breath. "I never appreciated everything you gave me. All I kept thinking about was what I didn't have. I'm sorry for the asinine things I said to you, especially when I left home."

"You were just a kid."

"I was nineteen. I knew better." I gripped his hand tighter on the table. "I was never ashamed of you. I love you, Daddy. You were *always* good enough."

I'd never seen Crush break down except at my mother's funeral. He was a hard man who locked his feelings up tight, but in the privacy of his kitchen, he wept.

We both did.

I wiped my eyes, unable to bear the sound of my father crying. "Did you stay sober?"

He wiped his face on a bandana sitting on the table. "There were nights when the demons kept me awake, but I never touched a drop."

For the first time in my life, I was finally seeing Crush as more than just a father. I was seeing him as a man.

"Are you happy?" he asked.

I thought about it. "I'm getting there. It's just hard not always knowing the right choices to make."

He chuckled softly. "I know a little something about that." He rested his fist against his cheek and just stared at me, and the twinkle in his eye gradually returned. In some parallel universe, we could have just been sitting there like father and daughter, sharing a cup of cocoa. Only no tragic past, no heartbreak. And for those few minutes, I tried to forget the truth.

We made small talk, and I caught up on the latest news with his buddies and how business was going at the shop. Crush owned a garage and had a good thing going. He said he'd socked away enough money to buy a house but decided he didn't need all that space. The real shock was when he told me he'd been saving his money all those years ago for me—in case I wanted to go to college or if I ever got in a jam. But mostly because he wanted me to have an inheritance when he finally died—something that might be enough. It broke my heart. Even now that we were going our separate ways, I knew Crush would never spend that money on himself.

I didn't have many funny stories to relay, but when I told him about the MoonPie truck, he laughed so hard that I joined in. I missed his laugh. Crush had a great rolling belly laugh that always sounded like he was going to piss himself. He didn't really understand most of the story, like why I was riding on top of a car roof to begin with, but I think he got the gist of what I did for a living.

"Remember when I used to braid your hair?" he asked.

I smiled wistfully. "You were terrible."

Crush scooted his chair all the way next to me and began to section off my hair to make two braids. I memorized the feel of his hands and that fatherly love.

"Does it have to be this way?" he asked. "Isn't there a way I can stay in your life?"

I shook my head. "It's too dangerous."

"Danger is my middle name."

"Where did you bury me?"

His hands paused for a moment before he worked on the plaits. "Next to your mama. Have you been out there lately?"

"No," I whispered.

"Maybe you should. I bet she'd like you to visit her sometime."

I turned in my chair to let him work on the left side. "Do you forgive me?"

"There's nothing to forgive. Sometimes we have to make tough choices. Like I said, there's nothing you could do that would make me stop loving you. I wasn't the best father, and you deserved to have a mom in your life. Maybe I should have settled down with someone so you'd have that softness a woman needs. But I did my best. I even bought you that damn rabbit."

I smiled wistfully as he finished up the braid.

We sat for a quiet moment, having said most everything that

needed to be said. I hadn't realized until I glanced up at the clock that it was after midnight, and I dreaded our good-bye. "I have to go."

He cradled my head and kissed me on the temple. "If you change your mind, I'm here. You got that? This doesn't have to be final."

I peered up at him. "Why aren't you shocked by my fangs?"

He shrugged. "I've seen a lot of weird shit. You're not a monster, Cookie."

I barked out a laugh. "I'm the Cookie Monster."

"It's not funny. I'm dead serious. Don't ever think that I could love you less. Maybe I can't be there anymore to give you advice or help protect you, but you know my door is always open. *Always.* You look like you can take care of yourself now, but find someone you can trust and accept their help. You were always stubborn about wanting to do things on your own. You can't live life alone. I have my friends, and we're tight. We're family. We'd bleed for each other. That's what you need to find, even if I can't be a part of it. But don't think that's me saying I'm okay with it. Fuck the rules, Raven. If you ever need to come back, we can pack our shit and move to Puerto Rico. You got that?"

I fell into his arms. "Thank you."

Crush squeezed me so tight I didn't think he'd ever let go, and I didn't want him to. I scrunched his long hair in one hand and stared into the empty living room as our hug dissolved.

"I need to talk to your friend," he said. "Tell him to get his ass in here."

I nodded.

Crush gave me three quick kisses on the cheek. I used to hate it because his whiskers and goatee would tickle. All those stupid times I'd pushed him away.

I brushed my hand down his cheek and tugged on his goatee. "Don't do anything I wouldn't do."

He gave me a tight grin and flashed a silver tooth. "That's *my* line."

"Find an old lady, will ya? You shouldn't be living out here alone, you old bulldog. Someone needs to make you pick up your dirty dishes and drag your ass to bed."

"I'll think about it, Cookie." He pressed his forehead against mine. "I love you, little girl. With all the fire in my heart."

After our final words, I collected my jewelry box and finally left my past behind.

Chapter 25

CHRISTIAN STOOD BY THE DOOR and watched Raven until she got inside the car. He didn't need to ask what had happened; he'd heard it all. Every word, every gasp, every teardrop hitting the tile, and even the fluttering of her heart when her father told her good-bye.

Christian empathized. When he'd left Ireland centuries ago, he did so knowing he'd never see his sister and father again. It was a bold move leaving home and sailing across the ocean. His father had refused to go, arguing that he was too old for such adventures. In truth, Ireland was all he'd ever known. While leaving his father was difficult, it was especially trying on Christian to say good-bye to Cassie, his younger sister. She was just a wee lass at the time, but Christian had always held a soft spot for her. She was adventurous and loved her big brothers, but there was no way he could drag a blind girl across an ocean to an unknown, savage land. He still remembered the way she held on to him so tightly that he'd had to forcefully push her away. That was long ago, yet hearing Raven's homecoming dredged up all those old memories.

He wanted to reach out and tell her it would get easier. But words were of little consolation, and black deeds often erased what little goodness remained in an immortal. Better she learn that for herself. He'd already complicated things enough with kissing her by the river. What they needed was more distance between them, but he found it increasingly impossible to do, and not just because of their partnership.

During the ambush back at the Bricks, Christian's chest had

constricted when she offered him her blood. That was a great honor among Vampires, and even though she'd done it so he could fight, it was by no measure a worthless offering. And hearing the soft whisper of her blood inside his veins made it even more impossible to keep his feelings neutral.

Seeing her fight those rogues had impressed him tremendously. The memory of her fangs gleaming white against her bloodstained lips stirred something deep within him. Raven looked like a comic book heroine—a svelte yet feminine body with midnight hair that came alive when she moved. She showed courage and tenacity when faced with an ambush, and that was something you were either born with or learned through years of experience. She wasn't polished or of noble blood. She didn't wear perfume, and half the time she brushed her hair with her fingers. There was a wildness in her that couldn't be tamed—a woman who wasn't sitting around waiting for anyone's help. She was raw and uncut, and that called to his Vampire heart.

Christian leaned on the railing. Raven had lowered the vanity mirror and was wiping her smeared eyeliner with a tissue. He gripped the wooden handrail, keenly aware that her heart rate had slowed. The flush of scarlet on her cheeks was a teasing sight to a Vampire. While he didn't know exactly how she felt about him, he sensed subtle changes in her body whenever he entered the room. Her pupils would dilate before she averted her gaze and pretended not to notice him. In a millisecond, he could block out all noise in a room except for the sound of her heart skipping a beat. He never should have encouraged those feelings. After all, what did he care? Christian was a man who fucked women with wild abandon, never bothering to ask for names afterward.

He despised himself for allowing the attraction to flourish. And on top of everything, *she* was the little girl from the fire.

Jaysus. In the past century, Christian had experienced a few moments of weakness in his Vampire life, and not one of them had ever yielded anything but regret. He brushed his hand over the sleeve of his coat, still remembering the searing pain from the burns.

"Get your ass in here," Crush said from inside. "I know how you Vamps like the cold."

Christian straightened his back like an arrow.

"I know you heard me," Crush said quietly.

Dumbfounded, Christian swung open the door and entered the trailer. "And what exactly do you know about Vampires?"

Crush laughed and tied back his long hair. "Enough to know you don't like being called Vamps. Why don't you shut the door, and we'll talk." He stood up and headed to the fridge. "Want a drink?"

Christian took a seat and rested his left arm on the table, drumming his fingers and watching with interest. "I'll have a scotch."

Crush returned and put an orange soda in front of him. When he sat down, he popped the lid off his own bottle and took a long drink. Christian could hear the fizz bubbling in Crush's throat with every gulp, so he focused on tuning out all the little sounds that were becoming an unwanted distraction.

"Raven doesn't know I know," Crush began, setting the bottle on the table.

"If you knew about Vampires all along, why didn't you tell her?"

"She looked torn, and I didn't want anything holding her back from moving on if that's what she needs. There would have been more explaining to do, and one quick visit isn't enough to fill in all the gaps."

"The gaps being that she finds out you're a liar."

"I'm her old man, and a father will do anything to keep his kid from hurting. But you wouldn't know anything about that."

"You're right." Christian flicked his thumb, and the lid popped off his soda and flew across the room. "How much do you know?"

Crush scratched his jaw. "Enough to know that her eyes should be coal black. Enough to know that her skin doesn't look like a Vampire's even though she has fangs."

Christian took a swig and grimaced at the sharp bite of the carbonated drink. He might as well learn what he could about

Crush since he was going to scrub it all away anyhow. "Raven's… special."

"Of course she's special. She's got her mama's blood running in her veins."

"What I mean is, she's not entirely Vampire."

Crush rested his right arm on the table and leaned forward. "Now you've got my attention."

"She's half Mage."

"You're shittin' me."

Christian stared directly at Crush, who was avoiding eye contact.

How intriguing.

He could easily imagine this guy wearing one of those black skullcaps that tie in the back, sitting on his Harley and spitting against the wind. The last guy he would have expected to know about the Breed world. His goatee and hair was mostly salt with a little pepper, and though his blue eyes weren't as light as Raven's, there was something familiar about them he couldn't put his finger on that reminded him of Raven. She hadn't inherited his big nose or rough skin, but she'd certainly acquired his straightforward personality and tough demeanor.

"How exactly did my daughter wind up a mutant?"

"I believe *crossbreed* is the word you're looking for." Christian waved his hand when Crush rinsed him with a cold stare. "I wasn't there. What happened to her is like hitting the genetic jackpot."

"And you're protecting her?"

Christian gave a throaty chuckle. "She does a fine job protecting herself."

"As a… bounty hunter," Crush said, making an educated guess.

"Not exactly. Think of it as bounty hunting on a larger scale without all the rules."

"She looks sick."

"That's only temporary. Raven helped bring down a murderer last night, and she saved a baby's life. She's all tuckered out."

Crush's chest swelled with pride, and he leaned back in his chair. "Then she's doing something that matters. I always knew she was better than just selling dresses at some fancy department store or being somebody's old lady."

Christian cocked his eyebrow. "So you're proud your baby girl's a killer?"

"Did you know that female lions do most of the hunting in a pride? Your first mistake is assuming that women are the weaker sex." Crush took a long drink until his bottle emptied. "You think your bluntness will shock me, but you're just a peckerhead in a *Matrix* coat. Did you ever see that movie? No, of course you haven't. That's why guys like you are still asleep. Even though half my buddies are Breed, I kept Raven away from the truth. They knew my rules and respected them. She didn't lead a conventional life, but I figured the last thing she'd want to know was that we were friends with Shifters, Relics, and a few others. I wanted her to have a normal life, because you and I know just how dark this world can be. Little did I know that when given the choice, she'd pick the red pill. I should have known. After all, she has my blood running through her."

Christian pretended to know what he was talking about and made a mental note to watch *The Matrix*. He studied Crush's tattoos. A skeleton riding a bike with flames behind him, and a dagger on his forearm with the name Cookie written across a banner in front.

"You like 'em?" Crush asked, turning his arms to show them off. Then he pulled his shirt up and revealed another one across his chest. The heart tattoo had flames on one side and a coy bluebird on the other. The banner across it had the name Bonnie. It was well done, shaded and given dimension. Crush stroked his finger over it. "It used to just be the bluebird. That was for Raven's mother."

"But you weren't married," Christian pointed out, remembering Raven's version of the story.

Crush laughed and pulled down his tight shirt, some of his belly sticking out. "A piece of jewelry doesn't prove your devotion. You can take off a ring, slip it into your pocket, and pretend it never happened. But this," he said, pointing at the tattoo. "This is my heart on my sleeve. Forever. I got the bird first because I called her Bonnie Bluebird. I got the rest after she died."

Christian put his hands in his lap and laced his fingers together. "I'm surprised Raven isn't covered in tattoos."

Crush tugged on his earlobe. "That was never her thing. But I have a pink unicorn on my ankle thanks to that girl. I passed out drunk, so she decided to teach me a lesson by having my buddy give me something extra," he said with a chuckle. "She has a sense of humor few men can appreciate."

"I know a little something about that."

"She also gives people what they deserve."

"I'm guessing that's why she never married."

Crush shook his head. "None of the bozos she dated were serious enough. They were also too clean-cut. One thing I know about that girl is Raven'll never give her whole heart to a man who doesn't ink himself for her. She grew up around that kind of devotion, so it's all she knows. You got any ink?"

"None that I'd like to share."

Crush squared his eyes on Christian and glowered. "Let's cut the bullshit. What kind of relationship do you have with my daughter?"

Christian felt himself blink more times than he should have. "We're partners."

"Uh-huh. I can tell you're not fucking her, but you've got some feelings for her, don't you?"

Awkward wasn't even the word. Christian peered out the window behind him and changed the subject. "You should get yourself a decent home with all that money you're hoarding."

"The first time I met Raven's mother, she slapped me in the face," Crush said, not letting Christian steer the conversation. "I deserved it for calling her a tramp when she didn't talk to me. I liked her, and men do dumb shit when they like a woman. I made it up to her later by treating her like a lady and taking her out. We used to live together, but when I knocked her up, she got serious about our relationship and wanted me to change my ways. You see, I had a demon called alcohol on my back. I loved alcohol more than Bonnie, and I wasn't willing to give it up. She threw me out, but we still loved each other. I took care of her financially and was a father to my kid. Bonnie never stopped me from being a part of Raven's life. But the booze… Sometimes we try to fool ourselves that we can be a better man when, deep down, we know we're not. Even after she died, I couldn't give up the booze. When I almost lost Raven because of it, I cleaned up my act."

"I don't think this is something I need to hear. Raven and I live in the present."

Crush's knee bounced up and down. "Your present just shit all over my life, so don't tell me the past doesn't matter. Don't think I didn't notice the way you were looking at her. She's a good girl, and good girls have no business with men like us. We're the hurricane that ruins their lives because we love something more. Maybe your demon is your own ego, or maybe it's something else. Love is easy. Commitment is a bitch. Commitment requires you to make sacrifices. So do me a favor and don't play with her heart. She's been through enough trauma in her life. She deserves a real man who isn't afraid to show his cards and be the love of her life."

Christian could feel the blood heating his face. He didn't like anyone holding a mirror up to him; he didn't like being transparent. But after meeting this brassy, uncouth man, it gave him a better understanding of Raven.

Crush sighed, his voice calmer. "You're her partner. Watch over and protect her since I'm not there to do it. She's always been tough with a mind of her own, but sometimes she doesn't know right from wrong. That's my fault. I didn't do a good enough job raising her like her mama would have. I fucked up—made mistakes. Getting clean wasn't good enough."

"Aye, I'll look after her." Christian's attention drifted when he heard *Für Elise* playing on Raven's music box outside.

He suddenly jumped when Crush stabbed between Christian's legs with a knife, sinking the blade into the chair. He'd been so distracted by the music that he hadn't heard the human pull the switchblade from his back pocket.

"One more thing," Crush said. "Now that I've got your undivided attention."

Christian's expression tightened, but he didn't remove the knife from the chair.

"I know why you tagged along," Crush continued. "But see, I already know about your world. You don't have to scrub my memory to keep your secret. I know how this favor thing works and how you immortals value it more than gold. Let me keep this memory of my daughter, and I'll owe you one."

Christian narrowed his eyes. "What could I possibly want from you?"

Crush sat back and folded his arms. "I'm sure something will come to mind. I've lived in your world for years. Why not get something out of it?"

"And what if I'm doing this as a favor to your daughter?"

"Then you'll have to figure out a way to repay her that favor without her knowing. Next time she needs something, you do it. No questions asked. Then whatever conscience you have is clean."

"And what if she asks me to do her laundry for eternity?"

Crush stood up and emptied his pockets, pulling the lining out. "I'm all out of fucks to give."

Christian freed the knife and set it on the table. It was a tempting offer. Scrubbing Crush's memory seemed superfluous, especially given the fact that he didn't just know about their world but was immersed in it. There was also a risk that if Christian left any holes, Crush's friends might sense something was off. It could backfire on him in a big way. Scrubbing his memory would be the easiest way to even his debt with Raven, but making a deal with Crush meant another favor in his pocket. He'd be a fool to turn down a favor owed, even from a human.

Christian rose to his feet and inclined his head. "I'll tell her it's done, but on one condition."

Crush slid his jaw to the side. "What's that?"

"You're mortal and probably one cheeseburger away from a coronary. The favor carries over after death to one of your friends. A Sensor can validate I'm telling the truth."

"Men like me don't die easily."

"You're human. You all die easily."

"My buddies won't trust a Vamp."

"Then my friend will hunt down your ghost and make you pay up from the afterworld."

Crush grimaced. "You know a Gravewalker?"

"Do we have a deal, or do we need to sit down and get to business?"

It took a minute, but Crush capitulated. "You can see my buddy Red. Just tell him he still owes me a favor for that piece-of-shit car. He'll know exactly what you're talking about, but I have a feeling you'll come asking long before the Reaper shows up at my door. Shake on it." Crush held out his hand.

Christian stared at it.

"Don't be such a pussy. I know you guys prefer to bow and shit, but I'm a man of honor, and we shake on things."

Christian held out his hand, and even though Crush was just a mortal, his grip was iron. "Then you and I have a deal."

Chapter 26

"How do you feel?" Gem watched me with keen interest as she rolled along on her skates.

"More like myself. I think my light's almost pure again," I said, rubbing my heavy-lidded eyes. It was already evening, another day lost. After coming home late from visiting my father the night before, I stayed in my room all day. I'd spent most of the time thinking about our conversation, but my body still needed to catch up on sleep.

She gave me an elfin grin. "I should hope so. You slept the entire day. Alas, you missed out on Christian's oatmeal extravaganza this morning. I finally know what wet sawdust tastes like. He also volunteered to make lunch, but everyone chipped in for Chinese delivery instead. Viktor's probably going to extend your cooking rotation since you haven't done much of it."

I slowed my gait and stared down at my white socks. "Dark light takes a lot out of me. I don't think you would have wanted me in the kitchen."

"Where did you and Christian go last night?"

"He wanted to talk to a guy about fixing his car. I slept most of the time. How's Claude?"

"Purrrfect." She giggled and skated ahead of me, her long black duster decorated with white butterflies flapping behind her. "He can't go to the party tonight since he's still recovering. Viktor ordered him to stay in bed, and he didn't put up a fight. So he *must* be in pain."

I snorted. "Or he doesn't care for going to fancy balls."

Gem twirled in a circle and then stopped. "Everyone likes balls."

I buried a laugh. "Why so glum?"

"I won't have my buddy to keep me company." Her violet lips turned down. "He always saves me from the awkward socialites who engage in dull conversations about how wretched modern-day living is compared to the Middle Ages when they had public beheadings and ate with their hands."

My gaze dragged up to the arched ceiling, and I marveled at the way the candlelight danced across every crevice of stone. Even though visiting my father and saying good-bye was the hardest thing I'd ever done, it had finally given me peace. The same kind of peace you feel when you get a funeral over with and you don't have that heavy weight on your shoulders of the final good-bye. My fangs had come as a shock to him, but why hadn't he asked more about it? Maybe it was too much to take in. I couldn't blame him. I mean, he thought he'd buried me, and there I was, drinking cocoa in his kitchen. He probably figured I'd joined a cult.

It didn't matter anymore. Christian had scrubbed his memory of the visit.

When we entered Wyatt's computer room, I saw the back of Christian's head. His arms were draped over the sides of a beanbag chair, and *The Matrix* was playing on the television. I frowned. Christian wasn't the kind of guy who sat around watching TV, let alone by himself.

I plopped down in Wyatt's leather chair and flicked a wrapper away from the keyboard.

Gem turned in a circle and then gripped the doorframe. "Well, I'm going to go downstairs and swim before it gets too late. Night, all!"

I switched on the desktop computer that Wyatt allowed the team to use. "Is Viktor repairing the van?"

"Aye. What are you doing in here?"

I typed in a few search words. "Some of those files I was looking at before this Cristo case came along have me curious."

"The Vampire trading? Let it go, Raven."

While Christian watched Morpheus offer Neo a choice between the blue or red pill, I tumbled down my own rabbit hole on the Internet. Now that Cristo's case was closed, I knew we would probably have downtime until our next assignment.

First, I typed in "people obsessed with Vampires." I read a few articles about the obsession with immortality, blood, and feeling chosen. I tried a few other search terms and scrolled through several pages until I found a comprehensive website about Vampires. The site contained a long list of categories. Vampire culture, history, clothing, folklore, social groups, photographs, facts, and media. The links with the facts had it mostly wrong. I supposed because the light hurt their eyes, people thought that Vampires couldn't come out in the daylight. Stakes paralyzed them, so one could easily assume it killed them. I wasn't sure where the whole myth with holy water and silver came in—probably from the church.

Thirty minutes later, I wound up on a message board. I had to create a name and password to log on, so I chose CookieMonster. Once in, I perused.

"Whoa. What a bunch of weirdos," I murmured. There was actually a board for people who bragged about drinking from their pets. When I saw a picture of someone licking a rat, I quickly scrolled down.

These humans either claimed to be Vampires or wanted to be a creature of the night. One section looked more like the personals where people were requesting to be slaves. A post with three hundred replies grabbed my attention. The message was an alleged Vampire asking for someone who wanted to be his chosen one. I scrolled down, looking at one reply after the next from people desperate to be selected.

"Christian, remember those files I was looking at? The black marketeer who's selling women?"

Christian held up his hand. "Bloody hell, he's in a pod! Have you seen this? If someone told me that was the real world, I'd shove my finger down my throat and vomit the drugs."

"It wasn't a real pill," I said. "He just opened his mind to the possibility."

Christian wasn't listening to me anymore.

I looked at the original post, in which the author had misspelled *discreet*, and jotted down the poster's name on a piece of paper. It was probably a coincidence; half the Internet couldn't spell. I printed out the page and folded it in half, deciding to include it in the file. Before closing the browser window, I left a message of my own. Most of them were long and looked like a résumé, while others were desperate pleas to be chosen. What were these guys looking for?

Dear Vampire, I'm a young woman with no family, no pets, no friends, and no future. I want someone to show me what's possible.

That sounded desperate enough. I hit Send and shut down. I'd really come in here to talk to Christian and find out if my father had said anything else, but he was so engrossed in the movie that I decided to leave.

"Raven?"

I glared at the back of his head. "Yes?"

"Do you ever wonder if there's any truth to this?" He turned around, his arms hugging the back of the beanbag. "What if we're all in a dream and none of this is real?"

"Then I guess it doesn't matter whether I cook dinner or not. See you later."

Keystone was enormous with its winding interior halls, courtyard, grand staircases, and a million rooms. Many of the halls looked the same, and I got easily lost when not paying attention. I opened the door to a balcony and stepped outside.

It was a beautiful view of the interior courtyard from the back of the house. Snow covered most of the grounds, except someone had dragged the cover away from the pool and turned on the lights. The velvet sky was blacker than I'd ever seen it. I drew in a breath of clean air, which had just a trace of burning wood from one of the many fireplaces. I had to admit, I'd never seen anything as magical as Keystone in wintertime.

"How are you feeling?" Niko asked.

He joined my side and placed his hands on the snow-covered railing, unable to see the blue and green lights glittering in the heated pool below, unable to see the stars sparkling in the sky like diamonds. But he could see what counted.

"I feel better," I admitted.

His long hair fell forward when he leaned on the railing. "I won't ask where you went last night, but your light is brighter."

"I feel brighter. How's Shepherd?"

Niko straightened up and wiped flecks of snow from his sleeves. "Only time can heal his wounds. He carries a lot of grief with him over the life he'll never have."

"Don't we all. I was looking at a message board tonight where all these humans are dying to be immortal. They think they can still have their cake and eat it too, but they don't know what they'd be giving up."

"Just one of many reasons why it's best we live in secret. If they knew immortality was possible, just imagine the bribery and desperate acts. People would be willing to do anything for just a chance."

I shivered. Niko was right. All it had taken for me to give up my life was a chance meeting with a stranger in a bar.

My gaze swung toward the courtyard when I heard a shriek below. Gem dashed across a snowy walkway before leaping into the pool.

"That is one crazy girl," I mused.

Niko rocked with laughter. He had a warm and honest laugh, and it changed his expression entirely—his blue eyes flickering with ancient light, his appearance seeming younger. I couldn't begin to guess his physical age—maybe late twenties or thirties? I only knew that he was over fifteen hundred years old, and most immortals who'd lived that long had lost their naivety, humor, and passion for life.

"Gem's light is interesting in water. It changes to a deeper shade of what I see as violet. And it…"

He made a gesture with his fingers in an outward motion.

"Sparkles?" I suggested.

"I suppose that's it. Sometimes I see her trail in the halls where she's been skating, and it's a perfect ribbon of light. Shepherd leaves behind flecks that crackle and burn out. Everyone's different."

"Don't you find it odd she swims in winter?"

"We all have our peculiarities."

I leaned against the wall behind me. "If we ever go out of the espionage business, Viktor should open the doors to this place and make it an orphanage."

Niko's brows touched his hairline. "What brought that to mind?"

"I was thinking about what's going to happen with that baby. You can't help but feel empathy for them."

Niko led me inside. "That's where these charity balls come into play. We don't have government funding like the humans. We have to encourage the wealthy to give, and public events such as these are more effective."

"Because they're all trying to show off."

"Exactly. Without that money, there wouldn't be enough funds to maintain the orphanages, and those children would be out on the streets. Viktor was generous to offer his cut. He is truly a benevolent man."

That was pretty unexpected of him, I thought to myself. Viktor's donation made me see him in a new light.

"We have influence," Niko said. "I believe that's why they continually invite us to these events. We witness firsthand what happens to these children, and while they don't know our affiliation, we're able to paint a more vivid picture about where these orphans really come from."

"What do they sell at these auctions?"

"Sometimes people are willing to offer their services to the highest bidder. But usually it's a way for people to offload valuables they've collected over the years. The organizers auction everything from jewelry to historical paintings."

I stopped in my tracks and gave him a quizzical stare. "And people are willing to give away their valuables for free?"

"Some. Though I suspect most of the items are from the deceased."

"I thought all that stuff was sent to places like Pawn of the Dead."

Niko tilted his head. "Your brain is always working. You can question the higher authority when you get there if you like."

"I'd rather just eat cake."

"That's probably a wise idea. If you ask too many questions, it raises suspicion. Inquisitive minds are not often as celebrated in our world as in the human one you came from. Would you like to join me downstairs for a cup of tea?"

I looked at the folded paper in my hand. "Sounds good. Give me a few minutes. I need to take care of something."

After we parted ways, I headed up to my bedroom and closed the door. A few candles burned low, barely enough light to see the furniture. I rounded my bed and approached the desk, setting the paper down on top of a file. I lifted the lid to my music box, and as the melody began, the tiny ballerina twirled in a circle.

I admired my modest collection of personal things, including a diary that had once belonged to a girl named Penny Burns. It wasn't really mine to keep, but I'd read it twice more since the case. I shoved some pens and paper aside to make room for the fake roses I usually kept on my nightstand. As insignificant as these things might have appeared, they belonged to me, and that made this place feel more like home.

As the melody slowed down, I lifted the heart-shaped necklace from my neck and placed it inside. Now I had a home for my heart. I took a seat in the wooden chair and fiddled with the metal puzzle box.

Viktor taking a chance on me had been the best thing that could have happened given the direction I was heading at the time he found me. Maybe I didn't have a completely functional moral compass, but with Keystone, I made a difference. If only my father could have seen us saving that baby. It made me regret that I hadn't told him every detail, but I'd been afraid Christian would have more to erase and might accidentally scrub something important, like the fact that I ever existed.

A click sounded in my hands, and I looked down. I'd pressed

the cube in two different spots, causing a piece of it to slide out. I took a close look to remember what I'd done, and then I forced the block to the side as far as it would go. I peered inside the hole, unable to see anything. After five minutes of messing with it, I triggered another opening. Curious, I tugged and pulled at the pieces until one side twisted away from the cube and revealed the core. It looked like a black box within the cube. I couldn't find a way to pry it open, but when I pushed it with my finger, another click sounded, and it opened like a door with tiny hinges.

I blinked at the contents.

Inside was a key pressed into foam.

All that trouble for a key. Probably someone's extra house key. I carefully closed the sides, remembering the order that allowed me to open it.

Before heading downstairs to chat with Niko over some hot tea—and he made a mean cup—I spotted something I hadn't noticed when coming into my room just moments ago. Neatly folded at the foot of my bed was a new coat, just like the one that I'd lost in the Bricks. Also at the foot of my bed, a pair of boots. But they weren't new, because I noticed scuffs on the toe. While I couldn't be certain, they looked a lot like the ones I'd traded underground.

I guess I had a few mysteries of my own.

Chapter 27

I LIFTED A CHAMPAGNE FLUTE FROM a tray and breezed through the crowd until I found an empty corner. This charity ball was no joke. People were dressed to the nines, and even my black dress looked plain. Maybe it was a little too short, but I thought cocktail parties with short dresses were the norm. The studded leather bracelet probably wasn't, but it was a prized possession. Not because it used to belong to me, but because it was one of the few personal effects of mine that my father had saved for sentimental reasons.

After gulping down my second glass, I decided to ease up on the booze. I recognized a familiar face across the room. Hooper stood behind a long table, mixing drinks. This was a far cry from working in the Nine Circles of Hell club, and he stuck out like a sore thumb with his lip rings and the designs shaved on each side of his head. White cloth covered the tables. Behind him, another long table where they kept the alcohol and glasses.

Gem looked dejected without Claude at her side, but she masked it well with a mechanical smile and all that silver glitter around her eyes. Claude was an attentive friend to her, and perhaps I wasn't gregarious enough to be good company during events like these. Gem didn't care much for dressing appropriately—she had a different approach when it came to style. Her fairy dress was made of chiffon and had a bustled skirt that didn't quite reach her knees. The colors were beautifully blended shades of violet and ivory, and she was decked out in crystal necklaces and bracelets that sparkled beneath the lights. She even had a crown of flowers on her head.

Guests at these functions didn't notice people who went over the top. The ones who got the side eye were people like Wyatt, who was wearing his THE FUCK I GAVE WENT THAT WAY T-shirt.

I set my empty glass on a tray when a waiter breezed by. Standing alone was awkward, but when I decided to head over and talk to Gem, my plan fell apart as I saw her getting chatty with Hooper. Gem didn't drink, so she couldn't have been requesting a complicated drink order. They both shared a funky sense of style, and since like generally attracts like, I decided to leave them be.

Shepherd slowly climbed the stairs, distancing himself from the crowd. Viktor had a glass of wine in his hand while two patrons listened with rapt attention as he told the story about how children sold on the black market are stolen from their mother's arms. Blue looked liked she wanted to dodge the attention she was receiving from a tall man who couldn't take his eyes off her sage gown and feather earrings, which he kept touching. But she was dutifully encouraging donations with her plunging neckline and guile.

Perhaps I needed to do the same.

I entered a grand room where a string quartet enchanted the crowd with heavenly music. It was as if my music box had come to life. Couples twirled and glided, every one of them in perfect form. Sumptuous gowns floated gracefully, creating a magnificent array of color and texture.

Christian appeared next to me.

"Holy fuck. I thought we were mercenaries, not ballroom dancers," I said, gawking at the dancers before us.

"Is bathing and putting on decent clothes the worst thing about your job?"

"No. Smelling your rancid cologne is."

He chuckled. "The ladies do like."

I stole a glance. Christian had on a suit vest—no jacket. The most dressed up I'd seen him was in a silk shirt or a Henley, but this was a whole new look to marvel over. Even his grey slacks matched his vest. While he had knotted his tie to precision, there was one thing unkempt about him—his sleeves were sloppily rolled up to the elbows. Christian didn't just look like a gentleman—he portrayed himself as a powerful man who belonged among these people, which just went to prove what a chameleon he was.

The only thing he hadn't done was shave, but I suspected that would happen on the day that pigs grew wings.

"Why don't you ask a lady to dance?"

He rocked on his heels and put his hands in his pockets. "Are you afflicted in some way? I don't dance. It's a frivolous custom for fools."

I glared up at him. "I've seen you grinding on women in the club."

He winked. "That's not dancing, lass."

"Ah, yes. I forgot. That's how you decide who's good in bed. For your information, how a woman moves on the dance floor won't tell you anything about what kind of lover she is."

"If you say so."

"Well, I'll just let you stand here and watch other people having virtual sex." I smiled and strutted alongside the wall to the other end of the room in search of the waiter carrying the champagne.

"Would you care to dance?" someone asked, his French accent collecting my attention.

I raised my head at the man standing just behind me, his black suit and tie blending him in with half the crowd. *Why not?*

"Sure."

He took my hand and led me to the floor. My palms began to sweat when couples turned and glided all around us, as if they were following an invisible pattern on the floor. Maybe this wasn't such a good idea.

If I could survive a hail of gunfire, surely dancing couldn't be that difficult. I clasped his hand and followed his lead. Thankfully, he went slowly at first. He must have sensed by my trembling knees and lack of eye contact that I'd never done this before.

"It takes practice," he said. "You must be young. Perhaps a Relic?"

"No, a Mage."

I glanced at those around us, mirroring their moves. What I couldn't do was mirror their confidence.

"These gatherings are such a bore," he continued. "Always the same food, the same people, the same music."

"Maybe someone should hire a DJ." I grimaced when I stepped on his foot. "Sorry."

"Stop trying to take the lead," he said. "Relax and follow me."

"Maybe I'm not a follower."

When I finally got the hang of the steps, I smiled and looked up.

The blond-haired man blinked in surprise, and his eyebrows gathered in a frown. "You lost a contact lens."

"Nope. These are my eyes." I stepped on his foot again. "Is there something here you're bidding on? The orphans could really use your support. I never realized what a problem we had with all the black market stuff until recently. It's sad that so many kids get caught up in it, don't you think?"

The man continued to stare, and it made me self-conscious. It wasn't so much the staring but the shift in his expression from uncertainty to what looked like revulsion. What was spinning in that little mind of his? Was he questioning my Breed? His gaze flicked from one eye to the other until I finally stomped on his foot.

"Ow!"

"What the fuck is your problem?" I spat.

A few people gawked as they glided around us.

The man gave me a sour look and simply walked off.

So there I stood in the middle of a ballroom after telling a nice man to fuck off.

Good job, Raven.

Embarrassment heated my cheeks as I fled the dance floor. But when a few dancers made way, I met eyes with Christian, who moved in my direction with a purposeful stride.

"Is there a problem?" he asked, not a hint of amusement in his voice.

"Apparently someone didn't like my moves. Why do immortals make such a big stink about physical features? There are people walking around with blue hair and nose rings, and nobody gives them a second glance. But I get shit all the time for something so innocuous."

"Because they're dolts," he replied, taking my hand in his.

Before I knew it, we were dancing. Only, Christian didn't move anything like the other man. His grip and moves were smooth and demanding, and I could sense his direction before he even turned. Christian knew how to lead, and there was something erotic in the way he locked eyes with me as our bodies drew closer together.

"What did you and my father talk about?"

"Oh, manly things."

"If there's one thing Crush doesn't lack, it's candor. I'm sure whatever he said was brutally honest. Just try not to hold it against him." I fell silent, the room spinning as Christian led me around the dance floor.

"I saw one of your pictures on the wall," he said. "You were a little badass."

"Was that the one of me in the short leather skirt? I went through a phase."

"You'll have to let me know when the phase ends."

Just when we found our stride, the music ended, and light applause fluttered through the room. When I looked to the right, I glimpsed a familiar bleach-blond haircut. My friend from Club Nine held eye contact with me for just a second in the doorway before disappearing. I needed to thank him for leading us to Cristo.

"There's nothing wrong with your moves," Christian said, giving me a wolfish grin. "Sometimes you just need the right partner."

I straightened his tie. "Thanks for the dance, Mr. Poe. I think it's time for us to mingle."

He inclined his head and swaggered across the room toward a bevy of women who were preening in hopes of receiving his exclusive attention. I smiled and watched him work his magic.

Christian was a wild mustang, and whether or not he could be tamed was irrelevant. He didn't want to be. I'd known men like that my whole life, including my father.

Maybe they had more in common than I'd first thought.

Shepherd wasn't feeling up to a party, but he continued with the charade at Viktor's request. What he really craved was a bottle of hard liquor. He was hanging back, looking for an excuse to leave, when he suddenly caught sight of a woman with wavy blond hair. She might have been a ghost from his past, but when she turned around, a stranger's face stared back at him. His heart clenched, and that sealed the deal. He needed to escape the crowd and be alone.

Killing Cristo had brought him an immense amount of pleasure and pain all at once. Shepherd had always imagined it in his head, but Cristo's death hadn't brought him the closure he'd expected would follow. In those final moments, Shepherd became the monster that lived in the dark corners of his soul. He wanted Cristo to beg for mercy and apologize, but all he got were screams as he stabbed the man who had tortured so many women, including Shepherd's only love. Cristo laughed when the alarms went off, as if the cavalry had come to save him. Enraged, Shepherd sliced him across the belly. Murdering Cristo was a fruitless task that brought him no joy. It didn't bring back Maggie. Instead, it pushed him even further away from the man he once was. Perhaps what really died in that room was the last piece of his soul.

Shepherd found a quiet spot upstairs and sat down in an ornate chair. Patrick had one hell of a mansion. Officials like him always lived lavish lifestyles.

Wyatt sent him another dumbass picture over the phone. This time, he had a mouthful of grapes and a wide smile. Shepherd deleted the picture and began scrolling through the others that his twisted partner had been sending him all night. It was Wyatt's way of cheering him up, but Shepherd just wasn't in the mood.

He swiped his finger across the screen and frowned at a blurry shot of a carpet. After deleting it, he noticed the next image was a small shoe. Then one of Raven reaching for the camera, but she wasn't wearing a black dress. These were from Patrick's dinner party. Shepherd continued deleting pictures of vases, the ceiling, hands, someone's tongue sticking out, and then… finally stopped.

Patrick's little boy had stolen his phone and taken all these photos, either intentionally or by accident. Probably the latter. Shepherd wasn't sure how much little kids knew about operating a phone.

It was the first time he'd seen the boy without his black mask, and the first thing he noticed were how blue his eyes were. They were rimmed in black and not a flat color at all. The inside of the irises had a paler shade that streaked outward like electricity. Shepherd couldn't stop staring. Something else caught his attention, and he zoomed in.

His heart rocketed in his chest when he noticed a scar across the boy's face. It started near the corner of his left eye and curved across his cheek to the center of his nose.

Cristo's words echoed in his mind. *"Thought I killed him, though. Cut his face when my knife went in, and I only got paid half for damaging the goods."*

Shepherd quickly scrolled through the remaining pics, but only one other showed the boy, and the mask obscured his face. He went back to the clear shot and drank it all in.

It couldn't be.

It had to be a coincidence. But to look at him, he was roughly the same age as when it happened. He had Maggie's eyes, only his hair was black. Shepherd had dark brown hair, but his mother had black hair. The look he gave the camera was serious and stony—an expression far too mature for a five-year-old.

Shepherd needed to see him in person.

Now.

He launched to his feet and flung open the doors to every room he passed. The kid wasn't hanging around Patrick tonight like usual, so he had to be upstairs somewhere. When he interrupted a couple making out in a closed room, the woman gave him a scathing glance. Shepherd left the door open and jogged upstairs to the third level. It was quieter up there. No guests or staff.

Shepherd opened the door to another room, and something caught his attention.

A child-size bed.

He flipped on the light and strode inside, looking across the room at the small bed shoved against the wall. The white bedspread didn't look like something a kid would have. Didn't they usually have shit like Batman and race cars? To the right, a wooden dresser and a small desk in the corner. In some ways, it reminded Shepherd of his own room in how basic it was. He opened the top dresser drawer and peered inside at tiny underwear. It had to be the kid's room, but where were the toys?

"Should I be concerned that a grown man is snooping through a child's underwear drawer?" Patrick asked, closing the door behind him.

Shepherd flattened his hands on the dresser and gave Patrick a baleful look over his shoulder.

Mr. Bane leaned against the door, hands in the pockets of his black trousers. "I never thought you'd put the pieces together. I knew this day might come. That's why I made the boy wear the mask in public, but I suppose there's no need for discretion anymore."

Shepherd was thunderstruck, caught in a whirlwind between a dream and a nightmare.

Patrick took a deep breath and made a melodic sound as he released it. "Cristo promised me you were dead, but he also botched the job and scarred the boy's face. I decided to look into it myself and discovered a victim was transported to the hospital, but I couldn't get myself involved to investigate, let alone finish the job. After all, I had a new baby to care for. Shortly after, you disappeared off the face of the earth. I see you changed your name. Even with the scars, I didn't begin to suspect you were that man until you mentioned the story and dated it five years ago."

"Why the hell didn't you confront me?" Shepherd bit out, turning to face him.

"I'm a man who believes in opportunity. You caught your own son and didn't know him by touch. I could have rescinded my offer or even killed you, but when you asked for Cristo's address, it hit me that I could kill two birds with one stone. Cristo is an elusive man, and I've wanted to kill him for years. The only thing that held me back was having his death trace back to me. See, I don't get my hands dirty if I don't have to, and I don't trust anyone enough to do the deed. It was only a matter of time before Cristo would grow desperate for money and threaten me with blackmail. So you see, our favor trade guaranteed my security. You were the perfect weapon."

Shepherd scanned the empty room. "What was it all for? Your sadistic need to torture a child?"

Patrick laughed haughtily. "Don't be ridiculous. He's fed, adequately dressed, socialized, and educated."

"And deprived."

The Mage cocked his head to the side. "Depriving the boy of sensory things sharpens his skills as a Sensor. The less he has to distract himself with, the more attuned he becomes to the world around him. I remove objects that provide pleasure or pain in order to simplify his life."

Shepherd held back his rage, because beneath the surface was immense sorrow, and he'd be damned if he'd give Patrick the satisfaction of one tear. He flicked his gaze at the door and clenched his teeth. Patrick looked like one of the later actors in the James Bond movies, but beneath the façade, he was in fact the villain.

Patrick gave him a tight-lipped grin. "It's soundproof. Sometimes when I have to talk to the boy, I don't want the servants eavesdropping."

"You keep calling him the boy."

"He hasn't earned the right to a name yet. A name gives him identity and individuality. This is how you train them."

Shepherd turned his back on Patrick and slammed his eyes shut. It was everything he could do not to unleash hell on the man, but he needed answers. "Why? Why would you steal a child when you could have adopted one? I mean, what the fuck are these charity auctions for?" He spun around and stared daggers at him.

"Do you think I'd want just *any* child?" Patrick clasped his hands behind his back and strode toward the center of the room. "Maggie and I had a special relationship. Who do you think got her a job at the hospital in the first place?"

Shepherd felt all the blood drain from his head. "What are you talking about?"

"Maggie was a unique girl with specific abilities. Not many Relics specialize in human genetics and pathogens. Unfortunately, she wasn't… cooperative. You can charm a person for information, but you can't make them loyal. Eventually it was brought to my attention that she was with child. Imagine my surprise, especially since she wasn't married. Poor Maggie. She couldn't hide her secret any longer from the higher authority, and they frown upon such things." Patrick turned on his heel and paced. "I had a private conversation, assuring I would secure her job on the condition she tell me the truth about the pregnancy. I can't exactly protect someone if I don't know what I'm protecting."

Shepherd didn't remember Maggie ever mentioning Patrick. "Why would she confide in you if she didn't want to work for you?"

"You're a smart fella. Can't figure it out yourself? She had no recollection of our previous interactions and my unique offer; I had a Vampire scrub her memory of our conversations. Maggie only knew me as the kind man offering to step in and secure her job at the hospital," he said absently.

"Why would you want a Relic's baby?"

Patrick turned a sharp eye at him. "I have my reasons. When she revealed the baby's father was a Sensor, I was dismayed. That would mean the gifts would be canceled out. What an absolute waste. Then she went on to say how much she needed the job to raise a baby. I suggested adoption, and she confided in me that the unborn baby would have *both* gifts. I was flabbergasted. Not only that, but the child would have the lifespan of a Sensor. What a rarity, and only a Relic could know such a secret. What goes on inside their bodies is a mystery among mysteries. But she knew with absolute certainty, and that made the child even more valuable to me. Just *imagine* having a Sensor in my possession."

"Someone to do your dirty work," Shepherd growled. "Why not wait until the baby was born? Why would you—" He choked on his own words.

"Yes, the whole thing was a messy affair. Cristo assured me it was better this way. Clearly the father was a Sensor, and without knowing who the man was, Cristo advised it was too dangerous to wait. The child could have distinct features that would identify him, or the father might hold him and always know him by touch. Maggie was of no use to me once I had the child. He'll grow up with the same knowledge as his mother, and under my control."

"What's to stop me from outing you right here, right now, in front of everyone?"

Patrick gave him a sardonic smile. "Because, dear boy, no one will believe you. I'm telling you the facts so you'll know what's at stake. You have no evidence, and slander against a member of the higher authority without concrete evidence is treason, punishable by death. They won't open an investigation on accusation alone. You know that as well as I do." He took a step forward, his eyes glacial. "Do you want me to bring down your entire organization? I can place every single one of your friends in Breed jail and throw away the key. Even if you could get him back, without Keystone, what kind of life could you give a child if you're living hand to mouth on the streets? You don't want to mess with me. I will tear your life apart."

Shepherd retrieved a blade from inside his jacket and stared at Patrick wordlessly.

Patrick's eyes drifted down to the dagger. "We both know you won't do anything. Your son will end up in an orphanage, if he's lucky. It's your word against mine."

"I'll come for him."

Patrick's lip curled. "Will you? I have something of yours that's very... fragile. Accidents happen. If you even think about organizing a mission to steal him away, I won't hunt you down. No. I'll hire the most ruthless hitman in the Breed world to hunt down that boy and kill him... right in front of you."

"You're using my son to do your dirty work!" Shepherd roared. "You have no right."

"There's nothing wrong with a life of servitude," Patrick said flatly. "The people in power may hire you, but if your operation was exposed for what it really is, do you think they would protect you? What can you give him that I cannot? A toy? And what will that teach him? It's certainly not love—something we both know you're incapable of. Love doesn't make a boy into a man. You've crossed a line somewhere and have no business raising a child. Your only stake in this is possession. The boy helps me with my position. His job allows me to know who is being truthful and who is not. I have you to thank for those gifts."

"You can't do this," Shepherd said with less conviction, gripping the handle of his blade so tightly that his joints began to ache. "I'll kill you."

"I have eyes and ears everywhere. I'm not someone you wish to trifle with. The Vampires underground are very helpful for the right price, and they informed me that Cristo died by your hand. I've placed that little incident in your record. And yes, you have a record. Everyone in Keystone does. I like to collect things. Just imagine what my colleagues would make of a man who killed an official, especially after reviewing your history of violence. You'll do your son more harm than good, and you can't protect him if your head is away from your shoulders."

Shepherd moved fast. He slammed Patrick against the door, pressing the sharp blade to his neck. A rivulet of blood dribbled down his gullet. "You don't have a damn thing to take me down. Maybe you've got yourself a nice little file, but it's not enough to put me away, or else I'd already be behind bars. But know this: every move you make, I'll be watching. You make one felonious move, and we'll be on your ass, because that's what we do. Remember who *I* am. I work for Keystone, and that means I don't play nice. *No one* is untouchable. One way or another, I'm going to get my kid back. But not before I put a knife through your black heart and cut off your head, you dirty fucking Mage. Cristo begged for his life, but you're going to beg me to end it."

Patrick's lips pressed into a mulish line. He leaned against the blade, pushing Shepherd back until there was distance between them. After taking a handkerchief from his pocket and dabbing his neck, he gave Shepherd one final look before leaving. "Now that I know who you are, I know who to teach your son to hate."

Chapter 28

THE CHARITY BALL CARRIED ON until the wee hours of the morning, and by the time we dragged ourselves home, dawn was approaching, and most everyone went straight to bed. Shepherd headed down to the training room without skipping a beat, and I decided to bake canned biscuits—just in case someone wandered down for breakfast.

No one had.

To keep myself busy, I threw a ton of pasta into a boiling pot of water and spent a long time chopping up peppers, onions, tomatoes, and pepperoni to make a pasta salad. It was one of the few meals I knew how to make and the kind of thing that would keep in the fridge until everyone was ready for lunch.

Afterward, I went upstairs and showered. While changing, I wound up my jewelry box and opened the lid to play the music. Instead of placing my necklace inside, I kept it on and tucked it beneath my shirt. Something was weighing heavily on my mind, and since it was a beautiful day, I decided to leave later, but before dark.

At around three in the afternoon, everyone began trickling into the dining room. Niko helped me set the table, and when Viktor got a look at my culinary masterpiece, he selected an enormous bottle of wine to go with it. I'd even baked garlic bread as an appetizer. Not too shabby for a girl who used to eat cold hot dogs right out of the package.

"You must have a thing for pasta," Wyatt remarked, taking a

seat in his chair. He pinched a black olive from the bowl and tossed it into his mouth.

Blue moseyed into the room, her outfit an afterthought. She had on her trademark feather earrings, but her hair was pulled up in a messy bun, strands hanging loose, and her clothes were baggy and casual. She sat in her seat and yawned. "I think I'm going to let my animal fly for a few hours. I need more rest, and she wants to spread her wings."

Viktor circled the table, pouring wine into each glass… except for Gem's. "Take care that you stay on the property."

"She's always good about that, but I'm giving her full control today. I want to catch up on some sleep, so I can't make any promises."

He filled her glass. "I worry about you."

"Needlessly." She motioned for him to stop pouring. "I shouldn't drink and fly."

"I drink and run."

She grinned, a twinkle in her eyes. "Is that so?"

I stared blankly at Wyatt while he loaded up his plate.

"Is Shepherd sleeping?" I asked. "I saw him go upstairs an hour ago."

Wyatt scratched his whiskery jaw and looked at me with one eye closed. "I ain't his keeper. If he wants to skip lunch, then more for me."

Gem reached over the chair between them and pinched his arm. "Meanie."

"Lay that guilt on someone else. I knocked on his door to invite him down, but he's busy staring at his phone and ignoring the living. Probably looking at all those sexy pics I sent him last night."

Gem snorted. "Of what? You making love to your MoonPies? They're not a basic food group, you know."

He stood up and reached for the bottle of wine. "Says you."

"Have you put on weight?"

He glanced down at his belly and gave it a long look. Despite his nerdy inclinations, Wyatt kept himself fit. "Doesn't matter anyhow. I had to send them all back."

She gave him an impish grin. "So I won't find a hidden stash if I dig in the back of your drawers?"

He winked and refilled his glass.

Claude swaggered into the room. Shirtless. "I would say that something smells good, but I don't smell much of anything except onions."

Wyatt rolled his eyes. "Man, put something on. This isn't a casting call for *Gladiator*. Your chesticles impress no one around here."

Gem reached out, and Claude leaned down to give her a hug.

"How are the injuries healing up?" Blue asked.

He sat down at the other end of the table, across from Niko. "I should be snipping hair in no time."

"I think someone is milking his vacation time," Wyatt said to me. "Breakfast in bed, a sponge bath..."

I erupted with laughter. "Who gave him a sponge bath?"

He pointed both thumbs at himself. "Yours truly. Viktor's orders. I just can't figure out why it is I can't offer my services to the opposite sex."

I gave him a pointed look. "If you ever come into my bathroom with a loofah, I'll lay you out."

Everyone dug in, complimenting my food and conversing about the weather and other unimportant matters. Maybe I wasn't such a bad cook after all, but I certainly didn't want to make it a habit.

I glanced at Christian's empty chair to my left but said nothing.

After Viktor finished his plate, he abruptly rose from his seat and tossed his napkin down. "Please excuse me."

A few moments later, he returned from the kitchen with a round cake pan. A flame lit the top of a short candle, and my brows arched. Breed didn't celebrate birthdays, so I looked around at everyone for a clue as to what was happening.

Viktor set the cake in front of me and took a seat.

"Uh, what's this for?"

"I made this yesterday, special for you."

"Day-old cake," Wyatt said with an amused look on his face. "You're special."

"Let me finish. *Spasibo.* Raven, your week in the kitchen has taught me that this rotation is not going to work out between all of us. You have no concept of meals or planning ahead, Wyatt never reads directions, Christian boils potatoes with abandon, and Gem puts candy sprinkles on everything. Effective immediately, I will begin searching for a live-in servant. Someone who will cook our meals, do the laundry, and—"

"Keep our secrets?" Niko asked. "That's a lot of trust to impart in someone."

Wyatt pointed his fork at him. "Niko's right. Maybe we should hire someone who's deaf."

Blue shook her head and laughed. "Deaf people aren't blind."

Viktor pinched the candle out and cut the cake as he would a pizza. "Would you all prefer to continue your life of servitude? I have a pile of underwear that could use a good ironing."

"No complaints here," I quickly added. "If you can find someone trustworthy, I fully support your endeavor."

Wyatt gave me a smug look. "You haven't cut your teeth in the kitchen like the rest of us. I say we let you practice for the next two months. You've already shirked your duties more than once."

"You sure woke up with a mean streak this morning," Gem remarked.

I picked up my fork and wiped off the prongs. "It's only mean if you're implying I can't cook."

She gave me a sheepish grin and scooped more pasta into her mouth.

Viktor passed out small plates, each with a slice of chocolate cake. It didn't look pretty, but to his credit, it smelled delicious.

Wyatt gulped down his wine and then reached for the bottle. "I'm taking the day off." He glanced at Gem, and they shared a private joke that had nothing to do with the wine or taking the day off.

The joke being Niko. Today he was wearing a hot-pink

shirt—the one Gem had snuck into his closet. It generated quiet amusement among the team, but it was even funnier to me since they weren't aware that Niko was in on their little secret. He drank his wine, pretending not to see the sparks of humor around him while Blue told a story about socking a male suitor in the mouth at the ball.

Claude suddenly spit his dessert out, a look of revulsion on his face. "What did you do to this cake?"

Gem's mouth turned down when she tasted hers. "There's no sugar."

Wyatt gobbled up another bite and shrugged. "Just like my great grandmammy used to make."

Claude pushed the cake away and resumed eating his pasta.

I mashed together the sweet icing and sugarless cake until I had a mushy pudding. "Looks good to me, Viktor. Sometimes you just have to be creative." I took a bite, and it wasn't half-bad. It wasn't half-good either, but I'd had worse things in my life. In a gesture of appreciation to Viktor, others copied me and gulped down their wine after the first bite.

I quickly finished my plate and stood up just as Viktor popped the cork on the second bottle of wine. "I think that's enough for me. There's somewhere I need to go. Can I borrow a car?"

Viktor smiled warmly, his mood lightened. I couldn't help but notice how the stress lifted off his shoulders after we closed a case. He was usually all business, but I liked when he cracked open a bottle and told stories about his childhood. "Take Shepherd's. The van is still under repair, and his Jeep is reliable on ice."

"Thanks."

I left the room, relieved that no one had asked me where I was going. It was nice to have that kind of freedom where no one pried into my business. The laughter and boisterous chatter commenced as I left the room and journeyed down the long hallway toward the foyer.

A light knock sounded at the front door.

"Lock yourself out again?" I mused. It wouldn't be the first time Christian had gone for a stroll and someone had locked the door.

When I opened the door, I looked up at a gentleman about Christian's height, maybe a hair over six feet. His bleached-white hair was styled in loose, chunky spikes, and though physically he looked my age, I got a vibe that he might have been a few centuries older than that.

His hazel eyes sparkled when he smiled, and two vertical lines etched in his face at the corners of his mouth.

"How did you get past the gate?" I asked, noticing there wasn't a car parked in the circular driveway.

While the collar on his grey coat was high, his earlobes around his black studs were bright red from the frosty air. "I walked."

"Would you like to wait inside while I get Viktor? He's just down the hall."

"No. I'm actually here to deliver a message." He handed me a sealed envelope. "You seem like you're in a hurry."

"I was on my way out, but I'll be sure Viktor gets this. Can I have your name?"

He offered a friendly smile. "Let's keep it simple. It was lovely to see you again, Butterfly." He inclined his head and stepped forward, never removing his eyes from mine.

"Do I know you?"

"You always ask me that," he said obliquely. "I wasn't here. You never saw me, and you won't recognize me if you see me again. You found the note slipped underneath the door."

When he turned around and closed the door, everything got fuzzy. I held the card in my hand and flipped it over, tracing my finger over the gold sticker. Why would someone slip mail beneath the door when there were delivery boys for that kind of thing? Someone might have accidentally kicked it beneath a rug or something.

Viktor entered the room. "I thought you were gone?"

I flourished the card in my hand as I headed toward the stairs. "Someone shoved this under the door. It's probably for you since I don't get love letters from secret admirers."

"Don't be dramatic. I have no admirers." He tore open the envelope and took out the paper.

"What's it say?"

He gave a dismissive shake of his head. "Someone who enjoys playing games."

Viktor handed me the letter to read.

"I'm taking what's mine. Signed Houdini. What's up with this Houdini guy and his cryptic letters?" I handed it back to Viktor. "Maybe he should just tell you what he wants instead of all the veiled threats."

"I'll have Wyatt add it to the collection of fan mail we receive. Christian and Shepherd looked into it but found nothing. We confiscate many goods from the pawnshops. Probably a disgruntled relative. Are you positive you won't join us for more wine?"

"Maybe tonight if the party's still going. There's plenty of leftover pasta in the fridge if anyone gets hungry for more."

"Splendid. Go. Have a good time. Shepherd's keys are in the ignition." Viktor strolled toward a room where he stored a modest collection of good wine.

"And, um… Mr. Kazan?"

The silver fox glanced over his shoulder, an inquisitive look in his eyes. "Da?"

"Thanks. For giving me a second shot in life. I don't know if I ever really thanked you." In some ways, Viktor was the closest thing I'd have to a father in my new life. I wasn't going to make the same mistake twice.

He gave a brisk nod. "Don't let me down."

Chapter 29

I NEVER IMAGINED THAT A GRAVEYARD could be so beautiful. My father would sometimes bring me out here to lay flowers on my mother's grave. He would always remain behind for a few minutes longer after I went back to his bike or truck, whichever he had driven. I never understood why he wanted to talk to a tombstone. It wasn't as if she were hanging around a graveyard. Then again, I never really knew her. Just a collection of random memories and a few photographs my father had kept.

"Sorry I haven't been around much," I said, still seated on the wet grass, the cold stone pressed against my back. I had kicked the snow away from my mother's grave, but my trench coat offered a little protection from the wet ground.

I drank in the spectacular view of the setting sun. A buttery glow lingered in the air, caught within a thin veil of fog. It reflected off the crystalline snow and landed on the headstones in front of me, casting long shadows behind. The twisted branches of the trees were barren of leaves but glistened with melted snow. Icicles clung to the wings on a statue like ornamental jewelry.

"I talked with Daddy," I continued. "I think we're all good now. He doesn't remember the conversation, but I'm sure you understand… wherever you are." A long stretch of silence passed, the only sound being a crow in the distance. "I miss you. I didn't really know you, but I can still remember the little things. Oh, who am I kidding? This is stupid. You can't hear me."

I packed a snowball and threw it.

When I thought of my mother, I didn't think about heavenly

angels or even ghosts. I thought about her remains locked in a coffin in the stone-cold earth, still wearing the same blue dress we'd buried her in, even though I never got to see it because it was a closed-casket funeral. I reflected upon my own death that would inevitably come, because even immortals could die. Even if I could live forever, who would want to? What would be the point?

Maybe the most depressing part about it all was that I wouldn't have anyone to set flowers on my grave. No one would be around who loved me, who cared. No children. No family. Maybe not even a tombstone. I'd be one of the forgotten ones.

"Well, isn't this a morose sight?" I heard Christian say.

Startled, I looked up to my left and saw him standing over my grave, which was next to my mother's. I'd been so lost in my thoughts that I'd somehow tuned out the sound of his footsteps in the snow.

He did a little jig in a circle. "Got any goose bumps? I always wondered if that worked."

I heaved a sigh. "How did you know I was here?"

"You drove me."

I regarded him for a moment, noticing his messy hair and long-sleeved black shirt with the buttons undone at the top. "What are you talking about?"

He sat on my tombstone. "I was lying on top of the Jeep before you came in. Sometimes a Vampire needs a little privacy."

"In the garage?"

"It's quiet like the dead in there. You're hardly one to judge a man's hiding place."

I stood up and wiped my hands. "So you rode all the way here on top of the car?"

He shrugged nonchalantly. "Always enjoyed a little wind in my hair." Christian looked between the two graves and patted mine. "Your da forked over good money for these."

"It doesn't take much to impress you, does it?"

He looked long and hard at my grave. "A headstone does offer a peculiar sense of belonging. Perhaps you should say your farewells. You've been here for over an hour."

I glanced down at my mother's headstone and then squatted in front of it. My fingertips traced the letters that spelled out *Bonnie*. The worst part about leaving was always remembering how she died. That kind of knowledge changes a person forever.

My lip quivered, and tears spilled down my cheeks. I collected my emotions and pressed a kiss to the cold stone. "I love you, Mama," I whispered.

As I hugged my mother's headstone, I felt Christian's hands on my shoulders. When I finally stood up, I turned around and didn't look back, each step easier than the last.

"I never understood why they put fences around cemeteries," Christian remarked, his breath clouding the air in front of his face. "Don't you think it's more likely that people want out... not in?"

"The spikes on top of the wrought iron fence are a nice touch. I almost impaled myself jumping over it."

"'Twould be a shame if I had to put you in the ground for real."

"As long as you put fake roses on my grave."

He clasped his hands behind his back. "Fake? I'd plant a real one covered in thorns, just as prickly as your tongue."

"If you had to care for a living thing, it would die from neglect."

"I'd water it myself, right after a pint of ale."

We laughed as we followed my trail toward the back where I'd snuck in. Visiting hours were over, because apparently the dead needed a break from the living. When we neared the mausoleums, I decided to get a better view of the grounds. One of them had a flat roof, so I climbed the statue next to it and pulled myself up. Once there, I kicked the snow away while Christian climbed up behind me.

"Would you look at that," he said. "All those fecking bodies. It just goes on forever."

With the sun at my back, I took a seat, my legs dangling over the edge. Seeing it from this angle gave me a new perspective. It suddenly occurred to me that death wasn't a personal thing but a practical one.

Everyone dies… eventually. That's the one thing we all have in common.

Christian kicked more snow away until half the roof was cleared. Instead of sitting next to me, he perched on the corner like a gargoyle overlooking his domain. "I never had a grave of my own. Even if someone had pretended to bury me, there would probably be a shopping strip over my coffin by now."

"It makes you wonder if we'll run out of land."

"Perhaps they should put the dead on display like the clothes at the dry cleaners. You just push a button, and the body of your loved one comes out on a hook."

"There you go again. Saying all the right things to make me feel better."

He cocked his head to the side when a white rabbit scurried over our tracks toward the grave.

My hands squeezed the stone ledge, and I looked up at him. "Can I ask you a question?"

"I don't see what's ever stopped you before."

"This necklace isn't a fake stone, is it?"

He scraped his teeth against his bottom lip and then stood up. "Did you steal it?"

"I don't know what you're prattling on about," he said, moving out of sight.

I scooted back and stood up to face him. "No more bullshit. Why did you give me a Burmese ruby necklace? And not just *any* ruby, but one worth a lot of money? Tell me the truth, or I'm giving it back."

Christian caught sight of me pulling it out from beneath my shirt. "Don't give it back," he quickly said.

"Someone could steal it."

He chuckled softly. "The chain is infused with magic. Let them try."

I blinked in surprise, his words tangling in my head.

Christian approached me and lifted the jewel between his fingers. "No one's going to steal your heart. They create stones in labs now, and most dolts can't tell the difference between dime-store jewels and the real thing. I've had it for a long time. Seemed a shame for it to spend eternity in a box. I'm sure they would agree," he said, jerking his head toward the graveyard.

"So then why not give it to Gem? She loves stones. Why me?"

A cryptic look flickered in his expression, and he gazed at me so intently that I found myself drawn to him. Christian had captivating eyes—like two obsidian stones encased in porcelain. Without warning, he cradled my neck and kissed me, his tongue delving deep and flooding my senses. It was the only warmth my body felt, and I surrendered myself completely. Christian's kiss was like a passionate tide rocking and swelling against my shore, but it was the undercurrent of emotion that threatened to pull me under.

Christian softened the kiss and spoke against my lips. "That's why."

He tasted decadent, and I didn't mind his scruffy beard or even the fact that there was a lingering flavor of mint on his breath. I melted beneath his touch, my heart quickening.

Christian drew back, his gaze so reverent that it gave me butterflies. "I'd walk through fire for you."

I struggled for words. "You have."

"And I'd do it again."

"Why would you give me something so valuable?"

His thumb swept across my cheek. "It's romantic, is it not?"

"But you're not a romantic."

"Aye. But maybe a heart made of fire is the best I can do."

He pulled me tight against him and kissed me hard, deep, so our tongues married and thoughts disintegrated. I touched his chest but didn't push him away. Energy flowed to my fingertips, and what would have knocked a grown man off his feet had no effect on this Vampire. Christian took his time savoring me, and my knees weakened at how tender he was. The kiss didn't just end—it burned out slowly like dying embers.

"When did all this begin?" I asked in disbelief.

"The night we met, when you put a blade to my groin. That's when I knew you were the one."

"Don't be funny. I'm serious."

He swept a lock of hair away from my eyes. "There's no one moment I can give you. Sometimes when we're at the table, I tune everything out and listen to the sound of your heart beating inside your chest. I can't help myself. You're an addiction I've never known before."

"I'm also a crossbreed."

"I've come to terms with that. Have you? Because I think it's time you realize how remarkable your Vampire nature is. The part of you that you're afraid of is the part that draws me nearer to you."

My breath caught. "Why are you saying all this? Getting a compliment out of you is like pulling teeth."

Instant regret flashed in his eyes.

"Wait a minute. I know what's going on here. You're going to scrub my memory, aren't you?" I pushed him away, putting distance between us. "You can't just write all over me like a chalkboard and erase whatever you say. I don't want you in my head."

"You can't remember any of this, Raven."

"You gave me your word you'd never fuck with my head again. This isn't like the last time; I'm not going to walk away from my job because of this attraction between us."

"It's already changed things, but I had to get it off my chest. I can make this conversation disappear so it won't vex you. Do you really think we can work together after this?"

I shrugged. "I can."

He wiped his hand down his mouth. "I don't know what the feck I'm doing. I get all soft when I see a woman weeping over her mother's grave."

"Don't pretend like you said any of this because you felt sorry for me." I looked right at him, but he avoided eye contact. "I thought we were going to be honest with each other?"

"If you remember this conversation, you'll regret it."

We both stood still as the wind blew. Christian was guarded with his emotions, and not being able to scrub my memory of his admission must have been a painful blow to his ego. But if this Vampire was willing to admit he felt something for me, then maybe he needed more than my silence or reproach. "If you're afraid that your feelings are just a one-way street, they're not."

His eyes darted up.

"I don't really know *what* this is, but I feel something for you I've never felt with another man. It's the same feeling like when we jumped off that bridge. Fear, excitement, and not being in control of what's going to happen. Maybe it's because we're more alike than different, or maybe it's because you don't get mad when I play jokes on you. I have strong feelings for you, Christian. Feelings that could go somewhere. But…"

"But?"

"A man will have to conquer my heart if he wants it. There's no halfway with me. That's how people get hurt. I can't commit to someone who isn't sure how he feels about me or how far he's willing to go. That's what happened to my parents. Commitment isn't a norm in my life, and clearly it's not in yours. Having feelings is one thing, but you're not ready, and you probably never will be. I'm not even sure if I'm capable of that kind of love. But I'm not going to hold it against you. Let's not forget this. Let's just see where it goes and try to get through it without hurting each other."

"That's the saddest oath I've ever heard."

I gave him a mirthless smile. "We're immortal, so marriage isn't exactly the endgame."

"And why not?"

"Do you really think you can spend an eternity with just one person? And besides, I'll never marry someone who doesn't ask for my father's permission."

Christian cocked his head to the side. "Your da isn't getting any younger. Not to mention he thinks you're dead."

"That's not my problem."

"You're making bold assumptions about me, Raven. I never said I wanted to marry you."

"Then what *do* you want?"

His eyes darkened. "It's what I don't want. I don't want to see you with another man. I don't want anyone else to taste your blood, to kiss your lips or put his hands on your body. I don't want you to look at anyone else with the same look that you're giving me right now."

I gave it a little thought. I'd never considered myself a traditional girl by any means, and this was a new journey I was embarking on with its own set of rules. "I can live with that."

He shook his head and took a step forward. "You deserve better. You should find yourself a good man, not one with a wounded heart made of stone."

I huffed out a laugh. "What would a good man want with a woman who's killed for sport? Don't try so hard to talk me out of this. What are you so afraid of? That I'll find out you're not a man who just sees women as sex objects? A man who's repeatedly saved my life can't be all bad."

"Aye, my heart has always been my weakness. But make no mistake, Raven. I'm a cold man. I'm broken beyond repair. There are things I have done in my life that no woman could overlook. I'm far too rough around the edges for anyone's liking, and I'm cynical. I've seen love ruin men, and I've never had much luck with it myself. You don't really know me like you think you do. I'm too dark for anyone to love."

"Let's not have a contest on who has the blacker soul. I might actually win."

My hair whipped wildly around me.

Christian gathered it together and tucked it behind my ears before cradling my neck. "What do you ask of me?"

I placed my hand on his heart. "Be honest. That's all I want."

"Aye, Precious. You have my truth. But we have to keep this between us. Viktor won't take kindly to a relationship brewing; it's against his rules."

"I'll agree to that. No sense in getting fired." I smiled softly. "Who does this before sex? Declares all these intense feelings? We might not even like each other in bed."

A dark hunger flickered in his eyes, and his voice became rough and sexy. "The things I'll do to you will make your ancestors blush. There's a nice spot over your grave if you want to test me."

I leaned in and kissed his mouth. "The mausoleum is warmer."

"I'll pass. I've developed a sudden appreciation for abstinence."

"Does that mean our relationship will be sexless?"

He smiled against my mouth, giving me tingles in all the right places. "Perhaps I'll wait until you want it more than I do."

I slipped my tongue between his lips and abruptly backed away, leaving him wanting. "I'll accept that challenge."

Once I climbed down the statue and hopped to the ground, I realized we could make up the rules as we went along. I couldn't give Christian words of love since they weren't all there yet, but I could give him hope. In return, he gave me butterflies. He gave me companionship. He sometimes gave me coffee in the morning. And most of all, he gave me his heart on a chain. Maybe sooner or later he'd give me a broken heart and a reason to leave Keystone, but I was willing to take the risk.

Christian jumped straight from the roof to the ground and then fell in step beside me. "You're not a jealous woman, are you?"

"We've never had sex, so I hardly have claim on anything. Maybe I'm just as skeptical about this whole thing as you are."

He clasped his hands behind his back. "You're unlike any woman I've ever met."

I snorted. "This is *so* us. Declaring our feelings in a cemetery."

He bumped shoulders with me. "And you thought I wasn't romantic."

"What I can't figure out is why you would spend a million dollars on a necklace when you're walking around with holes in your sweaters."

"It adds to the mystique."

Tiny snowflakes began to fall, and it felt like we were caught inside a snow globe after someone had violently shaken it.

"This weather can't seem to make up its mind," I said.

"That's why they call Mother Nature a woman."

"And Father Time drags his ass like a man?" I watched our footsteps fall in sync. "I really don't know a thing about you, Christian Poe. What's your favorite color?"

"Red."

"Dripping from the neck of your victim?"

"There's a lovely little vein on the groin I find most delicious. What makes *your* mouth water?"

I grinned, my stomach growling. "Angus burger with extra cheese and a milkshake."

"Don't forget the onion rings."

I hooked my arm in his. "Come on, Vamp. You're buying me dinner."

He squinted at the setting sun. "So… exactly what are we?"

"Why do we need a label? We're partners. Maybe prospective lovers."

"We're like two savages in the night."

"What's that supposed to mean?"

Christian began to recite a poem:

"Ships that pass in the night, and speak each other in passing,
Only a signal shown and a distant voice in the darkness;
So on the ocean of life we pass and speak one another,
Only a look and a voice, then darkness again and a silence."

Maybe it would have been easier to have erased his confession, but I needed to see what was possible. I was certain I had an impenetrable heart that would survive what became of us, but life was about taking chances… even if they turned into regrets.

Ancient souls below our feet cried out for us to live and seize the day.

I gazed up at him. "That's a depressing poem. How did I ever fall for such a morose guy?"

He stopped in his tracks. "You fell?"

I gave him a fragile smile. "Falling. I'm still falling."

Christian wrapped his arms around me. "Then I'll catch you."

CPSIA information can be obtained
at www.ICGtesting.com
Printed in the USA
BVHW032200140219
540362BV00001B/5/P